A DANGEROUS MAN

The viscount's eyes narrowed and his gaze ripped up and down her body. When he spoke, the soft huskiness of his voice alerted Liza to a new danger.

"You got something against makin' love, honey?"

Liza stopped herself from sidling backward.

"Making love, my lord? Mercy, what you want isn't making love. You don't even know me."

He said nothing at first, then, holding her gaze with his own, he pulled at one end of his necktie where it hung over his shoulder. The black silk slithered against his shirt and came loose.

"Sometimes there's just no talking with a woman."

The tie dangled from his fingers, and she found herself staring at it. Then he launched himself at her and caught her. She shrieked and tried to kick him, but he lifted her and squeezed. She gasped for breath.

"My lord."

He was so close she could feel his breath skimming across her cheek, and her vision filled with the sight of his lips.

"There ain't no lord here, honey, so don't bother," he said, and then he touched her lips to his. . . .

LADY
DANGEROUS

Suzanne
Robinson

BANTAM BOOKS

New York   Toronto   London   Sydney   Auckland

LADY DANGEROUS

A Bantam Book / March 1994

ISBN 0-553-29576-4

Published simultaneously in the United States and Canada

Bantam Books are published by Bantam Books, a division of Bantam Doubleday
Dell Publishing Group, Inc. Its trademark, consisting of the words
"Bantam Books" and the portrayal of a rooster, is Registered in U.S. Patent and
Trademark Office and in other countries. Marca Registrada. Bantam Books, 1540
Broadway, New York, New York 10036.

PRINTED IN THE UNITED STATES OF AMERICA

RAD   0 9 8 7 6 5 4 3 2 1

Few men possess all of these qualities—creativity, humor, and insight, combined with an abundance of intelligence. One such man is Russ Woods, to whom this book is dedicated.

LADY
DANGEROUS

1

LONDON, 1857

If she was caught spying in the home of a viscount, she'd end up in Newgate. Was she mad to have come to the house of such a man as Viscount Radcliffe? His reputation conjured up visions of hellfire and brimstone, dark caverns that glowed with flowing lava and echoed with the screams of the damned. He was said to dine on innocents. But what choice did she have? The Metropolitan Police hadn't believed her suspicions that he'd murdered two men.

Shuffling down the hall to the master suite carrying two buckets loaded with coal, Liza glanced back down the hall toward the servants' door. Deserted. Perhaps she'd have time to search his rooms this evening. She must succeed soon, for he was returning from America shortly.

She had just set the buckets down and grasped the doorknob when a crash signaled that Tessie had dropped a lamp on the marble front stairs. A wail confirmed Liza's guess, along with the outraged bellow of Choke, the butler. Then the volume of the noise rose. It seemed that everyone from the knife boy to the housekeeper was babbling and rushing to and fro. Doors slammed, and boots clattered on wooden and marble floors.

Liza hesitated on the threshold of the master suite. The coal wasn't actually intended for these rooms, since the viscount wasn't using them. The most she'd ever seen of him was the portrait in the blue saloon. She disliked the painting, for the man in it exuded the cold beauty of an aristocrat and gazed down on her with cat-green eyes that had no soul.

Perhaps he'd lost his soul somewhere in the American West in one of those gunfights she'd heard about. For some reason the viscount preferred the frontier to civilization. He'd spent several years in Texas and California after his military training. Liza knew of no other member of the peerage quite so willing to abandon civilization for the savagery of Indian territories and deserts. The man's reputation for recklessness matched his reputation as a marauder among the ladies of Society.

She resented the man for that reputation alone. He was one of those men who seemed never to be without a woman, though never with one who held his affections. Sledge had offered the opinion that the viscount seldom spent a night without a woman. Liza sniffed when she heard this. Some men were truly animals. Tessie said he had not just one mistress among the nobility, but several, because the company of one woman bored him. How dare he possess a title, wealth, and beauty, and value his boot scraper more than the women to whom he made love? Liza disliked selfish men.

She especially disliked this one for sailing off to Texas two days after her brother had been murdered. She'd had to wait eleven whole months for him to return.

She started at the sound of running feet. If someone saw her, she had been planning to claim she mistook her way. Having pretended to a slight lack of wits, she might succeed in the pretense. Her plans fell to ruins, however, when Choke's graying head and spindly shoulders appeared coming up the main stairs.

Liza stared, for she'd never seen the man run. Choke usually moved with the stateliness and care of a debutante at her royal presentation. The butler skittered down the hall shouting the names of the housekeeper and the two upstairs maids. He zoomed past Liza, the slick souls of his boots sliding on the polished tile floor as he tried to stop and veered around to confront her. His face, normally pale as Cook's flour, had turned a rosebud pink. Choke heaved in several deep breaths as a footman and maid carrying fresh linen raced upstairs and past them into the master suite. Liza heard the mad rustle of damask and silk.

"He's coming!" Choke had finally regained his breath. "Quick, girl, take those inside and build the fires."

Before Liza could move, a stranger appeared at the head of the stairs. She hadn't thought it possible that there could be a person of more dignity and

countenance than Choke, but this man had the demeanor of a pope. He managed to intimidate, though
he possessed the slightest bit of a paunch and a high,
glowing forehead ringed with brown hair. Choke
moaned as he beheld the stranger.

"Loveday, don't tell me he's here already."

"Five minutes," came the sedate reply.

"Five!" Choke's voice rose to a screech, then he
bawled with all the force of his gaunt frame. "Two
minutes, everyone lined up in front in two minutes!"

The footman who had carried the linens shoul-
dered Liza aside as he left the master suite. He started
upon hearing Choke's bellow. Now Sledge was a big
fellow, and young, and proud of his physical skills. He
boxed and was constantly alert for opportunities to
test his talent in the pubs and rowdy streets of East
London. Therefore, when Sledge's face drained of
color and he swallowed and ducked his head, Liza
understood just how fearsome the viscount must be.
She listened to the cries of the household. The
atmosphere was one of panic so tangible, the house
itself seemed to shake with apprehension.

Her throat went dry, and she swallowed. Dear
God, how was she to survive in such a household in
disguise? Her skin went cold despite the grossly
overpadded corset and dress. A bead of sweat trickled
from beneath the cap that concealed her hair. Just
then the man called Loveday appeared in front of her
and picked up the coal buckets as though he were
retrieving a queen's discarded jewels.

"I will put these inside the door. Run along, girl,
and make yourself ready to be presented to his
lordship."

Liza bobbed a curtsy, turned, and ran down the
back stairs. Dashing into the scullery, she dodged a

tearful Tessie and the knife boy, and found the old mirror that hung in a dark corner. She shoved her straggling hair up beneath her cap, glanced about surreptitiously, and shifted her whole dress to sit better on her shoulders.

The garment was lined with layers of cotton bunting to make her appear plump. She made sure the buttons at her wrists were secure. It wouldn't do for anyone to remark upon the size of her wrists compared to her arms. She found her mantle and shoved her arms through the sleeves. At the housekeeper's shout, she joined the stampede of servants as they rushed up the stairs and into the reception hall. Hanging back, she allowed the kitchen and laundry maids to pass her as they exited the house and clattered down the white stone steps.

It was one of those damp January evenings that made the prostitutes of Whitechapel shiver in the streets. Moisture dripped from the black iron fence that surrounded the house. Inside the fence, yellow fog curled about the trunks of the trees that formed a protective barrier between the street and the house. It spread, unwholesome and cloying, and rose to knee level while the staff arranged themselves beneath the carriage porch in order of precedence at the foot of the front steps. By the light of the great brass lamps on either side of the doors they stood, shivering and waiting. Beside her, a kitchen maid breathed in soot-laden mist and coughed.

Choke, a crystal lamp in hand, marched down the phalanx of servants. He snapped at the knife boy to button his coat, then took his place beside the housekeeper at the head of the line. The crystal lamp rattled in his hands, and Liza was sure the tremor wasn't caused by the cold.

Across the lawn, footmen opened the gates. To Liza's surprise, two men in long coats and top hats walked up the circular drive. They drew near, and Choke stepped forward.

"Your grace," the butler said.

"Not here yet. Good. Yale, we'll wait inside until the carriage comes."

Liza dared turn her head a fraction of an inch to glimpse the newcomers. The duke! The viscount's father, the Duke of Clairemont, had come, to welcome his son home from America. Her only comfort was that the duke lived nearby in Grosvenor Square and wouldn't be staying the night. The other man would be Lord Yale Marshall, the duke's brother. But where were the ladies, the duchess and the daughter, Lady Georgiana?

The noblemen disappeared inside, and the staff was left to wait in the disquieting stillness. The fog continued to curl upward, its chilly tendrils slithering up her skirts. She heard a cat yowl, and then, silence. Liza burrowed her nose in the collar of her coat. The hour was late and the house removed from the street so that it appeared like a white stone island in the midst of blackness. Finally, when she thought she would have to stuff her fingers in her ears to shut out the disturbing quiet, she heard the hollow clip-clop of horses' hooves in the distance. The sound bounced off stone walls and curbs, disembodied and eerie in deserted streets that normally roared with life.

Iron squealed against iron as the footmen swung the gates back again. Black horses trotted into view, two pairs, drawing a black lacquered carriage. Liza stirred uneasily as she realized that vehicle, tack, and coachman were all in unrelieved black. Polished brass lanterns and fittings provided the only contrast.

The carriage pulled up before the house, the horses stamping and snorting in the cold. The coachman, wrapped in a driving coat and muffled in a black scarf, made no sound as he controlled the ill-tempered menace of his animals. She couldn't help leaning forward a bit, in spite of her growing trepidation. Perhaps it was the eeriness of the fog-drenched night, or the unnerving appearance of the shining, black, and silent carriage, but no one moved.

Then she saw it. A boot. A black boot unlike any she'd ever seen. High of heel, tapered in the toe, scuffed, and sticking out of the carriage window. Its owner must be reclining inside. As she closed her mouth, which had fallen open, Liza saw a puff of smoke billow out from the interior. So aghast was she at this unorthodox arrival, she hadn't heard the duke and his brother come down the steps to stand near her.

The horses began to prance and toss their heads, causing the footmen to spring up to catch their bridles, and still the boot remained in the window. The only sound was that of the restive black beasts. Suddenly the boot was withdrawn. The head footman immediately jumped forward and opened the carriage door. The interior lamps hadn't been lit. From the darkness stepped a man so tall, he had to curl almost double to keep his hat from hitting the roof of the vehicle.

The footman retreated as the man straightened. Liza sucked in her breath, and a feeling of unreality swamped her other emotions. The man who stood before her wore clothing so dark, he seemed a part of the night and the gloom of the carriage that had borne him. A low-crowned hat with a wide brim concealed his face, and he wore a long coat that flared away from his body. It was open, and he brushed one edge of it back where it revealed pants, a vest, a black, low-slung belt and holster bearing a gleaming revolver.

He paused, undisturbed by the shock he'd created. Liza suddenly remembered a pamphlet she'd seen on the American West. That's where she'd seen a man like this. Not anywhere in England, but in illustrations of the American badlands.

At last the man moved. He struck a match on his belt and lit a thin cigar. The tip glowed, and for a moment his face was revealed in the light of the match. She glimpsed black, black hair, so dark it seemed to absorb the flame of the match. Thick lashes lifted to reveal the glitter of cat-green eyes, a straight nose, and a chin that bore a day's stubble. The match died and was tossed aside. The man hooked his thumbs in his belt and sauntered down the line of servants, ignoring them.

He stopped in front of the duke, puffed on the cigar, and stared at the older man. Another intimidating silence followed while Choke scuttled in the man's wake. As Choke halted behind him, the man gave a last puff that sent smoke wending its way toward the duke. Slowly, a pretense of a smile spread over his face. He removed the cigar from his mouth, shoved his hat back on his head, and spoke for the first time.

"Well, well, well. Evening, Daddy."

That accent, it was so strange—a hot, heavy drawl spiked with cool and nasty amusement. This man took his time with words, caressed them, savored them, and made his enemies wait in apprehension for him to complete them. The duke bristled, and his white hair almost stood out like a lion's mane as he gazed at his son.

"Jocelin, you forget yourself."

The cigar sailed to the ground and hissed as it hit the damp pavement. Liza longed to shrink back from the sudden viciousness that sprang from the viscount's eyes. The viscount smiled again and spoke softly, with relish and an evil amusement. The drawl vanished, to be supplanted by a clipped, aristocratic accent.

"I don't forget. I'll never forget. Forgetting is your vocation, one you've elevated to a sin, or you wouldn't bring my dear uncle where I could get my hands on him."

All gazes fastened on the man standing behind the duke. Though much younger than his brother, Yale Marshall had the same thick hair, black as his brother's had once been, only gray at the temples. Of high stature like his nephew, he reminded Liza of the illustrations of knights in *Le Morte d'Arthur,* for he personified doomed beauty and chivalry. He had the same startling green eyes as his nephew, and he gazed at the viscount sadly as the younger man faced him.

Yale murmured to his brother, "I told you I shouldn't have come."

With knightly dignity he stepped aside, and the movement brought him nearer to his nephew. Jocelin's left hand touched the revolver on his hip as his uncle turned. The duke hissed his name, and the hand dropped loosely to his side.

He lit another cigar. At a glance from his grace, Choke sprang into motion. He ran up the steps to open the door. The duke marched after him, leaving his son to follow, slowly, after taking a few leisurely puffs on his cigar.

"Ah, well," he murmured. "I can always kill him later."

Liza exchanged horrified glances with the knife

boy. As the noblemen vanished, Choke thrust the
crystal lamp at a footman and clapped his hands.

"Hurry. Cook, the food mustn't be late. Sledge,
his lordship's luggage." Choke turned on the knife
boy and two scullery maids who were chattering in
excitement. "Silence. Get yourselves belowstairs at
once. And you!"

Liza jumped as Choke barked at her. "Gamp.
That is your name, isn't it? Gamp, get those fires
made. Don't gawk at me, girl." Choke descended
upon her and shoved her by the shoulders. "Run. And
be out of there before his lordship goes upstairs."

Lifting her skirts, Liza bolted. In her haste she
took the main stairs. The hand of Robert Adam had
passed over the viscount's house, leaving airy, light
elegance. The entry hall was dominated by the central
marble stairs, which rose one flight, then split and
ascended to the right and left. Her boots clattering on
the ivory and black marble, Liza turned to the left,
dashed down the hall to the double doors of the
master suite, and burst into the sitting room. Once an
antechamber, it served as the viscount's study.

Liza snatched up her coal buckets, deposited
one in front of the fireplace in the sitting room, and
raced into the bedchamber to place the other on the
hearth there. As she straightened to catch her breath,
her gaze caught the half-made bed.

"Heavens!"

No time to fetch Tessie. She shoved aside the
hangings and burrowed under the mattress, stuffing
sheets in place. Her heart sped up as she realized how
much she was being delayed. People simply didn't
carry guns in civilized London—Her Majesty Queen
Victoria's London. People didn't, not even the worst
criminal. He did, though. She pulled the last cover

into place and stood back to survey her work. She tried not to think of the man downstairs.

The bed's trappings matched those of the chamber, a pearl gray shot with silver thread. The same brocaded silk covered the walls and draped the line of tall windows that made the room appear even larger than it was. An Adamesque white-and-silver plastered ceiling finished the chilly look in a foliated oval design. Liza shivered and realized she had yet to build the fire.

She ran back to the study, dumped the coal in the hearth, and began piling it correctly. Her hands, dress, and face were black by the time she had lit the coals and hurried into the bedchamber. She heard the rattle of a silver tea service. Tessie entered and placed a tray on a table between the windows and the fireplace.

"Hurry," the maid hissed as she skittered out of the room.

Liza knelt at the white marble fireplace and spilled the coals onto the hearth. Her hands moved rapidly, arranging the coals in a compact pile. She had to squint, for the only lamp she'd lit was sitting on the table by the silver teapot. She was engulfed in shadows.

Dropping the last coal on the pile, Liza sat back on her heels and fished in the darkness for her brush and dustpan. She heard a peculiar tapping sound and paused. She turned her head quickly and jumped at the sight of the viscount walking slowly from the sitting room into the bedchamber. The noise had been the heels of his boots as he stepped from the carpet to the polished wood floor.

He regained the carpet. Without glancing her way, he walked to the window near the tea table. He'd removed his coat downstairs. By the lighted lamp she could see the gleam of a coarse, white shirt beneath the vest and the tight buckskin that hugged his thighs. He wore that same expression he'd had when he first left his carriage—an expression that was no expression at all. Stretching out a brown-skinned hand, he moved a curtain aside to peer out into the night. Beaded with moisture, the glass revealed only the fog and a black, skeletal tree limb.

He dropped his hand, and as she sat there frozen, he sighed. She jumped again, for she hadn't expected him to make such a human sound. He belonged to a world of savagery in which sighs played no part. Then he did something that made Liza's jaw loosen and drop. He turned toward the tea table, giving her her first full glimpse of his face with its straight, dark brows and harsh planes softened by the smoothness of the skin that stretched over the sharp angles. To her amazement his long fingers slipped around the handle of the silver teapot with the ease and grace of long practice. Resting his free hand on the hilt of his revolver, he lifted the pot and poured steaming tea into a china cup edged with silver.

Brown liquid streamed into the cup to just the right height. He tilted the pot back and placed it on the tray. The whole scene added to her feeling of unreality. This man who wore a gun in a city where no one wore guns, this man who dressed in animal skins, poured tea like the son of a duke. A man who poured tea like that couldn't be a murderer, could he?

She was about to clear her throat to announce her presence as the viscount's hand moved toward the teacup. Before she could summon her wits, she saw a blur of movement and heard a metallic click. She found herself staring at the small, round hole at the end of the barrel of his revolver. Her mind slowed from shock, Liza gasped and lifted her gaze to Jocelin Marshall. He must have heard her, though he never betrayed surprise. He wiggled the barrel up and down.

"Come into the light, slow," he said quietly.

Liza maneuvered her padded self erect and took three steps. He narrowed his eyes as the lamplight danced over her soiled apron and voluminous cap. A muscle in his jaw twitched, but the revolver hadn't moved. It was still aimed at her stomach.

"Don't move."

There it was again, that slow, hot drawl. He went on.

"I can draw, cock, and fire in one move, without thinking. Takes years of practice. You grasp the gun by the handle with your wrist twisted down while your finger goes for the trigger and your thumb reaches for the hammer. An awkward maneuver, but if you do it careful, a deadly one. You got to learn to hit what you aim at the first time, 'cause the smoke obscures your view of the next shot." He holstered the pistol without taking his gaze from her. "At this distance, I wouldn't need no second shot."

She had been motionless with fear. As he lectured her in that lazy, uncouth accent, she recovered her sense, and then lost it in her rage.

"You nearly killed me!" Too late she remembered her own accent. Luckily she hadn't said much. Rubbing her grubby hands together, she wailed. "You give me a turn, my lord. I'm all twittered, Lord bless me."

At her whimper the viscount seemed to wake from some unknown reverie. He blinked rapidly. His hand dropped away from his holster. As she peeped at him from behind her hands, a change came over him.

His indolent slouch disappeared while his spine straightened. Wide shoulders stretched the seams of his shirt when he squared them. His chin lifted so that he looked down from an even greater height than before, and one hand balled into a loose fist, which he put behind his back. Uncannily, she almost heard in his voice a drum roll and pipes, and the sound of the parade of the Horse Guard.

"I'll not have a plump and peevish maid of all work take me to task." The aristocrat's sneer was back.

She clamped her fingers over her mouth, aghast that her zeal to cover her identity had brought her close to dismissal. Then she shrank back as he suddenly began to stalk toward her.

"I told you not to move." He stopped not two feet from her and scowled. "You're filthy, and shivering. Did they send you up here without allowing you to warm yourself? No doubt you've been standing outside in that damnable fog for an hour. Go away."

"Th-the fire, my lord."

"I'll attend to it." The clipped, university-bred accent was well in place now. "If I can start a fire in a Panhandle snowstorm, I can light coals. Off with you, miss."

"But, my lord—"

"Hang it all!"

The sound of a cleared throat interrupted the viscount's American curse. "Ah-hum. My lord."

Jocelin tapped his fingers against his holster and nodded for Loveday to enter. The valet glided over to him noiselessly.

"It seems, my lord, that our second pair of riding boots has been ruined by the new knife boy."

"Already?"

"Yes, my lord. We will have to wear our new ones. The knife boy has put black polish on them instead of brown. I fear our reputation has preceded us and caused a slight brain fever in the lad."

Liza's consternation renewed when, instead of launching into a peevish fit, the viscount shrugged and turned away. His hands went to his belt. Leather creaked as he loosened it, and it fell away from his hips, slithering over a taut buttock that caught and held Liza's gaze. An unexpected heat burst within her when he lowered himself into the chair by the tea table and the buckskin pants tightened over his thighs. Her glance seemed unmovable, fixed on the knot of muscle just above his knee.

"Get her out of here," he said wearily. Without glancing at her, he lay his holster and revolver next to the silver teapot and lifted the china cup.

She felt an elbow prod her arm. Loveday poked her again. Backing up, Liza turned and fled. Racing through the servant's door, she sprinted downstairs as if chased by rabid dogs. Once in the scullery, she found water and gave herself a wash. She noticed for the first time that her hands were shaking. Never had she seen anyone like Jocelin, Viscount Radcliffe— part gunman, part nobleman. What was worse, as barbaric as his American side appeared, she was beginning to realize that his aristocratic side might be as dangerous, and was certainly more sinister.

2

Jocelin leaned back in the Louis XVI chair, his legs crossed at the ankles, and listened to the plump little maid run from the room. He regretted drawing on her. But, hang it, she should have let him know she was there.

He'd been out west too long. He'd made the trip to California and back through Colorado and Texas to forget the war, to erase Balaklava and Scutari from his memory—and for other, less benign reasons. The cure had been successful, as long as he'd been in America, but the cure had its price. Tension had permeated his body and mind over the countless weeks on the trail. His senses had magnified. He heard single drops of rain in a storm, he smelled campfires across mountain ranges, sensed the mute presence of a Comanche. So he drew on little maids kneeling at a hearth in his town house.

Shifting uncomfortably, he pulled a pair of nickel-plated iron handcuffs from his back pocket. He tossed them on the tea table. The clank drew a glance from Loveday. Jocelin favored him with a bitter smile, but refused to react to the I've-just-smelled-rotten-pork expression on his valet's face. He fished in his vest pocket and withdrew the key to the handcuffs and a leather cigar holder.

Loveday floated over to the table and picked up the handcuffs with his fingertips, holding them at a distance from his body. "I may store these away along with our other American accoutrements, my lord?"

Jocelin took a big gulp of tea and grunted.

"I noticed that Mr. Tapley has not returned with your lordship."

Leaning back in his chair again, Jocelin folded his arms over his chest and closed his eyes. "Ah, yes, Mr. Tapley. Poor Tapley ran afoul of Comanches when we took the stage from Texas to California. Darned shame. But then, I warned him about how dangerous it was when I told him about all that gold in California. Real shame. The coach broke a wheel, and we were stranded on the road for the night. He wandered away from camp. Told him not to go gallivanting off by himself."

"How foolish of him, my lord."

Jocelin opened his eyes and met Loveday's drill-like gaze, unperturbed. "Yup, foolish. I had to do it, Loveday. It was the only way to get the bastard away from his victims."

Still dangling the handcuffs, Loveday nodded and withdrew a sealed envelope from his coat pocket.

"Our mail has been sorted, my lord, and it can wait until we've rested from our journey, but I saw this."

Taking the envelope, Jocelin sat up and drew the lamp nearer. He glanced at the seal. It bore the impression of a stylized guillotine. Nick had a taste for the macabre. He broke the seal and read the enclosed letter, then glanced at the sheet behind the missive. His gaze ran over a list of five names and addresses. The clammy chill of the fog outside his window seemed to creep into his body. Like a slave's burden, his own living nightmare settled on his shoulders again.

Loveday had lit the fire. Jocelin handed him the letter, and the valet touched it to a red coal. Rising abruptly, Jocelin began rolling the list into a cylinder as he left the room.

"My bath?" He heard himself pronounce the word with the accent he'd acquired at Sandhurst. The West was wearing off him a little.

"The footmen should be bringing the water shortly, my lord."

He went to the sitting room, ignoring the symmetrical delicacy of its silver-and-gray plasterwork. He walked to the fireplace. On the mantel rested three vessels. A Wedgwood urn, a nautilus shell Jacobean drinking cup, and a pedestaled flask carved of lapis lazuli. It was an antique from the Italian Renaissance, once owned by Francesco de' Medici. He grasped the flask. Trimmed in gold, it had a narrow neck and a hinged top. He opened it and slipped the cylinder of paper inside. Closing it, he replaced the vessel on the mantel and went to his desk.

He'd never cared for the desk, for it crawled with elaborate decoration, from the pictorial marquetry to the gilt ormolu mounts. However, it was big enough to hold most of his correspondence—at least, his ordinary correspondence. He unlocked and shoved back the top, selected a pen and plain paper.

By the time the footmen arrived with his bathwater, he'd finished a response to the writer of the list. He handed the envelope to Loveday to post and dismissed the valet for the night. He went to the bathing room and stripped. Not daring to remain in the hot water for fear of falling asleep, he got out and was soon in bed. He tried to sleep, but couldn't, in spite of his drowsiness. In desperation he retrieved his revolver from an armoire and slipped it under his pillow.

Still, he couldn't relax. He hadn't expected his father to be there when he arrived. He certainly hadn't expected Yale. He hadn't seen his uncle in over a year, and before that, seldom. Not since he was fourteen. Quickly his thoughts skimmed past the memories of his fourteenth year. He'd excised them and shoved them deep into the void inside his head where he kept other remembrances that brought pain or shame.

Instead, he concentrated on looking forward to seeing Asher. Dear old Asher was preparing to run for Parliament. Now that Jocelin was back, they could resume their political meetings. No doubt Asher had recruited several more allies, perhaps even that old scoundrel Palmerston. With Asher in the House of Commons and himself in the House of Lords, they could gain much.

He was beginning to grow drowsy when he heard tapping at one of the windows. His hand was instantly on his revolver. He whipped back the covers. Chilly air made goose bumps form on his bare flesh. He slipped on a fur-lined silk robe and parted the curtains over the window. A pale face floated in the mist outside. Jocelin cursed and opened the window. Two wet boots thrust inside and landed on the carpet.

Jocelin shivered as he closed the window. "Hang it, Nick. I got your note. You didn't have to come."

"Is he dead?"

Jocelin surveyed the young man who was stamping his dirty, wet boots on his Aubusson carpet. Damp brown hair sprang out from beneath a worn cap. His neck and chin were shrouded in a torn wool scarf, above which gleamed pale, angel-blue eyes. He remembered when he'd found Nick, years ago, in Houndsditch. He'd stumbled over what he thought was a pile of rags and bones. It had been Nick, who had run afoul of a procurer in a gin shop. Now Nick worked with him.

"Well, is he dead?"

From the first Nick had never called him "my lord."

"Yes."

"You got me note? Good. I come to—came to—see if you'll be wanting to do a prowl."

"Acquiring breeding, are you?" Jocelin asked as he returned to bed.

"I'm fixing me—my grammar. Now I got plenty of money, I got to act quality."

Tossing aside his robe, Jocelin slipped under a pile of blankets. "And dress like a costermonger?"

"You know I been on a prowl. I got wind of a place in Spitalfields. Lots of young ones for the gentry. Posh carriages, white silk scarves, and bleeding degenerates. Just your kind of place, love."

"Damn you, I just got home. I was trying to sleep."

"Well, we both know how much of that you do."

"This time I won't have any trouble. Now go away."

Nick shrugged and sauntered toward the sitting room.

"Not going back out the window?" Jocelin asked.

"Nah. Too much trouble, and I need practice sneaking around big houses. Don't want to lose me—my touch. Never know when I might need to steal something. Ta, love."

Jocelin groaned and burrowed down among the covers until they shrouded his head. He listened for an uproar among the servants, but it never came. He drifted off to sleep and dreamed of Nick climbing the walls of his house, and of a plump, peevish maid.

It was still dark when he roused. Lying motionless, he took stock of his situation. He was lying on his stomach, his arms and legs sprawling across the bed. What had awakened him? A rustle. He heard it again, near the bed. It was close to where he'd dropped the boots he'd been wearing last night. He waited until the rustling stopped, grabbed his revolver, and sprang up from the covers like a dragon launched from his cave. His free hand snatched hold of something as he cocked the revolver and aimed it at the intruder.

He heard a squeak and groaned. Yanking his prisoner close, he peered into the darkness to meet the terrified gaze of the plump maid. They gawked at each other, nose to nose. He had hold of her wrist. His thumb pressed into a small bone while his fingers sank into mushy flesh.

"Hang it, woman. What are you doing in here?"

"Th—the fires. I do the fires. And, and your boots, my lord." She held his boots before his nose. "I got to clean your boots. Mr. Choke sent me special, since the knife boy ruined your others."

He thrust her wrist away. Uncocking the revolver, he laid it aside and plumped his pillow. Furious at how she'd caught him unaware and made him act the barbarian, he lay back, allowing the covers to fall to his hips. He put his arms behind his head and watched her turn crimson. Irritated for no good reason other than being startled awake, he nodded at her.

"Continue. Do this hearth first."

She had been scuttling toward the sitting room when he spoke. Now she turned and stared at him.

"Light the lamp," he said.

When she had obeyed, he got a clearer view of her. She had a brown little face, oval and wide of forehead. Her lips were pursed, making them appear thinner than they were, and she kept her gaze away from him. Still, he got a glimpse of eyes of a strange, indeterminate color between brown and blue-gray. Squiggles of light brown hair corkscrewed at her forehead and temples. He waited while she built and lit the fire. She was almost to the door when he stopped her.

"You forgot something."

He almost smiled at the reluctance she displayed to turn around. He could read her thoughts. She was angry at his treatment of her, and furious that she couldn't show it. Her little hands were doubled into fists. Some perverse devil was prodding him to taunt and irritate her. As she turned, he sat up, allowing the covers to slip so that they barely covered his groin. He leaned over the bed, exposing a bare hip, and picked up his boots. Holding them up to her gaze, he smiled.

"Come and get them."

He could hear her grinding her back teeth. She

even glanced at the iron poker beside the fireplace, which caused Jocelin's grin to widen. She stalked to the bed. As she reached for the boots, he moved them so that she was forced to lean over him to catch hold. Then he slipped his arm around her waist and pulled. She lost balance and toppled onto him. Dropping the boots, he hugged her and laughed.

She tried to kick him in the groin, then gasped at her own audacity. "Let go of me! I mean, please, my lord, let go of me."

"Damn it, woman, you could have gelded me."

Clamping his teeth together against the pain near his sensitive parts, Jocelin wrestled with her as she pushed at his chest. Her blackened hands were cold against the heat of his flesh. He forced her chin up with one hand and met her horrified gaze.

"The next time you sneak into my room, you'll pay for it."

"I wasn't sneaking. I have to build the fires. Don't!"

Jocelin's brow furrowed as he squeezed her mushy body. He could feel her breasts, but they had an odd consistency. Before he could comment, she wrenched herself from his grasp. He let her go, having achieved his purpose. Her knee dug into his thigh. Flesh ground against bone, and he yelped. She hopped backward off the bed, dragging the covers with her. She faced him, gave a sharp cry, and turned her back to him. Jocelin rubbed his thigh, but his grimace of pain turned into a smile as he pulled a sheet back over his hips.

"Next time tell Choke to send a footman."

This time she ran. He heard the sitting room door slam. All at once, returning home didn't seem so bleak. Sparring with plump little maids did wonders for melancholy spirits. He sat up straight, his head cocked to the side as if he were listening, while he examined his feelings. Unprecedented. His anger, always just beneath the surface of his emotions, had faded to a murmur located somewhere deep inside his chest.

Where was that feeling of crabbed malice? The plump little maid had taken it with her. Jocelin smiled—a genuine smile free of mockery and rancor. He was still smiling when Loveday entered with his breakfast tray. Instead of lingering in bed, smoldering and thinking snakelike thoughts, he bounced through his morning toilet.

Dressing proceeded in companionable silence, for Loveday had been with him since he'd gone to Sandhurst Royal Military College. Father had sent him young, at sixteen, and not because Jocelin had been precocious, though he had been. The duke had wanted to put his son somewhere out of the way. His one concession to a lonely and distraught boy had been to hire Loveday as a combination valet and guardian. He hadn't anticipated that the servant would take upon himself the responsibilities of a fanatical and intelligent duenna.

As he brushed Jocelin's coat and creased the pleat in his trousers, Loveday raised a brow. "Shall I tell Mr. Choke to expect you for luncheon, my lord?"

"What? Oh, no. I'm going to call on Asher Fox, and a few others. I should be home by three." Jocelin took the gloves and top hat Loveday handed to him. "Loveday, have you . . ."

"If I have ascertained that Lady Octavia is At Home, my lord. As are the Honorable Miss Birch and Lady Alberta. Lady Octavia's husband, unfortunately, has been called to France on business of the Foreign Office."

"Thank you. Then I'll call on Lady Octavia after I've seen Asher, and possibly old Buggy Winthrop."

"Very good, my lord."

He descended the stairs, his good mood still uplifting him. He paused in the entry hall to retrieve a walking stick from the stand by the door. His gaze caught the glint of the silver calling card salver on the table beside the stand. His father's embossed crest caught his eye, and his spirits plummeted. Last night's arrival. . . . He'd been unprepared for his father's stupidity. The old man had cornered him in the library, taking advantage of Jocelin's loss of composure upon being forced to remain in the same room as Yale. He remembered little of the conversation. Its details had been blasted away, exploded starwise, by his almost uncontrollable hatred.

All he remembered was that the duke had harped on Jocelin's lack of heirs, his dissolute habits, his mistresses. Interspersed with these criticisms were admonishments to put aside his imagined griefs in favor of hunting, shooting, fishing, and attendance at church. These, the duke assured him, were the pursuits of a proper Englishman.

He remembered little else of his father's conversation. What he did remember was that disjointed feeling of unreality. It was as if the real Jocelin didn't exist—at least, not for his father. All the ugliness and violation sat across from him in the library in the person of his uncle, but the duke ignored them in favor of chastising his son. After a long absence Jocelin always forgot how his father was.

Why couldn't he give up hope that his family would change? He heard a loud crack, which sounded

all the more loud in the marble-and-stone entry hall.
He looked down at his hands. Each held a jagged-
edged portion of his walking stick. He stared at them
in surprise, but glanced over his shoulder as he heard
another sound. It had been a faint rustle followed by
a click. Careful not to make a racket, he placed the
pieces of the stick on the floor and hurried to the door
behind the stairs that led to the servants' area and
stairs down to the kitchen.

As he's suspected, the door was slightly ajar. He
grasped the knob and threw it open. Encountering
nothing but shadows, he slipped inside. He sped
along the hall to the next door. Throwing it open, he
found an empty cloakroom. The next door was
locked, the silver pantry. He was about to open a third
when he spotted the edge of a starched skirt disappearing around a corner toward the stairs that led
down to the kitchen and scullery. He sprang after it.

Jocelin rounded the corner and collided with a
maid. His foot came down on the hem of her uniform.
It ripped. She cried out and stumbled, her arms
flailing as she careened onto the top step. Jocelin
caught hold of the banister and the neck of the maid's
gown. Material rent, and the woman gasped as he
pulled her to safety on the landing. He caught a
glimpse of white skin, the rise of a breast, before she
clutched the ends of her bodice together and rounded
on him.

"You bleeding idiot—my lord!"

As he tugged on his coat and brushed a lock of
hair back from his face, he scowled at the plump maid.
"Were you in the hall?"

She squared her shoulders, tilted back her head
to meet his gaze, and looked down her nose. "I beg
your pardon, my lord?"

"Don't look at me as if I were a street Arab with the pox. Answer me. Were you in the hall just now?"

"No, my lord. If your lordship will remember, my task is to lay fires and clean boots this morning."

Her tone made it clear she thought he had no conception of heavy coal buckets and boot scraping. She stood there, as stiff and virtuously offended as a martyr at an orgy, waiting for him to apologize. The damned little nuisance was waiting for him to apologize.

"It was you," he snapped. "I know it."

"I beg leave to contradict your lordship."

He began walking toward her. In the dark hallway she stood her ground much longer than he thought she would, but finally, when his boot touched her torn hem, she shrank away. He followed, and her back hit the wall. Her shoulder nearly dislodged a portrait of some long dead and faithful Marshal butler. He reached out and steadied the painting. She dodged to the side to avoid his arm, but he braced his free hand on the wall so that she couldn't burrow into the corner.

Leaning over her so that he could make out her face, he said quietly, "Servants are supposed to be invisible, especially maids of all work."

"Yes, my lord. If you will excuse me, I will become invisible."

He flattened his other hand on the wall as she moved toward the stairs. "Too late." With satisfaction he watched her try to merge with the wall at her back.

"You were watching me," he said.

She glared at him. "I was not, you—my lord."

"I have bountiful leisure in which to await your confession."

He touched one of the wispy curls at her temple,

and she started. He hadn't realized how close to her
he'd moved until he smelled lemons. This maid of all
work, with her coal-grimed hands and her mussed
hair, smelled of lemons. He was used to the odor of
horse sweat and exploding artillery shells, accustomed
to the complex fragrance of Parisian perfumes. Thus,
when he swelled to near bursting upon catching a
whiff of lemons from a peevish housemaid, Jocelin
found himself unprepared.

Without thinking, he pressed his body against
her. She drew in her breath. Still clutching the neck of
her gown with one hand, she pressed the other against
his chest. Coal dust smudged the white cleanliness of
his shirt. He grinned when she noticed, pulled her
hand away as if it burned, then put it back as he
moved closer.

"Admit you were watching me," he breathed
near her lips. "You smell like lemons."

She had gone silent and stiff. At least he'd
achieved that much.

Their lips almost touched, and he whispered,
"You were watching me. Other women have, so don't
be ashamed. I want you too."

He kissed her then, because the smell of lemons
was driving him, as were her trembling and her
reluctance. His lips touched hers. Pliant, they opened,
and he tasted her. Then she stomped on his foot.

"Hang it!" Springing back, he fell against a wall
and grabbed for her at the same time.

She ducked under his arm, whirled, and scam-
pered down the stairs. Still cursing, Jocelin put his
weight down on his injured foot and grimaced. He
pulled off his boot and examined it. On the top he
made out the imprint of her heel.

"Hang it!"

A door slammed somewhere in the bowels of the scullery. Jocelin limped back the way he'd come. His gait sounded odd, since he walked on one booted and one stockinged foot. He swore at himself all the way back to his room.

Loveday had the habit of appearing magically, like a genie. He did so now. Jocelin expected him, since the man seemed to have the ability to know exactly when he would be required, no matter what his master was doing.

Throwing his boot on the floor, Jocelin stomped to a chair beside the fireplace and sat down. "Ice, Loveday."

"Indeed, my lord?"

"I hurt my foot, Loveday."

"How unfortunate, my lord."

"Not just for me, Loveday."

"Yes, my lord."

"I'm going to strangle that maid, Loveday."

"Which maid, if I may inquire, my lord?"

"The plump, lemony one, Loveday."

"Ah, Miss Gamp, my lord."

"Gamp? Gamp? Gamp, Loveday?"

"Yes, my lord. May I inquire if your lordship wishes the maid dismissed?"

Jocelin shot to his feet, grunted when he put his weight on his swelling foot, and sat down again. "No. No, no, no. If you get rid of her, I can't have revenge, Loveday."

"No, my lord."

"And don't say 'No, my lord' in that disapproving governess way of yours."

Loveday shoved an ottoman over to Jocelin's chair. "If I may say so, it has not been our custom to dally with the maids in our service. We have prided ourselves on this small virtue."

Jocelin flushed and propped his foot on the ottoman.

"Well, Loveday, we can't be so proud of our virtue anymore."

"No, my lord?"

"No."

"I will get the ice, my lord."

"She smells like lemons, Loveday."

"Indeed, my lord. A most wholesome fruit, the lemon."

With this comment Loveday left Jocelin slouched in his chair, staring at his foot and wishing he had a cup of hot tea—with lemon.

Strangling the neck of her gown, Liza ran downstairs. As she pattered over the thin carpet tacked to the risers, she listened for the viscount's footsteps, but heard none. She'd been in terror that he would follow her. The heels of her boots tapped the polished wood floor of the kitchen. No notice was taken, however, for a cry had gone up from the butler's pantry.

"Tea!" Choke called. "Tea, Mrs. Eustace. At once."

Liza tiptoed into the scullery, past the maid on her knees scrubbing the floor, and out a rear door. She reentered the house by a side door, reached the back stairs, and climbed to the attic, where she shared a

room with the third housemaid. She arrived breathless
and still shaking from her encounter with that uncivilized aristocrat. Choke would think her still occupied
with the bedchambers, so she had a few minutes to
repair the damage to her disguise.

The ragged edges of her gown fell open to reveal
the padding sewn into it. She'd been desperate to
conceal this lining and the stuffed corset when the
viscount had torn the dress. The man was mad. No,
not mad, but far too intelligent. He'd caught her
watching him, and now she'd alerted him to her
interest. Luckily he possessed the vanity of most men
and thought her interested in his glorious person.

She stripped off her gown and set about righting
her corset. Usually she and her roommate dressed in
the near total darkness of early morning and late night,
which prevented her from revealing her padding and
allowed her to stuff her hair beneath a cap. Without
the need for concealment, Liza pulled the cap off.

Cascades of hair tumbled forth. Liza thought of
it as neither-here-nor-there hair, for it was neither so
pale as to be blond nor so dark as to be brown. It was
an unsatisfying taupe, which she darkened with po-
made to complete her Miss Gamp disguise. What if
the viscount had dislodged her cap!

Liza pulled a fresh gown from the locked trunk
at the foot of her bed and stepped into it. Drawing it
up to her waist, she found that her hands were still
shaking. She'd been careless to let him hear her, but
she'd wanted so badly to see if he was leaving.

She'd searched the house everywhere except his
rooms. This morning she'd been able to examine the
last of the unoccupied bedrooms. What miserable luck
that he'd returned sooner than expected.

Her fingers were cold and trembled so, it was

difficult to button the gown. Not for the first time she was grateful for the lining that made the bodice warmer than it should have been. Her fingers slipped on a button, and she sank down on the bed to take several deep breaths.

If only the Metropolitan Police had believed her, but they'd sent her away with condescending smiles and secret laughter. She didn't care. Men had laughed at her before, and she'd lived.

She didn't care what they said. William Edward hadn't been the kind of man to skulk about the brothels and gin shops of Whitechapel and get himself garroted. She remembered thinking exactly that thought when the police came to her to identify him upon finding her card in his vest pocket. In her grief it had taken her months to make herself face the truth of her suspicions. More time had been wasted trying to get the Metropolitan Police to see her views. They never had. It would have been useless as well to try to convince Papa, since he'd taken the same opinion as the police. Finally she'd begun to inquire into the circumstances of William Edward's death herself— late, but determined.

Liza closed her eyes as she remembered her brother's bloated face. His tongue had been—no. No, she wouldn't see his face anymore. She'd promised herself.

Instead she thought back to that night last February, the night William Edward had been killed. He'd called on her unexpectedly. After leaving home, she'd kept in touch with him and her mother—secretly, because of her father. Papa would have nothing to do with a daughter he'd disowned for her stubborn unmaidenliness and quarrelsome nature. He hated it that she hadn't come back to him on her knees after he'd cast her out of his house. He was furious that she'd made herself independent in a trade. So William Edward had visited her secretly at her house, which doubled as her place of business, Pennant's Domestic Agency.

He'd been agitated that evening, and William Edward was never agitated. Part of his excitement had been on account of being admitted into Asher Fox's political committee.

"He'll get things done, Liza," William had said. "You should have seen him in the Crimea. He was the best lieutenant colonel in all the regiments. He saved bloody Marshall's life, and mine too. God, that idiot Raglan had us charging artillery."

"But your letters," Liza said. "You wrote that Marshall hated you."

William Edward flushed. "He wanted us to dress like savages. We're officers, her majesty's own cavalry officers, not bloody Indians. He wanted us to wear muddy buckskin, I tell you, and crawl around on our bellies—spying! But . . ."

"You changed your mind?"

William Edward traced the pattern on a lace curtain in her parlor-office, then cleared his throat. "I was with him when he took a vedette out one day shortly before Balaklava, and we came on a Russian troop unexpectedly. We were cut off, ripped to pieces. That fool Cardigan hadn't been where he was supposed to be with his men. Marshall and I and Sergeant Pawkins got away. But only because he made us take off our red coats and gold braid and roll in the mud. He'd spent too much time in Texas and California, and acquired a most ungentlemanly attitude toward war. You should have seen us, Liza. He made us cling to our horses along their sides and ride through the Russians. You should have seen their faces."

Walking over to sit on the edge of her desk, her brother looked down at her with haunted eyes. "That day I learned to ride bareback and crawl up to a Russian sentry on my belly and slit his throat from behind. He told me to do it or he'd kill me himself, since he wasn't going to die simply because real fighting wasn't 'quite the thing' among cavalry officers."

"This man made you crawl in the mud with a knife in your teeth and . . . and—"

"And I'm alive. But he's still a bastard, Liza. You don't know what he's like. Propriety forbids me to speak of his habits to you. When I think of a dukedom going to a murderous savage like him . . . Do you know that most of DeBrett's is wiped out? I don't think there are more than a handful of noble families with an heir left. And two weeks ago old Harry was killed."

William Edward played with her ivory letter opener as his voice lowered. "Poor old Harold Airey. Harry Airey, we used to call him. Always falling off his horse in drill. Never on parade, but always in drill. He got through Balaklava and then got himself strangled, garroted, they said. In Whitechapel. I didn't think old Harry Airey knew where Whitechapel was."

"Some of my best maids were born in Whitechapel."

William Edward waved a hand. "Well, maids, yes, but not Airey. He was a cavalry officer, Liza, a cavalry officer."

He said the words as if they were only slightly less honorable and noble than "her majesty." Liza had sympathized with William Edward, knowing that she could never make him understand the skin-and-bone poverty of the London slums, the stench-ridden sewers and soot-laden air. The children who slept in doorways and ended their short lives in ditches.

She had read about them in *The Times* and in pamphlets she secreted in her bedroom where her father couldn't find them. Papa didn't approve of women reading about such things. He would hand her mother portions of the paper that dealt with society, and Mama would pass them to her. Liza got the day-old papers from the butler, who was susceptible to bribery. The papers had been one of her few releases from day after day of grinding boredom. She wasn't bored anymore.

Liza shot to her feet. What was she doing, sitting here lost in the past? Choke would notice her absence if she didn't hurry. She thrust her cap on her head and pushed her long curls up inside it.

The memory of her last conversation with William Edward still haunted her. If it hadn't been for that chance remark about Harry Airey's being garroted, she might never have suspected William Edward's own death. But he'd gone from her house to a political meeting at the house of the viscount, whom he resented and with whom he'd quarreled, and never returned.

He'd died exactly the way the Honorable Harold Airey had died, and in the same nasty area of the city. William Edward was supposed to have been at a political meeting, not in Whitechapel. Two men from the same regiment, who attended the same political meetings, died the same way. The similarities were too great to be by chance. She was sure of it. And she was going to prove it.

William Edward had been the brightest and most loving of men. When Papa had raved at her for speaking her mind to suitors instead of pretending to have dried flowers for brains, William Edward had distracted him with tales of cavalry drills. William Edward had loved her in spite of her being different from other girls.

Enough musing. Liza patted her cap, then stuffed her torn dress in her trunk and locked it. She sneaked back into the kitchen and through the scullery to the small room where the knife boy polished boots and did other messy chores. She had yet to clean the viscount's boots. If she accomplished this task, she would have an excuse to go back to his rooms.

After what had just happened, she needed to search for clues to his guilt and escape the house quickly. Another encounter with him was not to be thought of. How she wished she'd been able to escape Choke's sharp eyes before the viscount arrived. Without the master in residence, however, both Choke and the housekeeper had had time to watch all the servants closely.

Liza paused as she crumpled up the newspaper upon which she'd scraped the muddy boots. He'd come at her out of the dark, cornered her. But when she should have been frightened, she'd been something else as well—she'd been drawn to him.

He wasn't what she'd anticipated. Despite his reputation for wildness and rapacity, she hadn't expected him to possess great personal beauty. Seductive men often didn't. Yet he could wear buckskin and cotton and turn a woman's spine to treacle.

She should be ashamed of herself. What happened to her every time she was in his presence? At first she'd put down her flustered feelings to fear of being caught, but now, now she knew better. She had only to look at him, and her mind stopped functioning. Several times she'd forgotten her role and nearly insulted him.

She had always prided herself on her good sense. Not for her the silliness and vapidity of other girls, the skittish niceness of other spinsters. Now look at her. She polished the boots quickly.

By the time she was ready to take them upstairs, Tessie came into the kitchen bearing a silver tea tray and sniffling. The teapot rattled against the tray when she set it on one of the big tables in the middle of the room.

"What are you blubbering for now, Tessie?" asked Cook as Liza passed by with the boots.

"H-he yelled at me."

Cook raised her eyes to the roof and crossed her arms over her chest. "What did you do?"

"Nothing," Tessie wailed. "He wanted lemon, and there was no lemon on the traaaaaaay!"

Liza hesitated, staring at Tessie as the woman bawled into her kerchief. A low, drawling voice whispered in her ear. *You smell like lemons. I want you too. You smell like lemons. I want you.*

Shivering, she put her hand on Tessie's arm. "Has he gone?"

"Yes. He'd hurt his foot somehow. Loveday bandaged it, and he went away. Thank God. He's never been like this. I shall speak to Mr. Choke. If his lordship's to continue like this, I'll look out for another place. Oh, are you going up, Miss Gamp? Would you take his shirts with you? I pressed them, but I just can't go up there again."

"I'd be might glad to do it. And I'll tidy the room so you don't got to do that either."

She followed Tessie to the laundry room. The maid placed a pile of ironed and folded shirts in her arms. She hooked her elbow around the handle of a coal scuttle filled with brushes, cloths, and a dustpan.

Loaded with the scuttle, silk, fine wool, and a pair of boots dangling from her fingertips, Liza marched upstairs. She passed Loveday on his way out, hat and gloves in hand. At last her luck was turning. She should have at least an hour to investigate the viscount's rooms.

Laying aside her burdens, she closed the door to the hall. She didn't dare lock it for fear of arousing suspicion should another servant have business in the suite. She glided quickly to the bathing and dressing rooms and searched them. Since she guessed they were the least likely places to hide anything, she wanted to deal with them first.

She found a battered trunk that had arrived with the viscount. She opened it and withdrew a brown horsehair rope, a strange, beaded bag containing eagle feathers on a thin, beaded band, and a pair of buckskin leggings. When she unfolded the leggings, an image came to her of Jocelin Marshall strapping them around his thighs. *Stop that.*

She set the leggings aside and dipped her hand into the trunk again. This time she retrieved the viscount's belt, holster, and revolver. The smell of freshly cleaned leather and gunmetal reminded her of him. She traced the intricate engraving on the belt buckle, remembering where it had rested on his hips. *Elizabeth Maud Elliot, you stop this depravity at once.* She rapidly searched through the remaining clothing and refrained from touching a double-barreled shotgun and shells. Then her hand touched fur.

Peering inside the dark trunk, she grasped an animal skin with black hair. When she pulled it out, her gaze caught the glint of metal. A hinged box

reinforced with metal. And it was padlocked. Faded
letters on its top spelled out "Wells Fargo." Liza felt
a burst of satisfaction as she hauled the box out and set
it on the floor of the dressing room.

From the pocket of her apron she drew a slim
metal tool acquired from Toby Inch. Inch was the
retired-thief-turned-butler she'd hired to pose as the
respectable Mr. Pennant when she'd first opened her
agency for domestic servants. Up to now she hadn't
required his criminal expertise.

She slipped the tool into the opening of the lock
and worked it slowly. After a few agonizing minutes,
the lock clicked. Liza opened the box—and groaned.
It was filled with dark, slim cigars.

Frustrated, she replaced the contents of the
trunk and rapidly searched through armoires and
chests filled with male clothing. She found neckties
and stocks, shirts and collars, morning coats, frock
coats, dress coats, and overcoats. She riffled through
dozens of half boots, military boots, unused slippers.
She opened drawers full of watches and chains, tie
pins, studs, and rings. And found nothing.

Next she tried the bedchamber itself, even
searching between the mattresses and bed frame.
Nothing. Liza ground her teeth together in frustration, then glanced at the desk in the sitting room.
Surely he wouldn't hide anything in that ornate
freight car. Still, she had to search. Poking through
every drawer and slot took time, and glancing at all the
letters took even longer.

Once she heard footsteps on the landing, but
they faded. The bulk of his correspondence concerned his estates, business interests, and political
dealings with men in government. For a man reputed
to be so dissolute, he was surprisingly concerned with

reform of the army and the controversy stirred up
when the queen tried to bestow upon the foreign-born
Prince Albert the title of king. Liza folded a letter and
replaced it in a slot. She had poked and prodded for
secret compartments to no avail.

Reluctantly she closed the desk, rose, and
straightened the chair in front of it. Slowly she turned
in a circle, inspecting the sitting room. She noted the
eighteenth-century armchairs, the curio cabinets that
had yielded nothing more sinister than Ming china,
the white mantel over the fireplace, an old secretary
too small to be of use except for decoration.

To expect a murderer to keep about him anything that would indict him in his crimes had been
foolish. She realized this now, after all her elaborate
schemes had failed. Dejected, Liza gathered her coal
scuttle, brushes, and cloths, and walked to the door.
She turned and gave the sitting room one last look.
Cool elegance, silver-gray, classical, sparsely decorated
except for a few ornaments like that blue thing on the
mantel.

Liza's hand was on the door. She paused in mid-
twist of the knob, cocked her head to the side, and
fixed her gaze on the blue vessel above the fireplace.
She set her coal scuttle on the floor, plucked a clean
dust rag from it, and darted to the mantel. She wiped
the rag along it until she came to a nautilus shell
contraption. Humming to herself, she poked her nose
into its interior. Empty. She gave the surface a swipe
with the rag and put it back.

The rag slid along the mantel to a Wedgwood
piece. She tipped it and stuck three fingers inside.
They swirled around in empty space. Muttering, Liza
pulled her hand free and dabbed along the mantel
again. She paused to consider the next vessel. The

blue thing looked like a flask. It had a small base. She would have to hold it with both hands to keep it from tipping over. The rag patted nearer and nearer the blue thing. She lifted both hands.

"Loveday said I should discharge you."

Liza jumped and shrieked. Whirling around, she beheld the viscount standing on the threshold. He was leaning on one shoulder and had his frock coat slung over the other and hooked over a finger. At her yelp, he grinned, came inside, and shoved the door closed while she gaped at him.

"He's right," the viscount continued. "I've never preyed upon my servants. Bad form." The frock coat sailed in the air and landed on an armchair as he stalked over to her. "Odd how I never noticed maids before you came. Loveday says you're new."

Liza scuttled sideways as he prowled toward her, but he changed direction as she did. She wrung the dust rag in both hands, backing up as he approached her. Her legs hit something solid, and she fell into one of the chairs near the fireplace. The viscount chuckled and swiftly bent to place his hands on the arms of the chair.

His body loomed over her. She could feel the heat from it. His head angled down so that he could meet her gaze. Brown, his skin was brown, not pale like that of most Englishmen, who spent their days indoors. Did all gunfighters have brown skin? Heavens, she was all atwitter again. He'd caught her snooping, and all she could think of was his skin.

"You needn't squirm so. I'm not going to hurt you."

"I got dusting to do, my lord."

"I saw you."

"My lord?"

"I saw you dusting. Diligently dusting. Forget the dusting."

His lips were drawing closer and closer. Liza's courage vanished. Bending almost double, she shoved her head under his arm and dove for freedom. She would have succeeded if he hadn't twisted around and slipped an arm about her waist.

With a teasing laugh, he scooped her up and spun in a circle. Liza shrieked and closed her eyes to shut out the spinning room. The spinning stopped, but she was flying in the air. She cried out again, fearing a hard landing on the floor, but her body landed on cushions.

Eyes flying open, she found herself sprawled on the couch by the windows. A knee planted itself beside her thigh. An expanse of white shirt blocked her view as another knee shoved between her thighs. Air rushed out of her lungs when Jocelin Marshall lay down upon her body. Too startled to move, Liza stared up at him.

She found her voice and snapped at him as she would a disobedient dog. "Get off me at once."

He didn't bother to answer. His gaze was fixed on her breasts, which jutted forth with the aid of all the stuffing over them. He was going to touch her. Dear God, she had to stop him before he realized she was all padding.

"They told me you was a bleeding degenerate," she cried as she began to shove him off her. "You ain't going to do no perversions on me."

His head came up then. All trace of humor vanished, and he jammed her back down on the couch by the weight of his body. Catching her wrists, he subdued her struggles and stuck his face close to hers.

"So, you've been gossiping about me with the

others. What did they tell you? Did they tell you about
my women? Did they tell you how many?"

"No!"

He wasn't listening, she could tell. In less than a
second the viscount vanished. She knew when it
happened, for after her denial, his eyes had changed.
No more amusement, no mockery. The gunfighter
was back, with his assessing, duelist's stare. Silence
filled the room, broken only by her labored breathing.
Afraid to challenge him again, she waited. She
shouldn't have, for his gaze dropped to her breasts
again, and then his weight settled on her.

"Been a long, long trip, honey."

"No."

He wasn't listening again, for his knee shoved
against the inside of her thigh, pressing her legs apart.
Truly frightened now, she was caught between the
desire to scream for help and the need to keep her
disguise intact. He got her legs apart and settled
between them.

"My lord, no. You said you didn't, not with
servants, and I don't want to."

"You will." He held her wrists with one hand and
touched his fingertip to her lips. "One thing you learn
out west, good loving is scarce. You got to take it when
you find it."

"No!"

His hand wandered to her hip, then brushed
down her thigh. Unfortunately, there was no padding
to protect her when he slipped his hand under her
skirts. His hand was warm as it caressed her ankle.

"You got small ankles for such a plump little
thing."

She kicked, dislodging his hand, but again he
seemed not to notice her reluctance. Then it came to

her. He wasn't going to stop. He'd forgotten where he was, who he was. She could tell by his drawl, by the way he moved his body, all loose-limbed and snake-like, but deliberate.

She raised her voice. "My lord, you must stop."

"Why?"

She met his gaze and encountered ruthlessness fed by something fierce and unknown, something that caused his skin to burn and his hips to move against her in a way she'd never experienced. In that moment she knew that none of her reasons, based as they were on propriety and honor, mattered to this man. If she couldn't stop him some other way, he would take what he wanted. He'd been doing it for too long in places where civilization wasn't even a word.

"You—you can't." Where were her wits?

"Yes, I can. Now be quiet. Soon that whining'll change to moaning. Then I won't mind you making noise."

"Ah-hum."

She started at the sound of another voice. At the same time, Jocelin Marshall sprang off her, slapped his hand to his hip, where a holster should have been, and turned to face Loveday. She scrambled off the couch. Loveday regarded his employer calmly, his hands full with a brush and a shining top hat. Liza glanced uneasily from the younger man to the older. The viscount stared at the valet, his brow furrowed.

"Our new evening outfit has come from the tailor, my lord. If we are to have dinner in Grosvenor Square, we must try our new raiment to be sure of the fit."

"Grosvenor Square," the viscount said as if he'd never heard the words.

"Indeed, my lord. Lady Georgiana and her grace

have both sent notes. Lady Georgiana spoke to me herself and expressly asked me to beg of you not to be late, as she has missed your lordship greatly."

"Lady—my sister."

As Loveday spoke, the viscount blinked several times, then glanced quickly at Liza. His hand balled into a fist. He straightened, assuming a military stance, and placed the fist behind his back.

"Thank you, Loveday. I shan't be late."

"I assume Miss Gamp may go about her other duties?" Loveday asked.

"Of course."

Liza's mouth almost fell open as the gunfighter vanished again beneath the cloak of a bored nobleman. Without another glance at her, the viscount turned his back and walked to the desk. When she left, he was idly perusing the stack of invitations lying upon it as if his greatest concern was whether he would have time to visit his club tonight.

4

The plump and peevish maid had vanished from Jocelin's thoughts. His family had accomplished this feat, though for a few hours he hadn't thought it possible even for the Marshalls. Yet here he was, listening to the perpetually hesitant rustle of his mother's skirts as she left the dining room, followed by the clicking of Georgiana's slippers against the floorboards. When the doors closed, he abandoned his officer's posture. Slouching down in his chair, he opened his coat, rested his ankle on his knee, and stuck his thumbs in his waistband.

He cocked his head and aimed a lazy, gunslinger's smile at his father, who scowled at him in silence because the butler was offering him port.

Jocelin shook his head at the proffered decanter. "Whiskey, please, Vincent."

When Vincent was gone, Jocelin downed his whiskey in one gulp.

"A sot's drink," the duke said.

Jocelin poured himself another glass and lifted it to his father. "To your newfound good sense in not inviting Yale this evening."

"I wanted to talk to you, not fight to keep you from murdering my brother in front of me, sir."

"As I said, good sense."

The duke shook his white head and glared at Jocelin. He had the straight Marshall nose, so well suited for looking down at others. He looked down it now at his son.

"I'll not argue with you. I sent for you because I've had enough of this useless wandering of yours. With—with Charles dead, it's up to you to marry and produce an heir."

Jocelin lifted a brow. "You sent for me?"

"Don't be any more difficult than you must," the duke said. "I sent a letter months ago."

"Do you really think I came home because you told me to?" Jocelin smiled at his father's consternation. "I came home because my business in America was finished, and I had more here in London."

"You mean you grew tired of picking gunfights with barbarians and frequenting the company of red savages."

Jocelin took a sip of whiskey and surveyed his father over the rim of the glass. Slowly he placed the whiskey on the tablecloth and traced its cut glass with the tip of a finger.

"I had business that needed attending to here," he said, "and I'm not getting married, ever."

The duke rose and walked down the length of the dining table to stand by Jocelin. He leaned over his son, his hand gripping the back of Jocelin's chair.

"I thought you'd say that."

Jocelin's fingers tightened their grip on his whiskey glass, uneasy at his father's ferociously pleased expression.

"I have but one answer for you," the duke said. He paused, drawing out the suspense. Finally he went on. "If you don't do your duty, the title will go to Yale."

Silence fell once again. Jocelin lowered his lashes and held himself still. Ice colder than that of the Never Summer Range settled over the burning core of rage that served as his heart. He tried to think clearly. In his hatred of Yale, he'd never considered what would happen if his uncle inherited the title, and along with it all that wealth and power. Yale would use that wealth and power to prey on other innocents. Disgusted with his father's ruthlessness, he retreated further into the protection of his gunfighter role, but the duke had caught him unaware. He didn't quite succeed.

Lifting his gaze to the pale green eyes of his opponent, he whispered, "May God damn you to everlasting hell."

"I'm so glad you understand your position."

Jocelin took another sip of whiskey and gave his father a nasty smile. "I understand, but you don't. I'm going to choose her." He lapsed into his drawl. "And just think of what I'm going to bring home, Daddy."

The duke straightened and looked down on his son. "For tonight I'm satisfied with one victory."

Jocelin didn't answer. He rose, snatched up his glass, and sauntered to the door.

"Mother and Georgiana are waiting."

"You will marry, Jocelin."

He turned on the duke, who took a step back upon perceiving the expression on his face.

"You're such a God-fearing old fool. Don't you shrink at what the Almighty will do to you for condemning a woman to marriage with me?"

"You exaggerate."

Jocelin laughed. "Do I?" His voice lowered to a catlike hiss. "I'm all that is corruption, dear sire. The queen says so. Wickedness and depravity lie down with me each night." He put a hand on his father's arm and leaned closer in confidentiality. "If you don't believe me, ask Yale."

When it was obvious the duke had no reply, Jocelin bowed and allowed his father to precede him into the drawing room. He went to his mother, who was running a scent bottle under her nose and dabbing her eyes with a lace handkerchief. She held out a trembling hand to him.

"My dear boy, how I've missed you."

"I missed you too, Mother."

His gaze ran over her. She cultivated a pale complexion, so it was difficult to judge whether her pallor was due to frailty or powder. He regretted leaving her, for she needed someone who could stand up to the duke for her. She was still in mourning for his older brother, though he'd been dead for three years.

"You must help me deal with your sister," the duchess said.

Jocelin glanced at Georgiana, who was thumbing through the pages of *The Times* with a deliberateness that warned him of trouble. She lifted her head and gazed at him over the gold rims of her spectacles.

They had both inherited the Marshall black hair and startling green eyes.

"Don't smirk at me, you little curse," he said. "What have you done?"

"Nothing, Jos, nothing at all."

"It will be the death of me, her come-out," the duchess said on a moan as she waved her scent bottle under her nose again.

"Mother, she's too young to come out."

The duke spoke up. "Nonsense. Next year she'll be eighteen. The perfect age to marry. Not too young to have some judgment, not too old to be guided by her husband."

"It's not her age," the duchess said. She touched her handkerchief to her lips, and tears made her eyes glassy. "It's what she's planning."

The duke poured a cup of coffee and brought it to his wife. "Now, now, Delia, you mustn't listen to her. She only says such things to set you in a twitter."

Jocelin marched over to his sister and planted himself beside her on the sofa. Plucking the newspaper from her hands, he tossed it on the floor.

He turned her to face him and said, "Out with it. What are you about, little curse?"

"I don't want to come out, Jos. I don't want to get married and have to obey every whim of some strange man, go where he wants to go, do what he wants to do, sit at home while he carouses at his clubs and plays with . . ." Georgiana glanced at her mother. "Other ladies."

Jocelin stared at his sister. "Where did you learn about such things?"

"Don't spout that superior-male drivel at me, Jocelin Paul Marshall." Georgiana pushed her spectacles back up the bridge of her nose and sniffed.

"Married women have no rights. Just look at Mother. She can only buy things if Father approves, read things he finds acceptable."

"But it's only proper that she be guided by his judgment," Jocelin said. "She wouldn't know how to decide such things for herself. She'd come over faint at having to deal with business affairs and politics. A woman's mind is a delicate thing, unsuited for such heavy matters."

Georgiana gave him a disgusted look. "I've solved the problem though."

"What problem?"

"The problem of having to marry. I'm going to marry an old man."

Jocelin grinned. "How old? Twenty-five? Thirty?"

"No, you simpleton. Eighty or ninety."

"Eight—that's not funny."

"I'm not joking," Georgiana said. She leaned down and retrieved the newspaper.

Jocelin watched her calmly flap the paper out between her hands to straighten it. He knew Georgiana. Once she decided upon a course, she could seldom be diverted from it. He still winced when he remembered the time she decided to ride his cavalry horse to church. Women! Women were one of the few subjects upon which Jocelin and his father agreed. He didn't want to think about how much this small point of accord meant to him. Early on Jocelin had witnessed his mother's dependence upon Father, her helplessness in the face of the roughness of the outside world. She needed protection. Women in general needed protection, sometimes from their own impetuous natures, as with Georgiana. It was one thing for a man to flout the conventions, another for a woman. He glanced suspiciously at his sister.

"And just why have you taken it in your head to marry a man who could die at any moment? Oh."

Georgiana looked up from the editorial she had been reading. "Exactly. While he's alive, he'll dote on me and give me what I want, and then he'll die. I'll be a widow, and I can do as I please. No playing the slave to a husband-master for me."

"You'll make Mother have heart palpitations again."

"Mother has palpitations when it suits her. They're useful in getting Father to do what she wants."

"Mother isn't like that."

"Oh?" She raised her brows and wiggled them at him.

He'd always hated Georgiana's cynical attitude about their parents. When Father hadn't believed him about Yale, Mother had given comfort. Although she hadn't been able to stand up to Father on his behalf, Jocelin had understood.

He frowned at his sister. "Women are delicate, Georgiana. And you can't disgrace yourself with such an indelicate course of action."

This comment earned him another disgusted look. He sighed and debated with himself as to the wisdom of arguing with Georgiana. Perhaps he should wait. She hadn't come out yet. He could round up eligible young men and cast them in her way next year. Yes, that was a far more advisable strategy. Arguing with Georgiana usually proved fruitless. His father's voice broke through his reverie.

"Jocelin has come to his senses, Delia, so you needn't worry any longer. He's going to make the rounds and look over the new crop next season. He can start with house parties. Old Clarendon has gone to his place up north. He's got three daughters, each with fifty thousand and good blood."

"I was thinking of Lucy Lyttleton," Jocelin said.

The duchess gasped and waved her handkerchief in front of her face. The duke flushed, patted his wife's arm, and snarled at his son.

"You watch your tongue in front of your mother and sister."

Jocelin stood, grinning, and buttoned his coat over his snowy evening shirt. Lucy Lyttleton was the scandalous widow of Lord Lyttleton. She'd seduced him when he was sixteen. At least, she thought she'd seduced him. In actuality he'd picked her out and allowed her to pursue him. He'd been at Sandhurst, angry, desperate for distraction.

He went over and kissed his mother's brow. "I must go. An appointment in the city, Mother."

Georgiana kissed his cheek. "So, we're both on the block, up for sale."

"Georgiana!" cried the duchess.

Jocelin laughed, bowed to his father, and left them. As he entered the foyer and nodded to Vincent for his coat, a footman escorted several men through the vestibule.

"Jos, I'm glad we found you."

Jocelin smiled a greeting at Asher Fox, who slung his coat at the footman. He shook hands with Alex Stapleton and Lawrence Winthrop. As usual, Stapleton's nose was red from drink. Winthrop, Lord Winthrop, pursed his lips and nodded to Jocelin as if he were a judge instructing a bailiff. He led them into the library, where Stapleton aimed himself at a liquor cabinet. Winthrop took the chair nearest the fire as if it were his right, but Asher Fox was too excited to sit. He pounded Jocelin on the back.

"Palmerston has come out for me at last, old fellow."

"Excellent," Jocelin said as he sat on the edge of his father's desk. "Now if he will refrain from antagonizing the queen, his support will mean a great deal."

Asher leaned on the desk next to him. They both had the tall, muscular build required to be a member of the Heavy Brigade cavalry, but Asher was the taller by a fraction of an inch. He had always reminded Jocelin of an old painting of a Charles II cavalier with his brown curls, heavy-lidded eyes, and crusading spirit. Asher appeared to consider Jocelin's words, then glanced sideways, causing the hair on Jocelin's arms to rise. When Asher Fox looked at him that way, it meant Jocelin was going to be hounded into doing something he didn't want to do.

"What?" Jocelin demanded.

"Speaking of the queen . . ."

"Oh, no."

"As the son of a duke, you can request an audience."

Jocelin pushed himself off the desk and shook his head.

Stapleton waved a brandy snifter at him. "Hear him out, old fellow."

"Yes," Winthrop said quietly from his throne. "Hear him out."

"The last time she allowed me into her presence, it was to tear into me for my sinful ways." Jocelin ran a hand through his hair. "She thinks I'm a satyr in evening dress."

"You are," said Stapleton with his nose in the snifter.

Jocelin threw up his hands. "She threatened to refuse to receive me."

"Well, Jos," Asher said with a grin, "she has her throne to keep, you know. Can't appear to tolerate debauchery, not our proper little German hausfrau queen."

"There. You see?" Jocelin rummaged through the liquor cabinet for whiskey.

"Cowardice is unbecoming to you," Asher said.

Jocelin glared at his friend and sloshed whiskey into a glass.

Asher continued. "I wouldn't have asked you if I hadn't thought you could do it." He came to Jocelin and placed a hand on his friend's arm. "Her majesty doesn't want to admit it, but she's drawn to you. I've seen it. Think, Jos, of how it must be for her, stuck with that stuffy prig of a husband. She doesn't realize it, but part of her longs for a bit of dash and go, a minuscule taste of what she'll never have—courting and romance."

"She disapproves of me," Jocelin said as he shook off Asher's hand.

"Not as much as you think." Asher lowered his voice so that only Jocelin could hear him. "Only I know the whole of it, my friend. Only I ever will."

Jocelin glanced at his friend briefly, unable to bear for long the sympathy he found there.

"You don't play fair, Ash."

"I don't know what you mean."

"That's just it," Jocelin said quietly with a smile. Turning to the others, he said, "Vincent will have announced you by now, and Mother will be wondering where you are."

Winthrop waited for Stapleton to open the door

for him, and the two left. Asher remained behind, his gaze fixed on Jocelin.

"Will you do it?" he asked.

Jocelin shrugged. "If I must. We need people like you in Parliament. And now you must excuse me. I've an appointment."

"Not with that Ross fellow. Dear God, I thought when you came back from this bloodletting of yours, you'd have purged yourself of this, this need."

"Nick Ross is a friend."

"But what you're about has nothing to do with friendship."

Asher approached him again. Jocelin concealed his surprise when the older man snatched his whiskey glass from his hand.

"You can't keep doing this," Asher said. "It's perilous beyond imagining, not only to your body, but to your soul."

Jocelin turned away from Asher. "I lost that long ago. I live my days in a dark night of the soul. I'm irredeemable, Ash. Let me go." He rang for Vincent.

"You're going to get yourself killed."

"But I won't go alone," Jocelin said as Vincent entered with his coat, hat, and gloves.

He donned the garment and took his hat and gloves from Vincent. Asher accompanied him to the door, and Jocelin slapped him with his gloves.

"Don't look at me like that," he said. "Such a mawkish face you put on. If the tzar's army couldn't kill me, I should be safe in London."

He left Asher staring at him with a worried frown, ran down the steps to the street, and climbed into his carriage without looking back. He hated the way Asher seemed to know without asking when he was going into East London. He disliked causing his friend pain.

Asher had taken him in that night fifteen years ago, when he'd fled Yale's house. He'd taken him in, heard his confession, and accepted him in spite of it. Throughout the ugliness that followed, Asher had remained his friend. As his commander during the war, he had taken from Jocelin more than most officers would take from a junior.

The carriage came to a halt in front of a town house of grand proportions. For a few minutes Jocelin remained inside, lost in memories. The interior was dark, but a street lamp cast a yellow glow in the mist. He heard the clip-clop of hooves as a hansom cab passed. It slowed, but drove on and turned a corner.

A flower vendor strolled by, but Jocelin's expression warned her, and she didn't try to sell him her wares. He sighed and touched the handle of the door. A woman walked by, a servant by her plain dress. He caught a glimpse of an apron and a cap.

He could have sworn he smelled lemons as he stepped to the ground. He whirled, took two steps after the woman, then stopped himself. His imagination, that's what it was. He had to get hold of himself. Loveday had lectured him like a disapproving school-master about Miss Gamp. Hang it! He couldn't be alone for more than five minutes without lusting after the woman, and he had yet to see her clearly in daylight.

Jocelin muttered to himself as he swerved and planted himself at the front door of the town house. A parlor maid answered, recognized him immediately, and conducted him into a drawing room warmed by a too-hot fire. He heard someone running downstairs, and Nick Ross sailed into the room, resplendent in evening dress. From his coat of finely woven Saxony to his white silk waistcoat, Nick could have passed for a nobleman.

"You're late, your highness."

"Asher delayed me."

"You go making these pissers wait, they'll have your carcass floating in the river come morning."

"You're fizzed because you don't like to wait."

Nick pulled on his coat, then stuck his hand in an inner pocket. Withdrawing a small revolver, he broke it open and examined it.

"I think this bloke's the one."

"Damn all," Jocelin said softly. "Are you sure?"

"Nah, but I will be once I get me—my hands on 'im."

"'Him,' Nick. Your *h*'s, remember, not 'im,' 'him.'"

"Yes, your h-h-h, h-h-highness. Come on, love. My carriage is out back."

Jocelin pressed his hand against his coat and felt his own revolver. The hammer gouged into his rib, and he adjusted the gun inside his pocket. The carriage pulled out into the street behind Nick's town house the moment he closed the door.

As they drove east, he settled back for the long drive to St. Giles. They passed Notting Hill, Kensington, and Hyde Park, then drove up Oxford Street. Buildings began to crowd close, and he lost the scent of Hyde Park greenery in the stench of broken drains. The deeper into St. Giles they went, the more frequent the beer shops became, until the streets seemed to consist of nothing but pubs. The carriage slowed as foot traffic increased. Here vendors hawked meat pies, and costermongers offered fruit and vegetables to hurried and wary pedestrians.

They turned down a street of broken cobbles with three gin shops and several boardinghouses. Jocelin pulled his white silk scarf from beneath his coat collar and wrapped it around the lower half of his face. Nick did the same. The carriage slowed to a walk as it approached the corner. The back right wheel sank into a hole and climbed out.

Jocelin looked through the window. The boardinghouse on the corner looked like the two across the street. Prostitutes sauntered by, only to be chased away by a doorman of monumental proportions. Two professional men stumbled out of the noisy pub next to it and weaved their way past the entrance. The doorman watched them until they rounded the corner, his hand on a bulge in his coat pocket.

Their carriage stopped in front of the boardinghouse. Jocelin eyed the doorman, who spat on the cracked pavement and grinned, revealing a picket fence of broken teeth.

Jocelin glanced at Nick and murmured, "'O God! that bread should be so dear, / And flesh and blood so cheap!' Time to buy flesh and blood, old chap."

5

Liza wiggled and bounced in the seat of the hansom cab, so great was her impatience to see the carriage they were following. Beside her, Toby Inch leaned to the side and craned his neck to see around the horses and down the street lit by a single gaslight.

She tugged on his coat. "Which way did they go?"

"Turned down Wigs Lane." Toby suddenly yelled, "Here now, you get out of the way!"

Liza dared to poke her head sideways out of the cab. She hadn't done so when there was a chance she might be seen by the driver of the carriage they were following. Two men rolled into the street at the feet of

the cab's horse while a blowsy woman stood over
them, screeching about pickpockets.

Toby leaped out of the cab and waded into the
fray while Liza sat back and twisted a cloth purse in
her hands. She was cold and tired and frustrated. She
had an out tomorrow, that one day in the week she
could call her own. After being thrown on that sofa by
Jocelin Marshall, she'd been planning to use it to
disappear from his household. That was before she'd
followed him into St. Giles. Having tracked the
viscount this evening since he left for dinner at the
duke's residence, she wasn't about to lose him because of a thief.

She heard a loud *thwack*, then the scuffle of feet.
Toby reappeared, straightening his cap and woolly
scarf. He jumped into the cab, and they were off. Liza
gave him a grateful glance. He had always been
behind her, even when her own father hadn't been.
She remembered that time too well and the circumstances that had brought them together. Enraged that
she hadn't turned out to be the epitome of womanly
graces, fragile in wits as well as body, Papa had grown
more and more furious at her refusal to behave like
the lady he wanted her to be so that she could catch a
titled husband. Liza had known what he asked was
impossible for her to do. When he threatened her, she
refused to cower. She never had responded well to
intimidation; it only infuriated her.

Finally he'd decided to break her spirit. He
disowned her and threw her out on the streets,
scoffing at her that she would crawl back to him in less
than a week. But Papa hadn't counted on Liza's
intelligence and gift for strategy. Before leaving, she
persuaded Mama to give her a character as if she were

a housemaid. Taking with her valuables inherited from her grandmother, she'd gone to London.

In London it was Toby who had given her a place in the same house in which he served as butler. A tall man without much bulk, he appeared more frail than he actually was, which his employer's eldest son discovered when Toby found out the young man had gotten his daughter with child.

Liza didn't like to think back to those days. Toby had been convicted of assaulting the young man and his daughter accused of prostitution. The household splintered, and the servants were given notice.

In her desperation to find safe employment, she'd conceived Pennant's Domestic Agency, an elite service that responded to the emergency needs of Society—the sudden illness of a chef just before a banquet, a miscalculation in the number of maids needed at a come-out ball. After serving his short sentence, Toby had come to her to pose as Hugo Pennant, for she soon found that Society had no intention of giving its custom to a woman, especially a young one.

"Here," Toby snapped at her as the cab's half door slammed shut. "You keep your little nose inside. I'm not going back to Pennant's and have to tell the others I let our lady get herself knocked in the head in St. Giles."

"Toby, there it is! Driver, that's the one, the one pulling away from that boardinghouse."

As they passed the building, Liza craned her neck to see inside. The door was closing as she went by, and all she could see was a foyer bare of furnishings. The doorman slammed the door shut and snarled at her. Liza retreated into the carriage.

"What was that place, Toby?"

Toby folded his arms across his chest and stared at the hind end of the horse.

"Oh," Liza said. She contemplated Toby's set features and gray hair. "One of those places. Then why didn't they stay there? You might as well answer. I'll ask the driver if you don't."

"They didn't stay, Miss Curiosity Cat, because they picked up what they wanted and now they're going someplace more comfortable."

"But didn't you say there were—well, nice places where gentlemen went for refined sin?"

"Some likes to come down in the dirt, so to speak," was all Toby would say.

Liza thought for a moment, then glanced outside. "We're going back west."

Her curiosity increased as they followed the carriage past Hyde Park. The vehicle abruptly turned north toward St. Mary's Hospital. Traffic thinned, and Liza began to worry that they would be noticed. She made the driver slow, then stop altogether when the carriage turned down a side street without lighting. Telling the driver to wait, she and Toby approached the intersection on foot, her friend grumbling all the way.

"See here," he hissed. "You let me go first."

The hour was late. There were few pedestrians, all of whom huddled in their cloaks and coats and paid them no notice in their haste to get out of the damp cold. Toby and Liza reached the corner and carefully looked down the street, which was little more than an alley. The carriage had stopped. As Liza peered around Toby's shoulder, the door opened.

A man in evening dress climbed out. His face was shrouded in the folds of a white silk scarf, but Liza recognized that posture. He stood in the street and put his fist behind his back, spine straight, as a door opened in the wall beside the carriage. He turned back to the open carriage door.

To Liza he appeared to be conversing with someone inside the vehicle. He leaned through the doorway, and though she couldn't understand what he was saying, she heard the coaxing tone in his voice. He held out his gloved hand. Slowly, with painful hesitation, another, bare hand appeared and surrendered itself to the gloved one.

Liza frowned, for the arm that followed it was swathed in a patched coat sleeve. The viscount gradually persuaded his guest from the carriage.

She glanced up at Toby and mouthed, "It's a boy?"

He said nothing, but nodded once.

Confused, Liza watched the viscount induce the boy to leave the carriage. Though he was dressed in tattered wool, someone had thrown a silk cape over his shoulders. Liza could just make out his features by the light of the carriage lamps.

Bronze hair, thick and smooth, a complexion without blemish, strongly sculpted cheekbones. The boy pulled his hand free and backed up until he hit the side of the carriage. His fear screamed at Liza.

The viscount spoke soothingly to him, but the youth started when a cloaked and hooded figure emerged from the doorway. The figure stood on the threshold, making no move toward the boy, but immediately the youth's whole body sagged from its rigid posture. Without warning, he brought his hands up to his face.

The viscount moved then, dropping an arm over the boy's shoulders and drawing him close. The youth was so distraught, he put up no resistance as the viscount handed him over to the cloaked figure. Liza shot Toby a questioning look, but Toby jerked his head in the direction of the carriage.

Another man in evening dress sprang from the vehicle. In his arms he held a girl. She wore a frilly dress and bright patent leather shoes, and her lips were a too, too bright red. She also was handed over to the cloaked figure, but the moment she was released, she wrapped her arms around the youth and buried her head in his shoulder.

The viscount spoke again to the boy, touching his shoulder. The boy shrank away from the touch, but nodded. His head hung wearily, and with a last frightened glance at the viscount, he allowed the cloaked figure to pull him inside the building.

The viscount stood staring at the closed door. His companion said something, and he shook his head, turned abruptly, and climbed into the carriage.

"Quickly," Liza said as she and Toby hurried back to the cab.

The doors had barely closed on them when the carriage turned the corner and drove past them. They were off again, this time toward the countryside beyond Fulham.

"What was that all about?" she asked.

"I don't like it," Toby said, chewing his lip. "And we can't follow them out of the city much farther without being noticed. Gor, missy, this business got a foul smell to it. Watch it!"

Liza lurched forward as the driver hauled on his reins, and Toby threw an arm in front of her.

"I think they stopped again. Can't go no farther without them seeing."

Toby opened the door that stretched across his

legs, stood up and peered into the darkness. "They did stop."

Several minutes passed with Liza anxiously waiting for some sign from Toby. Even if she stood up, she wasn't tall enough to see anything, for the road descended the other side of a hill and plunged into a stand of trees.

"Gor!" Without warning Toby jumped back into his seat. "They're coming back. Turn this cart around and scarper, lad."

They clambered ahead of their would-be quarry and managed to pull into a busy street in Fulham before being overtaken by the carriage. Tangled in a snarl of vending carts, omnibuses, and carriages, they watched the vehicle disappear.

Liza slumped back in the cab seat. "Let's go home, Toby."

It was well past midnight when they paid off the cab and entered the house that served as the offices of Pennant's Domestic Agency. Situated between Kings Cross and Shoreditch, it was near the wealthy, yet not so far from East London that working people couldn't reach it. Pennant's was the third in a row of terraced houses done in Grecian style with columns marching down the row one after the other.

The house was dark. Toby lit a lamp in the genteel drawing-waiting room before passing through the fictitious Pennant's reception room to the true center of the agency, Liza's office. Customers were never admitted here, where they could encounter the real owner. Indeed, not all of Pennant's employees knew who Liza was.

Liza trudged into the office as Toby lit another lamp. After pulling off her cloak hood, she removed her cap and rubbed her face with it. Her eyes felt as if they were coated with sand, and her back ached where she'd twisted it trying to wriggle away from Jocelin Marshall.

She collapsed on a settee and sighed. "Find out what that place was in St. Giles."

"Nasty, that." Toby stood over her, his arms folded.

"He's up to something," she said. "Damn him. I couldn't find anything in the house."

"You know he got that little girl and that boy from St. Giles." Toby cleared his throat. "Missy, there's goings-on you best not know about. Some things ladies shouldn't—"

"Don't bother," Liza snapped. "Ignorant ladies are helpless ladies, helpless and powerless. By now you'd think you'd have given up lecturing me on delicacy. Women aren't delicate, Toby, or they wouldn't survive childbirth, or the slums, or husbands who run off and leave them with the children. Oh, never mind. I'm too tired to argue. Just do as I say."

"It ain't proper," Toby growled.

"Go to bed."

"I'm going. Gor, who'd have thought a miss with a father as rich as King Solomon would turn out such a witchy, bluestocking shrew."

Groaning, Liza maneuvered herself off the settee, crossed the room, and carefully lay down on the longer sofa. She propped her head up on an embroidered pillow and snuggled down in her coat. She stared at a painting of a Scottish loch that hung above the couch.

What was Jocelin Marshall doing? Regardless of Toby's attempts to shield her, she had learned much since coming to London to work. She knew most men frequented women of low morals. What had shocked her was the little girl, and the boy. But if the viscount had taken the two children from that pretended boardinghouse, he hadn't done so for the same reasons the other patrons had. Why had he deposited them like bullion, in a place far away from their employer, when he would have to return them?

Such questions would have to wait for answers. Liza turned on her side and winced at the twinge in her back. Yes, she had expected depravity of the viscount, but never had she imagined that he would conceive a passion for her coal-dusty and fulsome self.

No gentleman had ever lusted after her. Even more unimaginable, she suspected that she was aroused by his interest. Why else would she fail to run from him when he advanced, when he might be a murderer? Even if he wasn't one, she should have run.

Elizabeth Maud Elliot, how unmaidenly. What improper conduct. How unbecoming. How dangerously foolish. Liza sighed and turned on her back to stare at the ceiling. She was a poor creature, a poor creature indeed. If she was going to succumb to a gentleman, she might as well have stayed at home and married one of Father's boorish, self-interested, and close-minded persons of title. But then, she'd never had difficulty conceiving a distaste for any of them.

Jocelin Marshall, now, he was different. He had but to set foot in her presence, and she became fascinated. She couldn't claim that her interest was all due to his pursuit either. From the moment his carriage had pulled up to the line of servants that night, she had been drawn to him. Heavens, she'd been captivated by his boots.

She could govern herself, however. She could. Dear Lord, she must keep her suspicions in mind for her own sake. She had the strength to do so. She was as strong as a house in her resolve. Therefore she needn't quit the viscount's household so precipitously. After all, any woman would be enticed by a man like that. Exotic, wondrous in his black-cat appearance, dangerous, he cast into shadow the effete society men of her acquaintance.

She would have to be more careful if she returned. No more cleaning his room. No more going above stairs when he was about. He seemed to have the ability to discern where she was and trap her. She would take greater care. That was all.

Having resolved most of her dilemmas, if not the mystery of her brother's death, she took herself off to bed. The next morning she was in her office going over receipts with Toby and his daughter, Betty. They'd been running Pennant's while she was gone.

Liza sat in her leather armchair behind the big cherrywood desk she'd found at an auction. Betty hauled out the leather-bound book of days in which they recorded their schedule by the week. While Liza gnawed on the end of a fountain pen, she detailed the activities of the past fortnight.

"And we have the Duke of Lessborough's banquet next week?" Liza asked.

"Yes, and his secretary has been hounding me about Monsieur Jacques. I've assured him that he would get Monsieur Jacques, but he's still atwitter."

Monsieur Jacques—really Elihu Diver, exseaman and ship's cook—was in great demand. He was in demand because Liza had started a rumor through her mother that his recipes had been handed down from Marie Antoinette's chef.

"Very well," Liza said as she turned a page of the schedule. "Toby, write a letter from Pennant's to the secretary promising Monsieur Jacques."

She glanced at the watch pinned to the shoulder of her gown. Ten o'clock. "Time to receive, Toby."

The rest of the day passed quickly, for there were bills to pay and new people to hire. Pennant's reputation had spread in the three years since she began. After Papa had thrown her out of her only home and she'd come to the town house run by Toby, she'd been confident that she could be a maid of all work. How hard could it be? She'd soon learned that there was more to dusting than just running a cloth over furniture, more to serving than just plopping plates down on a table. The first day, she'd tried to dust an arrangement of dried flowers and destroyed it.

Toby could have gotten rid of her, but he took pity on her ignorance and her desperation.

Liza had a headful of book learning. She couldn't empty slops. Under his tutelage, she learned to empty slops, clean boots, dust, sweep, lay fires, draw baths, polish silver, and serve a table. And she'd done it all out of rage at her father.

Thinking back over her life before she'd come into service, Liza could remember a time when she hadn't been hurt and angry. Long ago, when she was quite little and William Edward was a baby, then she'd had no notion of resentment and animosity. Her world transformed, however, one day when she was almost seven.

William Edward came down with diphtheria. Days passed in which her parents hardly left his room. She was terrified and bewildered. Longing to help, afraid to leave the house for fear of somehow losing her parents as well, she had stolen away from her governess and gone to William Edward's nursery. She crept toward his little bed, grasped the rail, and stared at her parents.

Her mother was crying, but Mama cried a lot, and Liza had seen her do it too often to be frightened of the sight. What terrified her was Papa's sobbing. She hesitated, afraid to remain, too frightened to leave. Then she put her hand on Papa's shoulder. He jerked his head up and stared at her. She drew back her hand as she met his gaze and encountered for the first time his undisguised resentment and rage.

"Why?" he said, wiping his tears with the back of his hand. "Why would the Almighty take my beautiful William Edward instead of you?"

When she only gaped at him, he buried his head in his hands. "Go away. God, why didn't you give me a son instead of her?"

That day she learned she'd been unwanted. Mama followed Papa's every wish and, under his sway, regretted her failure to give him a firstborn son. Not that she'd been neglected. She'd been given the upbringing of a proper gentlewoman. Papa, the son of a butcher, had seen to that for his pride's sake. But while Papa spared no expense to send William Edward, whom he'd almost lost, to Eton and on a tour of Europe, and later to Cambridge, he'd not been so inclined when it came to providing for his daughter.

Knowing her precarious position in his affections, she hadn't complained. Yet all the while she labored under the burden of knowing that she, not William Edward, would have flourished on the meat and bread of such an education. So she taught herself with the help of governesses handicapped by the same prejudice that had robbed her of opportunity.

She hadn't complained. Not until Papa sent William Edward to Europe. William Edward had only been fourteen, a lackluster student. After that, she screwed up her courage and asked for the same. Papa laughed. When she persisted, he grew angry, dismissing her longings without really listening to her. And so she stayed home.

The next year, when she was seventeen, Papa discovered an interest in her. This was because she had suddenly become useful. Having spent his life building a fortune in banking and investments, he now wanted more than riches. He wanted gentility. He wanted acceptance in Society. Never a man to settle, he chafed under the besmirching heritage of his common background. Papa wanted his son to marry well. He wanted his grandchildren to have titles. He wanted to see it happen before he died.

In order to do that, he would have to purchase a suitable bride for William Edward. Such a maneuver would take years to accomplish, for England's nobility didn't offer its daughters to butchers' grandsons— even if they were extremely wealthy. Thus Richard Elliot designed a plan. His daughter, with a properly splendid dowry, would spearhead his movement to conquer Society. He had clawed and slashed his way into a fortune using his sly cleverness. He could intrigue his way into the gentry using his daughter.

His one mistake was in failing to consider Liza. She was unknown to him. He saw her occasionally—at meals, after dinner. That is, he knew she was around. Other than to take note of her presence and pay her bills, he had left her upbringing to his wife. After all, how difficult could it be to teach a girl to play the piano and dress herself well? He launched her into country society first, as he would have launched one of those steamers in which he'd invested, never suspecting that his daughter would have anything to say about his plans for her. She had.

While he'd been absorbed in raising and indulging his son, Liza had been left much to herself. Mama too was enraptured with William Edward, when she could spare time from pursuit of her one real interest in life—herself. Left alone, Liza explored the world through study, since she couldn't do it in person. She used her allowance to buy books and prints. She read newspapers and magazines.

If he'd bothered to find out what she was doing, Papa wouldn't have approved. As it was, the unpleasant discovery of his daughter's bluestocking character came in the midst of her first party. Liza took perverse satisfaction every time she remembered that night. Papa had turned vermilion as he heard his daughter argue with an eligible son of a knight of the empire about the merits of a married woman's property act and the necessity of a divorce bill.

Well, it served him right. But then had come her first season, and the event that soured her already negligible taste for titled young men. It wasn't that she hated men. She wasn't so stupid as to think all men as parsimonious and close-fisted with their love as Papa. It was just that none of them seemed to understand that a young woman would want more than to sit at their feet and goggle at them in adoration.

Papa had been furious at her. He accused her of being "clever." It was social death for a girl to be thought clever. Still, it had been his own fault. Perhaps if he'd spared her some morsel of his affection, she wouldn't have insulted a total of five bigoted young men during the course of one ball and gotten herself ostracized from Society. Definitely, it had been

Papa's fault. After that had come his threat to disown her. She still couldn't think of the way he'd so easily cast her out without feeling a sharp jab of pain in her chest. Yes, the whole disaster had been Papa's fault, but this knowledge didn't take away the pain.

6

He watched Jocelin pour brandy into coffee cups. Jocelin, the gracious; Jocelin, the beautiful; Jocelin, the dangerous. He shouldn't have come tonight. He was feeling the beast, snarling, pawing, keening to come out in the open. On the way over in the carriage he'd almost stuck his head out the window and howled. And now they were talking about Stapleton's death in a cloud of after-dinner cigar smoke. Stapleton had drunk two bottles of brandy without stopping. A man can't do that and live, which had been the point.

The beast rolled over inside him, grunted, and snuffled. When he felt like this, he saw everything as if he were crouched on all fours, and everyone either as predator or as prey. His fingers curled into claws. His thoughts blurred into elemental instincts, flashing images of quarry scrambling for safety, of running, running, running through a battlefield. His horse was gone. Oh, God, his horse was gone.

On foot he was dead. Around him shells exploded. Pieces of his men spattered his coat. He screamed. Lieutenant Cheshire rode at him. Cheshire was wounded and slumped over his horse's neck. He grabbed the rider, who cried out as he was hauled from the saddle. He mounted. Cheshire grabbed his leg and pleaded. He kicked out, and Cheshire flew backward onto the lance of an advancing Russian.

He kicked the horse, and it sprang forward. He heard Cheshire's dying cries, swept by Sergeant Pawkins, saw Jocelin clash his saber against that of a Russian cavalry officer. He galloped on and on until he was safe. But he would never be safe, because someone besides Cheshire might have seen his cowardice. Someone else might know what he was.

The beast lifted its head, pointed its muzzle skyward, and howled. He heard a small sound in his throat—a little grunting whimper. That sound jolted him into the present.

Jocelin had finished pouring the brandy. No one seemed to have noticed his lapse. He tapped his cigar ash on the edge of his dessert plate. He was here because of Lieutenant Cheshire. Most of the old group were here, those who had survived. That was why he came, why he supported their political aims. He could watch them, especially Jocelin, who was so wild and on the edge, uncontrollable.

Jocelin had lain next to Sergeant Pawkins in hospital at Scutari. Jocelin had been delirious when he'd come to the ward that night and smothered

Pawkins. Jocelin didn't remember anything. And if his friend ever did, he would be there, at his side, watching, watching, watching.

Liza hiked her skirts and tiptoed up the back stairs. She had returned to her post determined to avoid the viscount. Not having seen him for almost two days, she had decided to risk sneaking into his rooms again for one last search. He was busy with his political meeting.

She had peeked at the guests and their host from behind a door as Choke and two footmen took coats and gloves. It seemed as if they had all arrived at once, and never had she seen such a collection of brilliant young men. They must be rather like their cavalry horses, all sleek, working muscle and blazing spirits.

She reached the door to the viscount's sitting room and slipped through it. Listening for Loveday, she concluded that the valet was still submerged in the evening paper in his own room. A fire burned in the fireplace, but there was no other light. Where had she been when that awful man came upon her? Ah, the mantel.

Liza went to the fireplace and stuck her hands out to warm them. Stiff fingers dropped things, and she couldn't afford to drop Wedgwood or anything else. After rubbing her hands for a few moments, she grasped the Wedgwood urn. Empty, as she remembered. The nautilus shell cup concealed nothing either, which left the antique blue thing with the hinged top. She took the vessel in both hands and lifted it from the mantel.

A delicate gold chain connected the top to the

neck of the flask. She pulled the top back and looked inside, but the interior was too dark. Carefully she touched her forefinger to the lip, then slid it down the neck slowly so that she didn't push anything too deep inside to be retrieved. Her finger hit something. She withdrew her forefinger and inserted her little finger. Snagging the object, she pulled it out.

A small roll of paper. At last. Excitement caused her to fumble with the blue thing, and it almost slipped through her hands. Gasping, she caught her upper lip between her teeth and set the vessel back on the mantel. Then she opened the paper and read it.

What disappointment. But then, had she expected a confession? Still, the list must be important, or the viscount wouldn't have hidden it. She read the five names. They were set out in two groups, one of three and one of two names. She read them over and over in order to memorize them: Griffin Poe, Nappie Carbuncle, Frank Fawn; Sir Morris Harter, Dr. Lucius Sinclair. Her lips moved as she repeated them. Later she would give the list to Toby, who would make inquiries about them among his widespread acquaintances, criminal and respectable.

She placed the rolled paper back in the blue thing and straightened it on the mantel. Then she tiptoed back to the door and opened it a crack. The hall was empty. Did she dare steal into the room that connected with the library? The viscount and his political friends had gathered there, and she might be able to hear something important. Jocelin Marshall wasn't the only man to have close dealings with her brother. He was merely the most credible suspect.

The night William Edward died he had gone to one of these political meetings and had words with the

viscount. He'd left in a miff, if the police were to be
believed, and gone drinking in Whitechapel. Fastidi-
ous, snobbish William Edward drink in Whitechapel?
Never.

The other man, Airey, had died the same way.
Such coincidences weren't to be believed. And now
this man Stapleton was dead, the Honorable Alex
Stapleton. He too had been a member of this select
group of ex-cavalry-officers-turned-political-aspirants.
Stapleton, however, had drunk himself to death. Too
much alcohol in his blood, the paper said. A hard-
drinking man like that would know not to swill
brandy. Three odd deaths. Three odd deaths. The
cadence reminded her of a nursery rhyme. *Three blind
mice, three blind mice. See how they run.* They ran or got
their tails chopped off.

It was late. She was supposed to be helping the
scullery maid with pots and pans, but she'd been
diligent about the washing up for two nights and done
the bulk of the work for the scullery. Her absence
wouldn't be resented.

Liza skimmed along the hall and down the front
stairs after looking to see that the foyer was uninhab-
ited. Darting into the parlor next to the library, she
shut herself in and crept to the door that connected
the room to the library. She had oiled its hinges and
lock only this morning.

She caught her breath, twisted the handle, and
eased the door open so that a sliver of light beamed
into the dark parlor. Letting the air out of her lungs
slowly, she waited a moment before risking a look
through the gap. The movement hadn't been detected, so she widened the crack.

All five of them were there, including Jocelin
Marshall. As she examined the group lounging about

the room, Asher Fox seemed to be listening to a muted discussion he found distasteful. His nostrils widened while his drooping eyelids swept down to conceal a gaze she'd often seen when a gentlewoman happened upon her while she emptied slops. From a family of military heroes, Fox was the grandson of old General Lord Peter Bingham Fox, of revered memory for his part in the battle of Waterloo. His father, the present Lord Peter, had served in the Horse Guards with distinction. His distant ancestor had fought for Charles II's restoration.

She'd seen the man warming himself nearest the fire. Lord Winthrop, he whose chin and hairline were in a race to see which could disappear faster. Even Liza, uninterested as she was in Society, knew that his mother was the offspring of a liaison between the daughter of one of the queen's uncles and of the Earl of Mumford. Winthrop was glaring at Arthur Thurston-Coombes, a son of mere gentry. Then there was the earl, martinet of the drill field and parade ground, Reginald Underwood, Earl Halloway.

The earl had settled himself in the chair opposite Winthrop. Halloway was known as a connoisseur of women. He leaned forward in his chair and followed Jocelin's every move. Choke, in a rare moment of gossip, had commented that Halloway resented Jocelin's attraction for the ladies, mostly because a certain Miss Birch had deserted him for the viscount.

Liza surveyed them all and marveled that the veneer of civility these men cultivated could contain all the seething resentments and personal foibles. Her gaze snapped back to Lord Winthrop when he made a sound of impatience.

"Blast it, Coombes, must you reveal your lack of

breeding? Take the band from around your cigar, man."

Thurston-Coombes, the youngest of the group, flushed, sucked on his cigar, and blew smoke at Winthrop. "You always were a bounder, Buggy old chap, but we're not in the regiment anymore, so stuff your pretensions up your ass."

Jocelin laughed softly. Halloway left his perch and walked over to him. He swirled the remaining port around in his glass.

"I saw you riding in the park yesterday," the earl said. The others went silent and watched the two. Jocelin glanced down at Halloway, then took a sip of whiskey.

"Keeping track of my social engagements?" he asked.

Halloway slammed his glass down on an end table. "You sneaking bastard, I saw you with her."

Jocelin carefully set his own glass down and selected a cigar from a box on the table. "My dear Hal, I never sneak where women are concerned. However, I am discreet. Now shut your mouth, for if you mean to taint a lady's reputation, I'll pull your spine out your ass."

"God," the earl said, flushing to the color of a geranium. "I'd like to see you try."

Arthur Thurston-Coombes guffawed. "Me too."

"Sod you all," Halloway said, as he glared at Jocelin and took a gulp of port.

Asher Fox pushed himself away from the mantel, on which he'd been leaning. "Please, old fellow, they're just baiting you, and you allow it. You're so touchy. Please, chaps, we're all on edge because of Stapleton."

Halloway shrugged and turned his back to the group.

"Odd, Stapleton's going like that," Thurston-Coombes said. "Still, he'd been upset about something the last few days. Emptying the bottle more than usual."

Halloway sighed and turned back around, his foul mood having evaporated. "And then last year we lost old Harry Airey and young Elliot. Wouldn't have thought they'd go in for slum crawling. Stupid, that."

"They had no sense of propriety," Lord Winthrop said as he held out his glass to Jocelin for a refill. "Airey was half mad, and Elliot, well, everyone knew his family wasn't quite the thing."

Thurston-Coombes swore at Winthrop. "Christ, you can be such a prick."

Asher Fox dropped an arm about Coombes's shoulders. "That's enough. I think we're all a bit coshed about Stapleton. We've finished our business, so let's go home. We've got a job of work to do if we're going to canvass for support among the members. No need to go savaging each other. Remember what it was like in the Crimea. We'd be dead if we'd gone at each other like this."

Thurston-Coombes waved his glass at the viscount. "Not old Jos. He'd have painted himself with mud, stolen into our tents, and slit our throats."

Jocelin grinned at the young man.

"Yours first, old boy."

"I'm honored," Coombes said with a bow.

Liza pulled back from the door as the men rose and filed out of the library. She went to the door that let out onto the foyer to watch them leave. The viscount said good-bye to his friends, dismissed Choke and the footmen, and ran upstairs. She heard his door shut. Racing belowstairs, she was just in time to receive Choke's instructions to tidy the library.

She trudged back upstairs and began collecting glasses, snifters, and ashtrays. While she worked, she repeated the list of names under her breath. Stumbling over the last one, she decided to write them down. A secretary desk surmounted by a cabinet with beveled glass contained paper and pens. She took a sheet, dipped a pen in an inkwell, and scribbled the names quickly. She closed the desktop, folded the paper, and slipped it inside the padded sleeve of her gown.

As she pulled the cuff down on her wrist, the door opened.

"I knew you'd come out if I waited long enough."

The viscount propped himself against the door frame and hooked a thumb in his waistband. He had pulled his necktie loose, and his top shirt studs were missing. He hadn't had his hair cut since he came home, and a lock of it fell over his brow. Although he'd brushed the rest of it back, it had dropped forward again, moonless-night black, soft, and gleaming as though sprinkled with starlight. Liza hadn't moved since he spoke. In that first moment, she had been afraid he had seen her writing or putting away the piece of paper, but he didn't remark upon it.

Instead he came into the room, shoved the door closed, and kept walking. This was what she'd been dreading. As he moved, she darted around a wingback chair. Scooping up two glasses, she put them on a tray. She was about to pick up the tray and run when he caught her.

Suddenly he was behind her. An arm reached around her and pushed the tray back down on the table. Liza let go of it and sidled away from him. He grabbed her arm, then caught her around the waist and drew her close. Pushing against his chest, Liza wondered how human flesh could feel so dense and unyielding. Did he suspect she'd been snooping? Frantic, she bent her knees and dropped straight down and out of his grasp.

He beat her to the door and put his back to it. Liza tried to swallow, but her mouth was too dry. Why did he have to have that disturbing body? She hadn't expected to see him. She'd been caught unprepared. Her skin tingled, and in spite of her dread, some unbalanced, animal part of her put mad thoughts in her head. *Don't run. Let him touch you. If he touches you, you can touch him.* Lord in heaven, she wanted to dig her fingers into his bare flesh. No, how wicked.

"Why do you run away?"

"Um, hmm."

"Um, hmm?" The viscount's hand snaked out and captured hers. "Why, you're shaking. Hang it, woman, I only want to seduce you, not beat you."

Liza yanked her hand out of his grasp. "I'm a respectable woman, my lord. I give you no reason to doubt it, so please keep your hands away."

Swearing, the viscount crossed his arms. "I never met such a cantankerous filly."

"You're angry."

"I am not."

"Yes, you are. You're talking in that drawl that makes you sound like you wished you could shoot me like those ruffians over in America, those, those gunfighter persons."

"Gunfighter persons? Hell, woman, all I want to do is kiss you."

Liza snorted, her courage shored up by the fact

that he hadn't tried to capture her again. "Kiss indeed."

She shouldn't have been so contemptuous. His eyes narrowed, and his gaze ripped up and down her body. When he spoke, the soft huskiness of his voice alerted her to a new danger.

"You got something against makin' love, honey?"

Liza stopped herself from sidling backward. She couldn't let him know how easily he could discompose her. Furious at the thought that she might want a man who sampled women like tea sandwiches, she lifted her chin.

"Making love, my lord? Mercy, what you want isn't making love. You don't even know me, so you can't love me, which means you just want to have relations with me. I got no use for being used."

He said nothing at first, then, holding her gaze with his own, he pulled at one end of his necktie where it hung over his shoulder. The black silk slithered against his shirt and came loose.

"Sometimes there's just no talking with a woman."

The tie dangled from his fingers, and she found herself staring at it. Then he launched himself at her. Startled, Liza was slow to react, and he caught her. She shrieked and tried to kick him, but he lifted her and squeezed. Her chest flattened against his. She gasped for breath, but his arms tightened. He walked over to the wingback chair by the fire, swung her into his arms, and sat down. Liza immediately tried to jump off him, but he clamped his hand to her waist. She couldn't break his hold, and stopped trying when he slipped the tie around her neck.

Going rigid, she directed her gaze at his face instead of his hands. Her back was to the fire, and light bathed his features. The viscount was gone, in spite of the evening clothes, the signet ring on his hand. Holding the tie at both ends, he drew her closer and closer.

"My lord."

He was so close, she could feel his breath skimming across her cheek, and her vision filled with the sight of his lips.

"There ain't no lord here, honey, so don't bother," he said as he touched her lips with his.

How amazing. Liza argued with herself: feel his lips, they're so soft; make him stop; God, he's putting his tongue in my mouth; make him stop; my blood, it's going to boil and turn to steam.

He pulled on the ends of the tie, forcing her to accept a deeper, more penetrating kiss. Liza lost all rigidity in her body. He released the tie. One hand cupped the back of her head while the other kneaded her waist. Then, without warning, he sucked on her mouth. Liza moaned, heard herself, and panicked.

Merciful heavens, what was she doing? She opened her eyes. She didn't even remember closing them. Grabbing a handful of soft, black hair, she yanked and propelled herself out of the chair. The viscount yelped and clutched at her. She scrambled out of reach, clamped a hand over her cap to rearrange it, and ran to the door. He thrust himself out of the chair, but stopped when she opened the door and took a step over the threshold.

"You come back here."

She shook her head violently and gasped for breath.

His chest was heaving.

"You make me chase you, you'll be mighty sorry."

"You're not civilized, you aren't."

"Look, honey. I just came from a place where women are scarce. A man who don't take what he wants ends up with no woman at all."

Liza gawked at him as she retied her apron. "This isn't the American frontier, my lord. I got me reputation to—"

"Hang your reputation."

He swooped at her while her hands were still tying a bow at her back. He surrounded her with his arms and planted his mouth on hers again. He kept it there for what seemed like a century, exploring her while she tried fruitlessly to make him release her. Then he lifted his lips just enough to allow him to whisper to her.

"Shit, honey, forget this silly idea you got about protecting your virtue. Give it to me, and I'll settle you someplace real nice. Someplace where I can light all the lamps and finally get a good look at you."

Fury enveloped her. As he lowered his mouth once again, she met his lips, and bit them. He cried out, and she pushed at his chest as hard as she could. He flew backward. Hitting the door, he stumbled and covered his mouth with one hand. Liza whirled and raced across the foyer, around the stairs and through the door that led to the back of the house. Hurtling downstairs, she paused to listen for him. She heard his footsteps on the landing above her head.

She ran through the dark kitchen, fumbled with the latch to the back door, and slipped outside. As she raced up the steps to the yard, she heard him.

"Wait!"

She paused on the top step and turned to face him. He was wiping blood from his lower lip. To her astonishment, he grinned at her.

"Damn all if you don't set me on fire."

His English accent had returned. Liza relaxed and breathed more easily.

He brushed a lock of hair back from his forehead. "Do you know how long it's been since a woman refused me?"

Liza shook her head.

"Neither do I." He glanced over her from head to toe. "I never knew what I was missing. No, don't bolt again."

"You touch me, and I'll scream for Mr. Choke."

He laughed and put his foot on the bottom step.

"I will," she said.

"I know."

He took another step. She would never be able to outrun him.

Frantic, Liza burst out, "I'll scream for Loveday!"

He stopped then, and glared at her.

"I'll scream louder than a steamship whistle, and Loveday will come out and find you."

"You sly little midge." His hand strangled the wrought-iron banister at his side. His glance raked over her again as silence fell. Suddenly he turned and stalked downstairs again.

"It worked this time," he snapped over his shoulder. "This time. It won't work again."

He vanished. Liza sighed as she heard a door slam inside the house. She waited until she was sure he wasn't coming back, then went to her room and began packing. She couldn't stay now. If she stayed, he would find her again. Somehow she brought out a ruthlessness in him he didn't even want to control. No, she couldn't stay, for in her heart she suspected she really didn't want to go.

7

Liza poured another cup of tea from the china pot on her desk as she read the information gathered so far by Toby. Glancing out the window at the back garden, she watched snowflakes fall, then yawned. She had reached Pennant's late last night, and hadn't calmed enough to sleep for several hours after that. The mantel clock struck four in the afternoon, and she returned to her reading.

That boardinghouse had been a place of prostitution, of course. Rumors about it said that the men who frequented the place had peculiar tastes. They also said that the manager pandered to these tastes most enthusiastically, since they coincided with his own. The manager's name was Frankie Fawn.

"Fawn."

Liza rummaged among the papers on her desk, found the note she'd scribbled last night, and jabbed her finger at one of the names.

"Frank Fawn. Merciful heavens." She jumped up from the desk and began to pace back and forth in front of it. "Toby!"

Toby, who had been seeing off a group of employees bound for an earl's military banquet, clattered through the house in his all-weather boots. Entering her office, he put his mittened fists on his hips and surveyed her.

"Read it, did you?"

Liza waved her list at him. "That man, the manager or procurer or whatever he is, he's on the list."

"That's real peculiar like," Toby said. "Old Bill just got in from the docks. Says they've found another floater."

"A what?"

"A corpse, missy. One floating in the river. It's our Frankie, it is."

Liza clutched the back of a chair. "Frank Fawn."

"Some blokes saw him fighting with a gentleman. Seems our Frankie came at him from behind with a knife. Picked the wrong gent, though, 'cause this one did for him good. Frankie stumbled and fell backwards off the dock. Must have hit his head on a pylon. Maybe that gent was the one who reported our Frankie to the rozzers, 'cause they raided his place. Didn't find no tykes though. None at all. Only regular whores."

"Dear me."

Liza's voice sounded faint even to her own ears.

She sank down on the chair and clasped her hands tightly in her lap.

"Toby, there are so many people dying. William Edward, Airey, Stapleton, this man Fawn."

"Nah," Toby said as he unwound a wool scarf from his neck. "London's a big city. With this many people in one place, there's bound to be some dying, and sorry creatures like Frankie get done all the time."

"But their names don't appear on lists hidden in the houses of dukes' sons."

Toby stopped unbuttoning his coat. "You're right there, missy. Good thing you scarpered, or you might have ended up a floater."

"I can't just leave off."

Groaning, Toby marched over to her and shook his forefinger at her. "Now you listen to me. You hire one of them gents who investigate crimes for folks."

"We've been through this," Liza said. "They're too expensive, and I'm not risking the financial health of Pennant's. Too many women with children work for us."

"That's not it."

"Oh?"

Toby stood erect and clasped his hands behind his back with a snort. "It's him. And don't look at me with them innocent eyes. Ever since you first saw him, you been acting peculiar. I seen your face go all soft and misty-eyed when you was thinking of him. I got a daughter of me own, so don't think I don't know what that look means. He's got to you, just like he meant to, and you'd better stay away from him if you don't want to end up like my Betty."

"Why, Toby, you're worried about me, and I can't imagine where you got such ideas."

Her answer was another snort, and a mimicking sneer. "Oh, gracious, I can't imagine."

"Besides, I've just thought of a plan."

"Gor, not another plan."

Liza gave him an affronted look. "It's a good one. Look, Toby, we can't stop now. Don't you see—there are children involved."

"Them two we saw are still with the old lady we saw. They don't need our help."

"How do you know that old woman isn't another procurer? How do you know she isn't keeping them for the same reason Frank Fawn kept them?"

"You make me sick, you do, with your canniness and your stubbornness."

"Then we're agreed," Liza said. She laid the list in her lap and smoothed her skirts. "Which is good, because I need you to post a letter for me at once. It's to my father."

"Gor!"

"I've found a way to be near Viscount Radcliffe and yet make sure he won't, um, pursue me."

"Not if you don't wear a padded dress."

"I'm going to be me, Toby, which should prevent any further interest."

Toby threw up his hands. "You're daft. Being you won't get in his way. Women. If a young hound like that comes sniffing around you plump, he'll sniff around you skinny."

"Papa wants me to marry well, especially now that William Edward is gone. He wants a grandson. Not a granddaughter, mind you, a grandson. I'll pretend Pennant's isn't doing well and that I've learned my lesson. That's what Papa's been waiting for me to do. I'm going to agree to hunt for a husband, and then get him to invite Jocelin Marshall to a house party. When Papa realizes I want to try for a duke's son, he'll be apoplectic with joy."

"Him visit your pa? Not likely."

"He will if Papa mentions he's thinking of supporting Asher Fox's bid for a seat in Parliament. The viscount has a great fondness for Mr. Fox, and political aims as well."

Dropping to his knees, Toby spoke to her quietly. "You listen to me, missy. Don't you go putting yourself in his way. If this high tone fellow is up to the nastiness I think he is, you're in danger."

Liza patted Toby's arm and rose from her chair.

"If he's killed my brother or done the things you say, he'll find me dangerous as well."

❧ ❦ ❧

Jocelin sat behind his desk in the library nine days after he refrained from seducing his plump maid. During the past week he'd fought a small war with his scruples and lost, which was why he'd sent for the housekeeper and Choke. The housekeeper sat on the edge of her chair. Her lace cap quivered with her shaking. Choke stood beside her, unperturbed at this abrupt summons.

"And since I'm going to be searching for my future wife, I'll be entertaining more," Jocelin said. He was gratified with his reasoning. It had taken him a while to come up with it. "Therefore I'm going to need more service abovestairs. I want you to make that new maid—Gamp is it—make her a parlor maid and hire another maid of all work."

The housekeeper's cap quivered. Choke and she exchanged glances, and the butler cleared his throat.

"Your lordship hitherto has left household matters in our hands. Ah-hum." Choke looked at his employer with mild reproach. "And since your lordship has had so many late night appointments and political meetings, there hasn't been an opportunity to take up certain matters."

"What matters?"

"Gamp, my lord. She's left your service. Quite abruptly, over a week ago. She left a note informing me that her aunt in Liverpool had taken ill and that she was forced to go to her."

Jocelin lowered his gaze to the correspondence on his desk. "She's gone, is she? Where?"

"Yes, my lord, and I replaced her," Choke said. "I can find another parlor maid quickly, however. The Pennant's Domestics are always available, and—"

"Where, I said."

"She didn't say, my lord."

"Never mind."

"But, my lord, if you are contemplating some new entertainments, we should begin hiring at once."

"I've changed my mind. Thank you, Choke."

He nodded and rose from his chair. Left with no other alternative, Choke and the housekeeper filed out of the room. When they were gone, Jocelin pounded his fist on the desk.

"Damn all!"

Ignoring the ache in his fist, he stuffed his hands in his pockets and glared at a portrait of George III hanging on the wall beside the desk. Then he pulled the bell cord and sent for Loveday. He was drumming his fingers on the desktop when the valet arrived.

"What have you done with her?" Jocelin asked.

"Whom, my lord?"

"The plump and peevish maid, Gamp. Did you send her away?"

Loveday's brow wrinkled, causing furrows in the bare scalp above them. Then they smoothed as he comprehended.

"Ah. We have been unable to rise above temptation, and have also just discovered Miss Gamp's disappearance."

"We're pissed, Loveday."

"Indeed, my lord."

"I thought she was hiding from me belowstairs. Where is she?"

"I don't know, my lord. But perhaps her absence is fortuitous." Loveday cast a meaningful glance at him. "If I may be frank?"

"Go on. You will be anyway."

"Since we encountered Miss Gamp, our manner has lacked a certain decorum. We have been temperamental with servants, which is quite unlike our usual gracious deportment when dealing with those in our service."

Jocelin stood up, put his hands on the desk, and leaned forward to grind out his words. "I don't care. If you think I've been temperamental, just watch me if I don't find Miss Gamp. We're going to have her, Loveday, and we don't care how we get her."

"Indeed, my lord?"

He sank back into his chair and clutched his head. "Indeed. Loveday, I'm desperate. I think I smell lemons everywhere. I accosted Lord Quay's scullery maid in the street because I thought she was Gamp. Damn those silly caps. They cover a woman's whole head."

"This is quite unlike you, my lord."

"I have to find her." Jocelin slumped over and buried his head in his arms and groaned out his frustration.

"This obsession is likely to interfere with our efforts to find a bride."

Jocelin talked into the pillow of his arms. "I can't think with my cock stiff as a cook's rolling pin. Sorry, Loveday."

"As I said, my lord, our decorum has lapsed since making the acquaintance of Miss Gamp." Loveday bent over the desk to peer at Jocelin. "If I may make a suggestion, my lord. We might avail ourselves of the services of a private inquiry agent. Such a person could find the whereabouts of Miss Gamp and put us in communication with her in a circumspect manner. Once this task has been accomplished, we would be free to entertain the young woman in our usual discreet fashion."

"You're a man of acumen and discernment, Loveday. Feel free to go around to that rare book store you like. Select several volumes that take your fancy, and have them send the bill to me."

"Your lordship is gracious." Loveday bowed regally. "And now, if I'm not mistaken, Mr. Ross was just arriving when I came in."

"Throw him in here, then."

Jocelin sat up, straightened his necktie, and brushed his fingers through his hair. Nick Ross sailed into the library, waving the morning paper at him. He grinned, but his smile faded when his friend spoke.

"*Delenda est Carthago,*" Nick chirped. "*Morituri te salutamus.*"

"Oh, God, you've hired another tutor."

"*Fas est et ab hoste doceri.*"

"It is right even to learn from an enemy?"

"Is that what it means? Clever of me." Nick dropped onto the couch, put his legs up on it, and flapped the newspaper at Jocelin. "Read it?"

"Not yet."

"They have found a partial list of Fawn's customers."

Jocelin turned away and gazed out the frosted windows behind the desk. Beyond the French doors lay a terrace, and beyond that a snow-shrouded garden.

"Has that boy told you how many others?"

"No. He doesn't want to talk about it. Give him time, Jos. Don't think about it. You always go black on me after we do one of our little jaunts. And don't bother denying it, because I heard that sigh." Nick jumped off the sofa and struck a dramatic pose. "Don't think about it. Listen to this:

> *'Teach me half the gladness*
> *That thy brain must know,*
> *Such harmonious madness,*
> *From my lips would flow. . . .'"*

Jocelin hunched his shoulders and turned around to stare in horror at Nick. "That's Shelley. You've hired an English tutor as well, blast you."

Nick put a hand on his breast and gazed at the ceiling. "'To be, or not to be: that is the question: / Whether 'tis nobler in the mind to suffer / The slings and arrows of outrageous fortune—'"

"No!"

Jocelin sprang at Nick and clamped a hand over his mouth. Nick shoved his hand away.

"Watch it, Jos."

"Please, please, Nick. Hamlet was murdered once in the play. Don't you do it a second time."

Nick flushed and turned his gaze from Jocelin.

Rising, he stalked to the fireplace, placed an arm on the mantel, and contemplated the coals.

Remorseful, Jocelin took a seat nearby. "Sorry, Nick, old fellow."

"I got to get me learning somehow. Missed it while you was pulling pranks at Eton and military school."

"I'm an ass, Nick. How can I make it up to you?"

"You can't."

Jocelin gazed up at Nick's set features and decided to change the subject to an innocuous one. He returned to his desk and shuffled through a pile of invitations.

"Father has been busy trumpeting that I'm for sale. I got a pile of invitations in the morning post."

"Don't get no invitations."

Hearing the bite in those words, Jocelin grinned. "Would you like to?"

Nick gave him a disgusted look. "Your people wouldn't have me in their barns, much less their houses."

"They will if I want you there."

"Jos, not even you can scrape the mud of St. Giles off me."

"Then we'll give you a new coat to cover it. We'll give you a pedigree. Nothing elaborate. Perhaps a distant relation to some Scottish family that's gone to America."

Jocelin dropped his invitations on the desk and rummaged through them. "Here we are. Mr. Richard Elliot. A butcher's son made good. Dying to get into Society. Elliot would let me bring a goat if I accepted his invitation to stay with him at his place in the country. Besides, he's offered to be of use politically. What do you say?"

"Humph."

"Come on, old boy." Jocelin frowned at the invitation. "I'll need support if I'm to make it through a whole month dodging the matrimonial traps of a financier and his solid and no doubt oafish daughter and do Asher some good at the same time."

"The duke wants you to look at a butcher's granddaughter?" Nick asked.

"Of course not. I've had a note from him warning me not to accept offers from anyone of less rank than an earl's daughter."

"So you're going to go just to make him puke."

"Want to come along?"

Nick's froth and insolence returned, and he smiled. "Never could resist a jaunt, now could I?"

"And I'm going to teach my father the cost of trying to use me like a stud put out to breed."

Shaking his head, Nick said, "'Double, double, toil and trouble; / Fire burn and caldron bubble.'"

8

The procession that set out from the train station at Little Stratfield-on-Willow rivaled any that had been seen in the last thirty years. First came the grand Stratfield Court landau carriage, black and yellow, drawn by four matched grays, two of which were ridden by postilions. Then came another, lighter vehicle bearing two valets and light luggage, followed by mounted grooms leading two hunters. At a slower pace in the rear struggled a wagon loaded with trunks. Liveried outriders trotted in advance.

In the landau, sitting opposite each other with the top down in spite of the cold, sat Jocelin Marshall, Viscount Radcliffe, and his friend, Nick Ross. Nick was facing forward and trying to keep his cheeks from turning red.

Above the noise of trotting horses and clattering wagons, he asked, "You always go visiting this way?"

"Of course not," Jocelin said. He rested his ankle on his knee and waved a glove in the general direction of the retinue behind them. "Elliot wants the whole county to know who has deigned to stay with him. What use would I be if no one knew I was here? So word will spread. I'm counting on it."

"So we're giving up our jaunts so you can visit this gent and annoy Daddy."

"Not quite. Dr. Lucius Sinclair lives nearby."

"Sinclair. He's on the list."

Jocelin nodded.

Nick whistled softly. "What are you going to do about him?"

"Take steps, Nick old fellow. Take steps. Not as severe as what he deserves, but steps nonetheless. And of course, I must begin this business of hunting for a bride and talk to Elliot about old Ash."

He didn't mention that his efforts to find the mysterious Miss Gamp had so far failed. Frustration gnawed at him, for he kept smelling lemon fragrances when he first woke up, at his club, in his bath. He suffered from unsatisfied lust in a way he had never experienced. The torture made him short-tempered and restless. Only the prospect of keeping himself busy with courting Elliot's political support had put him in a better mood.

He and Nick drove in companionable silence until they reached the gates of Stratfield Court. Wrought-iron grillwork swung open, and they drove through carefully preserved woodland. The train ride hadn't been too long, less than four hours to Wiltshire, but both men chafed at being confined to a railway carriage. Jocelin was gazing up at bare tree branches highlighted by weak afternoon sunlight when Nick made a strangling noise. He turned and glimpsed a monumental country house in the distance. As the trees gave way to an expanse of lawn, he understood Nick's consternation. The place looked as large as Windsor Castle.

Nick was frowning, and he squinted at Stratfield Court. "What's wrong with it?"

Jocelin's lips curled.

"Could it be all that depressingly dark red brick?"

Nick gazed at the house in confusion.

Jocelin took pity on him. "Calm yourself, old boy. The thing's part castle, part French château, and part cathedral. You're unaccustomed to seeing them all thrown into one monstrous effusion. Old Elliot must not have been able to make up his mind what he wanted, so he used what he liked from five or six types of architecture."

He pointed out the gables, the towers, the chimneys, the turrets and spires, the potpourri of roof types, the corbeling. Elaborate, asymmetrical, and irregular of plan, design, and decoration, the place seemed to crawl with gargoyles. They drove down the semicircle path to the carriage court.

"Jos," Nick said faintly.

Jocelin glanced at the couple and their servants waiting beneath the columns that supported the roof of the carriage porch. "Don't worry. It's old Elliot and his wife."

He descended from the carriage and urged Nick forward for introductions. Elliot wore an air of a lord of the manor greeting royalty on a state visit. He was one of the few men Jocelin didn't top in height, but the majesty of his frame suffered somewhat by the fact that he wore side-whiskers. These had turned gray before the hair on his head, thus giving him the appearance of having resorted to dyes. His mouth turned down at the corners, no doubt from his constant fits of pique.

His wife, Iphegenia Beaufort Elliot, suffered in comparison to her overwhelming spouse. Dressed in the bell-shaped and narrow-skirted fashion of the previous decade, she wore her fading blond hair in long ringlets to either side of her face and hardly ever finished her sentences. She didn't have to, for her husband usually spoke for her or told her what she meant to say. He'd married her for her position as eldest daughter of one of the county's oldest families, not for her mettle.

Jocelin fell into conversation with Elliot while Nick lent his arm to their hostess, and they all went inside. He saw Nick's jaw drop slightly as they walked beneath soaring Gothic arches and between long rows of columns of marble. Conducted in state through the entry, past the medieval screen, and into the entrance hall, they proceeded up the main staircase. Walking beneath cavernous fan vaulting, he glanced at their reflections in a succession of huge trefoil mirrors.

He concealed a smile when Nick winced at the busy carving, the gilding that touched almost every surface, the cavernous magnitude of each succeeding room. Poor Nick had never been to a country house before. His friend disliked formal, drafty mansions. He himself preferred his own, much smaller, seventeenth-century house. It had never been improved after the last century and remained comfortably small. He left the palaces and castles to his father.

"So glad you could stay with us, Radcliffe," Elliot was saying. "As I said, my girl took herself off with the guests to the pond for ice-skating. Ah, here's Thurston-Coombes. Coombes, old man, you're back."

Jocelin greeted his friend and introduced Nick again.

"Yes, sir," Thurston-Coombes said. "We all trooped back except Miss Elliot. She was going to visit one of the cottagers on the estate. Said she'd knitted the old lady mittens and a shawl."

Elliot glanced meaningfully at Jocelin. "A good girl, my Elizabeth. Always doing right by our dependents. Takes my position seriously, of course. One's Christian duty. She'll be along soon. Coombes, I was just showing Radcliffe and Ross their rooms. They're down from you."

"If you don't mind," Jocelin said before Elliot could go on, "I'd like to take my hunter out for a bit. He gets restive after a long train ride. He hates the noise."

Elliot gave him an expansive smile, rather like the grimace of a lion contemplating a zebra foal.

"Of course." He nodded at his butler. "Kimberley will show you to the stable block."

Jocelin glanced at Nick. "Come along, old fellow. Time for a short gallop before dinner." He bowed to Iphegenia Elliot. "If Mrs. Elliot permits."

"My pleasure, my lord. Dinner is at . . ."

"Eight," finished Mr. Elliot.

With a few more proper expressions of delight in their accommodations, they were left to themselves. In half an hour they were mounted on their hunters and trotting out of the back gate. A bridle path had been cleared of snow, and they followed it down a hill. Riding quickly across the park surrounding Stratfield

Court, they entered a wood. The trees closed in, and they had to walk their horses single file.

The moment they'd cleared the stables Nick had dropped his carefully guarded accent. "Bleeding toff. 'One's Christian duty,' he said. 'Our dependents,' he says."

"A solid landed proprietor, is our Mr. Elliot," Jocelin said with a glance back at Nick. "No doubt he wants to purchase a baronetcy."

"He's a butcher's son. Common stock, just like me," Nick said as he guided his hunter over a fallen log.

"He made his sovereigns by investing in railways when they first started building big. Now he's got his fingers into a lot of pies—wool, tea, salt mines, guano."

"Guano?"

"The excrement of seafowl, my dear man. Fertilizer."

"He's in birdshit?"

"Among other things."

"Disgusting."

"Lucrative." Jocelin reined in. "What's this? The pond?"

Nick pulled alongside him, and they gazed out at a snow-covered meadow that stretched to the edge of the wood. Several hundred yards away an ice-covered pond reflected the lowering sun's rays. A coach was parked near its banks, the driver holding the horses. A maid was shoving what looked like a woman's petticoats and hoop inside the vehicle. On the ice a woman in a voluminous crimson day dress and matching cape was skating.

Jocelin put his hand on Nick's arm to stop him from speaking. He followed the skater with his gaze as she sailed around the pond. All the ladies of his acquaintance skated, even his mother. This lady didn't just skate, she flew. Unlike most of her kind, she pushed her legs rapidly, gaining speed until he was sure she would lose control of her body and crash. Instead she turned around and sailed backward, working up more speed. Suddenly she stepped on one foot and jumped in the air. Her legs parted, then came together. She landed, still sailing backward, on one foot.

"Dear God," Jocelin said.

"The little fool's going to kill herself."

"Look!" Jocelin pointed at the woman.

Her brilliant skirts flying behind her, she now crossed her legs and stepped forward onto one foot, bringing her arms close to her body. Jocelin held his breath as she began to spin. Whirling faster and faster, her skirt billowed. Her bonnet flew off, and cascades of ash blond hair tumbled and fluttered. As suddenly as she'd begun, she slowed and stopped herself, then calmly set sail again.

She glided around the edge of the pond in a circle, then bent forward, lifted one leg in the air. She arched her back like a ballerina and drifted, a small, crimson sloop wafting across a glassy sea. Jocelin released Nick's arm, but continued to stare at the woman on the ice.

"Have you ever seen anything like that?"

"I seen people running about on the ice before."

"But not like that," Jocelin said. "Not as if she were dancing on a ballroom floor. And women never, never jump, and certainly they never spin until their skirts whirl up and expose their legs."

"Damned long legs. I'd like to—"

"Don't," Jocelin said.

Nick cast an irritated look at Jocelin. "Jesus, you've already picked her out for yourself."

"You'll be too busy distracting Miss Elizabeth Elliot for me."

"I got better things to do than hold some old maid's knitting. Damn it, Jos, the Elliot woman's twenty-four, a spinster. Probably a wide, lumpy one too."

At last Jocelin tore his gaze from the skating figure. "Come on, old chap. Be a good fellow and do this for me." When Nick snorted, he wheedled some more. "Do it, and I'll let you visit Miss Birch."

"You brought her?"

"She's promised to take rooms in Little Stratfield-on-Willow."

Without waiting for Nick's answer, he looked back at the object of his interest. She had left the ice to sit on a stump covered with a blanket. Removing her skates, she handed them to the maid and put on walking boots. Soon she had entered the waiting carriage, and the coachman had guided it out onto the path to the road that skirted the Elliot estate.

Jocelin kicked his hunter. "Come on," he shouted to Nick. "We can make it back before she does and be waiting when she comes down for dinner."

"Can't you ever leave women alone?"

"No."

"I thought you was going to have that maid."

Jocelin chewed his lip, for his discomfort had been growing since he'd encountered the skating lady. "I am, eventually." He continued with reluctance. "I've got to try for this one too."

"Why's that?"

"Because she's the first woman I've seen that I

don't compare to Miss Gamp." Jocelin leaned down and patted the neck of his hunter. "If you tell this to anyone, I'll call you out."

"Who am I going to tell?"

"Well, then, I've tried to forget about Miss Gamp. After all, a man has his needs, but . . . Hang it! I visited Miss Birch, and all I could do was criticize. Her waist was too small, her chest not full enough, her hips not wide enough, and damn all, she smelled of roses when she should have smelled like lemons."

Nick reined in and stared at Jocelin. "Time was, women were in-betweens for you. In between our jaunts, in between politics."

"Now I seem to exist in between ruminating about Miss Gamp and wanting her. Hang it, I haven't even seen her clearly yet, and I can't forget her. She's eating me alive."

They kicked their horses and rode slowly toward Stratfield Court.

"I know," Nick said after a few minutes. "It's 'cause you ain't—haven't had her yet. Come on, love. When's the last time you had to work for a woman?"

"I don't remember."

"See?"

"But now there's this skating lady." Jocelin sighed. "Perhaps I'm recovering."

"Then you can count on me to help with the medicine, old love. I'll even distract that old relic and his wife."

With their plans set, they returned to Stratfield Court. Eight o'clock saw them enter the drawing room side by side to join the rest of Richard Elliot's guests. Besides young Thurston-Coombes, several eligible men and a few ladies formed the house party. Jocelin suspected Elliot wanted him to realize his daughter was in demand, thus the other contestants.

He conducted a polite conversation with a dowager countess and her daughter who had just had a successful season in which the young lady had attracted and accepted an offer from one of Prince Albert's gentlemen-in-waiting. The dowager had another daughter on the market and was inspecting Nick, who smiled at her and quoted Shakespeare. When the dowager failed to recognize the source of his wit, Nick lost interest and maneuvered himself and Jocelin over to join Thurston-Coombes.

As they talked, another group of ladies entered the room. Jocelin glanced up as they manipulated their crinolines across the threshold. Luckily there were double doors. The last woman to enter slid gracefully past the danger by allowing her arms to rest on the layers of petticoats and crinoline frame. She turned suddenly as she cleared the door, and the quick movement brought a surge of recognition to him. The skating lady.

He watched her walk. She almost glided, as if she were still on ice. To take his gaze from her body seemed impossible now that he'd recognized that pliant tread. She had a habit of movement in which she paused and quickly turned her head back over her shoulder to glance at people. Jocelin found himself watching the sway of her upper body above the cascade of her skirts. Many women encased in yards of petticoats and silk and corsets moved like carousel animals. This one moved the way a woman ought to move. He could barely perceive the undulating of her breasts as she walked.

What was he doing? He shouldn't be staring at a lady's chest. He was frazzled indeed to make such a slip. The woman turned to glance over her shoulder and caught his gaze. He glimpsed wide, gold-brown-teal eyes, startled eyes. But she didn't look away at once. She seemed transfixed, and as he drank in the several hues of her gaze, Jocelin felt himself stir. He began to ache, which brought a curse to his lips. He was losing his composure for the second time in but a few weeks. Hang it. He wasn't going to plunge into rut over this one too.

The lady blushed and dropped her gaze, thus releasing him from the source of his growing discomfort. To his surprise, Richard Elliot bustled over to her, appropriated her hand, and led her to Jocelin and Nick.

He heard her name and nearly laughed. Miss Elizabeth Maud Elliot. The solid old spinster. Nick almost smirked at him, and he cast a warning glance at his friend as he bent over the lady's hand. Then his mind whirled into confusion. He smelled lemons. He made small talk with the Elliots while desire flooded through him and his brain reeled.

She smelled like lemons. Shooting unobtrusive glances, he noted her slimness. Her long legs were concealed by the gown. Her chest was flatter than Miss Gamp's, her hair the wrong color. Hang it! What was he thinking?

He studied the gleaming, dried-grass tawniness of her hair. This young woman, who cast down her eyes upon encountering his gaze, was no Miss Gamp. She was too slim, too graceful, too clean. His glance fastened on her hands. The nails were short, the fingers long.

He had felt the softness of her palm when he kissed her hand. But the lemons hadn't been his imagination. He'd definitely smelled lemons. Perhaps they used the same toilet water. Possible. After all, this was the granddaughter of a butcher. She might use the same scent as a maid of all work. Yes, that was the answer.

He smiled at some quip on the part of Richard Elliot. He managed to conduct a sensible conversation with the old man while Miss Elliot remained quiet. Exerting his will, he achieved a monumental accomplishment of taming his unruly desires. He'd done many things, but never had he swelled to readiness in front of a host and his spinster daughter. He wasn't going to let it happen.

At last he was able to incline his head regally when the old man ushered his daughter over to grace the presence of the son of a baronet. In reality the introduction and conversation had lasted less than five minutes. Clever of the old blister. Elliot knew better than to thrust his daughter at Jocelin.

Nick interrupted his speculations. "Well, well, well. So Miss Elliot is our skating lady. I've been relieved of my task." He dug his elbow into Jocelin's side. "Adequate, old fellow. She's quite adequate. Not a beauty, but then, you said you weren't looking for beauty in a wife."

"No," Jocelin said faintly.

"But why?"

Jocelin was staring at Miss Elliot. She looked his way and caught him. Instead of glancing away, he held her gaze for a long moment, then smiled sweetly at her. She blushed and looked away. He turned his back to her. No sense in looking too eager. Bad strategy.

"What did you say? Why not a beauty?" he asked Nick.

He needed a distraction before he succumbed to lust again. "Because beautiful women tend to be like that Wedgwood cup on my mantel. Excellent on the outside, old fellow, and empty of substance. They learn early that all that's required of them is appearance, so they devote their entire beings to taking care of themselves. And deep inside they're frightened that one day they'll lose their beauty. And without that, who would want them? They're right, of course, because no one wants to spend time pursuing a relationship with Wedgwood."

"And besides," Nick went on under his breath, "beautiful women can't be trusted not to fall into traps set by chaps like you."

Jocelin nodded in Miss Elliot's direction. "We're to be stunned by the lady's musical accomplishments, and before dinner too."

Miss Elliot seated herself at the piano that rested in an alcove. Resting her hands on the keys, she began a piece by Chopin. The room fell silent. She played the way she skated. He could feel the lightness of her touch, hear the delicacy of her interpretation. He exchanged surprised glances with Nick. Young ladies usually learned to play. He'd spent many a tortured evening enduring the efforts of some earnest debutante.

Elizabeth Maud Elliot's playing mocked such dilettantes. As he watched her, he could see that she'd forgotten her audience. She sailed through complex chords, carried on the waves of her own passion for the music. When she finished, he found himself longing for her to continue. Guests crowded around her and offered congratulations. He held back, for he didn't want to be one of the crowd.

Nick poked him again and hissed at him gleefully. "Just think what your father would say if you offered for Miss Elizabeth."

"I have no intention of offering for her, for I doubt we'd suit. However, if by some fantastical chance I did want to marry her, I wouldn't care what Father said. I've been thinking about it since Father forced me to, and I know what I want in a wife."

"You do? You surprise me."

"If I'm going to stop Yale from inheriting," Jocelin said, "I'll do it on my own terms. I may make Father suffer by appearing to consider tradesmen's daughters, or even a woman of light reputation, but I'm not a fool. There are too many dependents upon a duke for him not to consider how his choice of a wife will affect them."

Jocelin pulled his gaze away from Miss Elliot and looked at Nick. "I require certain attributes of a wife—softness, delicacy, modesty. A woman should concern herself with her household and children. She needn't concern herself with matters outside her home. I don't require great intelligence, just the ability to listen when I speak and the sense to be guided by me. And all the usual accomplishments she must have for entertaining and keeping me satisfied."

"And she's got to let you do what you want without interfering," Nick said.

"Of course. In return, I won't interfere with her domain."

They nodded at each other, in perfect agreement.

"Here they come again," Nick said. "You get to take her in to dinner."

Nick was right. Jocelin found himself offering his arm to Elizabeth Elliot. When Mr. Elliot made a joke about the contrast in their coloring, she aroused his protective instincts by blushing and looking as if she wished she could dive behind a sofa. He smelled lemons again and, in that moment, decided that he could make do with Miss Elliot if he couldn't have Miss Gamp right away.

"I'm delighted to have been given the privilege of escorting you." He leaned down and whispered to her. "And don't mind your father. It's only that he's proud of you, you know. And he's right to be, Miss Elliot."

The young lady looked up at him, but glanced at the floor again. Her cheeks flushed again, and for some strange reason, the sight of that rosy stain aroused him. She glanced up at him and smiled uncertainly.

"Thank you, my lord."

Her voice was soft, like her mother's, but she finished her sentences. He loved the way she said "my lord" in that tremulous way.

"You're welcome, Miss Elliot."

They entered the dining room, and he pulled back her chair for her. She sat and looked up at him, giving him a smile that jolted him from his eyes to his toes.

"Liza, my lord. My name is Liza."

9

She knew he'd be shocked
by the drawing room. Trying not to stare as the
viscount entered, Liza watched him pause, then recover his composure. She couldn't blame him. After
all, he lived in houses where Gothic arches belonged,
because they'd been built five hundred years ago.
Stratfield Court was new. He was looking at the
ceiling, and she cringed. Fan vaulting belonged in
cathedrals. It only made the drawing room seem like
an ornate cave made by trolls with good architectural
skills.

What was she doing worrying about whether this
man found her father's taste lacking? She needed to
concentrate on maintaining her ladylike demeanor.

Until he came, she hadn't had any difficulties. The moment he walked into the room, however, she'd begun to feel as tremulous as she pretended to be. And why? He behaved like the charming yet slightly aloof aristocrat he was, but when he looked at her, she saw the gunfighter. She saw the man who wore a gun with the nonchalance of a gentleman wearing his watch fob. She saw the man who paid no attention to her protests any more than he would to an enemy he faced in a gunfight.

With him looking at her with that ruthless gaze, she couldn't keep her voice from quivering, her hands from shaking, or her cheeks from turning red. Since she was supposed to be a shy and demure spinster, all this discomposure worked to her advantage. To find herself acting like human jelly irked her and caused her to resent the viscount. She hated all this pretense. If she hadn't suspected him of murder, she would have loved to revert to her old self.

He was ignoring her. On purpose. He'd made a mistake, though, for she knew better than to think he sought out her mother's company for its fascination. Mama wasn't interested in any of the things he was, not politics, or army reform or improvements in sanitation to prevent cholera. As he turned his back to her, Liza wished she could cast aside all propriety. She longed to march up to him and tell him she knew he didn't want to marry the granddaughter of a butcher, that he was interested only in her father's political support for his friend Asher Fox, and why didn't he just come out and admit the truth, and by the way, was he a murderer?

He was coming to her! Just when she'd worked herself up into a fit of indignation, he was coming to her.

"Miss Elliot, the few moments without your company have been as a century."

Liza glanced down at the floor, twisted the lace handkerchief in her hands, and wished she could stomp on his foot as she had as Miss Gamp. "How, um, how gallant of you, my lord."

He looked around the room at the various clusters of guests. "They're leaving us alone. Your father is a formidable strategist. Will he maneuver us into the music room for another demonstration of your skills?"

"Oh, I hope not."

Liza clamped a hand over her mouth, aghast at her slip. She hated playing for an audience. She hated the feeling she got when someone listened to her, for she hated to be judged. Then playing became a test, a test to be failed, a test conducted by her father. She had never passed his tests. Still, she shouldn't have lost her senses and revealed herself to the viscount. He was grinning at her now.

"We have something in common. I detest being put on display too."

"Like—like a prize cow." She could have bit her tongue.

He chuckled. "I beg to change the comparison. Like a prize bull."

As he spoke, his gaze drifted over her face, down her neck to her breasts and hips. This time she didn't have to remind herself to blush and drop her gaze. The lecher. Feeling ill-used, she nearly succumbed to the temptation to kick his shin. Instead she decided to do the one thing he wouldn't expect. Mama was leaving. She always retired early, usually with vapors or a sick headache.

"I see my mother is retiring, my lord. I too am exhausted and will say good night."

"You're leaving? Now?"

His disbelief and shock were comfort to her irritated soul.

"Yes, my lord."

No novice, the viscount quickly recovered and wished her a pleasant evening. She joined her mother, who became flustered at the thought of how her husband would view this desertion in the face of duty. Liza said her good evenings to the rest of the guests with her mother, however. But once the drawing room doors closed, she patted Mama on the arm, lifted her skirts, and raced through the picture gallery to the corridor that lead to the young ladies' stair. Papa's sense of propriety decreed that young ladies and gentlemen be housed on opposite sides of the house. With separate stairs, entrances, and corridors, they need never meet unescorted.

She turned right just inside the corridor and almost skidded on the marble floor. Regaining her balance, she raced toward the young ladies' stair. She heard a door close and glanced behind her. The valet Loveday emerged from the door that concealed the hall leading to the servants' wing. Liza stared at him. He bowed to her. She dropped her skirts and tried not to appear out of breath. Turning slowly, she mounted the steps at a decorous pace.

By the time she reached her room she was furious with herself. "Drat. Drat, drat, drat."

"Miss?"

Her maid, Emmeline, whom she'd recruited to join Pennant's, was laying out her nightgown.

"Oh, nothing," Liza said as she drew off her gloves.

"Ooo, miss, I never been in such a house before."

Liza nodded, not really listening.

"I never seen so many servants nor so many rooms." Emmeline counted them off on her fingers. "There's the cleaning room, brushing room, footman's room, gun room, odd room, and plate safe, not to mention the butler's pantry. That's all on the men's side. Then there's the women's side—workroom, still room, storeroom, housekeeper's room, kitchen and cook's closet, servery, two pantries and a larder, the scullery, and that's not all."

"Emmeline, what are you going on about?"

"This house, miss, it's a palace, it is."

Remembering Emmeline's hovel in St. Giles, Liza sighed and refrained from shattering the maid's illusions. "It's late, you go on to bed."

"Thank you, miss."

Alone in the grandeur of her bedroom, Liza glanced at the tasseled and skirted furniture, the nooks and crannies stuffed with figurines, the presumptuous canopy of state that hung over her bed. She sighed again. Her room at Pennant's held not one figurine, and the furniture didn't wear clothes. She went to the desk that rested near the fireplace and sat down to finish reading the latest letter from Toby. He and Betty had been left in charge of Pennant's.

More houses of prostitution had been raided after Frankie Fawn had been killed. Usually their lists of customers were missing. Their managers had been taken into custody, but ordinarily such misfortunes meant only a change of personnel. Curiously, in this latest round of raids, the owners of the property shut the houses down altogether, reopened them as pubs, or sold them.

Liza turned the page of her letter, and the name Dr. Lucius Sinclair jumped out at her. Toby had been investigating that list she'd found in the viscount's sitting room. She dropped the page and drummed her fingers on it. Dr. Lucius Sinclair was a respected medical man in Harley Street, with a house in the country—in Wiltshire, to be exact. Dr. Lucius Sinclair, it seemed, lived at the moment in his house in the market town of Willingham, not ten miles from Stratfield Court.

"So," Liza murmured to herself, "so, my lord, perhaps you've more than one reason to pretend amusement with the company of the Elliots."

"Elizabeth Maud!"

Liza started as her father burst into the room with barely a knock. She turned her letter facedown and curled her fingers. Papa stomped over to her, scowled for all of three seconds in silence, then harumphed.

"You'll never behave correctly, will you?"

"Papa, he spent most of his time ignoring me. I was showing him I didn't hang on his words and live to be in his presence." Liza leaned back in her chair. "But knowing his lordship, he no doubt thought I was overcome with his magnificent self and needed rest for my flustered sensitivities."

He stopped warming his hands at the fire and shook his finger at her. "Now you listen to me, miss. You're not letting this one get away. If you so much as mention women's property rights or, or . . ."

"Divorce rights?"

Richard Elliot turned crimson with suppressed rage. "Ungrateful, that's what you are. God, to think that my William is dead and I'm left with an ungrateful, unwomanly creature like you." Elliot approached her, his wrath making his lips twitch. "I'm warning

you. I want this boy for a son-in-law. He's a duke's son.
A duke's son, do you hear? A military man too."

"Your eyes are gleaming, Papa."

He hadn't heard her. He turned to contemplate
something in the coals in the fireplace.

"My grandson will be a duke."

"You can't be sure," Liza said. "I'm trying, Papa,
but you can't be sure."

He straightened, then glanced at her as if suddenly remembering she was in the room. "I'm sure.
One way or another, my grandson will be a duke."

He left as abruptly as he came. Liza stared after
him. All at once she grew uneasy. Papa hadn't gone
from being a lowly clerk at a provincial bank to a
gentleman of wealth and power by accident. Papa had
gotten what he wanted by some questionable prac-
tices. She had little knowledge of the details, but she
knew Papa. Papa's Christian principles stopped where
his business instinct began. Ah, well, there was nothing she could do to stop Papa. With luck, she would
discover whether the viscount was a murderer long
before Papa could do anything horrible. With luck.

Sleep came with difficulty for her that night.
The next morning she slept late, regardless of the
hunt scheduled for that day. Everyone was gone
except Mama by the time she descended to the
morning room. The day was overcast, and only dim
sunlight battled through the thick glass of the windows.

Mama huddled with her sewing beside the
fireplace. Although the morning room had been designed on a less lofty scale than the drawing room, it
still harbored drafts because of the arched ceiling and
columned arcade that bordered three of its sides. Liza
settled herself opposite Mama and took up a piece of

embroidery that would eventually become a pillow-case. She constructed French knots while she contemplated setting her personal footman to watching Jocelin Marshall. When he came back from the hunt, she wouldn't be able to keep him in sight all the time.

"I like your viscount, my dear."

Startled out of her schemes, Liza said. "That's nice, Mama."

"So charming. He knew my family. Of course it's only to be expected, since . . ."

"Since the Beauforts are such an old county family?"

"And I've been worried about you. So worried. I could hardly face my At Homes with a daughter who had become a—" Iphegenia lowered her voice as if speaking of a disgusting sin. "A spinster. And what if my dear Richard died suddenly, may the Almighty preserve him. Why, who would take care of me? Who would . . ."

Liza furrowed her brow and studied her mother. "Who would take care of you? Mama, you're a grown woman."

"I know, but . . ."

Useless to listen further. Mama was one of those women who complained and catastrophized without end. When a listener provided solutions or offered advice, her invariable reply was, "I know, but. . . ." After a lifetime of listening to moans and whimpers, Liza had decided that Mama enjoyed misery and helplessness, especially helplessness, for being incompetent meant Mama didn't have to take responsibility for herself or anyone else. Thus, when she heard "I know, but . . . ," Liza stopped listening.

Still, just knowing that Mama had launched into her list of reasons why she couldn't live her life without someone serving as a veritable parent to her caused Liza's chest to burn with irritation. She jabbed her needle through the middle of another French knot and yelped.

Dropping the material, she stuck her finger in her mouth and sucked. To her chagrin, Jocelin Marshall chose that moment to walk into the room. Caught off guard, she stared at him with her finger in her mouth as he greeted her mother. Turning to her, he fastened his gaze on her mouth. She hastily withdrew her finger. He glanced at her flushed cheeks, then returned to her mouth. His own lips parted slightly. All at once she realized he was remembering Miss Gamp. Flustered even more, she fumbled with her needle, thread, and material.

She was so agitated, she was too late to prevent Mama from excusing herself and leaving them alone. She scowled after Mama's retreating figure, certain that Papa had instructed her to commit this breach of propriety. One simply didn't leave a young lady alone in the presence of a man, especially a man with the viscount's reputation.

Glancing up at Jocelin Marshall, she caught him looking at her with amused speculation. "Um, Mama is . . ."

"You aren't going to start leaving your sentences unfinished, are you?"

Liza stared at the tips of her slippers and shook her head. She shrank back in her chair when he suddenly knelt beside her and picked up an enameled thimble.

"You dropped this," he said.

To her astonishment he took her hand, opened it, and placed the thimble in it. Curling the fingers, he covered them with his hand. Unlike her own, his hand was warm. He was doing it again, pursuing her. No man had ever approached her this way. None had shown the slightest desire to be near her. Liza sat frozen in confusion. Did all men try so relentlessly to seduce women?

She withdrew her hand. The movement should have been a signal for the viscount to remove himself from such proximity. He didn't. Now she could feel the heat of his body. Merciful heavens, he hadn't said a word, hadn't tried to recapture her hand, yet she felt a growing urge to put herself close to him.

"I've never met anyone so shy." "

Liza swallowed, darted a glance at him, and looked down at her hands. The brief glimpse was enough to plunge her into greater confusion. She hadn't counted on his pursuing her. She knew what it meant, that look of his. He was studying her mouth. If she didn't think of something to distract him, he was going to kiss her, perhaps more.

"You didn't join the hunt," she said.

"Nor did you."

Her embroidery hoop lay on her lap. He touched a French knot with one finger, and she jumped. His hand was near a place between her thighs that suddenly tingled. She looked at the glowing coals in the fireplace, but he didn't remove his hand.

His fingers traced the leaf and garland designs on the pillow. They pressed the hoop lightly against her, and her face flooded with color. Gasping, she jumped, trying to stand, but his hand slid up her stomach to press on her ribs just below her breast. Her embroidery dropped as she shrank back into the chair in a effort to escape his touch.

"Don't run away," he said softly. "You're so skittish."

The sensible Liza screamed a warning. The primitive part of her that responded to the gunfighter urged her to keep her mouth shut. Liza kept her mouth shut.

He hadn't moved his hand from beneath her breast. She squirmed, but he pressed it firmly against her ribs. He made no further advance, and they remained there without moving.

At last he said something in a whisper. "Dear God, Miss Elliot, Miss Liza Elliot, how can you make me burn by simply sitting in a room with your embroidery?"

Liza had been avoiding his gaze. She looked up at him in surprise and found him regarding her with undisguised hunger. The cool, elegant patrician had vanished.

"I've frightened you."

She nodded.

"Be still. I'm going to frighten you some more."

His hand moved, and she gasped as it slid up to cover her breast. She tried to thrust him away, but he captured her hands with his free one while keeping the other on her breast. Dear Lord, his hand moved when she breathed. She tried not to breathe.

"Don't be afraid," he murmured. "Listen to me, sweet Liza. 'She was a phantom of delight / When first she gleamed upon my sight; / A lovely apparition, sent / To be a moment's ornament.'"

His hand absorbed her attention. The heat of it burned through her gown.

"A—a moment?"

"An eternity."

Her lungs hurt. She expelled air, and he smiled, drawing near enough to touch her lips with his.

Keeping his mouth close to hers, he continued to whisper.

"Do you read sonnets, my accomplished Miss Liza?"

She made the mistake of nodding, and her mouth brushed across his. His tongue darted out, laved her lips, then retreated before she could object. Still he kept her frozen in place by the touch of his hand and his lips so near her own.

"'Being your slave,'" he said as he moved so that his mouth brushed her ear, "'what should I do but tend/Upon the hours and times of your desire?'"[1]

His breath in her ear caused her to tingle and inflamed her body in a way Liza had never experienced. Transfixed by the overwhelming sensations, she vaguely realized that he was deliberately wooing her into a state of his own design. Yet somehow she couldn't summon the fortitude to make him stop. To forgo that hot brandy voice, the heat of his body, the touch of his hand, these were impossible sacrifices. They became even more impossible when he began nuzzling her ear and gently brushing his palm over her breast.

"Do you know how you make me feel?" he asked. "Like Keats' Porphyro."

She failed to answer, but it seemed he hadn't expected her to speak, for he continued.

> "Beyond a mortal man impassion'd far
> At these voluptuous accents, he rose,
> Ethereal, flush'd, and like a throbbing star
> Seen mid the sapphire heaven's deep repose;
> Into her dream he melted . . ."[2]

[1]Shapespeare's Sonnet #73 (traditional numbering: LVII).
[2]John Keats. "The Eve of St. Agnes," lines 316–320.

By the time he finished the last line, she woke from the spell.

"Throbbing!" Liza shot upright and thrust him from her. Pressing her hands to her cheeks, she gaped at him.

He rested an elbow on the arm of her chair and smiled at her sweetly. "You're shocked."

"You shouldn't—ladies don't—it's improper, ill-bred."

"What is ill-bred about poetry? Ah, your mama has taught you that anything to do with bodily function is to be ignored." He leaned toward her like a conspirator, glanced around the room, then whispered. "We ladies don't have legs, my dear, we have limbs, and preferably not those."

He sounded so much like her mother, she forgot her embarrassment and laughed. He grinned at her in response, an honest, uncondemning grin that endeared him to her before she could summon her skepticism. Too late she reminded herself of who he was, what was said about him, and what he might have done. Too late, for he had smiled at her and taken care to show her how to accept her own feelings without shame. Hastily she gathered her embroidery so that she had an excuse to avoid looking into those green eyes.

"I must go to Willingham. I've a fitting at a dressmaker's." She heard herself chattering, but was powerless to stop herself. "I try to patronize the local seamstresses. Their livelihood is so precarious. If you will excuse me?"

The viscount was looking at her as if he could

tell how badly she wanted to escape. He rose as Mama came noisily into the room.

"Ah, my dear Mrs. Elliot. I was about to offer myself as escort for your daughter on her trip into town."

"How gallant of you, my lord."

Dismayed, Liza stuttered, then managed to regain some of her composure. "So kind of you, my lord, but I have my maid."

"We don't refuse such gracious offers, Elizabeth Maud," her mother said. "The others won't be home for a long time, and I'm sure Lord Jocelin will be glad . . ."

"Of the lovely, entertaining company," Jocelin finished.

He smiled at Liza, inclined his head, and offered his arm to her. Thus trapped, she had no choice but to place her hand on his arm. In too short a time she was wrapped in a cloak and ensconced in a carriage. The door closed, sealing her inside with the viscount. Liza gazed out the window as her mother waved good-bye. How in the name of the Almighty had she done this to herself? The last thing she'd expected was to be shut in a carriage, alone, with Jocelin, Viscount Radcliffe.

10

Jocelin conducted himself with propriety in the carriage partly because Miss Liza Elliot looked like she would throw herself out of the vehicle if he didn't. Mostly he did it to confuse her while assuaging her fears. She seemed so uncertain of herself, so retiring. He had thought his gentleman's training long buried under predatory instincts he deliberately encouraged in himself. To his surprise, Liza Elliot stirred a forgotten chivalry in him. Unfortunately for her, she stirred his more elementary cravings as well. These he succeeded in curbing for the half-hour drive to Willingham. He made polite conversation.

Nevertheless, all the while he was listening to

Liza's descriptions of the countryside, he was thinking about the way her breast felt and how he breathed in lemons while he was close to her. His trouble arose from the years he'd spent on the American frontier before the war, casting aside the conventions of society. So when Liza aroused him, he descended to the growling, ravening level of instinct, rather like a Rocky Mountain black bear.

Relief came when he deposited Liza at her dressmaker's. He excused himself on the pretext of exploring Willingham, promised to collect her in an hour, and set off in search of Dr. Lucius Sinclair. He had been waiting for an excuse to visit the town, and hadn't expected it to come so quickly. Liza would be occupied for some time. He could accomplish what he needed and be back without arousing suspicions.

The doctor's villa lay on the outskirts of Willingham, down a path called Larch Lane. Although the snow was melting and the path soggy, he left the Elliot carriage behind. It wouldn't do for the coachman to bring back tales of his visit to an obscure physician. The house lay on grounds surrounded by an ornamental wall. At this time of day the doctor would most likely be in his library or, if he was brave, out for a walk.

Jocelin chose to approach from the rear, and slipped through the back gate. Walking quickly through a snow-covered arbor, he stood behind a thick tree trunk just off the swept stone path through the garden. He surveyed the house for a while, but could perceive no movement through the lace curtains. He was about to go around to the front and present his card when a man came out and paused on the terrace while he buttoned his coat.

Of middle years, he had the appearance of

prosperity—tailored suit, silk waistcoat, boots that obviously cost more than he paid his housemaid in a year. With his neatly cut, graying hair and side-whiskers, he looked like what he was, a successful professional man, a churchgoer, a pillar of the community, God's own Englishman. Jocelin's lip curled in distaste.

Dr. Lucius Sinclair waved his arms back and forth, taking deep breaths and blowing mistily, then set off down the stone path through his garden. Jocelin let him march by at his brisk pace, then called after him.

"Dr. Lucius Sinclair?"

The man turned abruptly, bristled, and stalked back to Jocelin. "This is a private house, sir."

"You are Lucius Sinclair?"

Drawing himself up, the man nodded.

"I've come to tell you that Mr. Frank Fawn is dead."

The doctor gave no sign of recognition, but Jocelin was used to his kind.

"Therefore you will no longer be seeing either Millie or her cousin James."

Sinclair turned red, then vermilion, and shouted, "Get out! Get off my property!"

"Be quiet, Sinclair, or what I have to tell you will be said in front of an audience." Jocelin glanced at the house and back at the doctor. Sinclair clamped his jaw shut. "Excellent. I've little patience with monsters like you, Sinclair, so I will be brief. I know that you purchased the favors of the boy James Pryne and those of little Millie."

By now the doctor's face had lost its tomatolike hue. The longer Jocelin talked, the more Sinclair resembled a three-week-old cadaver. He interrupted Jocelin.

"She—she could have refused," he said. "It was her fault. The boy could have said no."

Jocelin lowered his lashes, and when he next looked at the doctor, Sinclair took a step backward at the loathing he encountered.

"Yes," Jocelin said softly. "I see. You're how old, doctor, forty-nine? James is barely fourteen. Millie's ten. Forty-nine, fourteen, ten. Yet these children are responsible for your abuse, not you. Do you know how many times I've heard that from men like you?"

"But—"

"If I hear it from you again, you'll regret it."

The doctor's eyes shifted from side to side, as if he were searching for a weapon in the frozen garden.

"Now, doctor, to the point. I'm not interested in whether you accept responsibility for your crime, and a crime it is, sir. As much a crime as murder. Worse, for you murder children's souls. No, I'm not interested in your repentance or your redemption. I'm only here to tell you that letters telling of your crimes are due to be sent by tomorrow's post to all your patients here and in London."

He paused when Sinclair uttered a strangled exclamation. Jocelin watched with mild interest as the doctor swayed on his feet.

"I'm so glad you believe me. And since you believe me, I'll take the trouble to point out that an English gentleman faced with a predicament such as yours must think of his family. Take the honorable way out, Sinclair. If you do, the letters will never be sent."

Not waiting for a reply, Jocelin left the doctor standing in his snow-covered garden and let himself out through the back gate. As the wrought-iron door clanged shut, he thought he glimpsed something down Larch Lane out of the corner of his eye, but when he turned, he saw nothing. A rabbit out foraging, no doubt. Jocelin set out for town, picking his way through the muddy snow. He was halfway there when he heard a shot from the direction of Sinclair's house. He paused as the sound echoed through the trees, then set out again, his pace brisk, his lips pursed in a whistle.

He arrived back in Willingham only a little late, and went directly to the dressmaker's shop. By the time he entered, the familiar blackness of spirits had descended upon him, the inevitable consequence of the ugly task he'd just completed. Fighting a growing sense of hopelessness, he asked for Miss Elliot.

She wasn't there. He was directed to the milliner's next door, where he found Miss Elliot trying on a new bonnet. He walked in as she was tying green silk ribbons under her chin. He paused and watched gloomily as she surveyed herself in a mirror. Her hand touched the stiff lace ruffles just beneath the brim, in which nestled pink roses. Suddenly he became alert.

He had left Sinclair feeling dirty; even after he'd heard the shot, he'd felt defiled. Yet as he watched Miss Elliot, his despondency faded a bit. She had removed her cloak to reveal skirts that hung from curved hips. They swept up, gathered by bows to reveal an underskirt of lace that rustled with her movements. He remained silent, listened to that feminine sound, luxuriated in the soft, quick touches of her hands to the bonnet, the roses, and lace.

Here was a world far removed from the evil of Lucius Sinclair and his brethren. Dear Miss Liza Elliot. Untouched by ugliness, with her lacy bonnet and rustling skirts, she wove a spell of peace, elegance, and femininity. She pulled at the ends of the silk ribbon that formed the bow under her chin. The material hissed, then fell under the gentle tugging of her hands. She lifted the bonnet. An attendant took it, and she patted stray curls back into place.

She selected another bonnet from a stand on a table. Pale blue satin ribbons fluttered as she spun in a circle while holding the bonnet at arm's length—and his heart spun in a circle with her. He tore his gaze from Liza Elliot and scowled at his wet boots. Silk, lace, and Miss Liza Elliot spinning in a circle.

God, what was this feeling? Why did he want this little scene to go on forever? He took a deep breath. It was dealing with that monster Sinclair. Putting himself in proximity of that kind always made him distraught. Yes, that was it. Nothing more than nerves. This wouldn't have happened to him out west. He could have fed Sinclair to the Comanches and then eaten a twelve-course meal.

"My lord, I didn't see you."

"What? Oh, yes, well, I didn't want to interrupt your labors, Miss Elliot."

"I'm ready."

Was it his imagination? She was looking at him steadily, with an unwavering gaze that was most unlike her. And she had the most peculiar expression on her face, as if she'd just discovered he was a saint. Perhaps she was remembering what he'd done in the morning room. After all, she was as pure a young lady as he'd ever encountered. He must remember to be gentle.

He handed her into the carriage and allowed the sound of swishing skirts to lull him away from unhappiness. Then he saw her boots. They were soaked.

Jolted into vigilance, ever suspicious, he briefly wondered if she'd followed him to Sinclair's house. After all, there had been that stealthy movement in Larch Lane.

"Your boots, Miss Elliot."

She glanced down at them as he took his place opposite her in the carriage and sighed. "Yes, my lord. I'm afraid I forgot myself and rushed across the street to say hello to an acquaintance I hadn't seen in a long time. I was in the snow before I realized what was happening."

He should have realized how ridiculous his suspicions had been. He could easily imagine Miss Elliot's becoming flustered and rushing into snow piles. It was much harder to imagine this delicately nurtured creature so lowering herself as to follow a gentleman about by herself.

Jocelin sat back against the leather cushions of the carriage. As his muscles relaxed, he realized how he'd shot from tranquillity to fierce unease and back again. The contrast showed him how great a toll his self-appointed crusade had taken on him. He hadn't thought about the cost in a long time, and now, with Miss Liza Elliot here in front of him, a gentle, compelling reminder, he longed for more of that tranquillity.

She hadn't noticed his silence, for she was busy arranging a blanket across her lap. Taking up another, she handed it to him. He leaned forward to accept it, and caught a whiff of lemons. His gaze strayed to the lace in her bonnet, to the kid gloves that encased her hands. She moved, and her skirts rustled again. His glance took in her dark blue gown and matching mantle. Her eyes had turned blue-green when he could have sworn in the milliner's shop they were brown. Hazel eyes, that's what they were.

"My lord, is something wrong?"

He blinked at her. What was he doing?

"No, no. I was just thinking that few ladies I know would trouble to provide custom to local dressmakers and milliners."

"Oh, but they need my help," Miss Elliot said. "Both women have families to support, my lord. Gentlemen don't realize how many women have to provide for their children all by themselves. It isn't a rare occurrence, you know."

She went on, but he wasn't listening. He was too busy castigating himself. What was wrong with him? He'd allowed himself to take on over a woman. A woman! He'd been sitting here languishing and smitten, like some fool in one of those poems by Byron. Disgusting. It was on account of Sinclair. Yes, that was it. He'd never been with a woman so soon after completing one of his tasks, and after all, Liza Elliot was a compelling distraction. Yes, no wonder he'd become distracted. He wanted her. That was it, just another symptom of his lust. No doubt he'd lost control because of the delay in acquiring Miss Gamp.

Jocelin smiled at Miss Elliot as he remembered the scent of lemons. Perhaps he needed a diversion. After he'd recovered from the wounds he'd gotten in the Crimea, he'd gone off to America, taking that monster Tapley with him. He hadn't really rested. Obviously he was in need of diversion. Nick said so. Loveday said so, though his recommendations to Jocelin regarding activities were much more staid than Nick's.

Miss Birch was ensconced at an inn in town, but somehow Miss Birch's expertise repelled him at the

moment. He'd grown tired of Octavia and the rest.
Jocelin watched Miss Elliot's lips move as she spoke
softly to him. They were a pale rose color.

It suddenly occurred to him that he'd never
been with an inexperienced woman. Always before
he'd been interested in diversion, and in proving to
himself that what Yale had said of him wasn't true. But
since he'd come back from the Crimea, he'd come to
realize what Nick and his friends had been telling him
for years. Efforts at luring women on his part were
superfluous. They swarmed to him, like fireflies on a
hot night in Texas.

Having come to this realization, the excitement
of conquest faded. More and more he found himself
dissatisfied, restless, uninterested in the women who
courted him. Some lusted after his person, some after
his title; none cared about his heart. No, that wasn't
true. Those who might have cared he had avoided,
thus opening himself to the rest—the predators. So
he had only himself to credit for his own unhappiness.
Perhaps his thoughtless course had brought him to
this point, where he was at last able to appreciate the
unique Miss Elliot.

Appreciate. That was the word. No need to
plunge into the use of words of excessive emotion.
Still, he'd never met anyone who could make him feel
as if he was riding on the tip of a lashing whip,
snapping from tranquillity to swollen lust until he was
dizzy with the rapid shifts. Perhaps he'd been wrong
to think they wouldn't suit. What was wrong with
him? He never vacillated like this. If he wanted a
woman, he pursued her with no thoughts of the future
or of marriage. And yet . . . they might suit. He
knew how he could find out.

"Miss Elliot, did you like Baudelaire's verses?"

He loved the way she started and turned pink.
"What?"

"Come, you needn't fear appearing unmaidenly."

She stuttered, then straightened her shoulders
and glared at him. "Your manners, my lord."

He chuckled and moved to sit beside her. They
engaged in a tug-of-war for her blanket. She lost, and
he slid under it. Miss Elliot burrowed into a corner of
the carriage, but he followed her.

"My lord, you forget yourself."

"I assure you. I don't."

Slipping an arm around her waist, he drew her to
him. She protested as he lifted her, and her voice grew
so loud, he put a hand over her mouth.

"Shh. Do you want to alarm the coachman?"

She scowled at him over his gloved hand and
shook her head. He lowered his hand, but replaced it
with his mouth. She gasped, pushing her sweet breath
between his lips. She had responded to him before,
and betrayed her desire for him. Her ignorance placed
her at a disadvantage. Unfortunately for her, he had no
conscience when it came to taking a woman he
wanted, not even an innocent, it seemed. And how
else was he to discover if they would get on well
together?

He sucked on her tongue, but she was pounding
on him. He managed to capture both her hands, yet
she kept squirming in his lap. The movements ground
her bottom into his groin. She twisted violently, up
and down, side to side, until his sex felt as if it would
burst.

He lifted his mouth. "Be still!"

Not giving her a chance to reply, he kissed her
again. This time he nibbled his way from her mouth to

her temple, then blew in her ear. As he did so, she arched her back and gasped. He smiled as he slid his hand up to her breast. There were a thousand little buttons at the back of her gown. He loosened them one by one while nuzzling her ears and whispering to her of how she made him feel. When he began speaking, she froze and stared at him as if she'd never had a man speak to her before. Perhaps she hadn't. Not like this. He kept her attention on his words, told her how soft she was, how different from himself.

Placing her hand on his chest, he whispered, "Feel me. Feel how hard." He cupped her breast. "So soft, incomparably soft."

He squeezed, touching the tip, and at last her eyes closed. She was breathing rapidly now. He loosened her gown, slipped his hands inside, and gently pulled it down. To distract her, he began kissing her, but she still tried to stop him.

Another distraction then, the legs. He slipped his hand beneath her skirts and touched her ankle. She gasped and twisted, and her gown slipped down below her shoulders. Her hands came up to her breasts. He moved his fingers along her calf to her knee. She moved her hands to her legs. He returned to her buttons, loosening several more. When she chased him away, he found her knees. She pursued him there, only to find that his mouth had fastened on her neck.

She was lying under him now, chest heaving, fighting him while at the same time trying not to make any noise. She had decided her legs were in more danger than her breasts, and both hands had fastened around his wrist to keep him from touching her thighs. He whispered reassurances to her, then kissed her throat, then tongued his way down to the neck of her gown, nuzzled aside the material, and found her breast. At the touch of his mouth, she cried out and clawed at the hand that stroked her thigh, but when he sucked on her, the clawing stopped.

Sensing victory, Jocelin grazed his teeth over her nipple, making her whimper. He took advantage of her confusion and sucked hard, moving his hand higher and higher on her thigh all the while. In a few moments she wouldn't want him to stop. Knowing this made the slowing of the carriage all that much harder to take. She didn't notice, but he could tell they were turning down the road that crossed the Stratfield Court lands.

He lifted his mouth from her breast. Murmuring in her ear, he stroked her thigh while he pulled her upright.

"Liza, Liza, sweet, come to me tonight."

He could barely hear her.

"Wh-what?"

Cupping her breast in his hand, he kneaded it gently as he put her from him. He kissed her, and between kisses he talked to her, carefully drawing her back from the brink of surrender.

"Liza, I need you. Are you listening, sweet? I need you."

Her eyes weren't focused. He drew her gown up and began buttoning it. When she felt the material cover her breast, she blinked and looked at him directly. He held her with his gaze and put all the force of his newly gained power over her behind his glance.

"I need you, Liza."

"My lord, I don't understand."

He buttoned the last button, drew on her mantle, and kissed her again. Withdrawing, he rubbed the pad of his thumb over her lower lip while he kissed her ear and spoke quietly to her so that the spell still imprisoned her.

"I need you, sweet, sweet Liza."

She frowned at him in bewilderment, so he touched his tongue to her lips, bathing them and making her press her body to his.

Then he whispered, "Listen to me. I need you, Liza, you, your enchanting sweetness, your soft body. 'Full nakedness! All joys are due thee, / As souls unbodied, bodies unclothed must be, / To taste whole joys.'"

He should have known she'd hear only one word. She bolted upright.

"Nakedness!" She catapulted out of his arms and across to the other seat, where she clutched her mantle to her chin and glared at him. "You . . . you . . . you."

Grinning at her, he nodded. "Yes?"

"You, you—"

"Beast?"

"No, you—"

"Scoundrel?"

"Monster!"

He laughed. She was so outraged over so little a sin. He hadn't encountered anyone so innocent in years. He couldn't remember a woman's cheeks turning that shade of violent pink. He was beginning to think they'd do quite well together. He captured her hands while she sputtered at him; then, as the carriage slowed in approaching the house, he spoke even as he chuckled.

"Now calm yourself, Liza, my sweet, or you'll betray yourself to the servants and everyone else. One look at that pretty red face, and the coachman will spread it around the county that I took your virginity while he drove us home. Shh!"

She wriggled in his grasp, and tried to kick him.

"God," he said as he dodged her foot, grinning all the while. "And I thought you a biddable, complaint little thing."

"You're a monster! Don't touch me."

"Accustom yourself to it, Liza, my sweet. I'm going to touch you, and touch you, and touch you, and you're going to let me."

He kissed her when she gaped at him, speechless.

"You're going to let me, Liza, sweet. If you think after this small taste of you that I'll ever be satisfied with less than all of you, you're more innocent than I thought."

11

Liza played the piano while one of her guests, Lady Honoria Nottle, sang. Liza wasn't paying much attention to Honoria, for if she did, the poor girl's habit of speech would drive her mad. Honoria couldn't pronounce the letter *l*. For the last two weeks Lady Honoria had been calling her "Wiza."

Honoria Nottle was one of those women designed to try Liza's forbearance to the utmost. She counted a summer evening lost if she couldn't stroll about a garden looking for "wee bunnies, the wittle deaws." Her life was filled with sentiment, oozy, drippy sentiment. If Liza hadn't needed her as a shield against Lord Jocelin, she would have poked Honoria in the nose for her intolerable mawkishness.

At the moment, however, she needed Honoria, because the gentlemen had returned from shooting and would be coming down to tea.

She'd suffered two weeks of playing the dutiful daughter. Two weeks of watching her words lest she betray her discovery about Jocelin Marshall. The day of their carriage ride she'd followed him down Larch Lane, intent upon knowing what he was about, and had been shivering behind the arbor when he cornered Lucius Sinclair. She heard Jocelin's accusations with stunned surprise and horror. Horror had turned to disgust and outrage as she comprehended the magnitude of Sinclair's perversion. And then there was Jocelin Marshall.

She'd always known the viscount was a killer. Tales of his deeds on the American frontier spoke of saloons, whiskey, and gunfights. Never had a word been whispered about his pursuits in England, and they were far more dangerous. She was still disturbed by what she'd heard. Obviously Lord Jocelin had discovered a coven of evil in that so-called boarding-house and had set out to rid the world of the infestation.

He was evidently bent on rescuing those children and assuring their safety by tracking down as many of their abusers as he could. In doing so he'd taken himself outside the law. What law? Liza knew all too well how people overlooked sins against the forgotten children of the slums. Indeed, according to Toby, much of the property on which such perversion took place was owned by bulwarks of Society.

She could still feel the reverberations of shock when she realized what Jocelin Marshall was doing. She still felt as if someone had dumped a tub of snow on her head. This man, who rescued children and tracked down muck like Sinclair, this man was no murderer. And so, at last, without meaning to, she had discovered the truth.

To her chagrin, knowing the truth had made her vulnerable. The viscount made an unlikely crusader. When he had turned seducer, she hadn't been prepared. It was hardly her fault. After all, her first season had lasted only a few weeks. Young men had been interested in her, or rather, her inheritance, but she had only to open her mouth to send them fleeing as before a plague of horseflies. No, she hadn't been prepared, for no one had ever made love to her. She should be ashamed of herself for liking it so much.

She was ashamed. The viscount had almost seduced her in her own carriage. Liza's fingers fumbled over the piano keys as she remembered the encounter in the morning room and the ride home from Willingham. Jocelin Marshall might be a compassionate savior of children, but he was ruthless when satisfying his own appetite. This knowledge was why, for the last two weeks, she'd attached her self like a shadow to the other female guests.

Her choices were limited, however, for only two ladies besides herself and Mama remained in the house party. Honoria was one, and the other was the dowager Lady Augusta Fowell, relict of Lord Watkin Fowell. The dowager wallowed in piety and was always recommending improving tracts for Liza to read.

In its composition, Papa had been quite obvious about the purpose of this house party. If she had been one of the gentlemen invited, she would have decamped upon surveying the dearth of female company. That none had left said more about Papa's wealth and influence than about Liza's attractions. Of this fact she was quite aware. To make matters worse, more gentlemen had arrived last week. Among them was Asher Fox, political aspirant and friend of the viscount. She suspected Papa had invited him at Marshall's instigation, for the three had had several prolonged conversations over port in the library.

Whatever Papa's intentions, Fox's presence enabled her to observe him in light of the possibility that he was a murderer. After discovering Jocelin's innocence, she'd tallied up her diminished list of suspects. It still included Arthur Thurston-Coombes, Halloway and Lord Winthrop. Fox was on the list as well, but she found herself reluctant to consider the heroic Fox among them, or the charming Coombes. In fact, the more she watched the two of them, the less they appeared as murderers. However, she couldn't logically exclude them yet. Dear Lord, she would be glad when she solved this horrible mystery.

Liza struck the last chord of the song as Arthur Thurston-Coombes and Nick Ross ambled into the room. Honoria curtsied as they applauded, and Liza tried to slip away unnoticed. However, Nick was too quick for her.

"Miss Elliot."

Nick bowed to her. Liza sighed, for Mr. Ross had taken to teasing her whenever they met. What made her suffering worse was that Mr. Ross was almost as handsome as his friend the viscount, though much easier of manner. To be teased by a man who resembled the fabled Tristan without his Isolt or his melancholy embarrassed her tremendously.

"Miss Elliot," Nick Ross said again. "Shy Miss Elliot, do you know that you're causing great suffering in this house?"

Liza rose from the piano bench, and Mr. Ross

was there to offer his arm, the pest. He conducted her
on a perambulation about the room.

"I?" she asked.

"Yes, you, Miss Elliot."

Mr. Ross smiled down at her, and Liza remembered to cast down her gaze. She was supposed to be
a reticent, maidenly thing.

"Can it be that you haven't noticed how old
Jocelin agonizes over your failure to give him your
company?"

Liza stiffened. "I feel I've shown his lordship
every courtesy."

"Of course you have, but poor old Jos had hoped
for more. He languishes, a pale knight sickening for
want of the company of his lady love."

"Really, Mr. Ross, you sound like Sir Walter
Scott."

"Won't you have pity on poor Jos?"

"I have every intention of seeing that my guests
are comfortable."

"How kind of you." Nick looked over her shoulder. "Then here's your chance."

Liza turned to find Jocelin Marshall bearing
down on her. One look at his dour countenance was
enough to send her scurrying from the room with
stuttered excuses to Nick. She skittered past the
viscount, causing him to hesitate and then scowl at
Nick.

Liza almost ran out of the music room. She
couldn't help it. Jocelin Marshall frightened her.
Mama and Papa would be furious, but she didn't care.
Her purpose in coming home had been served. She
couldn't endure another afternoon of conversation in
which Papa and his male guests talked politics while
she was expected to listen and nod in blind agree-

ment. And of course there would be the viscount, casting covert glances at her that made her cheeks burn.

He had a way of catching her eye and talking to her without speaking. He could be all the way across the room, but his gaze would say, "I want to kiss you again," or "Remember how I touched you, I want to do it again." Each unspoken phrase made her tingle and grow hot at the same time. She couldn't endure that again. Just contemplating the possibility had made her nervous. She would calm down by skating at the pond.

Leaving word that she'd gone poor-visiting, Liza escaped to the frozen pond with Emmeline and a pony cart. Bundled in her skating costume, she left the maid with hot tea and fruit turnovers while she glided across the ice. After a few minutes of racing around the pond, she began to make jumps and spins. The concentration necessary to leap in the air from thin blades on ice soon drove the tension from her body.

Throwing a leg out, she began a dizzying spin, the force of which made her feel as if she could whirl out of her own body. She smiled as the revolutions slowed, and gently touched her toe to the ice. Without waiting for her momentum to diminish, she began to glide again. Emmeline was watching her from the pony cart, and Liza waved. The maid waved back, then called out and pointed to something behind Liza.

Liza glanced over her shoulder in time to see a tall raven swooping down at her. Jocelin Marshall raced toward her, bent as he came near, and scooped her up in his arms. She gasped and clutched at the lapels of his long black coat.

"Put me down."

"Ah, the snow swan has much more spirit than the little house sparrow."

She dared not kick him, for he might drop her. His body shifted, and she realized he was going into a spin.

"Don't you dare."

"Hush. Trust me."

Without effort he twisted and launched into a spin. The sensation of floating made her grip him around the neck and bury her head in his shoulder. Feeling as though she were in the midst of a cyclone, Liza gritted her teeth and hung on to him. Finally he slowed and then stopped. She lifted her head to find him grinning at her. She scowled back and kicked her feet.

"Now, now, Miss Elliot," he said. "I'll start spinning again."

"Put me down!"

"Your cheeks are flushed." His gaze roamed over her face and settled on her lips. "I wonder how fast your heart is beating."

"Put me down, you, you—"

He dropped the arm that supported her legs, and she sank, leadlike, with a jolt. At the same time, he crushed her to him with his other arm. While she struggled to maintain her balance, he put a hand over her heart.

"I can't feel it at all," he said in mock surprise.

Then he slipped his hand inside her mantle. Liza squealed, then cut off her cry as she remembered Emmeline. His hand snaked over her breasts, then disappeared. He captured her hands while she sputtered in outrage.

Furious at being handled like a pony, she wrenched her hands free and sprang away from him.

She was off before he could stop her, but he came after her. His stride was much longer than hers. She looked over her shoulder to find him gaining on her as she raced across the pond. Suddenly a desire for revenge overcame her. Churning ahead of him, she turned quickly and sped in the opposite direction. She rushed headlong at him, then abruptly turned sideways. The blades on her skates shaved ice, plowing it up in front of her and into the viscount's face.

She heard him suck in his breath as ice battered his head and shoulders.

She laughed and shouted, "Don't breathe!"

Too late. He scrambled to a halt and inhaled with the shock of the barrage of ice, then choked. His eyes widened, and he coughed, spewing out ice. Then he shook his head and sent a spray of ice shooting at her as she circled him. Shielding her face with her arms, she giggled as Jocelin puffed and gasped. He scowled at her while he brushed his coat, his hair, his face. Ice speckled his shoulders, his brows, and there was one fleck on his nose.

She glided up to him and flicked the ice off his nose. "You missed some."

"Hang it!" He wiped a gloved hand over his face.

"There's more on your shoulders."

"You think I don't know that, woman." He slapped the lapels of his coat, missing the ice shavings on his shoulders completely.

Liza disciplined herself not to smile at his pique. She didn't think he knew that his cheeks were red with chagrin. Neither did he suspect he reminded her of a boy whose attempt to gain the notice of a girl by pulling her braids had elicited revenge instead of admiration. He shivered, and Liza began to feel remorse along with her amusement and gratification. Nevertheless, it served him right to be the one discomposed for once.

While he recovered, she had the chance to study him. His hair had fallen across his brow, which was furrowed from irritation. Straight, dark brows drew together. His lips, normally two lush curves, had thinned as they pressed together. His lower jaw was wide, his chin slightly dented.

Taken individually, each feature seemed pleasing. Put them together, and the whole called to mind a sensual, fallen angel, the lips soft, the eyes startling in their emerald brilliance. His looks suited his changeling temperament. He could dazzle and beguile, then without warning turn brooding and remote.

He sighed, then turned up the collar of his coat. He gazed at her, and his eyes burned bright against the glaring whiteness of the surrounding snow. Folding his arms across his chest, he braced himself on the ice.

"You're a dangerous little thing," he said.

She smirked at him. "I'm sorry, my lord."

"Jocelin, Miss Liza. After nearly freezing and choking me to death, you may as well call me Jocelin."

He shivered, and she grinned. "Serves you right." His eyes squeezed almost shut, like half-moons, as he scowled at her.

"It was your fault," she said. "You—you touched me."

"Damned if you aren't a different woman when you're out here."

She immediately stared at her skates and lowered her voice. "Oh, dear. Oh, dear. I'm so flustered."

"I don't believe you anymore, Liza." He

sounded bemused. "No, sweet Liza, I don't think I believe you're half so meek and timorous as I once thought. Or is it that I've brought out the viper in you?"

He was edging closer to her. Too late she noticed his proximity. When she tried to bolt, he caught her arm and swung her in a circle. She ended up in his arms. He captured the knot of hair at the back of her head and forced her to look up at him.

"God, you make me burn, Liza, sweet. I never knew how exciting it could be to educate an innocent."

"My lord, you forget yourself."

"Hardly. My self is in pain at the moment, and it's your fault."

"If you're cold, you should let me go and return to the house."

He frowned at her. "Cold?" He grinned at her as he ran a hand down her back to her buttocks and pressed her close to his groin. "Innocent indeed. I wasn't talking about the cold."

At this, her anger burst out of control. Crying out, she wrenched free and tried to shove him away. He slid backward on his skates and snatched her wrist as she thrust at him. He swung around, taking her with him, and before she could stop him, he was turning in a circle, rapidly. She yelped and grabbed his arm. Her body sailed around, faster and faster. She braced her legs and leaned into the spin, annoyed that he'd caught her unaware.

Burning wind cut at her face. He was grinning at her and laughing. Furious, she finally took a deep breath and shouted at him.

"Stop!"

"Promise me a forfeit."

"Please."

"Promise." He pulled her closer, as if to kiss her, while they spun.

"I promise!"

She felt a tug on her arms. Jocelin slowed and pulled her to him. Chest heaving, she stumbled against him, still annoyed. She turned her back to him and began patting her mussed hair and rumpled skirt. Her effort at ignoring him failed, however, because he glided up to her back and stood so close, she could feel him even though he hadn't touched her. She edged away from him under the pretense of adjusting her skate. She licked her lips. They were dry, and her throat was even drier. Still, her discomfort came more from contemplating what forfeit he would demand. Would he make her kiss him? Surely not in front of her maid. She looked up at him, but he seemed to be concentrating on some difficult problem. Finally he glanced down at her. Her discomfort grew, for he raked her face with a glance at once hungry and possessive.

"A forfeit, Liza, sweet. You owe me a forfeit, and I've decided what it is to be."

"I'll not kiss you."

He laughed and took her hand. "For shame. A lady of breeding never breaks her word."

"Let me go, you, you—"

"I had so hoped you wouldn't take after your mother in this habit of not finishing sentences."

"I won't pay. You . . . you lecher. Heavens, I hate the way you treat me as if I had the brains of a sheep."

He dropped her hand just as she yanked it, and she lost her balance. Liza fell on her bottom with a screech. She scrambled, trying to get her feet under her, but he stepped on her skirts. All she could do was glare up at him.

"Liza Elliot, you're a viper." He lifted his other foot and straddled her. "And a breaker of promises. And you lie to yourself."

"I do not," she ground out between clenched teeth.

Jocelin crossed his arms and let his gaze travel over her body. His tone softened. "I want your forfeit, and I'm going to get it."

"You will not. I'm not a child to play silly games."

She gasped when he dropped suddenly to one knee beside her.

"You gave me a taste, Liza. And then you let me starve. Had any other woman done that, I would have said she was trying to seduce me. I'm not going to starve any longer."

He touched her cheek with gloved fingers.

She pulled her head out of reach. "I don't know what you mean."

Leaning close to her, Jocelin favored her with a slow, deliberately magnetic smile.

"Does your father know about your skating?"

Her mouth fell open.

"I thought not. And I'm willing to bet he'd see to it that you never skated again if he found out about these little adventures of yours. What do you think?"

"I don't care," Liza said. "Tell him if you like."

"If I do, you'll be spending a lot more time with the fascinating Honoria Nottle, and Lady Augusta. How exciting for you, *Wiza*."

She almost cringed. She had over two more weeks remaining in her time at Stratfield Court. How could she bear all those days if they were spent with

Honoria and Lady Augusta? She couldn't leave suddenly and attract attention that might interfere with her inquiries. Were she to disappear abruptly, she wouldn't be able to spy on Asher Fox, or Arthur Thurston-Coombes. Drat. Drat, drat, drat.

"I'm waiting for your answer."

She hissed at Jocelin. "Blackmail, sir."

"Answer me."

"I'll pay, and I hope you catch a chill."

Jocelin smiled at her and cupped her chin. "You're going to pay dearly for your nasty temper, you proper little viper."

"Get it over with." She had lost the battle to remain demure long ago. "What do you want?"

"Meet me tonight in the conservatory."

She stared at him and found no remorse or guilt in his eyes. "No."

"Then I'll come to your room."

"No!"

"One o'clock."

He rose and offered her his hand. She ignored it, so he bent, slipped his hands under her arms, and set her on her feet.

"I won't. It's improper, and you're trying to, to . . ."

"You don't know what I'm trying to do," he said as he brushed a stray curl back from her face. "Now be a good girl and keep your promise. I'll wait ten minutes. If you aren't there, I'll come to your room." He leaned down and whispered in her ear. "I've found the way to the ladies' side, and I know which room is yours."

She shoved him away. "Don't you dare, you, you—my mother is in the room next to mine."

He laughed softly. "All the more reason to keep your promise."

No doubt he thought he could seduce her. Perhaps he needed to learn that all women didn't wilt at his touch. She would dearly love to be the woman who showed him. She gave him what she hoped resembled a calm glance that hid both her irritation and her uneasiness.

"I'll keep my promise if you promise in turn to behave with propriety."

Jocelin Marshall offered his arm in his most well-bred and noble manner. "I will, Miss Elliot."

Her apprehension faded until he continued.

"I'll mind my manners." He paused for a moment before giving her that gunfighter glance. "Honey, I'll behave. As long as you want me to, that is."

12

He was feeling the beast again, for while everyone else was standing about smoking and talking, he was on the floor, crouched and sniffing the air for the scent of danger. It was all he could do to remain quiet while the beast snorted and snuffled, rooted and crawled about. He suppressed a whine as he twisted around the leg of one of them.

The beast raised his snout. The nostrils worked. The muzzle waved back and forth in the air, then whipped around to point at Jocelin. Was he listening? Did he hear the furtive pawings and grunts? Did he remember yet?

Oh, God, any moment he was going to throw

back his head and bay. He should have known better than to come. Elliot had invited most of their group, most of the officers. When they were all together, the beast worked itself into a frenzy. It was snaking its way over to Jocelin, yellow fangs bare and dripping saliva. Curved claws scrabbled on the floorboards. He must get hold of the beast, for those claws, those claws, they could rake through flesh, carve bone, rip out his friend's beating heart.

Jocelin ran a fingertip around the rim of his crystal whiskey glass. His hands were shaking. They'd been shaking for days, always when he let himself dwell too long upon Miss Liza Elliot. Hang it. If only that fellow he'd hired had found Miss Gamp. Then at least he'd have one woman who smelled like lemons.

Two weeks. Two weeks of pretending interest in that Christian gentleman, Richard Elliot. Never had he gone to such lengths to have a woman, and now he'd expended time, money, and more on a futile search for one, and a fruitless chase of another. Damn Liza Elliot. Damn her for dangling relief from this black melancholy and then yanking it back. And thank God he'd lost his patience and followed her this afternoon. The more he saw of her, the more convinced he became that they suited each other, perhaps enough to—no, perhaps not that much.

Tonight he would have relief. How he craved it, this release he foresaw in the possession of Liza Elliot. During this eternal delay he'd worked himself into a state of churning, roiling arousal with the mere sight of her ash blond hair, the sound of her petticoats, the smell of lemon toilet water. God, he was a mess.

As if trying to test his endurance, old Elliot had expanded the house party to include some of Jocelin's regimental friends. Now Stratfield Court was bursting with ex-officers, Winthrop, Fox, Halloway. He couldn't blame Elliot, for the man had availed himself of the chance to gather his dead son's military companions under his roof. Unfortunately, he had then driven Jocelin mad with stories of William Edward's bravery. Since Jocelin had been forced to haul William Edward out of several deadly scrapes, he found it hard to listen and nod admiringly. He did it for Asher's sake, for Elliot had great influence with liberal members of Parliament.

Taking a sip of his whiskey, he glanced around the smoking room. The men had gathered here and in the adjoining billiard room, as was customary after the ladies had retired. He dreaded these evenings, for talk usually degenerated to the telling of juvenile sexual exploits.

The only solace came when Winthrop began tugging at his collar. Hang it if the fellow wasn't sweating. Pompous. No doubt he'd absorbed some of Prince Albert's uprightness. Poor old Winthrop never seemed to be able to bend from his semiroyal dignity.

Nick finished his game of billiards with Asher and joined Jocelin. "How much longer, old chap?"

"You can't go to bed until eleven. An hour."

Groaning, Nick puffed on a cigar, then scowled at the burning tip. A bout of laughter interrupted him. They turned to see Asher Fox throw up his hands and lay his cue down on the table. Nick gave Jocelin an inquiring glance.

"Asher's trying to perfect shooting with his eyes closed. Always bets he can sink a ball that way, always loses."

Across the table, Winthrop called to them. "Always loses to me. Even in the Crimea he lost wagers to me. Worst gambler in the regiment. Do you remember . . ."

Jocelin lapsed into silence as the talk turned to Balaklava. He hated reminiscing. Whenever they all gathered, Winthrop turned the conversation to Balaklava. In a few months he, Jocelin, and Asher were to receive the new Victoria Cross. Jocelin didn't want it. He wanted reform, an end to the purchase of commissions, modernization of the army so that officers didn't charge artillery and end up spread like paste over the surface of a battleground.

There had been that one encounter with the Russian cavalry, just before the charge of the Light Brigade. He remembered the screams, had heard them in his sleep for almost a year. He could still feel the shrapnel slicing through his chest and arm. That Russian officer, he could still see his face, his golden mustache, his smile as the man tried to finish him off. The saber glinted in a beam of light just before it pierced his thigh.

"Jos? Jos?"

He glanced at Nick as his friend whispered to him.

"It's nothing. Just bad memories." Jocelin managed a weak smile. "Balaklava, you know. I thought I'd put it behind me, but lately I've been dreaming of what happened when I was wounded."

Arthur Thurston-Coombes joined them, as did the others when Jocelin began talking. Asher shook his head and waved his glass of port.

"Don't, old boy."

"I can't help it," Jocelin said. "So many of us died just then. I should have. I keep remembering

Sergeant Pawkins. He was in the bed next to me at Scutari. Wounded at the same time. I thought he was going to make it, and then one night he just fell asleep and died. Then there was Cheshire. He shouted at me, warned me so that I turned before that Russian could get me through the ribs. I remember him riding toward me as we fought. I don't understand what happened to him."

Asher drew nearer. Winthrop and Thurston-Coombes were hanging their heads. Jocelin noticed that Halloway's color had faded, while Asher's bleak countenance reflected his own nightmares.

"Don't dwell on it, Jos," Asher said. "You'll probably never be clear about what happened just before you fell. You nearly died, and that does funny things to one's mind."

Jocelin grimaced, then smiled grimly. "Are you saying I'm dotty?"

"Of course not." Asher clapped him on the back and glanced at Nick. "What about you, Ross? Ever in the cavalry."

"I uh—"

"Nick's been in the Colonies. Haven't you, old man?" Jocelin raised his glass to his friend. "Chaps, you're looking at a man who owns a ten-thousand-acre ranch in Texas. He's been over there looking after his family's interests. Ten thousand acres, can you imagine it? And you should try riding through it in July. The sun's so hot, ice would melt in the shade before you could blink at it. Shrivel you up like a raisin and then turn you to dust. Rattlesnakes, horny toads, and longhorns. Right, Nick?"

Nick goggled at him. "Er, yes."

Winthrop wrinkled his nose. "Really, Jos, how disgustingly uncivilized. One needs one's club, one's stable, the opera. Now, what you were saying about Cheshire. You're right. He vanished just before you went down. Don't understand it. I seem to remember he was wounded and trying to retreat, and then, suddenly, he wasn't there anymore. Strange."

"We're never going to remember it all," Jocelin said. "Perhaps we shouldn't."

"I don't want to remember," Thurston-Coombes said. He lifted his glass. "To the dead, gentlemen. They died with honor, for the queen."

They all repeated, "With honor, for the queen," and drank.

After that the talk turned to women, but Jocelin's melancholy remained, made worse by the dredging up of old horrors. Being in the smoking room didn't help. Elliot had done it and the billiard room in the Moorish style, which meant a lot of dark wood, ugly tile borders, and brass.

Jocelin didn't like the gloom, nor did he particularly care for the way his host had split the house into masculine and feminine domains. The bachelors' side included the smoking and billiard rooms, the gun room and trophy room, Elliot's study and business office, and the single men's bedrooms.

Idiotic, really, to spend one's leisure among dead things, smoke, and bills. He preferred his own country house. God, he longed for Reverie. Sir Christopher Wren had built it for a Marshall ancestor.

The longer he remained at Stratfield Court, the more he found himself craving Reverie's balanced perfection. He would go to Reverie as soon as he'd convinced Elliot to support Asher—and as soon as he'd made up his mind about Liza. He'd never expected to have to make up his mind. Finding a woman who interested him had been so unexpected that he could hardly adjust to his own astonishment. He didn't trust his feelings. Perhaps he merely lusted after this woman more than most. He'd soon find out, but he already suspected that Liza meant more than gratification. But how could he be sure? He'd never found a woman like her. Whatever the case, he couldn't leave yet, not until he'd found the respite he knew he could obtain with her.

Both he and Nick were glad when the smoking marathon broke up. They said good night before anyone else and retired to Jocelin's room for a last drink before bed.

"Lord help me, I'll be glad to get out of here," Nick said as he poured himself a whiskey from the bottle beside Jocelin's bed. "I never had to watch me language so long. Now about this dinner. I never been to no big affairs like this one, and I only got three days to practice."

Jocelin pulled his silk tie loose and shrugged out of his coat. "Just don't quote Shakespeare too much. A proper English gentleman is more interested in hunting and shooting than literature."

"You ain't."

"Ah." Jocelin's face went bleak. "But I'm not like the others. You know that."

"Better than all of them. Now don't you go plunging into the deep again. Coo, you're worse this time than ever. Listen. Get your mind off it, love. Tell me about them etiquettes again."

Sighing, Jocelin dropped into an armchair and counted off a list on his fingers. "A gentleman doesn't wear gloves to dinner. He does wear gloves to a dance."

"Right."

"A gentleman doesn't smoke in a lady's presence unless invited."

"Right."

"If you're smoking and meet a lady, you get rid of your cigar."

"What a waste."

"And by the way," Jocelin said, "if you're out driving with your mistress, she should be placed on your left so everyone knows she's not your wife."

"Ain't got no wife."

"You will, and when you get one, you must receive letters from your mistress at your club. The servants will bring them to you address-down so no one else will see the handwriting."

Nick shrugged. "Why should I care?"

"In case some bounder decides to let your wife know, you fool."

"Come on, love. She's going to know."

"Yes, but if someone tells her, she can't ignore it."

"Stupid."

"I agree, but that's Society for you, old fellow." Jocelin glanced at his pocket watch.

Nick wandered over to stand beside him, staring. Jocelin grew uncomfortable under that steady gaze.

"What?" he demanded.

"You don't look so good. I been worried about you. You're taking on for a bout of melancholy again, ain't you. Got yourself all worked up over that bastard Sinclair."

"I'm fine."

"You ain't fine. I seen you staring out windows for hours. You didn't think I noticed." Nick put an arm across the back of Jocelin's chair, leaned down to him, and held his gaze. "You don't think I know, do you? I

seen the look on your face after you got back from
Willingham. You got it again when those blokes
started in on the war. I seen you stare out the window
at the snow when you come home from Willingham,
and I know you wished you could walk out into it and
lay down and not come back."

Jocelin tore his gaze from Nick's and stared into
his whiskey. "You're wrong."

"I ain't, love, and you better think about giving
up our jaunts. They're bad for you, 'cause unlike me,
you still got a heart."

His thoughts had wandered with the shock of
Nick's accusations. "So many of us in the old group
are dead, you see."

"Oh?"

"First Cheshire, then Pawkins, then Airey and
Elliot's son, William, and now Stapleton."

Nick whistled. "But still, it was war."

"Not the last three." Jocelin rested his forehead
on the side of his glass. "I thought the dying would be
over when we came home."

"Them bastards shouldn't have brought it up.
Look at you."

Jocelin glanced at Nick's troubled features and
smiled. "Don't worry about me, old chap. After tonight I'll be fine."

"Going to see Miss Birch?"

"No. You go see her."

"She's real pissed at you for not coming. Says
she's not going to loll about in a drafty old inn
forever."

"I've been busy."

Nick fixed him with an intense stare, then
grinned at Jocelin. "It's Miss Shyness, isn't it? Coo!
How'd you manage it?"

"A gentleman doesn't bandy a woman's name, old chap."

Downing his whiskey, Nick set his glass down and headed for the door. "Right. Another etiquette I got to remember. When can we get out of this vault and back to London?"

"Oh, I'd say about three days. I think the lady is definitely worth three days, and besides, we have to attend Elliot's dinner on Friday. Shall we catch the afternoon train on Saturday?"

Nick paused at the threshold. "You better think about what you're doing, love. Miss Shyness has got more to her than lace and embroidery."

"I know, Nick, and if she weren't a lady . . . Well, who knows, perhaps . . ." He was still thinking of what might happen when Nick closed the door.

His friend had been right about his state. He'd been upset by Sinclair, and by poor Millie, and Jamie. There were more Millies and Jamies out there where he couldn't help them. At this moment they were crying and suffering.

Jocelin squeezed his eyes shut. He couldn't think about that and remain sane. He would think about Liza. God, how long was it until he could go to meet her? Not long now.

He distracted himself by thinking of how she had looked at dinner. She'd been furious with him. Refused to look at him most of the night. He remembered her tawny hair, how it swept back from her face and nestled at the back of her neck.

That gown, she'd worn a midnight blue gown, silk over miles of petticoats that swished and rustled. He'd been content to listen to them and anticipate seeing them, briefly, before he got rid of them. Long ago he'd learned to distinguish the myriad types of petticoats, taffeta, lace, satin. Gloves, now, they required skill in their removal if a lady wasn't to be put off. They had to be unbuttoned and deftly slid down arms.

Jocelin broke off contemplation of petticoats and gloves to glance at the clock. Time, at last. He slipped into his coat again and left his room. Stratfield Court was quiet and dark. The servants had long since gone to bed, for they had to be up before dawn to clean and prepare fires. Family and guests had retired, and the men had drunk enough to keep them abed until midmorning.

He went down the bachelor stairs, across the entrance hall, and through a transverse corridor to the gentlemen's library. The conservatory ran the length of the gentlemen's library, morning room, and music room. Like all of Elliot's constructions, it was larger than necessary for a conservatory. The structure soared high on thin iron supports that were painted white in imitation of the fairylike Crystal Palace.

Jocelin let himself in through the connecting door from the gentlemen's library, then locked it. He made a circuit of the conservatory, dodged rubber trees, palms, ferns, and ivy. Elliot had heated the place with steam, and soon Jocelin was warm enough to be glad he hadn't worn an overcoat.

He took up a station near the door that connected with the music room, for Liza would come that way. He leaned against a pillar covered with ivy. Moonlight spilled through the glass roof, casting orchids into silver illumination. His boots sank into gravel. Loveday would be furious at him for scratching them. Minutes passed. The heavy, cloying scent of tropical flowers aggravated him. He wanted to smell lemons.

He reached out and touched the petal of an orchid. Orchids, the genus *Orchis*, from the Greek word *orchis*, an appropriate allusion, considering what was going to happen here. He tapped his pocket watch with his fingers, then glanced at it. Squinting, he could just make out the time. She was late.

"Hang it." She wasn't going to come. "Damn, damn, damn."

He'd been thinking about her, and now his body had responded. God, he was going to spend another night in pain because of her. Hang it, she knew he wouldn't really go to her room. She knew he wasn't the kind of man to do that, and she'd called his bluff. Blasted, stubborn little goad. She harried him, prodded, pricked, and excited him, and then ran away.

"God, I hate women."

He shoved away from the pillar and took two steps. His foot hit gravel, then something sharp and solid. He heard a *whoosh*, and a pole appeared out of nowhere to whack him square in the face. It cracked his forehead.

Jocelin yelped and stumbled backward. The pole dropped when his foot moved. He clapped his hand to his forehead and cursed. He heard a giggle and saw a gloved arm catch the pole. Bracing himself on spread legs, he rubbed his head and swore.

Liza Elliot walked up to him, holding a rake and giggling. Jocelin rubbed his nose. Peering at her over his cupped hand, he snarled.

"That hurt, you unfeeling wretch. Don't you dare laugh."

By this time Liza had propped the rake against a rubber tree and covered her mouth with her hand. Muffled giggles continued to issue from behind the glove. Finally she managed to stop long enough to say something.

"Oh! Oh, dear, did that hurt?" She looked at him half in pity, half in helpless amusement. She clapped her hand over her mouth as her laughter erupted.

Jocelin glared at her. Feeling his nose and forehead, he clenched his teeth together as her giggles escalated into full-blown laughter.

"You think it was funny, do you?" he muttered. "I'll teach you to laugh at me, you contrary little midge."

She stopped laughing and whirled, launching herself down the path toward the music room. He swooped after her and caught her in three steps. His arm snaked around her waist. Hoisting her on his hip, he turned and carried her back the way they had come.

"Put me down!"

"Shh, or you'll wake everyone. They wouldn't want to see you being lugged about like a sack of turnips."

She pounded at his legs, but he kept walking.

"Such bad manners, Miss Elliot, to laugh at a man when he's hurt. And bad manners require discipline, don't you agree?"

13

Liza gasped as Jocelin hoisted her higher on his hip. Her amusement had vanished the moment he picked her up, and now he was threatening to punish her like a child. She had a father who thought her a mental three-year-old because of her sex. She wasn't about to suffer the same treatment from his high and mighty lordship. She stopped beating at his legs, grabbed the nearest one, and pounded the kneecap.

He cried out and dropped her. She hit the ground and slumped against him as he hopped on one foot, clutching his knee. His other knee buckled, and he fell on her. Their heads bumped together. Liza clutched her forehead. Jocelin clutched his forehead.

Liza cried out. Jocelin cried out, and they sat side by side, rubbing their heads.

"Hang it!" Jocelin whispered fiercely. "You've given me a headache."

"You deserved it. I'll not be handled so, my lord. Not by anyone. And how dare you try to force me to, to—you, you . . ."

"Back to 'you, you' again, are we?" He glared at her in the moonlight, then moaned and put his palms to his forehead. "God, why is it that I can have any woman I want except those who smell like lemons? Miss Gamp was just like you when I touched her. I swear the two of you have given me brain fever."

Liza stopped rubbing her head and peered at him. "What did you say?"

Jocelin glanced at her, then quickly looked at the dark leaves of a rubber tree.

"Oh, nothing."

"You said a name, Gamp."

"It's nothing."

"You might as well tell me, for I'm not going to let it alone."

"Whatever happened to the meek Miss Elliot?"

"You made her vanish."

Jocelin sighed and tried to restore the crease in his trousers. "I came across a plump and peevish young woman named Gamp. I can't forget her. She's like malaria, she keeps coming back. And now she's vanished." He looked outside at the half-moon and whispered. "All for the good, probably. I'd be as bad for her as I am for you."

Liza's thoughts had been whirling. He hadn't forgotten her. He hadn't been able to forget her, despite the fact that he'd never even seen her clearly.

Her heart began to thump painfully, then her head felt light.

"So I hired a man to find this woman, but he hasn't been at all lucky. She's gone, and now I've made you hate me when you're the only one who makes me forget—things."

Never in her life could she remember being important to someone, as this man was telling her she was to him. He didn't know it, of course, but that wasn't the point. He hadn't forgotten her. He had wanted her, still wanted her.

For the first time, Liza considered the possibility that Jocelin Marshall might harbor more for her than a mild desire born of ennui. Now she could admit to herself that she'd always been afraid he was more interested in relieving the tedium of his visit than in her odd little self. She had been wrong about his being capable of murder, and she was wrong, it seemed, about his feelings for her. All at once the moon seemed brighter, the air filled with a more provocative scent.

Jocelin was muttering something about low spirits and lace. She hadn't heard the rest. Liza put her forefinger against his lips. He turned to look at her, his eyes in shadow. For a long moment he remained still and held his breath. Then he kissed her finger while taking her hand.

"Sweet Liza, are you going to forgive me?"

"I may."

"Shall I convince you to forgive me?" He glanced at the moon again, then put his cheek next to hers. "Look," he said, pointing. "'The moon like a flower / In heaven's high bower, / With silent delight—"

"'Sits and smiles on the night,'" Liza finished.

He turned to look at her, and she could feel more than see his smile.

"You know Blake?"

"It is I who should be surprised, my lord."

He stopped smiling. "I'm not really a killer."

"What?" Had he discovered her snooping?

"The cavalry, my skirmishes out west, all that isn't what I want."

"What do you want?"

He leaned toward her and placed light kisses on her cheeks and forehead. "I want love, Liza mine. 'Love to faults is always blind, / Always is to joy inclined, / Lawless, winged, and unconfined, / And breaks all chains from every mind.'" He poised above her lips. "Break my chains, Liza, break them for me."

Too caught up in the tickling sensations of his kisses, Liza hardly attended to his words. She felt his hand smooth down the length of her skirts to her ankle, where it dipped below to rest, warm and reassuring. All the while his lips drew nearer and nearer her mouth, until at last he kissed her.

For once she didn't fight, and because she allowed herself to enjoy the experience, her mouth began to feel like a hot whirlpool. When he sucked at her lips and tongue, she answered with her own forays. So concerned with his mouth was she that his slow movements didn't disturb her, not even when he stood with her in his arms. Still kissing her, he walked to the sitting area, where a long couch provided a resting place.

Instead of putting her down, however, he stood beside it, kissing her. She didn't mind, for he crushed her to him and devoured her mouth. Her hands began to roam over his shoulders then.

As if spurred on by their movements, Jocelin

began to kiss his way down her neck to the edge of her evening gown, just above her breasts. The feel of his mouth on her breasts made her gasp, which caused him to graze his teeth across her flesh.

Suddenly she was on the couch, and his hand was on her ankle again. It remained there, the fingers trailing over hollows and curves while he returned to her mouth. Her leg was bent, and she felt his fingers tracing the length of her calf. He whispered something to her, but she was more interested in how the presence of his hand made her tingle at her breasts and between her thighs.

Almighty in heaven, she couldn't bear it if he stopped. While she worried that he would stop, his lips nuzzled her breast, then fastened on it as his fingers brushed the inside of her thigh. Now she burned, and something tightened inside her, like a wet cloth being put through a wash wringer. As he approached the juncture between her thighs, the tightness grew and grew until she wanted to scream. When he touched her there, she sucked in her breath, but he immediately kissed her. With each caress, the tightness increased, and her hips began to move.

Jocelin made a delighted sound and whispered, "More, Liza, please."

Confused, she hardly listened. The tightness was going to drive her mad, so she moved against him. As her hips flexed, he smiled and nuzzled her ear, whispering encouragement. By now Liza didn't care if he was pleased or not. His hand twitched, and she cried out. He put his free hand over her mouth as she tried to twist from him. He kept touching her, and she exploded.

As she cried out into his hand, he moved, lifted over her. Vaguely, through her frenzy, she felt something long and hot between her legs. He prodded at her, and something elemental made her open. He slid inside her. She cried out as he lodged deeply and then remained still for a few moments.

Convulsions racked her again as he began to move. He rocked gently at first, but she clawed at his back and buttocks. A gentle pain traveled up inside her as he moved, but it paled beside the pleasure of having him so close. Liza slipped her arms inside his shirt and raked his back. She felt the muscles over his ribs work as he pumped gently inside her.

All at once he began to thrust quickly. Her eyes flew open as pain faded, swamped by that tightness. She cried out, then sank her teeth into his neck as the tightness burst again. He shoved back and forth in his own wildness, then, as she gasped for breath, cried out his pleasure with his face buried in her breast.

Liza felt him collapse on top of her. He was huge inside of her, and his convulsions snaked along her. She lay still, intent on feeling the whole of him and every quiver and twitch. She ran her hands down inside his clothing until they fastened on his buttocks. Digging her fingers into his flesh, she satisfied her long-held urge to explore him. When she raked her fingernails over his skin, his buttocks twitched, and she chuckled. At the sound, he lifted his head and looked at her.

"Oh, Liza . . ."

"Yes, my lord."

"Liza, Liza, Liza." He gazed into her eyes through a wild tangle of locks. "Liza, do you know what opium is?"

She nodded.

"No, you don't," he whispered. "It's you, Liza." He put his forehead to hers. "Oh, God, Liza. I've never been with an innocent before. Have I hurt you?"

He lifted his head and gave her a fearful look. His apprehension endeared him to her as nothing else he'd done this night. Liza smiled at him.

"No. Can we do this again?"

Blinking, he studied her. "Again?"

"Of course, my lord. Again and again."

"But you're supposed to be upset."

"I know, but you're so, so good at this. I'll be upset later. Now I want to know if you will do this with me again." She eyed him warily. "Don't you want to?"

He raised his eyes skyward. "Thank you, Heavenly Father." He kissed her. "And thank you, my sweet Liza."

When he pulled free of her and sat up, Liza sat up as well. Somehow her gown had come loose. It was falling about her hips. As she moved, she felt warm stickiness between her legs, but she was too distressed to worry about it.

"You don't want to," she said, her shoulders slumping.

Suddenly she was picked up and set on Jocelin's lap. He took her face in his hands and kissed her.

"Silly midge, how can you ask such a question? But you can't, not tonight."

"Oh."

"Do you understand why?"

He had ducked his head so that she had to look at him.

"I hadn't thought that it might be uncomfortable to be with you again," she said.

When he smiled at her, that new tightness started again, and she kissed him. At first he was still beneath her lips, then when she touched them with her tongue, he moaned and attacked her mouth with his. She twisted her fingers in his hair, shoved him against her mouth, and drove inside it with her tongue. He cried out and tore his lips free. Panting, he held her off.

"No!" He captured her hands. "If you continue, I won't be able to stop, and then you'll be hurt. Don't make me, Liza."

"Then promise we'll be together again, please. In the morning."

"But that might be too soon."

He didn't understand, and she couldn't tell him. That tightness was back, and growing, because of the low grating of his voice, because of the bunching of his thigh muscles under her hand. She couldn't survive this frustration he'd created.

"My lord, tomorrow morning, or now."

He stared at her. "You mean it."

She didn't reply, and he grinned at her. "I am at your command, Miss Elliot. Can you arrange to go poor-visiting?"

"I'll visit graveyards if it will bring you to me."

"The inn at Willingham would be more comfortable."

"I don't care," she said.

He laughed and turned her to face away from him so that he could fasten her gown. "You're most unusual."

"I know. I've been different all my life."

"How?"

She had said too much, and couldn't explain without revealing too much about herself. He was supposed to believe her a spinster.

"Well, I'm a spinster, of course."

He finished her gown and offered her gloves. "For no good reason that I can see."

Liza wrung her gloves and looked away from him. "I—I was unwilling to marry knowing that my husband would have been purchased. After my first season, I well . . ." She cleared her throat. "You see, I wanted to know the truth, so at one of my first balls I made the acquaintance of several gentlemen who had no knowledge of my income."

She swallowed, her speech dammed up behind a wall of hurt. No need to reveal so much to this man, who had never been within her reach at all.

"You were ignored," he finished for her.

Staring at her gloves, she nodded.

"I'm glad," he said, "for you don't deserve to be hawked about like strawberry tarts at a fair."

Surprised, she glanced up at him to find his brow furrowed.

"You're angry," she said.

"At them, at fellows who have the sensitivity of lard."

She smiled at him. "I like you, my lord."

"You do?"

"Why do you sound as if you don't believe me."

It was his turn to look away. "My experience has been that women come to me for something other than friendship."

She put her hand on his cheek and brushed her thumb across his lips. "They would."

His voice was so low, she could barely hear it. "And I'm tired of it, by God."

She took his hand in both of hers. "Then—" Her voice cracked with nervousness. "Then perhaps we can be friends, since we have so few people we can trust. I mean, aren't you weary of wondering if the lady you're with wants your title?"

"Friends? With a woman?"

Straightening her back, she put her hands on her hips and frowned at him. "It is possible, you know."

"Not if I can't have you," he snapped. "Not if being your friend means I can't have you."

"Why would it mean that?"

He let out a long breath. "You frightened me." He kissed her hand. "I've never had a woman as a friend. You're a rare little thing, Liza Elliot. And by the way, you have to stop calling me 'my lord' when we're alone."

"I'll try, but you don't know how very much a lord you are, my lord."

"Shall I take you to your room?" he asked as he helped her stand.

She glanced at his open shirt. If she touched his bare flesh, she would feel that maddening arousal again, and if he stayed with her much longer, she would touch that bare flesh. Her gaze fixed on the muscle over his breast, and her skin grew hot.

"My lord," she said on a tense note. "My lord, I don't think it would be wise for you to do that. In fact, you had better not stay here much longer if you don't want to find yourself on the floor again."

She blushed at her own frankness. When he gave her the smile of an innocently pleased cherub, her embarrassment vanished.

"You're a delight," he said.

She returned his smile, and he kissed her lightly before disappearing behind a wall of ferns. She heard his whisper as he left.

"I'm not going to sleep, my love, and it's your fault."

Grinning foolishly, she tiptoed all the way back to her room. There she washed at the porcelain basin and donned her nightgown. She stuffed her soiled clothes in a little-used trunk. Emmeline would take care of them discreetly.

She climbed into bed and lay with the covers clutched under her chin. That tightness had faded. Jocelin Marshall was gone, and her conscience was beginning to snipe at her. She had committed a sin. At the time, she hadn't cared, but now she was beginning to realize the magnitude of her actions. She had fornicated with a man. Good Christian women didn't do that. But then, she'd found out a long time ago, she wasn't a good Christian woman.

Sin. Mama and Papa would be ashamed of her if they knew what she'd done. But they'd been ashamed of her most of her life. She should give up Jocelin Marshall so that her parents and Society wouldn't disapprove of her. Liza gave an unhappy laugh. Giving him up wouldn't make anyone approve of her.

Why should she stop? She knew better than to think she would ever have another chance to love a man as beautiful and fascinating as Jocelin. His compassion and sensuality wrapped her in thrall.

No doubt he would pass through her life like quicksilver, and vanish. If she didn't have him now, she never would. This knowledge had spurred her on when she knew he was going to make love to her. No, a woman like herself, one of unexceptional appearance and unacceptable principles, a woman such as herself must snatch what small morsels and bits of love came her way.

She had gone to the conservatory determined to foil the viscount's plans for seduction. And then he'd mentioned Gamp. No man had ever been unable to forget her. The ones she'd met during her season had had no trouble forgetting her at all. Except for the ones who had made fun of her for her championing the cause of women's education and property rights. No doubt Jocelin would disapprove of her beliefs as well.

She wouldn't tell him. For no matter how much she longed for someone who would accept her, un-womanly principles and all, she knew she would never find someone like that. To her shame, she found that she craved Jocelin so much, she was willing to conceal her true beliefs, or at least not mention them. After all, they had so little time, no more than a few weeks.

Liza snuggled deeper under the covers. After that humiliating season in London she had made up her mind to forget marriage and the hope of someone's ever falling in love with her. Her greatest fear had been confirmed. She was too different, unable to be like other women, and thus no man had wanted her. Therefore, to save herself from shame and from pain, she had decided to forget marriage and love. She told herself not to think about them, and had succeeded so well that thoughts of men rarely troubled her—until Jocelin.

Jocelin she couldn't put out of her thoughts. He wouldn't let her. His pursuit had been so unexpected, so inconceivable, that he had slipped under her guard. Never had she imagined that a man so bewitching would want her. The very unexpectedness of such an occurrence had made her vulnerable.

Yet desperate as she was to have him, she wouldn't lie to herself. He might want her for a time, but not for long. And if she revealed her true self to him, his desire would vanish beneath a shower of distaste.

She would take what she could, grab her chance to be with him for the moment. He would tire of her, no doubt quickly, for she was no match for the women who pursued him. She could think of at least three Society beauties who were known to desire him, with or without marriage. Perhaps he'd already granted them favors. After all, he was generous.

No, she would seem a coot among swans when compared to them. Therefore she would watch closely and be ready. When he wanted to leave, she would be prepared. She would suggest they part first, so that the pain would be less for the lack of shame. If she let him go with grace and apparent equanimity, at least she would be spared shame.

He would never know the cost, never suspect that she longed for more. She would return to her old life. After all, she had a murderer to find. She couldn't fall in love and chase after Jocelin Marshall. How disgusted he would be if he knew her dreams of having him forever. She couldn't bear it if he looked at her with revulsion. To prevent that, she would give him only what he would accept, and never, never burden him with the knowledge of her longing and her love.

14

Jocelin lay between waking and sleep when someone who wanted to die grabbed his shoulder and shook him violently. He snarled, jerked his shoulder free, and sprang up from the covers. His hand met something solid, and he pushed.

"Blast it!"

Shoving strands of black hair back from his eyes, Jocelin peered over the bed to find Nick swearing at him from the floor. Nick scrambled to his feet and returned the shove.

"Slug-a-bed," he said. "It's almost nine o'clock."

Jocelin drew the covers back over his head. "Shove off. I don't want to go riding this morning."

He hunched down on the bed, then popped

back up again, glanced at the window as Nick drew
aside the curtains, and swore. He launched himself
out of bed. Pushing the bell for Loveday, he donned a
dressing gown. Nick watched him fly across the room
to a chest, yank open the top drawer, and begin
tossing shirts out of it.

Already attired, Nick watched him calmly from
the comfort of a settee. "Got news."

"Not now," Jocelin muttered. "I'm late for an
appointment."

"Sod your appointment. Our friend and the
friend of children everywhere, dear old Nappie Carbuncle, well, he's gone missing."

Jocelin paused in his search for a necktie. With
slow deliberation he closed a drawer and contemplated a daguerreotype of Mr. and Mrs. Elliot that
rested on the bureau. Nick's voice jolted him out of
his stillness.

"You're going to strangle that chest."

He relaxed his grip on the top of the chest and
squared his shoulders. "Then your arrangements have
been successful."

"Course. Alas, poor Nappie. 'I knew him well,
Horatio; a fellow of infinite jest, of most excellent
fancy.'"

"Damn you, Nick, it's not a joke."

Nick sprang off the settee and approached Jocelin. Taking him by the shoulder, Nick spun him
around so that they faced each other.

"You got to laugh or die, old love. That's why
you can't go on with this."

Nick folded his arms and surveyed Jocelin, who
glanced down at the shirts on the floor.

"How many times you going to kill your uncle?"
Nick went on quietly. "I see what you're doing to

yourself, old love. Might be better if you just killed Yale."

Jocelin walked away from Nick to stand at the window and stare at the frost-covered rooftops. "Don't you think I tried?" He lifted his gun hand and stared at it. "I held my Colt to his head once. Pulled back the trigger with my thumb. He was sweating and crying, and . . . I don't know." His hand dropped to his side.

Nick came to him and poked him in the shoulder. "You bleeding fool, he's just like all the others. Can't ever be trusted not to do it again."

"I have him watched."

"All the bleeding time?" Nick whistled when Jocelin nodded. "Cheaper to—"

Jocelin whirled on Nick. "I can't, damn you!" He swallowed and lowered his voice. "I can't. He's my father's brother, and at one time I loved him as I should have loved Father. I can't." Smiling bitterly, he continued, "Yale knows he's being watched, so he confines himself to those with sufficient years."

Nick shrugged and returned to the settee. "I still say you got to stop, but that ain't why I come. I got me own life, you know. It's just that I heard two of your cavalry chaps quarreling like they was still at war."

"Who?"

"Asher and the jealous earl, what's his name, Halloway. Halloway's taken himself off. Gone home, he has."

Jocelin went to an armoire and began sorting through morning coats. "Halloway's always fighting with someone, though I'm surprised he managed to do it with Asher."

"Why?" Nick asked. "Old Asher's not my favorite, always trying to charm everybody."

"Asher will be good for this country in Parliament."

"Asher's good for Asher," Nick replied.

Jocelin snagged a coat and threw it over his arm. "Go away, Nick. I have an appointment."

"Well, don't forget we're leaving Saturday."

"I won't, but, say, old fellow, perhaps not Saturday."

"I'm getting out of this crypt Saturday," Nick said, "whether you come or not."

"Yes, my lord."

Jocelin grinned at Nick as his friend left. Bearing a tray, Loveday passed Nick at the threshold. Jocelin wrinkled his nose and sniffed fresh, hot tea. Loveday set the breakfast tray on a table by the settee.

"Good morning, my lord."

"Great morning, Loveday. I'm going out immediately."

"Very good, my lord. Shall we be riding?"

"Yes, and I want my best outfit."

Jocelin gulped down half a cup of tea, stuffed toast in his mouth, and swallowed that. When Loveday remained in attendance beside him, he glanced up at the valet. Loveday wore his offended nun's expression, and Jocelin sighed.

"Why can I never keep any of my little offenses from your notice?"

"If we wish to keep a secret, we should take greater care with our apparel, my lord. The evening coat we wore last night smells of lemons and is disgracefully wrinkled."

"Oh."

"If I may be frank, my lord?"

"Do I have a choice?"

Loveday's brows climbed his forehead.

"Carry on," Jocelin said as he chomped on ham and eggs.

"Hitherto, our peccadillos have never extended to the frail and fair members of the maiden class. Hitherto, we have been most scrupulous to avoid besmirching the reputation of those we know quite well to be above reproach. Hitherto, we have behaved, shall we say, as a gentleman of honor and chivalry."

Jocelin set down his fork and contemplated the tea leaves in the bottom of his cup. After a few moments he shook his head.

"I can't help it. No, don't say anything." He waved a hand helplessly. "I've tried, Loveday. I've struggled ever since I first saw her skating on the pond. I lay awake nights fighting myself. I lost. And now it seems the lady wants me as much as I want her, so leave it. At first I thought we both had succumbed to simple desire, but now I'm not sure. We seem to get on so well together. We even fight well together. But what if it's only lust? God, I hate my father for making me endure this torture. I hate uncertainty. How do I know she's the right woman?"

He broke off and glanced at Loveday. "I only hope I can make a decision before she becomes truly besotted."

"I fear, my lord, that you are already too late."

Loveday produced a sealed envelope from his coat pocket. It was addressed to Jocelin in Liza's handwriting. Exchanging apprehensive glances with the valet, Jocelin opened it and read: "Ten o'clock at the inn. Take a room, and I will follow."

He released his in-held breath. "No cause for alarm." He handed the note back to Loveday, who placed it in the fireplace. "Not one syllable that could be called adoration, no effusions, no inflamed prose, no sentimental verse. Good. This way I can make a logical decision."

Loveday's skeptical look annoyed him.

"I can," he snapped.

"As you say, my lord."

He poured another cup of tea as Loveday prepared to draw his bath. "A logical decision. That's what I need. Careful thinking, which means I must be freed of this maddening lust first."

After sneaking out of Stratfield Court by way of the servants' hall, butler's pantry, and lamp room, he galloped most of the way to Willingham. He took a room and paced it so long in his agitated state that he was sure he'd grown gray hairs. At last he answered a knock, only to find a widow at his door.

"I fear you've got the wrong room, ma'am."

The widow brushed by him, and he smelled fresh lemons.

"Liza, you clever thing."

He grinned as she spun around and lifted her heavy veil. Yards of black satin trimmed with jet gleamed in the morning sunlight. He yanked at an inky ribbon and tore her bonnet away. Tossing it aside, he gathered her close. Jet beads poked at his chest through his shirt. He paid no attention to her as she began to speak and covered her mouth. She opened her lips and played with his tongue. When she slid her hands beneath his coat to knead his waist, he went wild. He forgot years of skill in the art of seduction.

"My lord?"

"Jocelin," he said before he submerged in a boiling sea of urgency.

He pressed her to him and dropped to the carpet. She seemed unable to stop kissing him long enough to frame her questions. Not that he could have answered. His fingertips burned when they raked through tawny curls. He lifted his mouth from hers, for mad as he was, he couldn't bear to frighten her. She paused in her kisses then and met his gaze. Relief flooded him when he perceived the heavy-lidded, burgeoning appetite he had created.

The relief prodded him, emancipated him from restraint. He held her gaze as he caressed and petted his way to her center. When her eyes closed and she moaned, he freed himself and entered her. Sinking deep, he allowed himself free rein until he heard her cry out. At the sound, he lost himself, engulfing himself in pleasureful insanity.

A long moment passed before he realized he was lying on top of her fully dressed and still inside her. He lifted his head, disconcerted, and looked down at her. Liza gazed up at him drowsily. She traced his lips with her fingertips, then nipped at them. He felt himself twitch. She gasped and then giggled.

"Hang it, woman. Don't laugh."

"Why not?"

Blast the silly midge, she was making him blush. He hadn't blushed in years. Years.

"Just don't," he said with his jaw clenched. "I'll explain some other time."

He left her then, righted his clothing, and sat with his head in his hands while she tended to herself.

"I'm a monster," he said. "I've ravished you. You, an innocent." He cast a sideways glance at her as she stepped out of her torn drawers and began using them as a cloth. "Have I frightened you?"

"A mite," she said with a smile. "At first, but after I touched your lips, I forgot everything else. You see, I had all these dreams last night. I must be quite sinful to have such dreams about you, but there you are, I'm beset by them and by you."

She rolled the drawers in a ball and stuffed them in her reticule. He watched her close it with an efficient snap, then look at him with uncertainty. He took her hand. Leading her to the unused bed, he sat beside her on it and cupped her chin.

"You're quite the most unusual young lady I've ever known, Miss Elizabeth Maud Elliot."

She winced. "Please, I hate the name Maud. Such an ugly name."

"Maud was a queen, and you're the queen of my delight."

"I am?"

"Why are you so astonished?"

"Oh, I don't know."

Intent on his own thoughts, he allowed this mystery to pass. "Will you come to London in the spring?"

She had been playing with his lips again. At his question, she dropped her hand and looked away.

"I don't think so."

"But your father is determined to marry you off, isn't he? It's the only prudent course, attending the season."

She turned then, and gazed at him with blank eyes. "Marry me off? Yes, how stupid of me to forget that you would know all about it. Yes, I'm to be put in the market again."

"Then, will you see me in London?"

She blinked at him, and suddenly he got the feeling she was only half listening to him. Something had alarmed her. Perhaps he'd been too cavalier about mentioning their irregular dealings so soon. Women like to preserve great fantasies about their affairs.

They wanted gushing avowals of everlasting devotion.
Well, she couldn't have them yet. He needed time.

As he thought, he struggled with the demands of
his body. She was sitting beside him, trussed from
neck to foot in tight black bombazine, not a bit of
ankle or breast showing, and he could feel himself
filling, swelling, pressing against his clothing. God, he
wanted Liza, wanted her again, now, as violently as
he'd wanted her but a few minutes past.

While he struggled for the presence not to leap
upon her in mindless rut, he realized he wasn't going
to get enough of her in a mere week or so. The way his
sex felt now, stiff as a fence post, he was going to need
Liza for a long time. He had to keep seeing her. But
old Elliot wanted her married. He frowned at the idea
of Liza's gracing the bed of some complacent and
neglectful blueblood. His annoyance made his tone
sharp when he repeated his question.

"Will you see me in London?"

"Perhaps."

She was avoiding his eyes. All at once he came
alert. Why this reluctance?

"What's wrong?"

Abruptly she sprang off the bed, turned to him,
and smiled brightly. "Nothing at all, my beautiful lord.
Can it be that you don't know how cataclysmic your
very presence is? You make love to me, turn me into
a screaming madwoman, and then expect me to make
sense." She hesitated, then said, "My lord—Jocelin, I
mean—may I touch you?"

He frowned at her, but she gave him a look of
tremulous longing. His suspicious mood vanished, and
he inclined his head. She came back to him and began
unbuttoning his shirt. Shoving him back so that he
rested on his elbows on the bed, she bared his chest

and smoothed her palms over his bare flesh. She traced the indentation that ran from the hollow of his throat and between his ribs.

Pressing her hand against the flat of his stomach below his navel, she tugged at his trousers and bared his hips. She discovered the indentation between his hip and his buttock. Scraping the backs of her nails along it, she pinched his flesh. He bit his lower lip, but tried to remain quiescent. She paused, blushed, and glanced at him again before relieving him of the rest of his clothing. However, when she stood beside the bed with her hands hovering over his chest, she stopped. Touching her hands to her inflamed cheeks, she whispered.

"Oh, you'll think me a—a, you'll think me shameless."

He smiled at her. If he told her how her ingenuous appreciation gave him more pleasure than any mistress's practiced compliments, he would embarrass her even more. Instead he sat up and took her hand. Placing it flat on his thigh, he looked into her eyes.

"God, Liza, if you set out to enslave me, you couldn't have thought of a more devastating manner in which to do it."

She gaped at him, and her lips formed a quavering smile. Her gaze dropped to his hips. To his delight and no little surprise, her hand slid upward, and she touched him. He gasped, lost control, and shoved against her. Liza's hand vanished. She shoved it behind her back and stared at him. He captured her hand and returned it to him.

"God, Liza, don't stop now."

She only shook her head, and he saw that she

was confused. He sighed, sat up, and pulled her down on top of him.

"I forgot," he said. "I'm sorry, my innocent. Let me teach you."

They spent a happy hour in lessons before he regained enough sense to put an end to it. Once they had dressed again, he sent her out first. The room overlooked the town's High Street, and as he buttoned his coat and ran his fingers through his hair, he could see her emerge from the inn. Smiling, he watched her pick her way down the sidewalk over cobbles and around several old men dozing in the sun in front of shops. She paused beside a red brick Georgian structure, gazed up at the polished brass nameplates beside the door, and mounted the front steps.

Jocelin's hands stilled on his necktie. As Liza reached the door, a young man came out of the building. He bowed to her and said something. She replied, and he offered his arm. They descended the front steps, still talking, and continued down High Street.

There was a roaring in his head. Jocelin gripped the windowsill and studied the retreating backs of his lover and her man friend. A man. He blinked in astonishment, for until now he'd never even wondered about whether a lover of his was faithful. Something was different now. Now he found that the idea of Liza's seeking the company of another man enraged him. She had gone from him to see a man. By God, he wouldn't have it. How dare she traipse about market towns meeting strange men?

Waves of jealousy crashed on the shores of his mind, obliterating reason and impelling him to act. He snatched up his hat, gloves, and riding crop. In seconds he had clattered downstairs, out of the inn, and into High Street. Jostling a grocer's assistant hauling grain bags, he cut his way through pedestrians, his gaze fixed on the black bonnet and mantle of Liza Elliot.

They were turning. He sped up and rounded a corner as the two entered another, newer building surrounded by a wrought-iron fence. The cut-glass-and-mahogany door shut. In the throes of unaccustomed and humiliating jealousy, he didn't stop to think. He burst through the gate, swept up the steps, and threw open the door. Inside, a parlor maid was walking away. She turned and gasped upon seeing him.

"Where are they?" His head would burst with the noise of his rage.

The parlor maid bristled. "Here now, sir. You can't—"

Jocelin snatched her wrist. "Where are they?"

"The master and Miss Elliot?"

"Yes, damn you."

"They're in the parlor, sir."

The maid bugged her eyes at him and pointed to a closed door to the right of the foyer. He turned his back on her, twisted the knob, and threw open the door. The panel banged against a wall.

The two people inside had been standing close to each other, heads bent. At the sound, they stepped apart and turned in alarm. Jocelin stalked into the parlor, located Liza, and went to her.

Speaking quietly, he asked, "Who is he?"

"My lord!"

"Damn your 'my lords,'" he ground out. "Who is he? And don't lie to me. I'll know the truth when I hear it."

The young man approached them then, and Jocelin spared him a glance. Pale, thin, ascetic, and ethereal in appearance, he nevertheless had enough daring to bark at Jocelin.

"See here, sir. Who are you?"

Jocelin inspected his adversary, noted the silky if receding gold locks and air of poetic delicacy. He narrowed his eyes. Some women loved artistic aesthetes who languished about pretending to intellect.

"My, my, my," he said.

He felt the heat of a Texas sun, heard the shake of a rattlesnake's tail. He hooked his thumbs in his waistband and stalked in a circle around the young man. At the change in Jocelin's accent, the stranger gave Liza a bewildered glance.

"What we got here, Liza, honey?" Jocelin continued to circle his prey. "Some womanish little varmint, I'd say."

He flicked a blond curl with his riding crop, then looked at Liza. "Yep, some varmint." He tapped the buttons of the young man's waistcoat with the crop. "You're sniffing around the wrong woman. I think we need to have a talk. A real, serious talk. Dead serious."

The young man's eyes widened to gooseberries as Jocelin smiled his cold, Colt smile.

"Yep," he said. "A real serious talk."

15

She knew the moment Jocelin decided to kill poor Ronald. He drawled his words, stretching them out and giving them a lazy caress, and like a cougar sunning on a rock, he turned slowly and beamed a narrow, green gaze at the solicitor that missed not a breath, not a flicker of a lash.

If she didn't stop him, she wasn't sure Ronald would survive much longer. Liza uttered a shout that nearly rattled the frames of the pictures on the walls.

"My lord!"

Jocelin didn't move or take his gaze from Ronald, but when he spoke, she sighed, for the gunfighter's drawl was gone.

"Bloody hell, don't interfere, woman. I'll deal with you when I've gotten rid of this bounder."

Liza closed her eyes, prayed that she wouldn't lose her temper, and put on the air of a queen faced with a leaking water closet.

"My lord." Picture frames clattered again. "This is my solicitor."

Jocelin stared hard at her. She watched a muscle in his jaw quiver, and his color rise. It faded swiftly as he let the riding crop fall to his side. It twitched and swished about his right boot, then stilled. He rounded on the solicitor and inclined his head.

"I've made an inexcusable error, sir. May I offer my apologies?" He held out his hand, which Ronald took reluctantly.

Liza hastened to intercede. "Jocelin, Viscount Radcliffe, may I present Mr. Ronald Varney, my solicitor."

Varney stuttered when he heard Jocelin's title. Glancing with quivering uncertainty from Liza to Jocelin, he fidgeted with his lapels. At last he found something to do with himself by calling for tea. He hurried over to a bell button on the wall next to the door.

"Oh, I forgot," he said. "It's broken. If you will excuse me, Miss Elliot, my lord?" Varney sidled out of the parlor in search of the kitchen.

Liza sat on the edge of a brocade sofa, her back stiff. Jocelin watched Varney leave, then discarded his hat, gloves, and crop. Feeling rather saintly in her endurance, Liza gawked at him when he rounded on her.

"*You* have a solicitor?" he hissed. "Why in sodding hell do you need a solicitor?"

"If you wish to speak to me, you'll keep your language clean."

He nearly growled at her, but folded his lips on each other. "You're going to make my head explode, Liza. Who is the bast—who is that little toad?"

By now it had occurred to her that the much pursued and coveted Jocelin Marshall was jealous, and she gloated at him. His brows drew together, and he gave her a thundercloud frown. When she grinned at him, he cursed, which elicited a chuckle from her. She threw up a hand when he plopped down on the couch beside her.

"No unbecoming behavior, my lord."

"If you don't tell me who he is, I'll, I'll—"

"Look at this." Liza withdrew a folded letter from her reticule and handed it to him. As he read, she continued. "That's from Miss Burdett-Coutts, with whom you and the queen are acquainted, if I'm correct. She and I are funding a kind of ragged school for the villages and towns surrounding Stratfield Court."

He had the grace to look chagrined. Handing her the letter, he sank back on the sofa and groaned.

The corner of Liza's mouth twitched. "Miss Burdett-Coutts and I intend to pay the children of poor families to go to school. We're going to pay them more than they could earn by working on farms and mills and such. Education, my lord, is the path out of poverty. Would you like to read an essay on the subject?"

He shook his head.

"I couldn't hear you," she said.

"I said, I'm sorry." He rose, took her hand, and kissed it. "I told you that you've given me a brain fever. No doubt I'll bay at the moon tonight, and don't you smirk at me, miss. I'm going to that pub down the street and wait for you."

"But I may be some time."

"Good. I need time to think."

He left as Ronald Varney returned from the kitchen. She heard him make a cordial excuse and apologized again. By the time he was gone, the solicitor was grinning, complacent and pink-cheeked with self-importance.

An hour later the viscount's hunter was tied behind her carriage. Tessie rode with the coachman while Liza and Jocelin were secluded inside the vehicle. Since he'd left Mr. Varney's, she'd had time to recover from the shock of being descended upon by an avenging, concupiscent male. Heavens, what a frightening experience. Now all she could do was beam at him like a locomotive lantern in startled amusement.

Liza sat gripping her reticule. She had removed her veil and stuffed it in the pocket of her mantle so that she didn't arouse curiosity when they got home. Jocelin had regained his poise, but stared moodily out the window at the countryside. The snow had melted, and March had brought sunshine and the promise of spring. Suddenly he turned and faced her.

"You should have taken your maid with you."

She rolled her eyes. "If you will remember, my lord, I sent Emmeline on errands because of you."

"Oh." Undaunted, he continued. "You should have left dealing with a solicitor to your father."

Liza folded her arms over her chest and impaled him with an irritated glance. "My father wouldn't approve. My brother would have helped me, but he's dead."

"If your father doesn't approve, you shouldn't

concern yourself with such matters. And I know your brother wouldn't have liked it that you gad about dabbling in worldly affairs."

Bristling, Liza gasped. "He would too."

"Are we talking about William Edward Elliot?"

At the sound of her brother's name, Liza's irritation vanished. Her eyes filled with tears, which she refused to shed. Fishing among her layers of clothing, she found a handkerchief and pressed it to her nose. A warm hand covered hers. Jocelin pressed his lips to her palm.

"Forgive me. I was insensitive."

His gentleness was her undoing. She sobbed, then wept openly into her handkerchief. Jocelin cursed as he lifted her onto his lap. She cried onto the shoulder of his overcoat until she had to blow her nose. Crumpling her handkerchief, she managed to speak at last.

"I saw him the night he died. I was, um, visiting friends in London, and he came to see me."

She went on, giving Jocelin as much of the truth as she dared. He listened without interrupting, his gaze fixed on her face.

"But I never will believe that he was killed by chance. I don't care what the police say. He wouldn't have gone to Whitechapel. You knew him. Much as I loved him, William Edward was a bit full of his consequence. He wouldn't even give his custom to a tailor he suspected of being not quite appropriate to his station. He despised people who don't know the right wines to drink, the proper dress for sailing or a picnic."

She gave Jocelin a look of appeal, and he squeezed her to him.

"Liza, sweet." He hesitated, then sighed.

"There are certain habits a fellow keeps from his sister."

"He wouldn't have taken a mistress who lived in Whitechapel."

"Liza!"

His utter consternation annoyed her, and she slipped off his lap and tossed her head.

"Well, he wouldn't."

Taking her by the shoulders, he demanded, "What do you know of such things?"

Liza wiggled out of his grasp. "Really, my lord. Ladies aren't blind and deaf."

He sputtered. "Well, well, they should be on such subjects."

"My brother was killed after he left your house, and he was suspicious of that man Airey's death," Liza said. "And now there have been more deaths. There is Stapleton."

Jocelin rubbed his chin for a few moments. "There have been an awful lot of deaths." He slapped his gloves against his palm while he remained silent. "I must think about this, Liza. I've been distracted by other—er—business of late. I'll consider what you've said."

"Do."

He glanced at her. "And you'll leave the matter in my hands. No, don't say a word. It's my place to attend to such things."

They had so little time left together, she was reluctant to argue with him. She was going to do more spying on his friends soon, but she couldn't very well tell him that. Instead she sighed and smiled at him.

"Very well, my lord."

"I mean it, Liza."

"Yes, my lord."

He was eyeing her in suspicion when the carriage turned into the Stratfield Court portico. They stepped out into a crowd. Disconcerted, Liza felt her mouth go dry with apprehension that they'd been discovered, but her father came forward to dispel her alarm.

"Ah, Radcliffe, Elizabeth, my dear. Thank the Almighty you've returned so soon. A most unfortunate accident. Poor Halloway has been killed. His carriage hit a mud hole, and the axle broke. The thing rolled down a hill. Poor fellow was thrown against the wall and broke his neck. Horses had to be put down. Dreadful."

Liza turned to look past her father's shoulder at Jocelin. He gazed back at her, his face set and blank. Her mother fluttered up, causing Papa to take his wife's arm and administer tower-of-strength comfort. Nick joined Jocelin, and she took advantage of her mother's ditherings to walk over to them as well.

"Nick, old fellow," Jocelin said as she came near. "Miss Elliot and I were just discussing the rash of deaths among my friends. Remember, we were talking about it as well."

"It seems to be rather unhealthy to have been an officer in your regiment," Nick said. "Come inside out of this draft, Miss Elliot."

The Elliots and their guest gathered in the vaulted music room. Liza sent for tea, the universal English tonic. Honoria and Lady Augusta joined them. Augusta looked upon Liza's attire with approval and cornered her for a discussion of a village funeral from which she'd just returned. Lady Augusta's chief entertainment was funeral-watching. Liza maneuvered the woman into attending upon Mama, who had progressed to a most enjoyable stage of vapors. Honoria hastened to fetch her scent bottle for Mrs. Elliot's relief, thus allowing Liza to rejoin Jocelin and his friend.

"Damnable waste," Nick was saying. "I rode out with him beside the carriage, you know. Must have gone afoul shortly after I left him."

When Arthur Thurston-Coombes asked Nick to tell his story, Liza and Jocelin were left alone. Liza nodded toward the group surrounding Nick, which included Lord Winthrop and Asher Fox.

"You're great friends with Mr. Ross."

"Yes, Nick's the best."

"Funny how his lordship broke his neck right after Nick left him."

Jocelin's head whipped around so that he could gape at her. "You're suggesting Nick had something to do with Halloway's accident?"

They both sealed their mouths while a maid handed teacups around. When she was gone, Liza continued.

"There aren't many of your friends left. Where was he when my brother was killed?"

Indignation rounded Jocelin's eyes. "Nowhere near him. Really, Liza, you shouldn't indulge in these feverish and weak-brained imaginings."

"Someone is killing your friends." Liza stirred her tea calmly and glanced at the group of men. "Mr. Ross, Lord Winthrop, Mr. Thurston-Coombes, Mr. Fox, and you. Five men left, my lord."

"I don't believe it," Jocelin said. "You're actually suggesting someone is ticking off my friends, one after the other. And why, pray tell? What reason could anyone have for committing such monstrous crimes? You don't know, do you?"

"My brother—"

"Was killed by some thief after his purse. God, why do women create such fantasies? No doubt it's because they have so little else to do. Nick Ross a murderer. What drivel. The illusion of your spinsterish little mind, my dear."

Liza set her cup and saucer down on a table with a clatter. "Spinsterish?"

"Nick once saved my life!"

Liza stuck her head forward and spat at Jocelin. "Spinsterish?"

"Asher is dear to me for reasons you can never understand."

Liza's chest heaved in jet-beaded fury. "Drivel. You said I spoke drivel."

Comprehension of his error seemed to erupt belatedly upon Jocelin. He made haste to set his own cup and saucer down.

"Now, Liza, perhaps I was a bit outspoken."

"Outspoken?" Liza began to rock back and forth on her heels while maintaining a stiffly correct posture. "So you don't retract your insult, you merely regret allowing me a glimpse of your true opinion of me."

Jocelin shook his head violently. "That's not what I meant."

Liza whirled in a sea of black satin and stalked out of the music room. She bustled through the gallery and marched up the young ladies' stairs, taking no care to ascend gracefully in the manner of a lady. She hiked her skirts above her boot tops and stomped her way to her room.

The hypocrite. She swished about the room, too furious to sit down. Spinsterish, indeed. He was just like her father, like—like a man! As long as she confined her interests to pleasing him and knitting baby clothes, she was his darling, his object of worship. But if she once hinted that she understood more than pie crust and corsets, he immediately slapped her down to the level of an idiot child.

"Confound him!"

Liza's hands absently curled around a porcelain figurine that rested on the Queen Anne desk in her sitting room. How she would love to hurl it against a wall, but ladies didn't commit violent acts of any kind. Ladies didn't have violent emotions, not even sexual ones, especially sexual ones. And at the moment, she was heartily sorry she had those violent sexual feelings for Jocelin Marshall. Why did she care about him at all? The hypocrite.

Since she had no way to release her anger, it festered and remained with her for the rest of the day and into the evening. Following her mother's example, Liza pretended to have a sick headache and spent the dinner hour in her room. She perused *Eliza Cook's Journal* and read Mary Carpenter's essays on reformatory schools, then wrote a letter to Caroline Chisholm, who was recruiting emigrants to Australia. Finally, after the solace of these activities, she regained some of her good humor. After all, what could she expect of Jocelin, who was, a nobleman?

She went to bed resolved to ignore her lover's prejudices toward her sex, and it wasn't as hard to fall asleep as she thought it would be. She woke from a deep sleep because her nose itched. She rubbed it, turned on her stomach, and scrunched her pillow under her cheek. Something tickled her nose again, and she flapped her hand in front of her face.

"Liza, sweet," Jocelin whispered.

Her eyes popped open to find him kneeling by

the bed, one of her curls dangling from his fingers. He'd lit a night candle by the bed.

"My lord!"

"Shh." He put a finger to his lips, then tugged at her curl. "'I arise from dreams of thee / In the first sweet sleep of night . . .'"

Liza yanked the curl from him and sat up. "What are you doing here?"

Jocelin slid a hip onto the bed next to her.

"I've come to grovel." He rubbed his hands together and ducked his head. "Forgive me, I beg of you, O mistress of my life."

"Fool." Liza tried not to smile even as she glanced about the room, as if worried that he'd brought the entire household with him.

Jocelin sank to the floor again, clasped his hands, and held them out to her. "I'm unworthy to kiss the hem of your gown, your rosy toes."

"Hush. What lunacy. Someone will hear you."

"I shan't stop until you forgive me." He sighed and lowered his head so that he could rub it against her thigh. "I'll languish and die of grief without your good favor, my lady love."

"I'm a spinster. Remember?"

"The loveliest, most enticing spinster this mortal coil has ever beheld." Jocelin straightened, put a hand over his heart, and swept the other before him. "'She walks in beauty, like the night / Of cloudless climes and starry skies; / And all that's best of dark and bright / Meet in her aspect and her eyes . . .'"

He glanced at her sideways with such a speculative look that Liza burst out with a giggle. Jocelin lunged at her and clamped a hand over her mouth. She swatted at his hand, but he held it there until he could climb on the bed and replace it with his mouth.

Liza was still chuckling, but the feel of his tongue inside her mouth quickly banished her mirth. Feeling warm from his good-humored overtures, she soon began to feel even warmer, only the heat came from her body rather than her mind.

As he kissed her, she felt him slip beneath her covers. Her hand skimmed over the silk of a dressing gown penetrated by the warmth of his body. His hands moved, and the robe came loose. Bare flesh pressed against her body as he released her mouth.

"Am I forgiven?"

Liza brushed her lips against his and wondered if there was a more enthralling feeling than their heat and texture.

"Liza."

She loved the way they felt when he spoke against her skin. "Ask me again."

"Will you forgive me?"

They felt like butterfly wings fluttering against her cheek.

"Again," she said.

He slithered down her body so that he could see her face. "You little devil, you aren't even listening."

Liza nipped at his lips. "Then you'll have to find some other way to forgive you."

"I will, if you'll promise not to absolve me too soon."

16

Jocelin ground his teeth together so that he couldn't yawn. Mrs. Elliot's idea of entertainment after her grand dinner was listening to a London tenor for over two hours. He glanced at the woman, but she gazed unblinkingly at the rotund singer, whose voice echoed off the vaults of the music room. Liza sat at his right, her lashes lowered. He saw her start, and realized that she too had nearly fallen into a doze. They hadn't slept much last night.

The twelve-course dinner hadn't helped, all that lobster and ptarmigan pie. He surreptitiously rolled his shoulders.

Beside him Liza muttered, "How much longer?"

He shook his head, but even as he contemplated

the disgrace of falling asleep in the midst of county
society, the tenor finished and applause filled the
room. Relieved, he stood with everyone else, but held
back as Mrs. Elliot rushed over to the singer.

He bent to whisper to Liza. "Tonight?"

Her answer was a sunburst smile.

"Oh, no, it's your father." Jocelin nodded to the
approaching figure of Richard Elliot.

"Heaven preserve me," Liza said. She gave him
a pleading look. "Would you mind if I bolted?"

"Run along. I'll distract him."

He watched Liza take refuge behind Lady Augusta's black silk bulk, then turned to cut off her
father.

"Ah, Elliot, capital dinner. Your chef's a good
man."

"Should be," Elliot said as he stopped a servant
and grasped a claret. "Brought him over from Paris,
you know."

"Excellent."

Elliot took hold of Jocelin's arm. "My dear
Radcliffe, might I have a word, in private?"

"If you wish."

He followed Elliot out of the music room and
across the house to the host's private study and office.
Wine-color leather and mahogany paneling lent an
impression of masculinity to the room. They settled in
two armchairs by a fire. Elliot offered cigars, which
Jocelin declined. Elliot lit one, puffed on it to get it
going, then stared at the glowing tip.

"You've been seeing quite a bit of my daughter,
Radcliffe."

"Miss Elliot is a charming lady."

"Quite a bit," Elliot said.

Jocelin merely looked at his host. More formidable papas than he had tried to force Jocelin to declare himself. Undisturbed, he allowed the silence to extend. He wasn't going to be rushed into marriage, even with Liza. Finally Elliot continued.

"So much that I find it necessary to ask you your plans, my lord."

Jocelin poured himself a whiskey from the decanter beside his chair. "I haven't any at the moment."

To Jocelin's surprise, Elliot only nodded.

"Thought you might say that. Know your reputation."

"You're a shrewd man, Elliot."

"More shrewd than you know," Elliot replied. He blew a ring of smoke and watched it float toward Jocelin. "May I be candid?"

Jocelin sipped his whiskey. "I would find it most interesting."

Elliot puffed on his cigar for a few moments and contemplated the resulting smoke clouds. After a while he glanced down at his guest. Jocelin at once grew wary, for he detected in that small-eyed gaze a hint of the usurer, the hard bargainer, the penny counter.

"You've toyed with my daughter," Elliot said suddenly. "I assume you'll propose to make it right."

The usual complaint, an unusually abrupt demand. The bastard had thrown the girl in his path like liver before a hound. By God, he wasn't going to be stampeded by this nouveau riche butcher.

"Your assumption is mistaken. Miss Elliot is a lady who has reached her majority. She knows what she wants." Jocelin smiled sweetly at Elliot. "She told me so."

He expected Elliot to turn scarlet and roar like a tiger deprived of a meal of villagers. Instead the old man nodded as if Jocelin had confirmed his presumptions. He chewed on his cigar for a while before responding.

"I like you, Radcliffe. You have pluck. Not many men could have survived what you've survived. The war, savages in America." Elliot caught and held Jocelin's gaze. "Other things."

Jocelin regarded his adversary calmly. The bastard was going to threaten him. Too bad, for the old buster couldn't touch him financially, and he didn't frighten easily. It was best that Elliot learn he couldn't bully him before Jocelin committed himself. He contented himself with raising a brow and taking another sip of his drink. Let Elliot raise the stakes.

"Oh, well," Elliot grumbled. "Thought I'd give you a way out, my boy, but you're a stubborn young colt. Then I'll just say a bit. Not much, for what I've discovered demands the utmost delicacy. So I'll just mention how I've heard that at one time, you and your uncle were quite fond of each other."

Silence surrounded him. He knew he was looking at Elliot, but he seemed to be enveloped in emptiness, cold, airless, isolating. He hadn't expected this particular threat.

"Perhaps 'fond' isn't the right word, or rather, your uncle was fond of you. I gather you didn't return the sentiment. How old were you?"

Jocelin heard his own voice as if it were a stranger's—thin and weak. "Fourteen."

He set his glass down and prayed his face hadn't lost all its color. He flicked a speck of lint off the arm of his chair.

"It won't work, you sodding old prick. I don't care who you tell."

Elliot chuckled, which made Jocelin stare at him.

"Knew you had pluck. Damned if I don't admire you for it. Too bad, though, if it came out. Bad for your young sister, that is, and your mother."

Elliot sucked on his cigar, but Jocelin said nothing. His mind twisted and writhed in an effort to see a way out. He heard the hissing of the fire. Elliot made obscene sucking noises on his cigar, noises that reminded Jocelin of Yale. He closed his eyes, the first movement he'd made since his host had stopped talking. Georgiana, dear, whimsical little Georgiana. And Mother. He couldn't let them endure the shame. He opened his eyes to meet the pitying gaze of his adversary.

"Checkmate, dear boy."

"Has she known all along?"

"Elizabeth Maud? Of course not. Never discuss such things with the women. Not done, and you very well know it. We need never speak of this again. If, that is, you agree to a ceremony in the parish church tomorrow."

Jocelin took a gulp of whiskey. He was recovering from his shock only to find himself in as great a rage as he'd ever experienced, but at least Liza hadn't done this to him.

"By God, you've had this planned all along."

Elliot waved his cigar. "Not all along, but for several weeks. Now, do I have your word, dear boy?"

Jocelin inclined his head, unable to trust himself to speak.

"Then you'll see to my daughter." Elliot rose. "I'll send her to you at once. Be eloquent, for your own sake. Wouldn't want to have to tell the dear girl anything about our little arrangement, now would we?"

Jocelin spoke quietly. "Get out of here before I decide to kill you instead of pay your price, you son of a—get out."

When Elliot had gone, he poured himself another whiskey and downed the whole thing in a gulp. He winced as he thought of Georgiana's face if she found out about him. He cursed, flew from his chair, and flung the glass at the fireplace. It hit the mantel and splintered. Crystal shards flew in all directions, and one cut his cheek. He brushed the splinter from his flesh, but ignored the cut.

He stared at the fire, unseeing. Bracing against the mantel, he forced himself to breathe steadily. His hands were shaking with rage. He couldn't see Liza like this. Covering his face with his hands, he forced his thoughts away from horror.

He'd learned to cut off ugly thoughts and memories long ago. Like a surgeon, he excised them now, splicing them from his awareness, separating them. Then he buried the ugliness deep inside himself in a hole so black and fathomless that even he couldn't retrieve them. By the time he heard a knock at the door, he was placid, undisturbed, remotely tranquil.

Turning to greet Liza, he felt confident he could play the part of a willing suitor, for what was left of him was surface, cake icing, a film of dew on grass. As she walked toward him, he concentrated on the swish of her silk skirts, the way she walked with her head slightly tilted, as though listening to a tune played by a distant flute. She drifted into his arms, and he breathed in lemons and Liza.

He kissed her. All at once his predicament didn't seem so terrible. Elliot's tactics were still unconscionable, but after all, he would have Liza. Liza, who could give him respite from his living nightmare, who craved him as much as he craved her. The last of his confusion about their ability to suit each other vanished as he held her. If she could give solace to him when he was so greatly disturbed, he couldn't bear not to have her.

In any case, he could justify his decision logically, couldn't he?

He required a wife, one suitable to his temperament, one who understood duty and who would accommodate herself to him, as a lady of rank should. He also required a wife whose very existence would rankle in his father's heart, whose children would deny Yale the hope of every polluting the family title by his inheriting it. Yes, he was being calm and reasonable in his decision to keep Liza for himself forever. He would marry her, and deal with Elliot later.

Lifting his mouth from Liza's, he set her in his armchair and knelt beside it. Liza was no fool. He would have to tell her some of the truth. He busied himself in removing her long gloves. He peeled one down her upper arm.

She watched him gravely. "Father sent me."

His fingers tugged at the material gathered at her elbow.

"He tried to get you to make an offer, didn't he?" she asked.

He nodded as he worked the glove down her forearm.

"You needn't worry," she said. "I'll not let him hound you."

The glove slid off her hand. He tossed it on the floor and began tracing straight lines from her hand to her elbow.

"But Liza, sweet, I'm not worried."

She shivered as his fingers skimmed up her arm. "Oh?"

"I'm grateful." He kissed her bare arm just below the shoulder, and she shivered again. "You see, your father jolted me out of my brain fever long enough to make me realize how stupid I've been."

She looked away from him. "I knew you wouldn't want me for long."

"What?" He caught her chin and turned her to face him. "What's this? Do you mean you've expected me to leave you all along?"

Liza closed her eyes and nodded. Jocelin sat back on his heels and put his hands on his hips.

"Is that so? You thought I'd taste and bolt." His voice rose. "And you let me! Elizabeth Maud Elliot, is that any way to behave? Where are your virtue and your sense of propriety?"

She faced him and snapped. "You didn't seem to miss them last night."

He quieted, realizing what he was saying. "Oh. Yes. Well. Hmm. Yes. Hmm." He burst out again, "But I'm different. You may trust me. I want to marry you."

She gripped the chair arms and stared at him wordlessly. He rose to his knees again and cursed himself for being so clumsy. He tried again.

"Liza, sweet, you're my bread and wine. I wake up needing to see your face and touch your hair. I spend my days listening for the rustle of your gowns and my nights dreaming of you skating on that pond and then gliding into my bed. You make me happy, and I can't conceive of a time when you wouldn't. Make me happy all the time, Liza."

She still didn't say anything. Her eyes had widened as he spoke until they were larger than his jacket buttons. He grew uneasy at the silence and decided to plead with her in a different way. While she gazed at him in confusion, he raised himself, bent over her, and took her lips. He snaked his tongue inside her mouth, bit lightly at her lips. His hand soothed her neck for long moments, then slipped beneath the sleeve of her gown to cup her bare shoulder. He brushed his mouth across her cheek, to her temple, to her ear, and whispered.

"Say yes."

"But we don't—"

He kissed her again. "Say yes."

"Yes."

He plunged into her mouth again, and she wrapped her arms about his neck. He straightened, bringing her with him, until they both stood erect. He shoved his body against hers and felt her hand stray down his back to his buttock. His blood churned. He felt as if his flesh were roasting on a spit. His fingers curled, dug into the bare flesh of her back, then fastened around the buttons that secured her gown.

The knock at the door almost made him tear one of them off her gown. Liza jumped. He swore and hugged her to him before setting her away and asking the intruder to enter. He walked away from Liza to stare at the fire while he battled with his unruly body. Richard Elliot bustled into the room. Jocelin put his fist behind his back and stiffened his spine.

Elliot waved his cigar. "Well, well, well, wonderful news. Wonderful news."

He kissed Liza on the cheek. She accepted the embrace, but gave her father a look of wary surmise. Jocelin tried to interrupt him, but Elliot slapped him on the back.

"Grand news, my boy, and I've arranged for the

parish church tomorrow night. Special permission
from the archbishop, you know."

Jocelin scowled at Elliot, then glanced at Liza,
who was frowning at her father. She had a hand on the
back of an armchair and was drumming her fingers on
the leather.

He hastened to interrupt her speculation by
returning to her side and slipping his arm around her
waist. "Your father has been playing Cupid. I told him
I couldn't bear to wait to make you my wife, and he
surprised me with these arrangements." He gave
Elliot a lynxlike glance. "Thoughtful of you, Elliot."

"Papa!"

Both men cringed.

"Papa," Liza said as she slipped from Jocelin's
grasp and rounded on her father. "Lord Radcliffe is
the heir to a dukedom. He can't marry in such haste.
There's the duke and his family, and don't forget her
majesty. Why, we don't even know if his father will
approve."

"My father already knows I'm looking for a
wife," Jocelin said.

Liza turned slowly to look at him. She cocked
her head to the side. "You've been searching all
along."

The lies were beginning to stick in his throat, so
he merely nodded.

"See there," Elliot said. "Nothing to worry
about. You don't want all that fuss, my dear."

Jocelin slipped his arm around her shoulders.
"No indeed. It's awful. And if Mother involves herself, we'll end up in St. Peter's in Eaton Square."

"Oh, no," she said.

"That is, of course, unless her majesty takes it

into her head to insist upon Buckingham Palace or Windsor."

"You're teasing me." Liza wet her lips and swallowed. "Aren't you?"

"No," Jocelin said.

"All settled, then," said Elliot. "No fuss. Have all the preparations in hand, dear boy."

As Elliot expounded, Jocelin noticed that Liza kept quiet. She was frowning at her father again. Suddenly she looked up at him. He smiled at her, but she didn't smile back. The darkness and gaslight brought out the teal in her eyes.

"I want to wait," she said, cutting her father off in midsentence.

Elliot's cheeks puffed out. "Wait!"

"Now, Liza, sweet," Jocelin said, kissing her hand and making her shiver. "I realize you've been taken by surprise. Perhaps we should speak to each other alone again."

He saw the muscles of her throat work as she swallowed, and gave her a smile that said he was quite aware of what he was doing to her. She yanked her hand from his grasp, snatched her glove, and began putting it on.

"I don't want to wait," he said.

"I need time." Her hands were trembling as she smoothed the glove over her arm. "Six months."

Elliot's curses exploded over them. "By God, you little fool, you can't wait six months!"

Liza gripped the chair back and stared at her father.

"Why not?"

"Don't make me—"

"Elliot," Jocelin said. "Leave this to me."

He repossessed Liza's hand and moved close to

her so that he could look into her eyes. He felt her body strain toward him and knew she was fighting her own urges. Bending over her, he lowered his voice and filled it with the somnolent heat of the Texas hill country in August.

"Liza, sweet, you don't want to make me wait, now do you?"

"Don't do that," she whispered.

"What, love?"

"Your voice, don't do that. It sounds like boiling honey. Don't do that. I can't think."

"You don't need to think. You said you'd marry me. We'll do it tomorrow."

He leaned down and kissed her temple. His tongue laved her skin, and she squirmed. He smiled and whispered something lurid in her ear. Crying out, Liza shied away from him.

"No," she said, holding out her hand to ward him off. "You're trying to rush me. I don't like it. Why have you changed so suddenly? What did Papa say to you?"

Elliot bellowed. "By God! You trample your own virtue in the mud and then quibble about a rushed marriage?"

"What have you done, Papa? You're too pleased with yourself. You can't treat Jocelin like some pimply apprentice."

Chest swelling, face coloring to the hue of a tomato, Elliot raised his arm and pointed at his daughter. "'A whore is a deep ditch,' my girl. And it's my shame that I should be forced to speak so to a woman. You would do well to read your Bible and spend this night on your knees in prayer, for the word of God says that we should abstain from fleshly lusts."

Elliot subsided, out of breath and biblical references. Jocelin moved to stand between Liza, who had gone pale and silent, and her father. He stood over the man, who backed up until his back hit the mantel.

Jocelin drawled quietly, "If you ever speak to my lady like that again, I'll stuff that cigar down your throat."

Mouth popping open and closed like a beached salmon, Elliot couldn't seem to find a retort. Jocelin returned to Liza, took her hand, and gazed at her anxiously, worried that her father's cruelty had wounded her. As he had feared, her eyes were bright with unshed tears. He squeezed her hand and brought it to his cheek.

"Don't listen to him," he said.

She drew in a ragged breath and released his hand. "I haven't for a long time. I will marry you, my lord, but not in haste and secret. Why, your mother and sister will want to be at your wedding."

The mention of Mother and Georgiana spurred him, called up the fear he'd thought he had banished.

"Damn it, Liza, why must you be so stubborn?"

"I'm not being stubborn," Liza cried as she paced back and forth and shook her head. She was trembling as she burst out, "This isn't what I expected. It's not what I planned."

To Jocelin the room seemed to jolt on its foundations at the sound of that one word. "Planned? Did you say planned?"

"I meant—"

"Wait a moment. Wait." They stared at him while he thought furiously, then raised his gaze to Liza. "You said planned." His voice faded as dread strangled him. "By God, you're a clever girl, far more clever than I'd imagined. You want a grand wedding all right."

"Of course she does," snapped Elliot. "Only natural."

"That one word doesn't mean anything," Liza said. "You don't—"

Jocelin stopped her with a raised hand. He could barely hear his own voice, it was so low. "One little word betrayed you."

Liza put her hands on her hips and glared up into his face. "Dear Lord, he thinks I've concocted some ornate plot."

"Don't, Liza," Jocelin whispered. "Don't lie anymore."

Liza threw up her hands. "I'm not a liar, but perhaps you're used to liars. Are your family liars that you expect to meet them under every sofa cushion? Is your father a liar? Is your uncle one too?"

There was a long silence. Jocelin felt the blood drain from his face. He'd thought his rage at Elliot immense, but when Liza spoke of his uncle, his mind turned to burning acid.

"You know," he said on a note of wondering horror. "Bloody hell, you've known all along."

"Known what?"

Liza was looking from him to her father. Once he would have been fooled by those fluttering lashes and that air of innocence. God, why had he ever thought her innocent?

Careful, he thought. Be careful. They know, and they could hurt Georgiana and Mother.

He sliced away his rage once again and stuffed it in a corner of his awareness. Summoning a veneer of calm, he allowed his body to relax.

"Very well," he said quietly. "Now we understand each other, which is all to the good."

Liza pointed to herself. "I don't understand."

Laughing nastily, Jocelin continued as if she hadn't spoken. "The wedding you've been working like a sweaty peasant to get will take place tomorrow."

Liza pounded her fist on a leather chair. "Now you wait, Jocelin Marshall. I'm not agreeing to anything while you're behaving so madly."

"No need to pretend outrage," he said. "After all, your methods were only slightly more disgusting than those of other women I've refused. God, women are shabby, always trying to trap a man. And by the Almighty, I do believe you'd not stop at murder."

Liza had turned more and more red the longer he spoke. She balled her hands into fists and trembled, glaring at him.

Elliot glowered at him as well. "See here, Radcliffe—"

"Shut up, Father." Liza's normally soft tones had roughened into a snarl.

Elliot's cigar burned a brighter red. "I'll not have my daughter talk to me in such a manner."

Liza turned on her father and yelled. "Father, damn you, shut up!" She turned back to Jocelin. "And as for you, my lord. I don't know what has happened between you and Papa, but I had nothing to do with it."

She stopped long enough to swallow and gain control of herself. When she resumed, her voice shook.

"However, if you'd loved me as you said, if you had trusted me, you would have asked me, not accused me. Then I would have told you the truth. But it's clear you aren't interested in the truth or anything about me that's real. I'm like all women to you, something hardly more deserving of esteem and respect than a dairy cow. Therefore, my lord, I think

I'll change my mind and not marry you, thank you very much."

Jocelin gawked at Liza. Elliot had long since collapsed into an armchair in consternation. Liza turned on her heel and, without a word to Jocelin, marched out of the room.

Liza slammed the door to the study, grabbed hunks of her silk skirt, and ran. Her vision blurred by tears, she stumbled down the corridor. She could hear her father yelling at Jocelin, a dangerous thing to do. She hoped they killed each other. Lord, what if they came after her?

She tripped over her skirts, lifting them higher, and turned into another corridor. Tears ran down her nose and cheeks. She covered her mouth to muffle the ugly gulping sounds she couldn't stop making. The servants' stair appeared, and she raced past it. Papa would never look for her in the servants' wing.

Blundering by the gun room and footman's room, she turned down the housekeeper's corridor, turned again and slipped through the kitchen entrance and servery. Shoving open another door, she tripped over the threshold of the kitchen. The place was dark, but the high, louvered roof let in moonlight.

Liza bumped into a sink, then thrust out her hands and felt her way to one of the long central tables. Dropping to the floor, she ducked beneath it, nearly striking her head on a drawer. Thus concealed, she huddled with her knees drawn and her arms wrapped around them. She buried her face in the puffy clouds of her skirts and wept.

To have been offered a glimpse of something for which she never dared hope—keeping Jocelin—and then to have lost it gashed at her heart. Papa had destroyed their love. Hadn't they felt love? She had. And Jocelin jettisoned that love at the first sign of danger. He had cast her into the sea storm and then shot his cannons at her instead of asking her to fight on his side. At the first sign of trouble, she had been tossed aside, accused of monstrous plots, and condemned.

Liza moaned at the physical pain her grief brought. She felt as if Jocelin had taken her heart and run it through a laundry wringer, squeezing it flat as paper, and as bloodless. And she was afraid, afraid to encounter him again and see the disgust in his eyes. Her father had looked at her like that all her life. To see the same revulsion in Jocelin's eyes was to encounter hell on earth. She'd spent years telling herself she wasn't unnatural, peculiar, an object of abhorrence; in a few moments Jocelin had shown her that her secret dread was true.

Minutes passed, during which Liza used her gloves as handkerchiefs. She hugged herself and endured the pain. After a long while she noticed a slight change in the darkness. In her grief she'd been oblivious to the passage of time, and dawn was coming. She couldn't stay here. She couldn't stay at Stratfield Court.

There was a train before six o'clock. She would leave on it. Crawling from beneath the table, she trudged back across the house and up the young ladies' staircase. The house seemed deserted, for everyone had gone to bed long ago. Liza woke Emmeline and sent her to rouse the head groom. They would take a pony cart to the station before anyone but the servants had stirred. She would sneak out of Jocelin's life before he had a chance to hurt her again, because if he did, she didn't think she could survive.

Several weeks went by, during which Liza tried to resume her old routine at Pennant's.

She left a note telling her parents without detail that she had decided not to pursue a husband. A few days later her mother wrote to describe her father's anger. Mama had been surprised at its mildness, and could think of no explanation for it. Liza was too upset to feel anything more than brief interest in the puzzle. March turned to April, but for once she failed to notice the appearance of new leaves on trees or the coming of daffodils in the garden that surrounded the house on three sides. She even ignored a song thrush that had made its nest there.

Finally her old concern roused her. A murderer still went free and most likely had killed again. The earl had been buried, and Toby had made inquiries for her. The accident with the carriage had been caused by a hole in the road concealed by mud and slush. The carriage axle had been extraordinarily weak. Toby thought someone had tampered with it.

One morning in mid-April, Liza sat at her desk organizing her notes on the men in whom she was interested. Halloway and Stapleton were gone. She had sorted through the information on them and stowed it away in large envelopes upon which she had written their names. Now she stuffed pages into another, with Jocelin's name on it.

She came across a sketch of herself in her fat dress. Betty had done it on the night before she first set out for the viscount's residence. Liza examined the pen drawing. Betty had drawn her from the side, and she appeared far more buxom than she really was as a result of all that padding. However, Liza could recognize her own face beneath the voluminous, lace-trimmed cap. While she'd worn it, she'd been afraid Jocelin would dislodge it when he held her. Liza closed her eyes as she remembered his strength, his unyielding green gaze.

Hastily opening her eyes, she thrust the sketch into the envelope and placed it on top of the stack of men she no longer suspected. Next she opened a drawer and pulled out several folders, each with the name of a man on it. She had to consider whose house in which to obtain employment. Asher Fox and Lord Winthrop lived near Jocelin. If she went to either, she would have to change her appearance slightly on the chance that someone might recognize her. Perhaps she should go to Arthur Thurston-Coombes first.

She was leafing through the file on Arthur Thurston-Coombes when she heard raised voices outside the office. Without warning the door slammed open. Liza glanced up from the file. Jocelin paused on the threshold, rigid and slightly out of breath. Toby shoved past him to stand barring his way.

"Gor, you're a cheeky sot. You get out of here quick like, or I'll toss you out on your bum."

Jocelin left off glaring at Liza to look briefly at Toby and dismiss him. Before Toby risked injury, Liza stood.

"Never mind," she said. "I'll deal with him."

Toby gave her a quizzical look, tugged on his lapels, and walked out. He muttered something to Jocelin on the way, and Jocelin moved his head in what could have been a nod. The door closed, and Jocelin walked over to stand in front of her. She remained behind the desk in silence.

Jocelin inclined his head. "Mr. Pennant."

"How did you find me?"

"An inquiry agent. He's no good at finding lost domestics, but he's capable of tracing ladies, even when they pretend to be men. I asked your father where you were, but he seemed most anxious that I not find you myself. Said he'd find a way to bring you back. Now I know why. I knew I could find you without his help."

"Congratulations. Now leave."

"You still smell like lemons."

"And you're still a fool."

She nearly smiled when his mouth twitched in annoyance. Instead she smoothed her skirts and seated herself in her desk chair. Taking up a pen, she opened an account book and began writing.

"When my agent told me about you and Pennant's, I didn't believe him at first." He swept his arm, indicating her office. "How could you pursue such an inappropriate activity?"

"I enjoy eating and not having to sleep in the streets," Liza said without looking up.

"Never mind Pennant's right now. We've more important matters to consider."

"I've nothing to say to you. Good day, sir."

"It's 'my lord,' not 'sir.'"

Liza scribbled a sum and turned the page. "Good day."

A shadow crossed the page, and she looked up to find Jocelin leaning over her. She made a mistake in looking at him. He deliberately held her gaze. His eyes widened, and he seemed to drink in her soul.

"We've unfinished business," he said softly.

She started, then fumed. "Am I to understand you're talking about marriage?"

"You're clever, for a woman."

Dropping the pen, Liza snapped the account book closed.

"By the Almighty in heaven, you're serious."

"I'm trying to be sensible." Jocelin sighed. "I was upset, and I made some wrong conclusions, but now you're just being stubborn."

Liza stood slowly. "Stubborn, am I? I trusted you. I love—damn you, listen carefully. I don't want your title. I don't want your riches. And I don't want you."

She felt a tremor of fear as the conciliatory gleam vanished from Jocelin's eyes. Shoving away from the desk, he met her gaze with the chill stare of a tomb effigy.

"Unfortunate. However, you are going to become my wife. We'll marry quietly, and you'll come with me to my house in Kent. I'm not enduring a season in London with you at my side and having . . ."

He stopped, and Liza followed the direction of his glance. His hand had been resting on the stack of envelopes. She'd forgotten them, but a shiver of dread came over her as she watched him read his own name. Without thought she tried to snatch the envelope. He knocked her hand aside and grabbed it. Opening the flap, he withdrew the stack of papers.

The clock on the mantel ticked louder than Big Ben as he read. The papers dropped from his hands and scattered on the desk. The sketch sailed from between two pages. He caught it. Slowly he looked up from it to her. Liza gripped the edge of her desk, unable to speak. His face went blank. He glanced again at the sketch, and when he looked at her again, he might as well have been staring at her over the barrel of his Colt.

"So I was right about you and your marriage traps. Did I frighten you when I found out about your plan? Is that why you ran away? Did you realize how dangerous it would be to force me and lose your backbone?"

Liza shook her head, but Jocelin didn't seem to notice. He kept her snared in his gaze. "What a thorough little bitch you are in your quest for a husband, Miss Elliot." Without dropping his gaze, he folded the sketch and stuffed it in his coat pocket. "My one consolation is that in marrying you, I'll be able to get my hands on you. You're going to pay, Liza. Don't think you aren't."

Truly frightened, Liza held on to the desk with one hand and raised her arm to point at the door. "I'm not marrying you, and I'm not paying for something I didn't do. Get out, or do I have to call Toby?"

She wished he hadn't smiled. His smile reminded

her of Dante: "The hellish hurricane, which never rests, drives on the spirits with its violence . . ."

"Be at my house in an hour, Liza. Don't make me wait."

She said nothing as he raked her with his gaze, turned, and left her. Her hand hurt. She looked down to find herself gripping the edge of the desk so hard, she would have bruises on her fingers tomorrow. Forcing her hand to loosen, she gasped in belated reaction to the violence in Jocelin's eyes. Her knees buckled, and she dropped into her chair.

Toby burst into the room, startling her. "Gor! What did he want?"

"He—he still wants to marry me. Papa must have done something horrible to him." Liza stared at a wall without seeing it. "He found out about Gamp, and now he hates me."

"Gor," Toby said. "See here, miss. It's time to scarper. That one's not a gent you can come up against and not get hurt. You get yourself out of London."

Liza rubbed her cold hands together and fidgeted in her chair. "I can't. I've got to see what I can find out about Winthrop and Fox and Coombes. And then there's that Mr. Ross. I nearly forgot about him. He's always with the viscount, and I don't trust him."

"You don't fool me, miss. You're so scared, you're hopping like a sparrow."

"I'll recover. What can he do?"

"I don't even want to think about that," Toby said.

He left, grumbling, and Liza tried to return to her perusal of her files. Her attempts proved useless, for much as she would have liked to pretend otherwise, Jocelin had frightened her. That night she went to bed, but didn't sleep.

At first she thought the trouble just part of the ordinary inconveniences of a domestic agency. Patrons canceled plans at the last minute without thinking about the consequences to Pennant's, any more than they would think about inconveniencing their shoes. Lord and Lady Quince rescinded their order for seven additional parlor maids and footmen for their daughter's engagement ball. The ambassador of France no longer required three new scullery maids, while Amberton's Gentlemen's Club requested the return of their deposit on Monsieur Jacques.

When the cancellations escalated the next week, Liza grew uneasy. Then one morning Toby ushered a blubbering Maisy Twoffle into her office. Maisy was one of her latest finds, a former occupant of the rookeries of St. Giles. Liza had come upon her trying to sell violets on the streets near Parliament in the middle of winter. The girl was hardly more than nineteen and desperate to put more food into the mouths of her three little girls. No husband.

"Now stop your sniffing, girl, and tell Miss what happened," Toby said as he shoved a handkerchief at Maisy.

"Th-they turned me away at the door." Maisy snuffled into the handkerchief. "That old fart—pardon, miss—that old man, the butler, that is, h-he shoved me out before I could get over the doorsill." Maisy began to hiccup. "And they was all looking at me, and then, h-he called me a wh-wh-whore!"

Liza met Toby's gaze over Maisy's head as she patted the maid's shoulder. She smoothed the starched ruffles of the girl's apron.

"There's been some mistake," she said, drawing Maisy to her feet. "You go back to the kitchen and tell Mrs. Ripple I said to fix you a nice tea with scones. And don't you worry."

Maisy rubbed her nose with the handkerchief. "But, miss, yesterday Hester got turned off of a place you sent her to, and so did Mr. Humewood."

"I'll deal with it," Liza said as she turned the maid around and marched her to the door.

She returned to her desk and spread out the large monthly schedule. Giant *X* marks slashed through over half the appointments for the last two weeks. She took a pen, dipped it in the inkwell, and marked through Maisy's engagement. Tapping the pen on the calendar, she pondered for a moment, then glanced up at the waiting Toby.

"No need," he said, holding up his hand. "I'll find out what's stewing. Maisy's ass of a butler is one of them that's only good at bullying girls and unfortunates under him."

Toby returned several hours later with his lip cut and his collar askew. He beamed at her as she offered him a chair and poured a glass of water for him.

"Took a bit of persuading, that butler did, but I got it out of him." He dabbed at his lip with the back of his hand. "The old bast—the old fool's daughter is in service at Lord Quince's, and she heard this rumor from her son's employer's butler."

Liza only needed confirmation of her suspicions. "Who is?"

"Choke, of course." Toby slapped the arm of his chair. "I knew it. His mighty lordship's gone and tampered with Pennant's reputation. Know what he's spreading? Seems Pennant's hires women of the street, so to speak, and thieves too. Monsieur Jacques just might be a well-known pickpocket on the Continent."

Liza sank down on the sofa. She could hear its old frame creak. He was going to ruin her. Everything she'd built would flounder under a bloated and greasy mountain of scandal. Society worshipped at the altar of superficial propriety. This propriety had to extend to servants as well as masters. Pennant's wouldn't survive another week.

Jocelin was proving what she'd always known. A frightening ruthlessness lay just below the cloak of civilized behavior he wore so loosely. In her calmer moments she could understand how betrayed he felt. She also knew he was being driven by some threat from Papa. That much she had thought out over the last few weeks. Papa had meddled and created a disaster, but Jocelin wasn't the kind of man to bow under threats for long. He'd find some way to flout Papa, but meanwhile she would suffer.

She had to find a way out of this tangle. Papa never listened to her, which left Jocelin. Jocelin wouldn't listen to her explanations. He was too hurt to listen to her defense, and she was too hurt and humiliated to risk trying to give it. Perhaps, however, she could make him understand that others shouldn't be made to suffer.

"Toby, I want you to send for Maisy and her children. Who else is available? Get Hiram and his two little brothers, and Mrs. Peak, and Aggie and her little ones, and Dora and her mother. That's fifteen. Have them here at one."

She went to her desk and penned a note. Blotting it, she sealed it in an envelope and handed it to Toby. "But first deliver this."

Toby looked at the address, then at Liza. "You're going to him ain't you. Take me with you."

"You'll only lose your temper," Liza said. "I can't have that. Pennant's is at stake."

With her arrangements in hand, Liza left Pennant's to make a visit to her bank. She had set funds aside for an emergency, but they wouldn't last forever, and there were over thirty people for whom she had to care. And they had to feed and clothe their families, pay rent, care for their health. She transferred funds from savings to Pennant's account under the disapproving eye of the bank manager and returned home.

By tea time she had bundled her people into an omnibus. She stepped into a cab and led the small procession west to Grosvenor Square. Soon they drove through the gates of Viscount Radcliffe's home and pulled up at the carriage entrance. She composed herself while the others spilled out of the omnibus, then descended.

A confrontation with the son of a duke was no time to skimp on her appearance. Having no reason to disguise herself, she had put on her best afternoon dress. Heavy, patterned silk in peacock blue and black, tailored and pulled snug at her waist with a wide black belt. She looked at the world through the fragile black veil of her bonnet, her expression as severe as the cut of her gown.

Marching up the steps, she paused to give Choke a look of distaste as he opened the doors. She sailed past him, noting that he resembled a startled turkey.

"Madam!" He clucked. "Madam, your card, if you please."

She ignored him, calling over her shoulder, "Come along, Maisy, Aggie, all of you!"

She hesitated in the foyer long enough to snap at Choke. "Where is he?"

Choke only gaped at her, so she reached out a hand gloved in black silk and grasped his necktie.

"Where (jerk) is (jerk) he (jerk)?" she demanded, yanking on his necktie after every word.

Choke sputtered, then pulled at the necktie. She reached for it again, and he scrambled out of her way.

"Si-sitting room."

She waved her hand at Maisy and the others. Two girls were scooting across the marble floor, while a toddler crowed at them. Other children crowded past Sledge, the footman, and made faces at him.

"Come along, everyone."

Twirling in a half circle, her skirts billowing, she set sail again, this time mounting the stairs. She wasted no time in knocking, and threw open the door to Jocelin's sitting room. A child skidded past her and aimed for the fragile baroque desk. Other infants spilled in waves after her as she strode over to Jocelin. He had looked up from the desk as the invasion began, only to be sidetracked by a three-year-old boy who crawled between his legs.

Liza stopped in front of him and waited while her employees crowded into the room. Jocelin yelped as Maisy's little Peg tried to climb his leg and grabbed a vulnerable body part. He tore the child from his leg and held her at arm's length in the air like a dirty shirt. Unfortunately for him, Peg had a round, rosy face, unending black curls and great, dark eyes of spaniel-brown. She kicked her feet in the air. He nearly dropped her and instinctively whipped her close and set her on his hip. Too late he looked around to find his sitting room filled with a seething stew of women, children, and an old man.

The quiet eye of this human hurricane, Liza
watched Jocelin glare at her people and then turn on
her.

"What do you think you're about?"

"I told you I was coming."

He glared at her over the child's head. "You're
early."

"Really?"

"And you said nothing about, about these persons."

Jocelin tried to shove Peg at her, but she kept
her hands clasped around her reticule. Peg had become fascinated with his hair, and when he thrust her
away, she didn't let go of it. He cried out, and Liza
smirked.

"Let go, you little varmint."

That drawl, the American wording. He was
upset. Good.

Jocelin pried his charge's fingers from his hair
and set her on the floor. Maisy called her, and she
toddled over to her mother. Something porcelain and
no doubt valuable crashed to the floor, and a little boy
screamed his frustration. Jocelin winced at the sound
and pointed at the boy.

"Get that child away from there!" He glared at
Liza. "What are you about, woman?"

Liza smiled at him. She turned and guided an
old man with cloudy eyes and a shuffle to stand in
front of Jocelin. Then she took a baby from Aggie's
arms and, before Jocelin could react, thrust the
squirming bundle into his arms.

"You're trying to ruin Pennant's, my lord. I
thought you should see who Pennant's really is."

Jocelin had paled and was gazing from her to the
baby.

Liza folded her arms over her chest and gave him a long, pleased look. "Hold her head up, my lord. You don't want to break her neck. But come to think of it, you might as well, since she and her mother will soon be living in doorways and alleys in Whitechapel anyway."

18

Jocelin glanced down at the baby in the crook of his arm. He could hardly feel her weight. She had a pink nose smaller than the tip of his little finger and a bright red bow of a mouth. If he moved, he might drop her, or break her. Alarm spurred him into action. He grasped the bundle firmly, charged into the crowd before him, and thrust the baby at her mother.

"Take her!"

He hadn't meant to shout. The baby woke and began to wail. Jocelin winced. Shrinking away from the source of that painful shriek, he bumped into Liza. He scowled at her and retreated to his desk.

Pressing a button on the wall behind him, he rang for Loveday.

A girl in a frilly coat chased a little boy between the damask curtains of a window. The boy stumbled and would have fallen if the girl hadn't caught him.

"You," he snarled at them. "Back."

He pointed to the milling group standing in the middle of the room. They stared at him for a moment, assessing the risk of disobeying, then returned to their mothers. Loveday entered. It was a tribute to Liza's ingenuity that the sight of her brood evoked so blatant a display of emotion from the valet. He raised both brows.

"Shall I conduct these persons belowstairs, my lord?"

Jocelin braced his spine and his shoulders, put his fist behind his back, and directed a questioning look at Liza. "You've made your point."

"Maisy, Aggie," Liza said. "Go with Mr. Loveday."

The churning sea wash of mamas and children receded. As he watched them go, Jocelin marshaled his composure. He'd been so intent on protecting Georgiana, so enraged at Liza, that he'd failed to consider who else might suffer. But she wasn't going to gain the high moral ground here.

She was the one who'd been spying on him, spying on him all along. For weeks he'd been worried about whether they felt love or lust, whether they would suit. For weeks he'd not dared to admit to himself how frightened he was, frightened that he—with his soiled past, his desecrated body—that he didn't deserve her. God in heaven, when he'd found those papers, that drawing, and realized how she'd tricked him, he'd wanted to die, just as he'd wanted to die when Yale . . .

Bloody hell. She'd made him feel the shame all over again. She'd plunged him into hell when he'd spent years climbing out of it. Liza and Yale, there was little to choose between them. He'd trusted both of them, and they'd each used him. Was there nothing for him in this life but betrayal?

The Pennant's people were gone. He had to regain the advantage. He remembered some advice he'd gotten from an old drunk in San Antonio—never let a man see you flinch; never let a woman know how much you care about her. Liza Elliot would see neither.

"Well, well, well," he drawled. "Spooked you real good, didn't I, honey?"

Liza's satisfied look vanished. "You're going to persecute babies?"

"Won't need to."

"Why not?"

"Once we're married, I'll have Pennant's reinstated, you might say. Once we're married."

He walked around her to stand at her back. Leaning over her, he said quietly near her ear, "That's what this show was about, wasn't it? A mighty good bluff. You're here to surrender, but since it sticks in your gullet to admit I've won, you're trying to kick sand in my eyes."

She moved away from him. Peacock blue skirts rustled, and he gritted his teeth to keep from allowing the sound to eat away at his rage. Removing her gloves, she rubbed her hands over the clasp of her reticule. They were white with cold, yet the room was warm. Jocelin smiled. He could tell she wanted to kick him in the belly and was furious that she couldn't.

"If I agree, you'll restore Pennant's reputation?"

"Yep."

She threw up her hands. "Will you please stop that?"

"What?"

"You're doing it again. You sound like a ruffian, and I hate that lazy drawl. You sound like you're half asleep, when all the time I expect you to draw that horrible silver gun."

"My Colt?"

"Yes, I suppose."

"What drawl, honey?"

"Stop!"

Jocelin laughed and noted the way she gave him a skittish look and dropped her gaze to his hips. He unbuttoned his coat and swept it back from his hips.

"Not wearing it."

Her gaze remained on his hips, and he forgot the gun. Hate didn't matter. Blackmail didn't matter when she looked at him like that. He went to her and touched her cheek.

"Maybe you got other reasons for marrying I didn't think about. Maybe you like what I do to you. I sure like what you do to me."

She slapped his hand away with a cry. "You stay away from me."

He ignored her and, encircling her with his arms, gave her a hard squeeze. "Come on, honey. What'll it be—the streets or me?"

Liza jabbed him in the ribs. He grimaced and released her. She scuttled out of reach, clutched at her bonnet, and held out her free hand to ward him off.

"You stay where you are. All right, all right, I'll do it."

"Say it, Liza. Say I've won."

Some of his grand wrath drained away as he watched her struggle with her pride and her desire to punch him in the face.

"What did you say?" he asked innocently. "I can't hear well since those little animals of yours came screaming into my sitting room like pallid Comanches."

"I said, you've won. I'll marry you, but only to save Pennant's and Toby and the rest. I can't let them be destroyed because of me. I couldn't bear it."

"I don't care why you're doing it. I only care that you'll do it. And you will, at once."

"At once!" Liza shook her head. "I can't. I have to find out what really happened to my brother. Perhaps you don't care, but I'm convinced all these deaths in your regiment can't be coincidence."

Jocelin's mind felt as if it were burning. His skull ached, and he felt pain just looking at her. The effort of will it took to fight the anguish left no room for contemplation of her unlikely theories.

"We'll talk about your brother later."

He reached out to take her hand. She slapped at his arm. Swearing, he grabbed her wrist and forced himself to speak politely.

"I won't discuss the subject, Liza. Right now I'm concerned with a much more urgent matter, one that won't wait. Your father won't wait. If you're a good girl, I'll consider making inquiries of the police on your behalf. Later. At the moment, we've our wedding to attend. Loveday will have already sent for everyone, the vicar, my witnesses, the carriages, everything."

"The police didn't believe me. I have to inquire for myself or—"

"I said I would handle the matter after we're married." He heard his own voice grow distant. "You really must accustom yourself to my rule, Liza. Ah, I see you hadn't thought of that when you planned your dirty little trap. Think of it now, while you're waiting. Your blasted father and I have already signed the marriage settlement. Once we're married, I'll have control of your funds, and of you. My one piece of luck in this whole mess is that your dear papa isn't so mad as to believe a woman should be left in control of her fortune."

She tugged her wrist. "I don't care about his money. I didn't need it to start Pennant's. I don't need it now. What I need is to find out who among your friends killed my brother. And if you would only listen, I could explain so much."

Jocelin closed his eyes for a moment. "Stop."

"But—"

"Bloody hell!" He tightened his grip on her wrist, but quickly loosened it when she winced. "If you're wise," he said through his teeth, "you won't broach that subject again."

Breathing rapidly, his pulse thudding in his ears, he glared at Liza. "We'll speak about murders and killers when I've have my inquiry agent investigate your brother's death and the others. I agree there may be something going on, but it may have nothing to do with my friends. Right now we've other business to accomplish. You'll leave Pennant's for that man Toby to deal with from now on. You're coming with me to Kent, where you'll learn to conduct yourself with propriety as my wife."

"I'll marry you, but that's all."

"You're making a point of some kind?"

She tried to pry his fingers from her wrist. "You're not to touch me."

He understood her, and threw her wrist from him in disgust. Stalking her, he crowded her so that she backed away from him.

"Your father may have forced me into this marriage, but by God you'll not presume to give orders to me. In a short time, my dear Miss Elliot, I'm going to own you."

Liza retreated until her back hit the desk.

"You will not, and you're to keep away from me."

He bent over her, scouring her face with his gaze. "Listen to me. Every single time I've wanted you, I've had you, in one way or another. It took little effort. Indeed, I marveled at how easily you opened yourself to me." He rubbed his thumb over her lips. "Think about it, honey. You might as well have begged me."

He brushed his thumb over her lower lip, and she nipped at it. Yelping, he jerked free.

She stood there glaring at him and breathing rapidly, tears in her eyes. "I wish it had been your— your—"

"Damn you!" He grabbed her and crushed her against his chest. "You're going to pay for that." He stopped and laughed. "I've just thought of an appropriate punishment. When I have the time, I'll make you fulfill that wish, but in a way that gives me pleasure. No doubt you'll balk at first, but in the end, you're going to like it, Liza. That I promise."

"You're evil, and I won't touch you."

He clicked his tongue again and began guiding

Liza toward the bedroom. When she realized their destination, she began to fight him.

"You needn't make this difficult," he said as he stopped and picked her up.

She kicked her legs and writhed in his arms, but he tossed her on the bed before she could escape. While he locked the connecting door to his bathing chamber, she struggled beneath a mountain of petticoats and skirts. She shot off the bed as he reached the door to the sitting room. Skidding to a halt, she eyed him with apprehension as he touched the knob.

"I'll kill you first," she said.

"I don't think you're fast enough."

With a gloating smirk, he slipped through the door, closed and locked it. There was a pause, then the sound of light, running steps. The door shook as she pounded it. He chuckled.

"I'm just beginning to realize the consolations I may take for enduring marriage to you. Did I tell you the other condition your father put on our agreement? Oh, perhaps I forgot. You see, dear Papa wants the promise of a grandchild within six months. I had thought never to touch you again as a punishment, but it seems I'm going to have to touch you a lot, and frequently. Think about it, Liza. Think about what I'm going to do to you while I get a child on you."

The pounding stopped. He listened for a moment, but no sound came from his bedroom. As he waited, he began to notice his body. It was cold, as if he'd jumped in a stream during a blizzard. He looked down at his hands. They were trembling. Balling them into fists, he stuck them behind his back. Taking a deep breath, he let it out unsteadily. He had to control himself a while longer, no matter the lowering thought of a future bound to a woman who had betrayed him.

Leaving the doorway, he went downstairs. His already desperate mood blackened further as he descended.

Unknown to him, a wish had remained concealed within the tangled and dry underbrush of his soul—a desire for something different than what he'd had. He didn't like to think of that desire, for it seemed weak and rather trite to hanker after a loving wife and family, a home. Yet there it was, that fancy. He wanted what his life should have been like with his parents, what he'd glimpsed in his love for Mother and Georgiana. No use pining after it now. No use at all.

He gained the entrance hall and noticed that Choke and Loveday had carried out his instructions. Upon observing Liza's presence, they had begun preparations for closing the house. Maids were throwing dust sheets over the furniture. Footmen were carrying trunks and boxes to a waiting coach. The vicar and his friends would be here soon, but not soon enough to distract him from this anguish. He had wanted Liza as his wife, but she'd betrayed him. Now he'd be satisfied if she would just behave as a wife should. How had Tennyson put it?

> *Man for the field and woman for the hearth:*
> *Man for the sword and for the needle she:*
> *Man with the head and woman with the heart:*
> *Man to command and woman to obey;*
> *All else confusion.*

He shut himself in the library. All else confusion. That's where the danger lay in women like Miss

Elizabeth Maud Elliot. They, with their lack of principles and mannish behavior, they couldn't be trusted.

He glanced around him, beset with wrath and frustration. Like the rest of the house, the library was shrouded in dust sheets, and the curtains were drawn, shutting out the late afternoon sun. He cursed and went to the liquor cabinet. Pouring himself a whiskey, he gulped it down in one try, poured again and made the liquid disappear in two gulps, poured again. This time he sank into a chair and stared at the blackened fireplace as the minutes passed. He had finished that glass and poured another when Loveday knocked and entered.

"Mr. Fox and Mr. Ross, my lord."

"Yeah," Jocelin muttered.

He loosened his necktie and opened his shirt as Asher and Nick came in. They hesitated upon seeing him, then moved together to hover over him.

Chin resting on his chest, Jocelin glanced up at them without smiling. "Where're the others?"

Exchanging glances with Nick, Asher responded. "You're foxed."

"Accurate, old man." Jocelin took another drink from his glass. "I'm foxed, Mr. Fox."

Asher snatched Jocelin's glass. "But why? And why this sneaking and scurrying to be married? You shouldn't be doing this at all. The girl's unsuitable, as I've told you over and over. No breeding, no family, and you've no need of her money. Why, Jos?"

Jocelin shrugged and snatched his glass back from Asher. Nick was too quick for him, and plucked the vessel from his fingers as he brought it to his lips.

Asher peered at Jocelin's face. "You can't marry in this condition. Marriage vows are for life, and you can't take them when you're drunk and look as if you'd like to throw yourself into the gullet of a volcano."

Speaking for the first time, Nick folded his arms and joined Asher in staring at Jocelin. "No use, Fox old chap. I've tried to dissuade him for days and days. He's going to do it. Odd how after the dinner he suddenly developed a distaste for Miss Elliot and yet couldn't wait to marry her."

Jocelin snorted and slumped in his chair. Nick met Asher's gaze. They communicated silently, then turned their stares on Jocelin again. He had buried his chin deeper in his chest and cast a resentful look at the two.

"No interference from either of you," he said, taking care to enunciate clearly.

"How did they run you to ground?" Asher asked.

Jocelin looked at the liquor cabinet and half rose in his chair. Nick put a hand on his chest and shoved. Jocelin's feet slipped out from under him, and he plopped back down with a curse. He listened to Nick's swearing retort, too miserable to realize his friend had slipped back into his natural accent.

"Coo! You're right tipsy, you are, old love."

"Dear God," Asher whispered as he gawked at Nick.

"Don't whimper like a pup," Nick said to Asher. "You knew about me, and we got no time for niceties. Jos listens better when I'm meself."

Jocelin launched out of his chair and thrust past his friends to aim for the liquor cabinet. "I should have known. Loveday told you about it, didn't he?"

"His words were, 'We are not ourselves this evening, and we have locked our fiancée in our bedroom,'" Asher said. "And since I'm not accustomed to having servants appeal to me in such a manner, especially not Loveday, I understood the gravity of your circumstances."

Nick joined Jocelin at the cabinet. "Right. Knew you were cocked the minute I got Loveday's note."

Jocelin managed to spill into his glass most of the whiskey he was pouring. Nick took the decanter from him.

"No more for you, love. Me mum used to say liquor was the devil's brew."

Weaving back to his chair, Jocelin gave a snuffling laugh. "You sound like old Pawkins."

As he finished, Loveday announced Winthrop and Thurston-Coombes. Jocelin waved his glass in salute.

"Ah, my other witnesses. Come in. Have a drink. We were just talking about old Pawkins. Old Nick here reminds me of him. Good old Sergeant Pawkins. Thought he was going to recover. Like me."

Winthrop wrinkled his nose and looked down it at Jocelin. "He's drunk."

"Can't blame him," Thurston-Coombes said. "After all, he's getting married in a while."

Jocelin continued in his own direction. "Pawkins was married. Asked me to see to his wife in case he didn't make it." He deposited his chin on his chest again, ignoring Nick's attempts to get him to sit up. "He was sleeping beside me that night in hospital at Scutari. Fevered, he was, but I never thought he'd die like that. I woke in darkness. I don't know why. I think I must have heard him gagging, because the doctors said he probably strangled on his fluids. He'd have rather died fighting."

Asher knelt beside him, and Jocelin gave him a bleak smile. "We're never going to leave the Crimea behind. Are we?"

"I have," Asher said softly. "And you can."

"How? You were there. You saw what happened to Cheshire and the others. At least I think you were there. Weren't you?"

"Not so close as Winthrop and Thurston-Coombes, but near enough."

"Bloody hell," Nick snapped. He'd resumed his refined accent now that the others had come. "You're doing him no good wallowing in the beastly past."

"Pawkins kept raving about a horse," Jocelin murmured. He glanced up when he realized that everyone was staring at him. "He did. He kept raving about a horse. Cheshire and the horse, he said. Over and over. Cheshire, Cheshire's horse, the horse."

Winthrop had taken the other armchair as his throne and now pronounced his judgment from it. "He's mad."

Thurston-Coombes gave him an irritated glance. Asher waved a hand for silence and shook Jocelin's arm.

"Jos, old boy, you were delirious too. Forget Pawkins. You're only trying to avoid thinking about this marriage."

"I say." Thurston-Coombes brightened and clapped his hands together. "I've always wanted to do something scandalous like attend a forbidden marriage. It is forbidden, isn't it?"

Nick laughed. "It would be if his grace found out."

A light tapping signaled Loveday's entrance. "The vicar has arrived, my lord. He awaits you in the drawing room."

Winthrop rose in all his dignity and brushed invisible lint from his coat sleeves. "I shall keep the vicar company. Fox, do something about Jos at once."

"Coombes," Nick said. "Find Loveday and tell him we need coffee."

Jocelin rose carefully as Coombes left. He listed to the right, then planted his feet apart and cleared his throat.

"Gentlemen, it's time to fetch my doting bride."

"Not yet." Asher poked him in the shoulder, and he toppled back into the chair.

"None of your interfering," Jocelin said. "I'm going to marry Miss Elliot, and then I'm going to teach her manners and principles and obedience. She wants all of those. And I've found out she's trying to set herself up as some kind of female police constable. She's certain her brother was murdered, along with Airey and Stapleton and Halloway. God, not only is she deceitful, but she's mad, thinking she could investigate such a thing."

Jocelin sighed and blew hair off his forehead. "Yep, deceitful. That's what she is. Well, she'll soon see what her loathsome trap has done for her."

Nick was pacing beside the chair, and Jocelin caught his arm. "She's going to pay, Nick, old chap."

Freeing his arm, Nick looked at the worried Asher. "Doesn't look good."

"No," Asher said. "Not good at all. Perhaps I should go to Kent as well. I've a place not far from Reverie. Perhaps we should all go."

"Got my own place," Nick said. "I'll stay there so I don't have to put up with his holiness Winthrop."

Asher gave Nick a distracted smile as he studied Jocelin. "Then it's agreed."

"Excellent," Jocelin said as he beamed at his friends. "Perhaps if you fellows are about, you can keep me from killing her."

19

Liza had stopped crying a few minutes after Jocelin left. Frightened, she now measured the length of Jocelin's bedroom with her tread. Movement seemed to keep the fear at bey.

He wasn't the kind of man to fulfill his threats. Was he? Then a thought occurred to her. Jocelin couldn't rescue children and turn around and become the embodiment of the men he punished. He was, however, capable of a fury that transformed him into that kill-you-with-a-smile-on-my-lips gunfighter.

She couldn't show fear. If he sensed it, he would use it against her. She would face him down, stand up to him.

"Dear Lord, let me be brave."

The door lock clicked as someone turned the key. Liza whirled around in a flurry of peacock skirts, squared her frame, and lifted her chin. Nick Ross strode into the room and slammed and locked the door behind him. Pointing an accusing finger at her, he snapped, "You bleeding tart, what have you done to Jos?"

Liza stared at him, caught off guard by the change in his speech. "You're not Society."

"You're right, missy, so spill it before I paddle your bum for you. I ain't got no high-flown manners to stop me neither. What have you done to Jos?"

Throwing up her hands, Liza said, "I've done nothing. I've said it over and over. My father acted without my knowledge."

"Oh sure, and that's why you're all fizzed at not having a great big Society wedding. Bleeding tarts, that's what you quality women are, just more expensive than those in the gin shops."

Liza felt blood and fire rush to her face. She marched up to Nick, stopped directly in front of him, and slapped his face.

"By the Almighty in heaven, I'll not be spoken to like that. And I'll have you know that I want no wedding at all, much less a big one."

"Fu—what?" Nick rubbed his stinging cheek. "What?"

Liza poked him in the chest with each word. "I don't want to marry him." She poked him again for emphasis.

"Here now." Nick backed out of her reach. "You stop that. You're lying."

"Let me out of here, and I'll vanish without so much as an engagement ring."

Nick studied her while he massaged his chest. "Jos says he's got to marry you."

"It's my father."

"Handy for you."

It was Liza who shouted now. "I don't want to marry him, damn you!"

Nick walked away from her. He stood leaning against the bedpost and contemplated the design woven into the carpet. After a long while he looked up at her.

"I can read people pretty good. You can't survive in the rookeries without you know how to size a bloke. Until that night at the dinner party, I never thought you was a money-grubber or a title chaser, no matter your ma and pa."

Liza eased her tense stance. "I'm not." She came nearer and spoke quietly. "If I were, I could have forced Jocelin into marriage long ago. You see, I've been making inquiries about him for other reasons."

She continued, telling Nick most of the truth about William Edward, about her disguise as Gamp, about following him and Jocelin. Nick made it difficult, for he fixed her with an unwavering gaze of such sagacity that the devil himself would have found deceit impossible. When she finished, he gave a low whistle and shook his head.

"Christ." Nick stared at her with his brows drawn together. "Then you don't know about old Yale?"

"What about Lord Yale?"

"Oh, nothing important, just testing you out."

Liza gave an impatient sigh. "Why would I spy on Yale when he had nothing to do with my brother? Well? Now do you understand?"

He sat on the edge of the bed, propped his chin on his palm, and stared at her. "You never said a word."

"No."

"Why?"

Liza went to a chair and picked up her reticule, which she opened and closed without looking inside. "I decided that a man who went about saving children from . . . from evil couldn't be the man I was looking for. And later I realized that Jocelin couldn't murder anyone."

"Bleeding hell, you're in love with him."

Liza threw her reticule to the floor. "I am not!"

"And I damned well know he's in love with you."

"He is not, or he couldn't have accused me of trapping him. He would have trusted me. He hates me. He said so. And I dislike him immensely."

"Immensely is it?"

Liza glared at Nick. He grinned at her and looked at his pocket watch.

"Almost time."

Rushing to him, she touched his coat sleeve. "You have to let me go."

"Not bloody likely. Jos wants you, and I'm going to see that he gets you."

"But he doesn't really."

"He does, or he'd have hung your father up by his balls—excuse me language—until he gave over. No, old Jos don't know it, but the reason he's going through with the marriage is 'cause he damned well wants to. And I always see to it that Jos gets what he wants. He saved me life, so I like to help him get on, I do. Besides, you're in love with him."

"Not anymore. And I don't marry where I'm not wanted."

Nick took her arm and guided her to the door. "You just let him know about how you could have blackmailed him yourself if you'd been after his title."

"I don't care what he thinks now."

"You better, missy. You better."

The beast had crawled up the damask curtains in the library and lay curled up on top of a book cabinet. Red eyes gazed down on the party gathered before the vicar. A lip lifted to reveal a curved canine, then the beast lowered its head to rest on its paws and watched, patient, silent, learning a new scent.

The female. A new danger, a scent to be inhaled and remembered for the hunt. And Jocelin, who was remembering again, much too well.

The beast stirred. Nostrils quivered, and its snout raised to weave back and forth in the air. Snuffling. Sniffing. Paws flexed to reveal nails discolored with dried blood. It had caught the scent. He could hear the snuffles grow louder.

The nostrils worked, rapidly sucking in the scent and blowing out, in and out, faster and faster. As the beast rose to crouch above them, the girl uttered her vows. Peacock blue skirts rustled as Jocelin moved close, drew her in his arms, and kissed her. Now, now when they were both together. No, no, too many others. The beast whined, clawed at the cabinet, and hunkered down to wait.

Now Liza knew what a real nightmare was. It was having a dream come to life in a perverted and distorted way that turned hope into dread and love into terror.

He hated her, and he had just obtained total power over her. She started as he bent down to kiss her. What froze her in place was how familiar and alluring his body remained in spite of their estrangement. His lips felt as warm and soft, his body as hard and yet gentle when it encountered hers. He devoted his passion to the kiss in the same way, drawing her so close, she could feel him breathe. But when he drew back, his eyes were as cold as the barrel of his Colt.

And he was drunk. Oh, he could stand. He could conduct conversation as if he were out for a drive in Hyde Park. But Nick stood at his side, surreptitiously supporting him with a steadying arm.

She hadn't let herself think about her own wedding in many years. Not since her botched season. She had never thought to find a man who would want her as she was. Why dream of something you couldn't have? Yet all the while, somewhere, she had cherished a girl's wish—ivory lace, roses, a country chapel. Foolish, trite, unattainable. Gone now, forever.

She had married a man who didn't want her, and who had to drink himself into numbness to make himself say his vows. The thought brought stinging tears to her eyes, and she hissed at herself silently not to disgrace herself by bawling in front of six men. *Think of Toby and Aggie and Maisy. Think of little Peg and all the other children. You can't send them to the streets.* She gripped her reticule, which should have been a bouquet.

Jocelin guided her to a table. She signed something. He signed too, as did the others. Before she recovered from her battle with unshed tears, she

found herself in the entrance hall. Jocelin settled her
mantle on her shoulder, and she glanced up at him.

He gave her a bored smile. "Time to go, my dear
wife."

She glanced about for protection, but everyone
had gone except Nick, who was stuffing Jocelin into
his coat.

"Now you leave off, Jos."

Jocelin mumbled something she couldn't hear.

"I'm coming along to see you don't do any such
thing," Nick said. "So you behave yourself. She's not
to blame for the old bastard's doings."

"Go away, Nick."

"Not just yet, old love. I can't let you loose when
you're as drunk as a costermonger on Boxing Day."

To Liza's surprise and gratitude, Nick escorted
them to the train station and deposited Jocelin in his
private car. Jocelin refused to be helped aboard, so
Nick lifted Liza up the steps after him. Jocelin
marched ahead of them with a kind of swaying stomp,
crashed into a sideboard, ricocheted over to a sofa, and
collapsed on it. He remained there, staring out the
window at the gaslit station.

She didn't know whether to be offended or
relieved. Nick cheerfully lifted his friend's legs onto
the sofa. He removed Jocelin's hat and admonished
him to rest. Loveday appeared, carrying Liza's night
case and another, which must have been Jocelin's. At
Liza's wild glance, he bowed and nodded at Jocelin.

"We have provided for your ladyship's comfort
by sending for your ladyship's things." Loveday made
a rumbling sound in his throat when his master
refused to take his gaze from the window. "We seem
to have begun our connubial celebrations a trifle
early."

"He's damned drunk," Nick said.

"Indeed, sir." Loveday left looking as if one of the palace guard had told secrets to the enemy.

Liza dropped onto an ottoman and stared around her helplessly at the velvet drapes, the bright brass-trimmed stove, the leather upholstery, her new husband. He hadn't. Yes, he had. He'd slid down on the sofa and closed his eyes. The beast was taking a nap.

One of Jocelin's hands lay on top of the blanket he'd pulled over himself. The long, slim fingers splayed out. It could have been the hand of an artist, if not for the rough areas on the forefinger caused by handling a revolver and the reins of a horse. She remembered how strong those fingers were, and yet how gentle they could be when they touched her cheek. Biting her lip to keep from shedding more tears, Liza glanced away from him.

"How long, Nick?"

"Hold on, old girl. We'll be there just after midnight."

Nick was right. They arrived in a deserted station close onto half past twelve. Liza had been in no mood to confide further in Nick, especially since he kept urging her to bare herself to Jocelin. Finally he gave up his attempts when Jocelin woke.

Two carriages drove up as they alighted, and soon they were on their way, leaving Loveday to attend to the heavy luggage. Nick took the second carriage to his own house, while Liza was left with her furious husband. After a silent carriage ride through dark countryside, they drove past a long, rectangular pond and up to a lighted house built entirely of white stone.

This was Jocelin's idea of a small house. A set of massive glass doors were flanked by columns built to resemble Roman triumphal arches. Behind them rose a dome over what was probably a salon. Double, curved flights of stairs led up to the entrance and softened the formal lines of the house.

Even in her misery Liza could perceive the tranquil beauty of Reverie's design. Once she would have longed to explore it, but now she wouldn't have time. She'd already made up her mind not to stay.

A butler and housekeeper and several footmen came out to greet them. Liza stepped into what seemed to be an ancient Roman atrium. Surrounded by fluted alabaster columns, she glanced up at the curved ceiling. Putti bearing garlands frolicked around the perimeter. She glanced to her right and left down galleries in the same muted color. No garish red damask here.

While she gazed at a succession of Greek and Roman statues in alcoves. Jocelin spoke to the butler and left. Then the housekeeper, whose name was, improbably, Mrs. Kettle, showed Liza to her chamber.

Exhausted, Liza tried to be complimentary about the room for the housekeeper's sake. She praised the parchment-color plasterwork with its gilded garlands that swept in graceful curves around the crown molding. She nodded her appreciation when the woman pointed out the columned recess that sheltered a bed with a headboard carved with a great double shell design.

After appropriately praising the cream-and-gold hangings, she dismissed Mrs. Kettle. She was removing her mantle when she heard voices. Throwing open a set of double doors, she encountered two footmen dragging Jocelin's trunks into a room done in white and pale green and dominated by a four-poster rosewood bed.

Liza clasped her hands and squeezed tight. The butler came in to direct his underlings.

"Is there anything you require before I make his lordship comfortable, my lady?"

How had they known she'd married him? As Liza shook her head wordlessly, a man's figure filled the threshold. Jocelin paused there, hair tousled and black waves about his face, his jaw set. Liza hastened back the way she came. Praying he wouldn't follow, she closed the doors. There was a key in the lock. She turned it, and sighed her relief. Rushing to the door that led to the landing, she locked it as well.

As she began to unbutton the bodice of her afternoon gown, she muttered to herself. "He didn't fool me. Swimming in whiskey. I hope he's sick as a pregnant girl in the morning. I hope he pukes until his tonsils fly out of his throat. I hope his head swells until it's the size of a pumpkin."

She stopped unbuttoning her gown. What was she doing? He might try to come in. He might do anything in his state. How much had he drunk? She began fastening her gown while she listened to the sounds of unpacking next door. The footmen left, but she heard Loveday's voice, moderated, polite, firm. She heard a querulous protest from Jocelin. A quiet repetition from Loveday. Soft sounds of drawers being opened and shut. A door closed. Silence.

She waited, hardly daring to draw breath. Minutes passed in a torment of uncertainty. She couldn't endure this waiting. Tiptoeing to the connecting door, she unlocked it and eased it open a crack. The room was dark. Good.

Made brave by the lack of light, she crept inside to listen to the sound of Jocelin's breathing. Deep, heavy breaths. Liza sighed as she stepped into the

dim path of light cast from her own room. It bathed a
bare arm and shoulder. He moved, and she almost
cried out. Then she realized he'd turned on his side
toward her. His face rested on his hand, and she
wondered how he could look so defenseless when
she knew how unfeeling and vicious he could be.

As she watched, those eyes opened, and she
cried out. Poised to run, she nearly screamed when he
spoke.

"Sorry to disappoint you, honey. If I touch you
right now, I'll puke."

She whirled, bolted into her room, and locked
herself inside. As she hovered on the other side of the
door, she heard his laugh, muffled by pillows. Sparks
of lightning arced up her spine while she listened. She
couldn't endure this fear, the worry that he might
suddenly pounce upon her. Furious at being intimi-
dated, she gathered her courage along with a candle,
and threw the door open again. He wasn't going to
treat her like an ill-fitting boot.

She tramped into the room and slammed the
candle holder down on a night table. Jocelin sprang
upright. He fumbled beneath his pillow and cursed at
finding nothing beneath it. Brushing back a shock of
black hair from his face, he blinked at Liza.

"Are you awake?"

"Hang it! I am now. Ow, my head."

Liza went to a cabinet and found a decanter. She
returned to the bed and thrust it into his hands.
"Drink this. It will make you feel much worse."

Jocelin glared at her and put the decanter on the
night table. The movement must have cost him, for
he subsided into his pillows, moaned, and buried his
forehead in his palms.

"Go away."

"I intend to. That's what I've come to tell you. I don't know why I let you terrify me into coming here."

With his head still buried, Jocelin mumbled at her. "Because if you don't obey me, I won't save Pennant's."

"But I married you."

"And because I'm your husband and it is my wish that you remain here. Now go away like an obedient little wife. Loveday gave me a headache powder, and I want to get some sleep."

"Are you going to undo the damage you've done to my business?"

"Bloody hell. Not married a full day and already beset with a nagging wife."

"My insisting that you keep your word isn't nagging," she said.

"Yes, yes, yes, yes. I'll fix it tomorrow morning if it will get you to leave me alone tonight. Oh, my head."

"And you're not going to . . . to . . . to . . ."

Jocelin sunk down under the covers and clutched his head. "Not tonight. Ow! See what you've done? I raise my voice because of you, and now my head feels like a boiled onion."

"I'm not staying here."

"Bloody hell."

He sprang from the bed before she could retreat. He grabbed her arm and swung her around to face him. Why was it that he seemed larger naked than clothed? Liza edged away from him and kept her gaze from dipping below his chest.

"I can always set about ruining Pennant's again if you leave," he said. "But you won't. You've worked too hard to be called 'my lady.' Once you're over your

snit about your fancy wedding, you'll calm down.
Next you'll begin whining about balls and cotillions
and dinner parties. God, I'm doomed."

"Then why did you do it?" Liza's fears of being
pounced upon eased as she watched Jocelin rub his
temple with his free hand. "Is Nick telling the truth?"

"What are you talking about, woman?" He
groaned and pressed his palm to his forehead.

Liza dared a glance at him from head to foot.
Jocelin was taller than her father by several inches,
and much broader in the shoulders. His muscles
curved inward toward the center of his chest to form a
deep valley that pointed down toward his groin. She
hadn't the nerve to examine him there, and directed
her gaze to the long, thick curve of his thigh. Her
glance strayed to his face. His eyes were closed as he
rubbed his forehead, so she darted a look at his hips,
then looked down at his ankles. Heavens, what a man.
Were they all so . . . so generously made?

And he possessed a frightening ruthlessness.
Calming, now that he wasn't using that ruthlessness
against her, she began to consider Nick's opinions
seriously for the first time. Certainly she would never
have expected Jocelin to submit so easily to Papa.

Jocelin released her to sink back down on the
bed and groaned while pinching the bridge of his
nose. As he did so, Liza's curiosity, which had been
buried under the weight of her own fears, surfaced.
Why hadn't he simply stuck his Colt in Papa's face and
threatened to kill him? Even Papa would have given
over upon being faced with Jocelin in his tranquil
killer guise.

Her husband toppled over on his side and
groaned again. Liza surveyed him while she tapped a
contemplative finger against her chin.

"My lord, we have to talk."

He moaned. "Not now. And don't try to leave."

"We have to thrash this muddle out calmly."

Jocelin rose up abruptly and lunged at her. He hauled her close and snarled at her.

"I'm not so drunk I can't throw up your skirts and consummate this hell-cursed marriage."

Liza wrenched out of his grasp. His fingers curled in the mass of her skirts as she twisted. The silk ripped, but she raced for the safety of her bedroom. Once more she began to close the door, and as it shut, she caught a glimpse of him, blatantly naked and confident. He lay back, leering at her, the blue silk trailing from his fingers.

"Next time, honey, I won't stop at your skirts."

She slammed the door once again. The lock clicked, and she heard him chuckle. Heavens, she wanted to kick the door. No, she wanted to kick him as usual.

She had to talk to him. She had to, before he decided to avenge himself on her by trying to make her into his so-called proper wife. Ha! What he wanted was a sort of connubial bond servant. He wasn't going to get one though.

How could she stop him? She could threaten to tell Papa. Papa wouldn't care. She could threaten to reveal his secret crusade. No. Jocelin didn't react well to her threats. Besides, she couldn't really expose him, and thus couldn't back up her threat. And there was no telling what he might do to her if she angered him further.

Liza stared at the closed door. What was wrong with her? Why had she baited him? She was Miss Elliot, owner of Pennant's Domestic Agency. She managed dozens of employees. She could reason with the most capricious of customers. Why hadn't she reasoned with this man?

Reason, that was the answer. Logic and reason. Calm discussion in the light of day. By tomorrow both she and Jocelin would have composed themselves. Surely they could work out an understanding, some sort of detached rapprochement. She could see that Jocelin was suffering, despite his show of belligerence.

After all, she had to admit, if only to herself, that he had been the victim. Perhaps she'd been hasty in condemning him for suspecting her. Especially since she really had been spying on him. Yes, she'd been as foolhardy as he in placing blame before listening to explanations.

If she could convince Jocelin that she hadn't been a part of Papa's scheme, they could stop fighting. Perhaps they could even remain married. The nobility abounded with marriages in which the two partners rarely saw each other.

She would reason with him tomorrow. She only hoped that he was capable of reason. So far he reacted to her only with anger and lust. Somehow she would reason with him, because, as unhappy as he made her, if she remained at Reverie, she might fall in love with him again. That she couldn't allow. No matter how beautiful he was, she wouldn't love him again.

20

Jocelin had managed to avoid pain and temptation for five whole days. He fanned his cards out and stared at them without seeing them as Nick, Asher, Winthrop, and Coombes took turns betting. He'd entertained them at dinner and gambling for the past week, thus sparing himself the torture of having to be with Liza.

This evening had been the same as the last four. Liza had dined in her room while he and his friends had eaten below. He congratulated himself on conceiving a strategy for living with his new wife. He wouldn't see her, except in passing.

He'd awakened the morning after their marriage with a swollen head and twitchy stomach to find her standing over him. She had demanded that they talk when all he wanted to do was find a chamber pot. Later, after his bout with the chamber pot, she had attacked again. Exhorting him to listen to her, she launched into an explanation of her behavior that he hadn't understood because of the surgical needles ripping at his eyes and the throbbing at the back of his head. His temper exploded like a misfired cannon, and they fought.

To end the battle, he'd thrust her into her room and locked the door only to be confronted with Loveday's disapproval.

"We have engaged in nothing but unbecoming conduct in our dealings with our wife."

"Is that so? Then you can deal with her. We haven't the patience."

Thus he conceived the Rules of Matrimony, which he passed on to his wife through Loveday. There weren't many. To make certain she understood, he'd written then down. Liza was to take her meals in her room. He would eat in the dining room. (After all, it was his house.) She wasn't to ride or walk when he was riding or walking. (His house and gardens and lands.) She wasn't to occupy a room if he was in it. She was to take tea in the morning room, while he refreshed himself in the blue room upstairs. She wasn't to talk to him or write notes to him. She could communicate with him through Loveday.

The Rules of Matrimony would save him from his own desire for revenge, from his desire for her, from the pain of being confronted with a woman who pretended to care for him when all she wanted was a title. Loveday had taken to calling her Lady Elizabeth. The attribution rankled. She didn't deserve it.

He had expected protests at the rules. She never

did what he expected. Liza had followed the guide-
lines scrupulously. Now she was a whiff of lemon in a
passageway, the swish of silk and lace in the next
room, the scrape of pen on paper, the tap of heels on
floorboards. He hated it.

Jocelin threw down his cards. Leaning back, he
drew on his cigar and watched the others play. Intent
on his own thoughts, he was slow to notice when the
others paused. Nick kicked him under the table, and
he turned to find Liza standing on the threshold of the
smoking room.

It was the first time he'd looked at her in days.
How had she grown so pale? She'd been given the
same fare as he. Perhaps it was that dress, pink and
mauve organdy, that gave her a frail air to which he
wasn't accustomed. Her first words dispelled the air of
delicacy.

"I want to talk to you."

He scowled at Nick and the others as they all
stood. He remained seated and puffed on his cigar.

"I have guests."

"I don't care."

He glanced at Archer, who was studying him
with a pained expression.

"Ah, gentlemen," Jocelin said lightly. "As you
can see, brides are a trial. So excitable. Women and
their frail nerves, their limited understanding. No
doubt my lady has upset herself over some domestic
trifle. I'll see you in the morning, Liza."

He had hoped to embarrass her into leaving. She
did flush, but instead of crumpling under the weight
of masculine condescension, she put her hands on her
corseted waist and narrowed her eyes at him.

"If you don't talk to me, your flock of fellow

roosters are going to hear what I have to say along with you."

Jocelin tossed his cigar on the table, thrust his chair back, and walked to her. He bent over her and whispered so that only she could hear.

"You're leaving, and if you ever embarrass me in front of my friends again, I'll flip your skirts and burn your bottom for you. And you'll be lucky if I don't do it where they can cheer me on."

Without waiting for her to reply, he escorted her into the hall, upstairs, and into her room. He went so fast, she had no breath to spare in her efforts to keep from being dragged the whole way. As he shoved her into the room, she wrenched free. He hesitated in his retreat, for as she turned away, he glimpsed a wet cheek. She was crying, but silently. She didn't complain. She didn't beg him to stay and speak with her. Back straight, head held erect, she walked to a small writing desk and placed one hand on it for support.

In that moment he realized what had been bothering him since he'd made up his rules. She had reacted with dignity, with grace. No tearful entreaties, no foul-tempered screeching passed her lips. He contemplated her stiff back, the curve of her shoulder above the filmy organdy sleeve of her gown. Had he made a mistake?

"Get out," she said quietly. "And if you ever embarrass me before others again, you'll wish you'd married Medusa instead of me."

No, he hadn't made a mistake. He returned to his friends, leaving her standing alone by the desk, her back as straight as ever. In the smoking room he found Nick waiting for him.

"Where are the others?"

Nick waved a brandy glass. "Gone home, love.

You frightened them off, tearing into the lady like that."

"Damn."

Jocelin found his cigar and lit it again in the fireplace.

"No use brooding," Nick said as he joined him by the fire. "Take my advice and talk to the girl. She's a sweet thing. Not at all like her pa."

"If she's so sweet, you take her."

"And have you come after me with that revolver of yours? No, thank you." Nick waited, sipping his brandy. "Oh, come on. None of us can stick you like this."

Jocelin cursed and braced himself against the mantel.

"Do you know what it's like to want a woman who's tricked you and used you? God, I want to beat her and take her to bed at the same time. I can't sleep. I can't read. I can't ride without thinking of her. If I'm not hating her, I'm lusting after her. She's killing me."

"You bloody fool, why don't you settle with her?"

"There's no solution to having a wife who trapped you into marriage."

"Damned if you aren't a stubborn sod." Nick swirled his brandy while they listened to the hiss of the fire. "Got a new fowling piece. Been collecting, you know. Got a lot of antique weapons in me new gun room at the lodge. Come over tomorrow morning."

Jocelin shrugged.

"Now don't you be turning your nose up at me, old love. I got something to show you at the lodge. You be there."

"I'm not interested in old guns."

"It ain't a gun, simpleton."

"Go away, Nick. I'll come if you'll just go away."

After a sleepless night, Jocelin kept his promise to visit Nick's lodge. A former Elizabethan hunting box, the Hart Lodge lay on the estate Nick had purchased next to Jocelin's lands. He rode his hunter there and hardly noticed the bright spring sunshine and new grass that rippled in the still-cold breeze.

At Hart Lodge he endured a lecture on single-shot muzzle-loading pistols, flintlock and wheellock pistols, flintlock rifles and muzzle-loading rifles. He was examining a French flintlock holster pistol when he heard the crunch of carriage wheels on the gravel drive. He gave Nick a questioning look, but his friend shook his head.

"Probably the new estate manager."

He handed Jocelin a muzzle-loading fowling piece. Jocelin gripped the long barrel and settled the butt into his shoulder. As he aimed at a budding tree through the window, someone came into the gun room. He swung around, still aiming the fowling piece. Into his sights swam curves upholstered in a dove gray traveling suit. Jet black curls, violet eyes. Jocelin swore and lowered the gun.

"Ida Birch, what are you doing here?"

"Now don't you come all over high and mighty," Nick said as he went to greet Miss Birch. "I invited her to stay with me."

Jocelin cradled the fowling piece in his arms and lifted a brow. "You invited my mistress for a visit?"

"Why not?" Miss Birch said as she removed her gloves and cast a hurt glance at him. "I've had nothing to do for ages."

"You still have your house and your allowance," Jocelin said.

Miss Birch shook her gloves at him. "For how

long? I know what it means when a gentleman pays the bills but never calls. You're sticking your fingers in other pies." She put her hand on Nick's shoulder. "Nicky said you were sorry for neglecting me and thought you needed cheering up, so of course I came. I require tea and cakes and then a bath. And then you may take me riding. Now where is my maid? Elsie? Elsie, mind you don't lose my jeweled bow."

Calling to her maid in her high, little girl's voice, Miss Birch left. Jocelin lifted the fowling piece and slowly walked toward Nick, who threw out his hands and backed away.

"You bastard," Jocelin said.

"Now wait, love. I was thinking of you."

"Two women. Two." Jocelin changed direction when Nick did and backed him into a corner. "You were thinking of me? How were you thinking of me? Thinking of new and more exquisite ways for me to suffer? A wife and a mistress. Both. Within a few miles of each other."

"But you said you didn't want to touch your wife."

"I want to touch her all right. Hang it, that's all I want, day and night."

"Well then," Nick said with a satisfied smile, "there you are. Console yourself with Miss Birch until you can redeem yourself to Liza."

"Redeem myself? Me? I'm the victim here. Not her."

"Whatever."

Nick brushed past him and began replacing antique guns in their mountings on the walls of the gun room. He kept one aside, a small Italian snaphance pistol with engraved gold fittings.

"I've got to take this to a gunsmith in the

village," he said. "You will give Miss Birch my regrets."

"Oh, no. You stay here."

Nick was already out the door. Jocelin followed him, speeding up as he realized that Nick's hunter was already out front and ready.

"You come back here."

He grabbed the reins as Nick turned his horse, but Nick hauled them out of reach.

"Won't be gone long, old love."

Gravel sprayed over Jocelin's boots as the animal launched into a trot. Jocelin cursed his friend, then stomped around to a stable to call for his own mount. His frustration elevated when he found that his hunter had been released in a back paddock to graze. A groom would have to find and catch the animal, then groom and saddle him. Sorely tried, Jocelin trudged back to the lodge, where he was forced to endure taking tea with Miss Birch.

Birch, he had to admit, had been an excellent mistress. She never asked for more than he was willing to give, never objected to any pleasure he desired, always vanished when he wished her to, until now. His neglect had soured her normally amiable disposition. Once she had reminded him of a sort of human confectionery, but the meringue had spoiled. Now she even sipped tea with the air of a martyr.

He counted the ticks on the grandfather clock in the hall while Miss Birch consumed orange cake. He'd reached three hundred seventy when he heard the clatter of china. Miss Birch had finished her tea, and while he wasn't looking, she had left her chair. He watched her approach, noted the determined set to her mouth, and tried to rise. Too late. She reached him first and planted her bottom in his lap. He sank beneath yards of dove gray merino, a crinoline, and great swaths of lace.

Taking his face in her hands, she breathed orange cake at him. "Darling Jocelin, haven't you missed me?"

"Enormously," he muttered as he tried to get a grip on her through the ocean of skirts, petticoats, and hoops.

He searched fruitlessly for a way to lever her off of him. At last he found a stiff wall that had to be a corset. He clamped his hands on either side of it, but he wasn't in time to prevent her from lowering her lips to his. He turned his face to the side, but she pursued him. Catching his mouth, she sucked hard. He tried to speak, but her tongue occupied his mouth.

Then he gasped as she burrowed beneath his coat, into his trousers, and cupped him. His hands scrabbled through and around whalebone, merino, and lace in a frantic search for a path to her hands. At the same moment that she began to pinch him, he found her hands and began pulling at them.

"Ida!"

"Here," said a new voice. "Let me help you."

He glimpsed a black beaver hat and veil, a rifle cloth riding habit, and ash blond curls. Black kid gloves sank into the chignon at the back of Ida's head and yanked. Ida yelped and sailed backward to land in a heap at his feet. Liza released her quarry, stepped between Jocelin and Ida, and removed a familiar-looking gold-trimmed pistol from her belt. She pointed it at Ida.

"This is your mistress," she said calmly.

Jocelin swallowed, then sneered at her. "One of them."

She hardly winced at all. To his consternation,

she nodded and then sank to her knees beside Ida. Touching the barrel of the pistol to Ida's breast, she smiled at her.

"Good morning, Miss Birch."

"Ooo."

Liza continued as if conducting a morning call. "I am his lordship's new wife, Lady Radcliffe. This is the only conversation you and I will ever have, so listen carefully." The pistol tapped its way up the buttons on Ida's gown and came to rest beneath her chin. "If you ever touch my husband again, I will shoot a lovely hole through your—hat." The barrel touched Ida's nose.

Miss Birch screamed. "Jocelin!"

Fascinated, unsure of whether to risk grabbing for the pistol, Jocelin kept his mouth shut and didn't move.

Liza rose and flipped the pistol at Ida. "Run along, Miss Birch. I'm sure you can catch a train if you hurry."

Ida was swelling with pique and blustering like a frightened guinea fowl. "You're demented. Quite demented."

Liza put an arm around her victim, squeezed her as if they were close friends, and addressed the woman in confiding, serious tones.

"All the more reason for you to be frightened."

With a shriek Ida fled, calling for her maid and a carriage. Jocelin couldn't stop himself from smiling. Never in all his dealings with women had one exhibited such wild jealousy, or had the boldness to draw a gun on her rival. She was jealous, which meant she cared for him. His smile spread into a pleased grin as Liza turned from watching Miss Birch's retreat. The grin vanished when she pointed the pistol at him this time.

"No mistresses," she said. "No gin shop ladies, no opera dancers, no actresses. No maids, no young housekeepers, no plump and frisky young cousins. Not even a dressmaker. Is that clear?"

"Now just a moment."

"I know how to fire a gun. Toby taught me. I don't often have occasion to use one, but my aim is excellent."

Jocelin sprang to his feet. He felt a tingle of anticipation as he beheld Liza's tapping foot, her narrowed eyes, and the way she squared off in front of him. Why hadn't he realized how much she excited him when they brawled? He couldn't resist the challenge.

Folding his arms over his chest, he said, "I'll not be dictated to by my own wife."

"And I'll not sit at home tatting lace while you cavort with other women."

He smiled, delighted that she'd accepted the challenge. "You'll keep to your place. And I'll do as I please. A man has rights, and a woman's duty is to see to his home and keep her nose out of his affairs."

"Absurd."

Jocelin stared at her as if unable to believe she was disagreeing with the civilized customs by which everyone abided.

"You're one of those women," he said.

"What women?"

"Those women who want—" he lowered his voice. "Rights, education." He lowered his voice again and stepped toward her with great drama. "Divorce, and, and the vote."

Liza stepped back and tossed her head. "Oh, that. Of course I do, but that's not the point."

He laughed then, but stopped when he heard her curse. "It is the point. Such desires are unwomanly."

"I know your backward views on women, my lord. I'm not interested in them. I'm only interested in making you understand your situation. You can behave yourself and adhere to the same standards of conduct that you expect of me, or you can hop from bed to bed and risk what I'll do to you."

His amusement vanished at this comment. She'd gone too far. His jaw worked, but he couldn't think of anything he'd care to say to a lady.

"And by the way, there will be no excuses." Liza waggled the gun at him. "No hiding behind the proverbial animal nature of men, those ungovernable urges that are supposed to exempt you from responsibility for your actions. Illogical nonsense."

Disbelief turned to outrage. He felt his blood thicken and gush painfully through the small veins at his neck and temples. No one told him how to conduct himself, especially not a woman. Grinding his teeth, he slowly began to walk, not directly toward her, but sideways, so that she moved away from the door.

"My, my, my," he drawled. "You sure got firecrackers in your petticoats, honey."

"What are you talking about?" She edged away from him as he closed the distance between them.

"If you're so hot to keep me from other women, you must want me for yourself."

"I didn't say that!"

He smiled as the pistol wavered.

"The thought of me and another woman curdles

your milk, honey. Admit it." They were circling now, but Liza's attention was on the argument.

"Absurd."

He laughed and inched closer to her. "You were ready to scalp poor Miss Birch. But you got to realize, honey, that the only way you're ever gonna be sure I'm not in someone else's bed is to keep me in yours."

She sputtered. The pistol barrel dipped, and he lunged, knocking the gun from her hand. It hit the floor. The trigger snapped, but nothing happened as Jocelin dove for Liza. He flew at her, taking her with him as he plunged to the floor. He landed on top of her, but managed to cradle her head so that it didn't hit the floor. She gasped as he bounced onto her. Transferring his weight to his lower body, he captured her arms and smiled at her.

"Now you're going to find out why I'm the master and you're the obedient wife." She bucked under him, and he laughed again. "I'll make a bargain with you. The day you can make me let you go, I'll consider all those arguments you just spit at me."

She writhed and swore at him, but couldn't break free. He kept a grip on her wrists, careful not to hurt her. At last, out of breath and curses, crimson from her neck to her scalp, she subsided. Jocelin could feel the heat from her face. He touched his cheek to hers, in spite of her protest. Then he kissed her temple. She jerked her head, but he captured her chin with one hand while holding her wrists with the other. Slowly he brought his lips nearer to hers.

"Come on, honey, I like to scrap, but we've got better things we can do."

21

When Jocelin plunged to the floor with her, Liza was abruptly thrust from the fugue in which she'd been submerged ever since she'd seen Miss Birch get out of her carriage. She heard him vow to give her his unabridged attentions, saw his lips descend toward her. Then, to her frustration, she burst into tears. This man, whom she feared she loved still, wanted to take pleasure of her as if she were a poor substitute for the mistress he'd just lost. The thought made her cry harder. She heard his alarmed inquiries, but couldn't respond.

She had followed Jocelin, after days of being shunned and ill-used, with the intention of cornering him and having it out with him. As she'd ridden down the lane to Nick's lodge, a carriage had passed her, bearing a woman of dark and voluptuous appearance. Knowing Jocelin, Liza's suspicions had been aroused.

She'd followed the carriage and met Nick riding down the drive to the lodge in the opposite direction. He had asked her the purpose of her visit, listened with satisfaction, and handed her an ancient pistol with the remark that she might need it. After she came upon Jocelin and the woman plastered together, her thoughts and actions seemed to occur within a crimson haze of rivalry and covetousness so unexpected and so violent that she felt as if she'd contracted some kind of dementia.

That dementia only vanished when Jocelin crashed to the floor with her and threatened to master her. Now she stared up at him through a watery screen of tears. Jocelin raised himself to sit straddling her. He released her hands, then took one of them and began to pat it distractedly.

"Hang it. What's wrong? I thought you were enjoying our little brawl."

Liza covered her eyes with her forearm and bawled. She'd already let him see her cry, so she had nothing to lose by unburdening herself. She felt Jocelin pat her hand, then her shoulder, and heard him mutter helpless consolation

"Did I hurt you?" he asked in a confused tone.

"Ah-hem."

Liza moved her arm and looked up at the length of a well-creased trouser leg. Jocelin glared at Loveday.

Before he could say anything, the valet clasped his hands behind his back and nodded to his master. "Good morning, my lord."

Liza glanced at Jocelin, who seemed to have lost his urge to conquer.

Loveday continued when Jocelin failed to reply. "Forgive me for intruding, my lord. A matter of some urgency." His gaze trickled over Liza and his employer. "I assume that some great catastrophe has taken place that would require us to sit upon a weeping lady?"

Liza wiped her eyes and stared at Loveday. Jocelin tossed his head, throwing a stray black lock off his brow, and removed himself from Liza. Offering his hand to her, he assisted her in rising. She freed her hand as soon as she was on her feet.

Jocelin marched to the door and held it open. "Get out, Loveday."

"No, don't," Liza cried out. "He's still playing the gunfighter."

"I am not!"

Liza set her jaw and stuck it out. "You are."

Swearing under his breath, Jocelin shut his eyes, then opened them and spoke more evenly. "Perhaps you are accustomed to discussing private matters before servants. It's not done."

"Loveday is different. Even I know that."

Jocelin began striding toward her. "I'm a tolerant man, but you're not to contradict me in front of a servant."

"My lord," came the gentle voice of civility. "We seem to have forgotten our own good breeding. We do not accost ladies."

"I told you to go away!"

Liza cast a glance of entreaty at Loveday, who raised his voice. "My lord, I said that we do not accost young ladies. We once remarked that such behavior reminded us of certain actions once directed at ourselves."

At this remark Jocelin halted in midstride. Surprised and relieved, Liza watched him flush. Then the color drained from his face, and he cast his gaze down at the floor.

"If your lordship will excuse me," Loveday said as he left the room.

Jocelin nodded, then swept his arm toward the chair he'd vacated. Liza circled him at a distance and seated herself. Jocelin stood several paces away, his spine as straight as a Greek column, and opened his mouth.

"No," Liza said. "Let me speak. If you do, we'll only fight again. You're going to listen to me if I have to haul down one of those muskets and point it at you. Nod if you agree."

He nodded.

"Good." She stood up. She felt more at an advantage standing. "I can't endure this purgatory you've designed for me for groundless and unreasonable reasons. Therefore, my lord, you're going to listen to me. I did not plot to make you marry me. No, don't say anything."

She began to pace back and forth in front of him. "I admit spying on you, but only to find my brother's murderer. And once I realized you couldn't have murdered William Edward, well, I stopped." No need to tell him she also fell in love with him. "And do you know why I realized you weren't a murderer? I'll tell you. It was because that first day we drove to Willingham, I followed you to Dr. Sinclair's house."

"Bloody hell."

She took satisfaction in the shock on his face.

"I heard what you said to him, and realized what

you'd done when you took that boy and that little girl from St. Giles."

"Dear God."

Now he was looking at her as if she had sprouted snakes on her head.

"Yes," Liza said. "I, whom you consider too weak-brained to vote or own property, am capable of stalking you without your knowledge and discovering your secret crusade. And on top of that, I've kept the secret." She paused while she watched his jaw work. "Now, my lord, if I truly wanted to trap you into marriage, I could have done it long ago, and with no help at all from my bigoted father."

If she hadn't cared so deeply about this infuriating man, she could have watched the cascade of his emotions with detachment. The columnlike stature melted. He ran a hand through his hair, and she noticed that it trembled slightly.

He whispered. "How much do you know?"

"Only what I've said. You and Mr. Ross have a secret quest to save maltreated children and rid the world of men who prey upon them."

"Nothing more? You swear it?"

Liza frowned, but nodded. "If you wish."

He confused her by sighing as though comforted by a miracle. Then he walked away from her so that all she could see was the back of his figure, regimental and aloof. She waited while he stared at a cabinet filled with medieval daggers. After a while he turned suddenly and walked back to her with a quick tread that spoke of a decision made.

She gripped the finial of a chair, prepared to bolt if he came at her. Her gaze followed his movements as he bent, took her hand, and kissed it. His lips barely touched the back of her hand, but she shivered at the contact. When he looked up, she caught her breath.

It was back, that look of admiration and amused fascination. It was back, that look she thought she'd never see again. It was back, and filled with more love than she ever thought to encounter, especially directed at herself.

He brought her hand to his cheek. "Liza, sweet. Sweet, sweet Liza. Will you forgive me?"

Her jaw dropped, and she stuttered, which made her flush and try to withdraw her hand. He tightened his grip and laughed softly, drawing her to him.

"I take it you do forgive me?"

She wobbled her head, not daring to lift her chin from its safe perch on her chest. He lifted it for her, murmured another disconcerting apology, and kissed her. His tongue tickled her mouth, and she forgot her shyness. She protested when he stopped, and opened her eyes. He was contemplating her as though faced with something as rare as the Holy Grail.

"I didn't know a woman could be like you."

"Odd?" she asked fearfully.

He laughed. "No, so accepting of what I am."

"I like what you are."

He threw back his head and laughed again, sending a thrill down her body to her toes.

She smiled and went on. "Then you don't mind?"

"Mind what?"

"You said I was accepting. Then you don't mind about the rest."

"Liza, I don't understand."

"About my principles. About women being educated and owning their own property and conducting—"

"Nonsense."

She frowned. "I see. It's for me to accept what you are, but I mustn't ask you to respond in the same manner."

"It's different for a woman."

Liza considered Jocelin fortunate that Loveday interrupted them again.

"Forgive me, my lord, but I dare not delay. It's your father and uncle."

"Jocelin!"

Liza jumped at the bellow that announced the arrival of the Duke of Clairemont and his brother Yale. The duke charged into the gun room, lacking only a destrier to complete the impression of an avenging and offended knight. Yale followed in his wake, a quiet and saintly yeoman.

The duke pointed at Jocelin with his walking stick and nearly hit his son with it. "God damn you to everlasting hell."

Jocelin wasn't even looking at his father. His gaze had fastened upon Yale the moment the man came into sight. Liza edged over to stand at Jocelin's side, uneasy at the way his features had chilled. As she watched him, he became a predator, encased in wary, voracious silence.

"Is this the person with whom you've allied yourself?"

Jocelin inclined his head, but his attention never wavered from Yale. Liza, on the other hand, felt the prick of resentment, hurt, and anger. Stepping up to the duke, she curtsied as gracefully as a princess at a coronation.

"Good morning, your grace. I'm afraid his lordship is distracted at the moment. I am Elizabeth Elliot—no—Marshall."

The duke's cheeks had reddened, and his features stilled so that they resembled the painted face of a marionette.

The duke ignored Liza. "Damn and blast. You've really done it, haven't you? You've married the granddaughter of a butcher. You'll get an annulment, sir. At once."

At last Jocelin released Yale from that hunting-hawk stare and glanced at his father.

"You wanted me to marry. I have done so, and an annulment isn't possible."

The duke's complexion began to resemble a geranium, and he barked at his son. "And I thought you'd done your worst when you made up those lies about Yale. You disgust me, sir."

The rope Liza had tied to her temper upon the duke's entrance snapped. She advanced on his grace, wishing she hadn't lost her pistol.

"You leave Jocelin be, you old goat."

For once the duke noticed her. His mouth worked open and closed, fishlike. "Keep silent, girl. You don't know the evil my son is capable of."

Jocelin headed for his father, but Yale restrained him. The moment the older man's hand touched his sleeve, Jocelin whirled and raised his voice.

"Back off, you bastard."

"You see," the duke said.

Liza spared an irritated glance at his grace, but returned her gaze to Jocelin, who had suddenly become quiet.

After a moment he smiled and said in a sleepy drawl, "Well, well, well, Daddy."

"Now look what you've done," Liza said to the duke.

"Maybe you need convincing," Jocelin said as he

transferred his lazy glance to his uncle. "What do you say?"

Yale shook his head and spread his arms in a gesture of helplessness. "What can I say, dear boy? I can only endure your dislike, though I must say I haven't deserved it all these years. I regret that your unstable nature has caused you to build a fantasy around my giving you shelter when you ran away from your family."

Jocelin walked over to stand in front of his uncle and smiled at him. "My unstable nature."

Liza's uneasiness heightened, for Jocelin's voice had grown soft, and he moved closer to his uncle.

"I'll not have another attack on Yale, sir," said the duke.

"Perhaps I've been wrong," Jocelin said as he came within half a foot of Yale, who began to retreat. "Perhaps I've harbored ill feelings too long."

The two men stopped moving when Yale backed into a gun cabinet. Jocelin placed his body so that it almost touched Yale's and looked into his uncle's eyes. Goose bumps formed on Liza's arms, for Yale appeared confused, wary, and somehow intrigued. Couldn't he see the danger he was in? Heavens! Was Jocelin armed? Liza sidled across the room to stand near the two. Jocelin glanced at her, but resumed his too-close contemplation of his uncle.

"Perhaps," he said, "perhaps the calming influence of my wife has made me realize how wrong my actions have been."

"Calming," Liza said. "Me?"

Jocelin suddenly thrust himself away from his uncle and snatched her hand. "Yes, of course. You, my dear." He drew her close and whispered, "When you leave, take my father outside and have him listen at the window." He glanced at the window that looked out on a small terrace and garden.

"Am I leaving?" Liza asked.

Jocelin raised his voice. "My wife has suggested that a few moments' privacy with Yale might resolve our misunderstandings. May we be private, Yale?"

"Do you mean this?" the duke asked.

Jocelin gave his father a chilly smile. "I'm quite serious."

"Come, girl."

Liza scowled at the duke, but followed him out. In the hall she grabbed his coat sleeve.

"Come on, your grace."

"Young woman, release me at once."

Liza yanked on the sleeve and scurried outside, dragging the duke behind her.

"What are you doing?" he asked as he pulled his sleeve free of her grasp.

She put her finger to her lips and began to tiptoe around the house to the gun room window. Left by himself, the duke followed.

"What—"

"Shhh!" She hovered at the sill and pointed.

Inside, Jocelin and Yale were facing each other beside a low display cabinet laden with several crossbows. The window was open, and she could hear clearly.

"If she's wrought such a change in you, I'm grateful."

Jocelin flattened his hand on the glass that enclosed the crossbows and cast his gaze down as if in shame and regret. "She has changed me. I don't understand it, and can't explain it to you, but she makes me feel that the past isn't so important as I once thought."

Yale drew nearer. "I could intercede for her with your father."

"Could you?"

"His anger is frightening, Jocelin, as you know. And his influence is indispensable if your wife is to be accepted by the family and by Society."

Jocelin sounded lost. "I don't want her to be hurt." He sighed, but appeared not to notice that Yale had come close. "I would be grateful for your help."

"Would you?" Yale's hand slowly reached out to touch Jocelin's as it lay on the glass. As it closed over his nephew's, Yale went on. "I will champion her to the last, if she's brought you back to me after all these years."

The duke made a noise, and Liza poked him with her elbow.

"Has your little wife made you realize the truth at last?" Yale asked as he lifted Jocelin's hand.

"I—I don't know."

Liza ground her teeth at the uncertainly in Jocelin's tone. He was an excellent actor, for Yale appeared much encouraged. As Liza watched, astounded, Yale leaned close and began to whisper intimately to Jocelin. The older man's hand slid up Jocelin's arm. A click stopped him. He went still, then spread his arms, releasing Jocelin, who stepped back and lifted the gold-engraved pistol to aim at Yale's heart.

"Well, well," Jocelin said as he glanced at the window. "What do you say now, Daddy? Kinda like having Judas for a brother, ain't it?"

Liza goggled at the two men, then yelped at the explosive roar that erupted from the duke. She lifted her skirts and ran after him as he charged back to the gun room. They arrived to find Yale still held at bay with his hands held up and his body quivering. Liza skidded to a halt upon beholding the expression in Jocelin's eyes.

"Don't," she whispered to him. "Don't kill him, please."

Jocelin seemed not to hear her, so she crept over to him and laid a hand on his arm. His lashes fluttered, but he still reamed Yale with his gaze.

At last she heard a distant murmur. "Liza?"

"Please, don't do this. If you do, I'll lose you."

The duke had been momentarily stalled by the sight of Jocelin on the point of shooting his uncle. Now he approached his son, chest swelling, collar askew and silver hair wild. "May God have mercy on your perverted soul. You're trying to twist the meaning of what just happened."

Jocelin turned a stunned glance on his father, then slowly lowered the pistol to his side. At the expression on his face, Liza slipped between her husband and his father.

"You're mad," she said to his grace. She pointed at Yale. "He's the one with the misplaced affections."

The duke rounded on her. "I saw nothing but the natural concern of an uncle for a loved nephew!"

Yale went to stand beside his brother. He gave a sigh of such patient humility that Liza wanted to punch him.

"Should I have let him have me?" Jocelin said quietly to the duke. "Then would you be convinced?"

The duke bellowed, and launched into a stream of imprecations against Jocelin.

Liza put her fists on her hips and shouted, "Shut up, you fool!"

The duke went quiet out of shock, but Jocelin intervened before Liza could attack.

"It's no use," he said to her in a dead tone. He lay the pistol on the glass top of the cabinet and turned his back. "I should have known. He chose long ago, and he didn't choose me."

"He's deliberately blind," Liza snapped.

Jocelin shook his head and sighed. "Leave it. I can't do this anymore. Leave it."

Frightened at the thin, strained quality in his voice, Liza rounded on the duke and Yale. Snatching up the pistol, she waved it at them.

"Get out." She advanced on the duke, who retreated huffily. "Don't you say a word. You get yourself and your brother on the first train to London, or this butcher's granddaughter just might slaughter herself some fresh, blueblooded pig."

She took great pleasure in watching the duke and Yale fall over each other in an undignified scramble for safety. When they were gone, she put down the pistol and approached Jocelin. He was staring out the window and had adopted his military stance, with his fist clutched at his back. She stood beside him and contemplated the lawn and the beds of irises and tulips. After a while he spoke.

"I—" He stopped to clear his throat. "I will give you an allowance. You needn't remain with me. I shan't expect it of you."

Liza clasped her hands behind her back and rocked on her heels. "I'm not going anywhere."

Jocelin's head snapped to the side, and he gave her a searing look.

"What do you mean?" he asked.

"I mean that I'm not going anywhere." She gave him a sidelong glance. "If you think I'm going to let you out of my sight when I've all those mistresses for rivals and your uncle as well, you're a fool, Jocelin Marshall."

"But you saw. You know now."

Liza shrugged. "You're an enticing person. I ought to know. So why do you expect me to be surprised and outraged just because your silly uncle finds you as fascinating as I do? Just don't expect me to share you with anyone."

He faced her and gave her a startled examination. "You're serious. Hang it if you're not serious."

"Yes." She gave a mock sigh. "I suppose I'll have to endure many years of people flirting with you, men and women."

"Don't you find it . . . dreadful?"

"What? Yale? Yale's an idiot."

Jocelin touched her arm, then hesitantly clasped her hand. "I was never—"

"I know that," Liza said. She rested her hand on his shoulder. "It happened. It's over. You don't have to tell me what happened between you and Yale. But I think I've already guessed, and you don't have to hide it from me. Like I said, Yale's an idiot, and I'll always be on your side, my love. Always."

She had controlled her own sympathy for Jocelin, knowing he would hate it. She waited for his response, hardly daring to breathe. A breeze brought the scent of cut grass wafting at them through the window. It touched her skin like invisible silk. Sunlight flooded into the room in waves of golden light. Then, when she'd almost given up hope, he began to tell her, slowly, softly.

22

Four days passed, during which Jocelin, beneath his happiness, expected Liza to turn on him without warning and look upon him with repulsion and accusatory shame. He kept mentally looking over his shoulder. She didn't turn on him.

They made love, and she remained in a state of what she called Marital Bliss. She would float up to him while he was writing to his estate manager, kiss him on the ear, and say, "I'm still in Marital Bliss." Then she would rub her hand along the inside of his thigh, and he'd forget to look over his shoulder.

Marital Bliss even survived his friends, who, with the exception of Nick, reacted to his change of conduct as if he'd contracted the grippe and would soon recover. When he forgot his political meeting with Asher and the rest at Asher's place, his old friend seemed hurt. Ten days after the confrontation at Nick's lodge, Asher, Winthrop, and Thurston-Coombes invaded.

"This won't do, old chap," Thurston-Coombes said as Jocelin handed around cups of coffee in the drawing room.

Winthrop frowned at not being served first, according to his right as a secret royal. "Indeed not."

"I'm sorry," Asher said as he stirred his coffee. "But there's to be a by-election in three months over in Hamptly-cum-Spiddow, and everyone agrees that this is my chance. I'm standing for Parliament at last, Jos."

"Disraeli will be furious," Jos said, but he lost interest when Liza appeared, her arms loaded with the post.

"Good morning, gentlemen."

He went to her at once, not caring that the others stared at him. "Shall I help you?"

"No, my lord. Most of it's for me. Toby sent a lot from Pennant's."

He stopped her by putting a finger to her lips and whispering to her. "Not here. Run along, and I'll join you when my business is done then."

Her brow wrinkled, but he only smiled at her and returned to the discussion of the by-election. An hour later he went to Liza's sitting room, where he found her submerged in correspondence. He frowned at the ledger that lay open on her writing desk. A wide sheet marked as a calendar earned an irritated flick of his finger. Liza hadn't looked up when he entered, which was contrary to her practice of hopping to her feet and flitting to him at his first appearance. When he reached her chair, he glanced at the object that had won the battle for her attention. A contract.

"That's a contract," he said. "A business contract."

Liza glanced up at him, smiled, and returned to her perusal of the document. "Only a standard one. For an engagement banquet and ball in July. The Devonshires' youngest daughter."

"I don't care if it's the queen's youngest daughter."

"Hmmm?"

He wasn't used to waiting for her attention. His greed for it allowed for no interference by boring contracts. He folded his arms across his chest. She didn't notice. He remained silent, frowning. She didn't look up. He tapped his foot. Her hand came out to pat his arm as if he were a querulous child. She was tolerating him, actually tolerating him! Still uncertain of this new love, this uncontrollable craving for her company, he grew frightened at the pain he knew he would feel if she had no time for him.

"Hang it!"

"In a moment," she said as she dipped her pen in the inkwell and signed the last page of the contract.

When she began to blot the ink instead of setting the document aside, he threw up his hands and walked away. Swinging around the desk, he planted himself opposite her and slammed his palms down on top of the letters, ledger, and calendars. His eye caught the signature on one of the letters. Brontë. He shoved it aside to glance at the address on an envelope—Barbara Leigh Smith.

Barbara Leigh Smith, the name was familiar—no, notorious. The woman had written a scandalous pamphlet attacking the legal position of married women, whose property, even to their corsets, belonged to their husbands. Suspicious, he studied the pile of correspondence, spotted a thin booklet, and fished it from beneath the clutter.

He read aloud. "'A Brief Summary, in Plain Language, of the Most Important Laws of England Concerning Women.'"

Liza glanced up from her blotting and met his gaze, which he hoped was as stern as he meant it to be. He let the pamphlet drop from his fingers, folded his arms over his chest again, and walked a path from the desk to the fireplace and back in offended meditation. She must understand how displeased he was, and never suspect how fearful of losing her to other interests.

"I thought we had reached an understanding," he said as he took up his judge's stance in front of the desk.

"About what?"

She seemed confused, and with good reason. Jocelin knew he wasn't himself or he wouldn't become jealous of books, papers, and contracts, but he couldn't seem to stop himself. Liza had gotten along so well before they met. Why would she need him, except to please her in bed, and he knew all too well how ephemeral desire could be. Damn it. He wouldn't compete with books and papers, but he'd reason with her calmly.

"Liza, sweet, you're my wife now." He gestured at the desk. "All this, this dealing in commerce can't continue. I will appoint a business manager for you."

She set the contract aside and clasped her hands on top of the desk. "Are you saying I don't know my own business?"

Women! "Of course not. But I can't have my

wife in trade. No lady concerns herself with such activities."

Her scowl alerted him to his failure. Somehow he had to convince her without showing this humiliating fear. Knowing his opponent, he changed tactics. He went to her, slipped his arm about her shoulders, and grazed his lips across her cheek. She was stiff in his arms, but she shivered, and he smiled.

"Don't you understand," he said. "I want to take care of you, protect you. I love you, and will always consider your welfare above all. You don't have to struggle anymore, Liza. I'm going to provide for you and guide you."

She turned to look at him. "Rather like an idiot child."

"Hang it!" Jocelin launched himself to his feet and stood over her. "I love you, so why do you need to involve yourself in worldly affairs?"

Liza jumped to her feet and faced him. "Is that your love? It sounds like the love of a master for a favorite hound! Well, you just change your mind about that kind of love. I won't have it. I've seen too many women raising children in poverty. They have husbands, husbands who are supposed to protect and provide for them because they're too frail to do it themselves. If they're so frail and weak-brained, why is it they can sew from morning until night, hawk vegetables all over London, scrub filthy floors and chamber pots?"

Jocelin shook his head and groaned. "You don't have to slave like that."

"No, I only have to damn myself to a life of unremitting inanity—drives in Hyde Park, morning calls, endless shopping, balls, dinner parties, picnics, more calls, more drives in Hyde Park." Liza scoured him with a glance that took in his entire body. "What you want, my lord, is a charming doll with less intelligence than a trained poodle."

Jocelin drew himself up to attention and placed his fist behind his back. "I do not! But we're going to have certain responsibilities, and eventually the reputation of the title to think of, and children." She was glaring at him, still, and he felt a surge of anger at her for evoking this new, unreasoning fear. "Or don't you feel a woman's desire for children?"

He was furious with himself as soon as he'd uttered those words, but his damned pride stopped him from saying so.

She was quiet then. Perhaps she'd seen his point. He straightened, shot his cuffs, and struggled to master his whirlwind emotions.

"If you will excuse me, my lord, I have correspondence to attend to."

He opened his eyes as wide as they would go, disbelieving what he'd heard. She was going to ignore him. Bloody hell, he'd get her attention. He turned his back to her and took a chair by the fireplace, from which he spoke quietly.

"You forget. When we married, I became the owner of Pennant's, and all your other property." He gave her desk a contemptuous glance. "Perhaps you should read your pamphlet again."

Liza marched over to him. "Now you listen to me. I don't care what the law says. Pennant's is mine, and I'm not turning myself into a poodle to gratify your pride."

He spun around to face her. "That's not what I said! God, give me patience. Women can be so obtuse. No wonder your father threw you out of his house."

Almost cringing as he realized what a stupid

thing he'd just said, Jocelin was too late to block the slap Liza delivered to his cheek. Pain and embarrassment made him lose what was left of his temper. He snatched her hand.

Lifting her, he strode into the next room and threw her on her bed. She landed on her back with her skirts over her head. To delay her, he grabbed the covers and tossed them over her. Then he rolled the bundle into a neat tube. He heard muffled imprecations and grinned as he left. Shutting the door, he turned the key in the lock and shouted at her.

"You stay there until we've both calmed down."

Liza pounded on the bedroom door.

He called to her. "You're not getting out of there until you're ready to listen to me without losing your temper."

After a while, when he refused to answer her again or let her out, she stopped. He glanced distractedly at the cluttered desk, then sat at it to pen a letter to his solicitors, asking them to arrange for Toby to be able to sign contracts and conduct legal business for Pennant's so that Liza wouldn't be burdened with so much work. Opening a drawer in search of clean paper, he came upon more correspondence from Toby. Its contents proved he'd been right to take Liza in hand. Not only had she been trying to run her agency all along, but she'd also resumed her prying into the deaths of her brother and his fellow soldiers.

Jocelin perused the summaries of the events surrounding the deaths of William Edward, Airey, Stapleton, and Halloway. Were they accidents and encounters with criminals? Shaking his head, he folded the papers and placed them in his coat pocket. He'd give them to his inquiry agent and set the man to work. Something was wrong, but he wasn't sure what it was.

Near the desk he noticed a bookshelf. As he'd thought, its contents were as unconventional as those of the desk—Brontë upon her dissatisfaction with women's lot in life, more tracts by Barbara Leigh Smith and by, of all unlikely things, a lady doctor named Elizabeth Blackwell. Replacing the Barbara Leigh Smith volume, he went downstairs to his library, where he placed Liza's murder information in an envelope, addressed it, and rang for Choke.

The butler appeared, and Jocelin handed him the envelopes for Toby and the inquiry agent. "Choke, please have these mailed."

"Yes, my lord."

"And, Choke, um, her ladyship is feeling fatigued and wishes to remain undisturbed, completely undisturbed, in her room. Please tell the staff not to go near the master suite."

"Yes, my lord."

It was a tribute to Choke's twenty years as a butler that he accepted these instructions without reaction. Jocelin watched in admiration as the butler left. If only Liza were so obedient. She wasn't though, and he couldn't suppress a slight feeling of uneasiness. He had to make her understand that her work shouldn't interfere in their life together. Why couldn't she have been a little more compliant—like his mistresses, and his mother?

Mother, now Mother was an example Liza should follow. Mother embodied all that was best in woman—modesty, delicacy, dependency, respect for her husband. He was sure Liza would never defer to him as his mother did to his father. Would it do any good to recommend his mother to Liza as a model of

propriety? Through all his battles with his family,
Mother had remained a solace to him.

True, she had been unable to stand against his
father. That day he'd first tried to tell his parents
about Yale, Father hadn't believed him, and he'd
pleaded with his mother for help. But it wasn't her
fault that she couldn't take his side. She, who was so
delicate and frail, couldn't be expected to fight against
the duke. However, Mother's good breeding and her
duty would urge her to take Liza in hand.

But first he must come to a rapprochement with
Father. He'd been a fool to expect the old buster to
face the truth after all these years. Jocelin went to his
desk and took up his pen. If Father wanted an heir,
and Father desired a grandson above anything, he
would have to apologize to Liza and make amends.
He began to smile as his pen scratched across a piece
of stationery embossed with his crest. He was going to
enjoy making Father writhe, and writhe he would at
the prospect of taking to his bosom the granddaughter
of a butcher and introducing her to Society. Jocelin
laughed aloud. Father was going to piss bullets.

He finished his letter quickly and went riding.
Remaining in the house with Liza locked upstairs sat
ill with him. He visited Asher, then Nick, whom he
brought back for dinner. Cards and conversation allowed him to forget his quarrel with his wife so that it
was well past midnight before he took a tray of hot tea
up to Liza's bedroom.

Setting the tray aside, he turned the key. As he
did so, he heard weeping. He swallowed against
the thickening in his throat. Had he been too harsh?
She did love him, the misguided little midge. He
knew it now, and relished the near worship with which
she gazed at him. Still, he had to come to some kind

of agreement with her. Straightening his shoulders, he put a fist behind his back and entered.

The room was dark except for light from a candelabra beside the bed. He walked over to the heap of skirts and petticoats on the bed and watched Liza's shoulders heave. He clenched his jaw, then touched her arm. She sucked in her breath and turned over, still sobbing. Holding himself back through great effort, he was unprepared when she cast herself into his arms and wailed into his lapel. He wrapped his arms around her and squeezed, pressing her close. Burying his face in her tousled hair, he murmured endearments.

In between sobs, she stuttered, "I h-hate it when we quarrel."

"It's all right," he said as he kissed her hair. "We don't have to fight anymore. We'll talk later, when you're not so distressed, my love."

"I'm s-sorry I slapped you. Do you hate me?"

"Never, my love."

He stroked her hair and smiled. That was his Liza, a termagant on the surface, and a noodle beneath. He cradled her in his arms while she wept, then held her while she fell asleep. She was exhausted, but he felt sure she would be more reasonable now that she'd learned the limits of his patience. She would listen to him, now, and he wouldn't have to reveal his fear of losing her.

The night passed quickly for him. He spent it beside Liza, not having bothered to return to his own room to change. The next morning she was still asleep when he woke. Not wanting to disturb her, he went to his own rooms. He washed and dressed, and had breakfast.

Eager to see Liza, but unwilling to interfere with

her rest, he decided to collect Nick and go for a long ride about the estate. Nick was willing, since he'd just purchased a new Thoroughbred and was eager to test the animal. They galloped across meadows and jumped ditches until they came to Jocelin's favorite path through his preserve of woodland. By late afternoon they were riding through a coppice of hornbeam, alder, hazel, and chestnuts.

Nick pulled alongside him and patted the neck of his roan stallion. "You're in a much better humor. Yesterday you looked like Oberon after a fight with Titania."

"Oh, God, you've been reading *A Midsummer Night's Dream*."

Nick grinned devilishly at him, put a hand to his breast, and recited as they rode beneath the branches of a hornbeam.

> *"I know a bank where the wild thyme blows,*
> *Where oxlips and the nodding violet grows,*
> *Quite overcanopied with luscious woodbine,*
> *With sweet musk roses, and with eglantine.*
> *There sleeps Titania sometime of the night,*
> *Lulled in these flowers with dances and*
>   *delight."*

Jocelin clapped a hand over one ear, but Nick pulled it away and raised his voice to declaim with fervid drama:

> *"And there the snake throws her enameled skin,*
> *Weed wide enough to wrap a fairy in.*
> *And with the juice of this I'll streak her*
>   *eyes,*
> *And make her full of hateful fantasies."*

Jocelin rolled his eyes. "Are you finished?"

"What's the matter, old love, your Titania giving you a hard chase?"

"Oh, we had a little quarrel, you might say, but it's over now."

"You apologized, did you, old chap? It's the only way with women."

"Of course I didn't apologize. She did."

Nick raised his brows and pulled up on his reins so that his mount halted. "Liza? Liza apologized? What for?"

"Oh, for losing her temper and quarreling with me." Jocelin gave his friend a placid smile. "It's over though. She said she hates quarreling with me, so I expect she'll be more amenable to handing Pennant's over to a manager now and not working herself so hard. I was quite firm, so she understood how it's to be between us."

"She did, did she? This is Liza Elliot that we're talking about?"

"What do you mean?"

Nick propped his forearms on his saddle and shook his head at Jocelin. "She's just going to abandon Pennant's completely? You're not describing the Liza I know."

"Perhaps not completely, but she's changed. She loves me."

"How do you know she's changed?"

"I told you. Last night when I went to unlock her door, she threw herself into my arms and told me how sorry she was."

"Let me understand this, old dear. You locked Liza Elliot in her room like a naughty tyke. You told her not to bother with her beloved Pennant's and lectured her on how much smarter you are than she.

And she let you? And she begged pardon for her naughtiness?"

Jocelin frowned and stroked his hunter's mane. "Now that you say it like that, she never really said she would do as I asked."

"Damned cert, old love."

"She never has before, given in easily, that is."

"You know what," Nick said as he contemplated a spray of violets nearby. "I'd be worried if I were you."

"I'm starting to be."

They stared at the violets in silence.

"Nick."

"Yes, dear Oberon."

"I think I'll go home."

"Good plan."

Jocelin wheeled his horse about, and Nick followed. They galloped most of the way. Careening across the lawn, Jocelin nearly climbed the front steps with his hunter. Dismounting before the animal came to a complete stop, he threw his reins at Nick and dashed inside. He ran into Loveday on the stairs. The valet handed him an envelope.

"I just found this lying upon our silk neckties, my lord." Loveday exited swiftly.

As Nick clattered up the stairs to stand beside him, Jocelin tore open the envelope and read the enclosed note.

My lord,

I won't endure a master. You don't want me unless I'm a slave. I have a life to lead, and I'll grieve until I die that I couldn't lead it with you.

Liza.

Jocelin crumpled the note in his fist and stared through Nick without seeing him. Nick took the note, read it, and whistled.

"Now, that's Liza."

"Bloody hell," Jocelin said.

"Where is she?"

"Gone. Don't bother to look for her." Jocelin looked down at the crumpled note. "She disappeared on me once before. She's good at it."

"What are you going to do?"

Jocelin gave Nick a pained smile. "Find her, of course."

"How?"

"I don't know, Nick old man, because this time she'll be much more careful than the last."

23

Liza set the last boot next to its mate on the shelf and stored the polish and cloths away in a wooden box. She wished she could put away her unhappiness as easily. Standing, she pressed the small of her back and rubbed polish on the tip of her nose with her forefinger. Damn, no time to wash, for she had to clean the front steps and then finish the hearth in Lord Winthrop's study before he came downstairs this morning.

Gathering her rags and buckets, Liza scurried upstairs, into the foyer, and onto the threshold. It had rained yesterday, and the sill, steps, and boot scraper all wore jackets of mud. As she scraped clumps into a bucket, Liza chewed her lip and tried not to think

about Jocelin. Why did he have to be so unbending?
No—no use in treading that well-worn footpath.

She had fled Reverie because he left her no
choice. She could no more give up her principles than
she could spend her life standing on her head, which
was what Jocelin wanted her to do. So she'd left, taken
refuge with Toby's Betty, and grieved. Leaving Jocelin
had cost her. At first she felt as if she didn't want to
live. Each night she stayed awake as long as she could
so she'd be too exhausted to dream of him.

She vacillated between hating him and wishing he
would come after her. When she was in her office, she
imagined him bursting in on her again, all glowering
male fury. He was so enthralling when aroused. Then
she would remember how he discounted her beliefs and
her principles, and got angry all over again. Then she
plunged into work to forget.

After a few days, however, she needed better
distraction. There was still the matter of William
Edward's murder. She'd never given up searching for
an answer to that mystery. Despondent but resolute,
she had taken a place in Arthur Thurston-Coombes's
house. An excellent start, for she soon found that the
young man had been with his mistress at the time
William Edward died.

This news allowed her to move on to Lord
Winthrop's household at the height of the season.
June was new when she took a place there in her
disguise as a maid of all work. Winthrop was a surprise.
Although the owner of a large income, he kept a
sparse staff and watched every expense, down to the
number of coals in each fireplace. He also had a
disturbing fondness for watching her do chores. Not
making beds or dusting, but the dirtiest chores, such
as cleaning the stoop or the hearths.

She was wiping the steps with a cloth after washing them when a carriage pulled up. Hurrying to finish, she picked up her rags and brushes and tossed them into an empty bucket. She spied a stray dust pan on the top step, reached across, and retrieved it as two pairs of polished boots ascended the stairs. She drew back, then paused as she heard a clipped, military order given to the coachman. Jocelin! She was kneeling on the front steps, and Jocelin had come to call.

Her hair was concealed beneath a frizzy brown wig, but it wouldn't be enough if he got a good look at her. Liza picked up her brushes and buckets, held them high so that they hid her face, and curtsied as the two men entered the house. Turning, she went down the steps, but she didn't breathe until the footman closed the door.

"The coffee!"

She scurried around to the tradesmen's entrance and discarded her cleaning materials. Rushing to a sink, she cleaned face and hands while the cook and scullery rushed to prepare refreshments for his lordship's callers. Liza bounded up three flights of stairs before she could be ordered to perform more tasks. In her room she applied a fresh coat of paste that darkened her skin, drew her eyebrows heavier, and tightened her corset. She had padded herself at her chest and hips so that she appeared to have a figure of Venusian proportions.

Racing back to the kitchen, she was just in time to carry the tray of coffee and scones up to his lordship's study. Praying that her disguise would deceive Jocelin, she went in and deposited the tray on a table. Asher Fox, Jocelin, and Winthrop were engaged in a discussion regarding the lingering war in the Crimea and took no notice of her entrance.

Keeping her face averted from her husband, she prayed that Winthrop would act as host rather than make her hand the cups and saucers around. He did, and she stood near the door awaiting a dismissal. Jocelin's back was to her, that wide-shouldered, parade ground posture revealing no clue as to whether he'd recognized her. As Winthrop handed around scones, she slipped out of the room.

A little over an hour later the butler found her in the scullery and ordered her to resume cleaning the hearths in the study and parlor. Liza closed her eyes and said a quick prayer. Jocelin and Asher must have left.

She gathered her brushes and pans and the coal scuttle and went to the study. She opened the door, but Winthrop was still there.

"Oh, don't go away," he said from his perch behind his desk. "Clean, girl, clean."

While he wrote a letter, she began scooping ashes. Her nose tickled, and she rubbed it.

"Now there's a spot on your nose, my dear."

Liza turned to find Lord Winthrop standing beside her. She patted her nose. Winthrop stuck out his boot and examined it.

"I seem to have a bit of dust on my boot. Please use your rag on it."

She brushed nonexistent dust from the shoe and started when Winthrop bent and touched her arm. She'd rolled up her sleeves before beginning the dirty job. He rubbed a spot on her wrist where ashes had fallen.

"Here you are," he said as though savoring a pastry. "Here you are, all in your dirt, come to serve me so humbly."

Liza pulled her wrist away, but Winthrop was on her, slobbering a wet kiss on her neck.

"Quit that!"

She shoved at him, but he buried his face in her false bosom. Disgusted, Liza grabbed a handful of hair and yanked. Winthrop squawked and fell back on his semiroyal bottom. Liza picked up her dust pan and crashed it down on his head. As she hit him, someone chuckled, and it wasn't Winthrop. His lordship yelped, and Liza hopped to her feet as Jocelin crossed the study threshold.

He kept coming, and she took refuge behind Winthrop's desk. While Winthrop groaned, Jocelin stalked her.

She tried courtesy. "Good morning, my lord."

"I've been looking for you." He lunged for her, missed, and circled the desk when she did.

"Really?"

"I sent inquiry agents to Pennant's. I threatened Toby. I had him followed."

Liza dodged an armchair and skipped around the desk again as Jocelin came at her.

"There's no need for this," she said.

"She's a trollop!" Winthrop had regained his senses, what there was of them.

"Shut up," Jocelin said. "This is my wife."

Winthrop goggled at them, but Liza came to an abrupt stop.

"Jocelin, don't!"

"Whyever not? You don't seem to care about your reputation, your station as my wife, your own safety." He leaped at her, snagged her arm, and lifted her in the air.

"You've told him who I am, damn you." Liza pounded once at his chest.

"Your wife?" Winthrop had risen and was massaging his head. "What's your wife doing masquerading as a maid of all work? I've never heard of such conduct."

Jocelin headed for the door with Liza in his arms. "Oh, don't worry about it. She's says that the officers in our old regiment are being killed off. She may be right, but I'll not have her trying to prove it in this manner. And by the way, old dear, if you ever touch her again, I'll drown you in your own royal blood."

Liza squirmed and twisted, furious at her inability to free herself. As she was carried out of the house, her wig came askew, then fell off her head onto the front steps. Jocelin kicked it out of the way and tossed her into the carriage. Liza landed on someone, who picked her up and set her beside Jocelin.

Asher Fox recovered his walking stick from the floor of the vehicle. "I say, Jos, you were right. It is your lady."

Jocelin shook a finger at Liza. "You be quiet."

Liza opened her mouth. Jocelin gave her a furious look, and she shut her mouth.

"I told you," Jocelin said to his friend with a grin of triumph. "It took me weeks of searching until I realized that she wouldn't hide in the country or on the Continent. The stubborn little widgeon can't give up on an idea once she's latched on to it. She's been spying on Winthrop, who is the one she most suspects. Ouch! Hang it, Liza."

Jocelin rubbed his ribs where Liza had elbowed him. She glared at him, so furious that she couldn't trust herself to speak. She folded her arms, whipped her body around, and stared straight ahead for the rest of the drive to Jocelin's house.

Asher continued in the carriage, while Liza was

tugged inside like a runaway urchin. In the marble hall, she got tired of being herded, set her feet, and halted. Jocelin stumbled, then turned and growled at her.

"You need a good thrashing. Don't tempt me."

"You're a self-satisfied fool," Liza said as she yanked her hand free of his grasp. "You've just blurted out my suspicions to the man I've begun to suspect of murder."

She might have held her temper if he hadn't laughed at her.

"Old Winthrop? To kill anyone would be beneath his royal dignity."

Smiling, Liza approached him while he laughed. "Do you know what you are?"

She flicked the end of his nose gently with a forefinger. Jocelin blinked. Then his jaw sank as he stared at her.

"You're a conceited bigot."

Sidestepping his stunned figure, Liza headed for the door. She wasn't quick enough. A roar echoed off the marble floor and columns. She sprang for freedom, but he lunged at her, encircled her waist, and lifted her. She sailed over his shoulder. Air rushed from her lungs as she was jounced upstairs. He plopped her down on a bed, and she rolled in time to escape Jocelin's descending body.

"Liza, you come back here and talk to me," he said on a note of controlled irritation.

Springing from the bed, she raced into Jocelin's sitting room. He caught up with her before she was halfway across the carpet. His arms dropped lightly around her, pinning her against his chest with her back to him. Then she felt something soft on her neck. His lips. The bastard. Kissing her when she was so furious with him. She was about to snarl at him when someone knocked on the door.

Jocelin lifted his mouth from her neck. "Go away."

Nick Ross came in anyway. He sauntered over to them, his gaze taking in Liza's disheveled and humble garb and Jocelin's determined face.

"So," he said, "you've found her. Knew you would, love. A fellow never misplaces a wife for long. But you're still playing Oberon and Titania, I see."

"Get out," Jocelin said between his teeth.

"Shall I play Puck or Bottom?"

"I said, go away. I'm taming a shrew, not wooing a faerie queen."

"Ah," Nick said. "'Such duty as the subject owes the prince, / Even such a woman oweth to her husband.'"

Liza wriggled in Jocelin's arms. "I oweth him not a damned thing!"

"Silly woman," Jocelin said. He glanced at Nick. "She loves me, you know.

At the complacent tone in his voice, Liza lost all forbearance. She dropped down through Jocelin's encircling arms, dodged him as he grabbed for her, and sprang away from him. However, Nick's hand darted out and caught hers.

"Sorry, me lady. Old Jos would never forgive me if I let you scarper."

Jocelin walked over to her. Liza shrank from him at the sight of his determined solemnity.

"Now, Jos," Nick said. "You just hold on." He stepped between them.

"Get out of the way."

"Not until you listen."

"She's my wife." Jocelin tried to step around Nick, who moved to bar his way again.

"Do you want to keep her this time?"

No answer.

"Do you?"

Liza looked over Nick's shoulder and saw Jocelin give his friend a curt nod.

"Last time she ran away, it took you weeks to find her. This time, you may not find her at all. She don't have to stay in England, old love. She's got pluck enough to go just about anywhere if you drive her to it."

Jocelin tossed his head. "I won't let her. Eventually she'll have to listen to me."

"What are you going to do? Lock her up until she's too old and ridden with gout to run away?"

"Well, no." Jocelin appeared to lapse into thought.

Nick turned to Liza. "And what are you about, miss? Going to spend your days hiding from him?"

"He treats me like a spaniel." Liza sighed and pushed locks of hair back from her face with her free hand. "He won't listen to me. He thinks the moment I became his wife I lost what little intelligence he ever credited me with having."

"I do not." Jocelin threw up his hands. "She spends too much time dealing with that domestic agency, and now she's skulking about my friends' houses in disguise. Ladies shouldn't do such things and, hang it, she could be in danger."

"My lord."

They all turned to find Loveday hovering nearby.

"Mr. Fox has called again, my lord. Shall I send him up?"

"Oh, why not. Most of London's here anyway." Jocelin said in disgust. He pointed to a chair and snapped at Liza. "You sit down and don't think of running away. I'll catch you before you reach the hall."

Nick released her, but Liza only stared at her husband.

"Sit down!"

Nick intervened before Jocelin reached her. Taking her hand, he kissed it.

"My lady, may I offer you a chair?"

Liza left off glaring at Jocelin, gave Nick a sweet, compliant smile, and allowed him to escort her to the chair. Jocelin cursed, but was interrupted by Asher Fox.

He came in, his collar askew, his face drawn, and went directly to Jocelin. "May I speak with you privately?"

"What's wrong?" Jocelin asked.

"I—I can't. Not in front of others."

Asher put his lips near Jocelin's ear. Liza strained to hear what he was saying. She thought she heard the name Yale, but could make out nothing else. Jocelin said nothing in response, but she could see him withdraw into himself.

"Nick, watch her."

"What's wrong?" Liza asked as he walked out of the room, followed by Asher.

He called over his shoulder. "You'd better be here when I return."

She leaped from her chair, intent on pursuing him, but Nick stopped her by closing the door and locking it. He slipped the key into his vest pocket.

"Sorry, old girl."

"Something's wrong. Please, Nick."

"Jos will take care of whatever's wrong."

"You don't understand, I heard Mr. Fox say something important."

Nick shrugged. "I got my orders."

"Oooo! You men, you're all in a plot to drive women mad." Liza went to him and plucked at his lapel. "I heard him say something about Jocelin's family."

"Maybe. Jos is still furious about—something that happened a long time ago."

"You know about that?" Liza gaped at Nick.

Nick gaped back at her. "Bloody hell, you know?"

She nodded her head violently.

Cursing, Nick whirled away from her. "That's why you left then."

"Of course not. What a silly thing to say."

Slowly, as though he couldn't believe what he'd heard, Nick turned around. "Bloody hell, you're a right one, you are. A peach."

"Never mind," Liza said. "Asher said something about Yale. Nick, if Jocelin has to face Yale again, I don't think he'll be able to control himself."

"Bloody hell." Nick found the key and unlocked the door. "Come on, before they get too far ahead."

They plunged downstairs. Nick shouted for Choke, who appeared, startled and scandalized, but ignorant of Jocelin's destination. Liza wasted no time on the man, and called for Loveday. The valet appeared from behind the servants' door.

In response to Liza's question, he nodded. "Yes, my lady. His lordship mentioned Lord Yale. Perhaps he's gone to Grosvenor Square."

She and Nick bolted for his carriage, and they clattered out of the drive as the sun reached its apex in the sky. Their appearance at the duke's residence rivaled that of a cyclone. Liza burst out of the still-rolling vehicle with Nick in pursuit. They crashed through the brass and cut glass doors, past an outraged butler and parlor maid.

Nick passed Liza on their dash for the drawing room, where they burst upon his grace, the duchess, and a young lady. Liza rushed up to the duke, panting.

"Jocelin, where is he?"

The duke rose and waved away his butler and two footmen who had chased after the intruders. He looked down his nose at Liza.

"Miss Elliot? Is that you?"

"Lady Radcliffe," Nick said, "and you know it."

Liza had no time for pettiness. "Where is Jocelin?"

"Young woman, I haven't seen my son since he staged that disgraceful scene with his uncle."

"Then he hasn't been here?"

"No. Will you please leave?"

Ignoring him, Liza turned to Nick. "Then where can he have gone?"

"He must be searching for Yale," Nick said.

"Nonsense. Jocelin detests poor Yale and refuses to see him unless forced," the duke said. "And in any case, my brother is at his club in Symmonds Street, not here."

They chased through midday traffic in the heart of London. Careening down the Strand, they were delayed by an overturned omnibus and arrived in Symmonds Street too late. Nick inquired within the club, for ladies weren't allowed. Liza waited in a fidgety state until Nick returned to the carriage. Yale had left over an hour ago. Jocelin and Asher had called for him, then left abruptly when it became apparent that no one at the club knew his destination.

"I'm worried," she said as she twisted her hands in her lap. "You didn't see Jocelin with his uncle."

"I don't have to."

Nick was drumming his fingers on the carriage window. The drumming slowed, then stopped. "Wait."

"What?"

"Now wait a minute." Nick began to tap out a rhythm again. "Jocelin has Yale followed. Constantly. Has for years. To make sure like."

"But then why would Asher—

"Old Asher's never concerned himself too close with Yale's doings."

Liza grabbed Nick's arm. "Dear God in heaven. It's not Yale at all. Asher heard about my spying. Jocelin told him my idea about the murders."

"Bloody hell."

Shaking Nick's arm, Liza hissed at him. "It's Asher, and he has Jocelin."

24

As the carriage left White-chapel Road and turned north into Spitalfields, Jocelin touched the ivory handle of his Colt. He'd stuffed it into his waistband as he left the house with Asher.

They passed block after block of dirty brick and clapboard structures that looked worse in the afternoon sunlight than in gloom. Refuse hugged the bases of buildings. Broken drains emitted their nauseating perfume, and the streets grew more and more narrow until the buildings on either side seemed to bend toward each other. Dirty, vacant windows stared down at him.

A match vendor scuffled alongside the carriage as it stopped for a water wagon. Shoeless and dirty children pounded on the carriage and ran off laughing.

The carriage turned a corner out of the bustle of foot and vehicle traffic and stopped at the corner of Little Thyme Hill and Liverpool Lane. Asher started to get out, but Jocelin put an arm across the door.

"Are you sure the boy said Spitalfields? This corner?"

"Of course. Do you think I could mistake Spitalfields?"

They got out, and Jocelin waited while Asher paid the driver to wait for them. He glanced at the red brick wall behind him. Its surface was layered with a century's worth of advertisements—notices of theater performances, livestock sales, tobacco for sale. He glanced down Little Thyme Hill past row after row of blank-faced houses. The breeze shifted, and he smelled the sweet, heavy scent of opium.

"I don't understand it," he said when Asher finished with the driver. "Why would Mott send a boy with a message about Yale to you?"

"Think," Asher said as he surveyed their unhealthy surroundings. "I was coming up the steps to your house, and the boy thought I was you. Obviously your man hadn't described you to him."

Jocelin examined the mews and storehouses on Liverpool Lane. "It's not like Yale to come to an area like this."

"Jos, look."

Asher pointed down Little Thyme Hill. "Blast it, he's gone down that alley. Come on."

Without waiting for Jocelin, Asher plunged down the street. Jocelin chased after him, turned a corner, and found himself in an alley faced with boarded windows and locked doors. At the end an intersection was partly blocked by a high fence. Asher was just disappearing around the fence.

"Ash, wait."

Jocelin raced after his friend. Squeezing between a wall and the fence, he emerged in a court littered with old grain bags, bits of muddy clothing, and broken barrels. There was only one way out, through a door in the face of a building Jocelin knew better than to enter. Unfortunately he saw Asher go through it and into a dark passage.

Now wasn't the time to call out. The fool had blundered into one of the rookeries. Inhabited entirely by criminals, these labyrinths sheltered London's most dangerous inhabitants. Creative murderers and thieves had cut holes into walls and ceilings, cellars and roofs so that a man could disappear into the maze and never be found. Jocelin drew his Colt, crept up to the door, and listened.

At first he heard nothing. Then came footsteps toward him, and Asher's voice.

"Come on. Mott's in here."

Colt first, Jocelin stepped into the darkness. He could see a vague shadow that must be Asher and went toward it, furious with his friend for disregarding their safety. He opened his mouth to deliver a lecture, but pain exploded at the back of his head. He dropped to his knees, his world shrinking to the agony in his skull. Darkness became a spinning vertigo, then nothing at all.

He woke sick to his stomach and moaning with the pain in his head. His face was buried in a pallet stuffed with moldy straw. He tasted bile and smelled a sickly sweet odor. Opium.

Instinct held him in his position on his stomach. Through his lashes he tried to examine his surroundings.

All he could see was a lighted lamp with a blackened glass on the floor and a large, empty crate. He was in a room bare of any other furnishings, and he was alone.

Unfortunately he was also bound. Rope encircled his wrists behind him, and tied his ankles as well. Since he had little feeling in either hands or feet, he must have been in this position for some time. Gradually, by working his hands and feet, he forced sensation back into them. Then he tried to sit up. As he turned on his side, he heard footsteps, and Asher came into the room. Behind him he dragged a girl with hair dyed greenish blond. She giggled and swayed as he tugged her into the room.

Tottering toward Jocelin, she snorted and fell in a heap beside the pallet. He got a whiff of unwashed body and cheap perfume as she patted his cheek.

"You were right, luv," she said in a gurgling voice. "He don't want to do it. Cheer up, luv. We'll soon have you stiff and ready, we will."

"Ash," Jocelin said as he looked from the girl to his friend. "Ash, what are you doing?"

"Here you are," Asher said to the girl as he held out a brown glass bottle. "Have some more before we start."

The girl snatched the bottle from Asher and downed its contents.

"You're a right gentleman, you are." She let the bottle fall, crawled away to prop herself against the opposite wall, and grinned at them.

Jocelin tried again as they both regarded the girl. "What are you doing?"

"Doing?" Asher appeared to be concentrating on something else. "Oh, doing. You're going to kill yourself, of course. After giving this poor lady too much brandy to drink. Too much alcohol in the blood, you see. Remorse, self-blame, too much for you."

Jocelin gaped at his friend, then shook his head slowly. "No. No, it's not you. You didn't do all those murders. You couldn't. It's not you. I don't want it to be you. Damn you, Ash. Damn you."

Asher wasn't listening. He knelt beside Jocelin and tested his bonds. Then he sat back on his heels and rubbed his face over and over, as if he couldn't wake from some nightmare.

"Ash, let me go."

Hands over his face, Asher didn't respond. Jocelin said his name again, but all he got was a low, whimpering moan, rather like that of a hungry wolf cub. The whimpering sent a sensation up Jocelin's arms and back that felt rather like roaches scurrying for their nest. Then the whimpering stopped suddenly, choked off on what sounded like a growl. The hands lowered, and Jocelin stared into agony.

"What's wrong?" he asked. "Ash, untie me."

Asher shook his head. "Ohhhh, God, why did it have to be you? Sooner or later you would have listened to Liza."

Without warning Asher leaped up and fetched a coil of rope from outside the door. When he returned, he was panting and his gaze was fixed on the rope. He slung it over an exposed roof beam and, with shaking hands, looped it into a noose. He disappeared through the door with the other end of the rope, evidently to tie it off. Returning, he knelt by Jocelin again. As Asher lifted him to a sitting position, Jocelin tried again to force a response.

"Damn you, answer me!"

Asher lifted Jocelin to a standing position and leaned him against a wall. He shoved the crate beneath the noose, then returned to Jocelin. As he reached out, Jocelin flung himself out of reach and toppled to the floor again. His head almost burst open, or so it seemed, from the pain. He lay gasping until Asher turned him over on his back. A hand gently brushed hair from his eyes. He was breathing rapidly, trying to fight the pain while Asher stroked his hair and rested a palm against his cheek.

"I'm sorry. It's the beast. He smelled the danger."

Jocelin bit his lip and remained quiet. At last he was able to open his eyes and gaze up at Asher.

"If only you'd stopped remembering," Asher said. "If only you hadn't married that little drudge. Unnatural, prying little beast, if she hadn't spouted suspicions and disturbed your memory . . . but you would have listened to her sooner or later, so now I must let the beast loose."

"God, Ash, what have you done?"

Asher crouched beside Jocelin, his hand gently stroking his friend's hair, and began to weep. "I lost my horse at Balaklava, and I took Cheshire's. I, who came from generations of military heroes, I ran, and I took another man's horse. There was so much confusion, I didn't think anyone saw except you, and you were wounded and sick. But then Pawkins said something, and I had to kill him, or everyone would know. I couldn't bear the disgrace."

"Oh, no." Jocelin clenched his teeth against the horror of what he was hearing. Asher kept stroking his hair. "How many? Cheshire, Pawkins, Airey, Elliot?"

Asher sobbed and lifted Jocelin so that he was resting against his lap. He rocked back and forth, head bent over his prisoner, weeping.

"You don't know what it was like. My great-grandfather, my grandfather, my father, all heroes in the regiment—ancestor after ancestor, I could tell you about each one—Waterloo, Italy, France, America. They triumphed everywhere, until me."

"Ash, listen to me." All he heard was weeping. Closing his mind to the utter madness, he shoved his shoulder into Asher's chest. "Ash!"

The weeping stopped abruptly. Jocelin felt a hand pat his face.

"I'm sorry."

Jocelin cursed when Asher lifted him again and dragged him to the crate. The noose dropped over his head, and Asher tightened it.

"You don't want to do this." He dared not throw himself from the crate and tighten the noose.

With unexpected strength Asher hauled Jocelin to a standing position on the crate. There was barely room for both of them to stand. Jocelin swayed, but Asher steadied him and further tightened the rope around his neck.

Jocelin had to make Asher look at him, listen to him. "Don't. I won't tell anyone. You're my closest friend."

"No, not since that Ross fellow came."

Asher pulled Jocelin's collar free of the rope so that the noose bit into bare flesh.

Jocelin strained to lower his head and caught Asher's gaze. "You can't kill me. If you could, you would have at Scutari."

Tears flooding, Asher threw his arms around Jocelin and hugged him.

"Untie me, Ash."

With a groaning wail Asher thrust himself off the crate and put his shoulder to it.

Jocelin cried out as the box shifted. Still weeping, Asher heaved against the crate again, and it creaked and scraped a few inches. Boots slipping, his throat on fire, Jocelin choked and tried to get his balance. He slipped again as Asher gave another shove, accompanied by a cry of grief and desperation. Jocelin's lungs caught fire, and his head erupted in agony again.

He heard another cry, but the crate didn't move. Something wrapped around his legs at the same time that he heard Asher's enraged scream. The crate moved back under his feet. He heard a shot, and a crash, as someone appeared in front of him. Vision blurred, all he could see was a pair of hands reaching for his neck. The noose came free, and he toppled off the crate to the floor.

Someone cried out his name, but he was engaged in a monumental effort to breathe. Dizziness assaulted him, and his awareness faded. When he opened his eyes, Liza and Nick were bending over him, frowning. He scowled and railed at them hoarsely.

"Bleeding hell, Liza, what are you doing—ah-hum—doing here?" He winced. Then his eyes flew open again. "Asher."

Nick helped him sit. Asher was lying on his back, bleeding from a hole in his chest. Bending over him was a Metropolitan policeman, the brass buttons of his coat gleaming dully in the lamplight.

"Gone, sir. He just shouldn't of pulled that revolver. Mr. Ross had no choice."

Jocelin stared at the body of his friend as Liza slipped her hand in his.

"I'm sorry," she said. "He wouldn't stop. It was horrible. He was growling like some kind of animal. I'm so sorry, my love."

As Nick spoke quietly with the policeman, Jocelin continued to stare at Asher's body.

"You were right all along," he said to her. The

thing that had tried to kill him hadn't been Ash. He winced and turned his face away from the body. The room seemed to tilt and grow colder as he remembered how his friend had transformed into a beast of grunts and howls. Asher seemed to have split into man and animal. The man part had contained his friend, the one who had saved him from Yale all those years ago. The animal? Who knew what abuse and idiosyncracies of nature had produced Ash's ability to transform into that creature?

All along, Ash had stalked them all, from within the close-knit circle of their friends. Ash, who had been a bulwark, more than a brother, had twisted and fermented and putrefied without Jocelin's ever knowing. His senses were reeling with the effort to reconcile the ravening beast with his friend Ash. And Liza, Liza had been steadfast in her insistence upon the existence of a murderer. But even she hadn't guessed at the atrocity they'd found.

He should have taken her more seriously. She deserved that, and she deserved his respect. She sat beside him. He sighed and took her hand.

Without warning Liza threw herself into his arms and began to cry. Bewildered, he ignored his aching head and held her tightly.

"I thought you'd be killed," she said between sobs.

"Near enough."

"We went to your father's house, and to Yale's club. We searched the streets until we found a hack driver who said he'd seen you, and then we set off in the direction you'd gone. It took us hours, but Nick found your hired carriage. He'd given up on waiting for you and was heading back to the West End."

He rubbed his temples, then began patting her trembling back as she continued.

"I can't believe it. I've been looking for a murderer all along, but now that I've found him . . . Poor, poor William Edward." She lifted her wet face to stare into his eyes. "It won't bring him back. God in heaven, it won't bring him back."

She ended on a wailing sob. Her head dropped to his shoulder, and Jocelin wrapped his arms more tightly around her as she cried. Suddenly he leaned his head back carefully against the wall while his vision blurred. "Liza, thank you for saving me, and I regret that I'm in no shape to give you proper comfort. But I seem to have a bitch of a headache."

He tried to stay awake to hear her reply, but somehow he sank into a state of confused half sleep. He roused briefly when Nick lifted him, then roused again as he was being put into a carriage. The next moment of awareness came when he woke in his own room.

He was lying on his side. Opening his eyes, he saw silvery gray damask and sunlight. Something was weighing down his legs. He moved, and looked down to find Liza half lying on top of the covers, still in her maid's gown. He sat up slowly, grateful that his head only throbbed a little. He frowned at the sight of Liza's apron and work-roughened hands, then fell to studying her mussed hair and augmented curves.

A sigh escaped him. He'd already lost the battle to remain stern and authoritarian. After all, she'd saved his life, along with Nick. He would have to persuade her into good behavior somehow.

Then there was Asher.

He still couldn't reconcile the animal with the friend. He had waking dreams in which Ash's eyes appeared, disembodied, in front of him. In his vision they gazed at him without recognition with a reptilian mercilessness, predatory, without a trace of humanity. He would never know exactly what had turned Ash into that. What unbearable atrocities had been committed upon him that would create such a beast within a good man, a beast that could be called up by fear of death, fear of shame.

While bathing and dressing, Jocelin finally gave up trying to understand the sickness in Asher only to remember Liza. She'd saved his life. Dear, stubborn Liza of the rustling petticoats and lemon scent. He could see now that his fears regarding her business dealings hadn't been warranted. At least, he thought so. Loveday told him she'd remained awake at his side through the night. She was asleep on his bed now.

Policemen came, spent hours taking evidence from him about Asher's death, and left. Nick called to assure himself of Jocelin's health. Then, to his great misfortune, his family came. He was resting on the sofa in the library with a pot of coffee at his side when his father, mother, and sister invaded. Georgiana and the duchess fussed over him while his father demanded a complete account of Jocelin's calamity.

As Jocelin finished his story, Liza came into the room, the picture of Society in blue-green foulard silk that billowed about her as she walked. He blinked at the change from maid of all work to viscount's lady. She curtsied gracefully to his parents as he presented her, and gave his sister an uncertain smile. They spent an uncomfortable half hour in meaningless conversation. His mother eyed Liza as if she expected her to chew tobacco or belch.

"Well," his father said, breaking into Jocelin's reverie, "all this time you've harped about some unfortunate misunderstanding with Yale, when all along your closest friend was a blasted murderer."

His head began to throb. "Go away, Father."

"What?" the duke barked.

He thrust up from the couch to shout in his father's face. "I said go away!"

Body trembling with the effort not to punch the duke in the nose, Jocelin stuck a fist behind his back, turned on his heel, and walked to the fireplace mantel. He kept his back to the room, but he didn't have to face it to know how his father behaved. There was a long silence, during which he was certain his father mastered his temper. It wouldn't do for a duke to disgrace himself a second time before the granddaughter of a butcher. Jocelin could see Liza out of the corner of his eye. She was staring at his father with a little, well-bred sneer on her face that made her look as if she'd just smelled horse dung on someone's boots.

Jocelin heard Georgiana persuade the duke out of the room. The knot between his shoulders unsnarled a bit, but his head ached and he couldn't seemed to keep images of Ash and Yale from darting at him in his imagination. He needed to talk to Liza. Talking to Liza always brought peace, or at least relief.

"Jocelin." His mother approached, her voice lowered as she glanced at the closed door through which her husband had gone. "Jocelin, you really must learn not to confront your father. It only makes him worse, and then he becomes vicious. If you could just learn to take care and not offend him."

As his mother spoke, Liza came to stand beside him. When she moved, he heard the swish and whisper of silk, caught the miniature breeze of starched petticoats and lemons. Something shifted inside him, like the movement of land in an earthquake. Jocelin glanced from Liza, who was a small, fuming steam engine, to his dithering mother. Enlightenment burst upon him. Never had he blamed his mother for not coming to his aid against his father and Yale. He should have. All her efforts had been toward peace for herself—the price had been his shame, his expulsion from the family. Disoriented by this insight, he failed to intervene when Liza spoke to the duchess.

"Your grace, bullies don't leave off if you lie down and let them stomp on you."

"Young woman!"

"I'm sorry," Liza said without appearing in the least to be sorry. "But if you take abuse, you invite abuse. Now you may like being continually tyrannized and kicked about, but you can't expect your son to like it."

The duchess made sounds like a hen caught in a lightening storm. "Jocelin, this, this person has insulted your mother."

He had been smiling at his wife and turned to shake his head at the duchess. "No she hasn't, Mother, she's disagreed with you. There's a difference."

"Oh!" The duchess quivered and bristled all the way out of the library.

Jocelin turned to Liza, smiling, and kissed her hand. To his surprise she pulled free and skipped around the sofa. She faced him from behind it.

"What's wrong?" he asked.

"You're not going to kiss my hand or any other part of me until we settle some things."

"It's ill bred for a wife to order a husband about."

He began walking toward her, but halted opposite her with the sofa between them when she started to retreat. He lifted his hands in a gesture of peace, then sprang at her. Catching her by the waist, he lifted her over the sofa. He swung around and sat down with her on his lap. Capturing her flailing arms, he held on to her while she bounced and kicked.

Finally, when she refused to listen to him or stop wrestling, he twisted and plunged down on top of her so that they lay full-length on the couch.

"Will you be quiet now?" he asked.

"Can't breathe."

He shifted his weight, and she gulped in air. Then he lowered his body again, and she gasped.

"Are you going to be quiet and listen?"

"Ye—uh, yes."

Holding her wrists, he stared down into her eyes. The blue-green silk had turned them teal, and they reminded him of a stream darkened by the threat of a thunderstorm.

"We're going to come to an understanding," he said in his best officer's voice. "I can't have a wife in trade."

"But—"

"And I'm not letting you go. You're my wife, and your place is with me."

"Now just—"

"And if you ever venture into East London again, I'll whip you until you can't put your delightful bottom on a chair for a week."

Liza glared at him. "Try it, and see what happens."

He studied her for a moment. "What an intriguing threat."

"I'm not stupid. I didn't go alone."

"True."

"But I'm not going to—"

"Will you be quiet, or do I have to squeeze you again? I warn you, it's giving me great pleasure."

She turned her head away and refused to look at him.

"At last you're beginning to see the benefits of cooperation. I marvel that I ever thought you a delicate little featherhead. No reply? Excellent. Now, as I was about to say before you interrupted, I can't have a wife in trade. However, I see no reason why Mr. Hugo Pennant shouldn't carry on his activities as usual."

She turned her head then and stared at him. "I'm Pennant."

"I know, but I'm the only one who's to have that knowledge. If Society knew, they'd abandon Pennant's in a flash."

"George Sand."

"What?"

Liza smiled at him. "Women have had to disguise their competence for a long time. George Sand, George Eliot."

"Hugo Pennant." He studied her lips, suddenly weary of arguments and much more interested in compromise. "Liza, honey, do you think we can agree?"

Her gaze drifted over his face. "Why have you changed your mind?"

He glanced aside, hoping his face wasn't as flushed as it felt.

"Jocelin?" Liza's voice was filled with consternation. "Jocelin Marshall, you're blushing."

Clenching his jaw, he turned back to her. "If you don't be quiet, I won't explain."

"Yes, my lord."

Damn her. She was biting her lip to keep from smiling. He plunged on before his courage deserted him.

"I was afr—. Hang it. I was afra—." He stopped,

cleared his throat, and stared at her chin. "I was afraid you'd want that damned Pennant's more than me."

He waited, but she didn't laugh. He changed a quick look, and found her staring at him in disbelief.

"You were jealous of Pennant's? Dear heavens, you actually thought I would care more for work than I do for you. Jocelin Marshall, you're mad, and I'm mad to love you so desperately that I see your face in every ledger and contract, hear your wicked laugh instead of the conversation of my employees, wish I were in your bed instead of sitting at my desk."

Relief and happiness crowded into his soul. Jocelin heard himself ask a question he'd never put to any woman.

"Are you sure?"

Liza's lips darted up and fastened on his. He forgot the question. He was beginning to feel tingles in his unruly loins when she broke off to question him again.

"And now you understand? You've really changed your mind?"

"I am capable of change and compromise, woman, even if I do have to be kicked in the head to make me do it. I also have realized that if you'd been as helpless and cloth-headed as women are trained to be, I'd be dead."

"Heavens, you're right. I never thought about it."

"I did. And then there's Mother."

"She might as well have 'Stomp on Me' sewn on the backs of her gowns."

He watched her lips as she spoke. "Liza."

"Yes."

"I don't want to talk about Mother, or Pennant's. I really don't want to talk at all."

She squirmed beneath him. "Now that you mention it, I don't either."

He put his lips on hers and snaked his tongue into her mouth. Sinking down on her further, he felt her legs part. Memorizing her face with the brush of his lips on her skin, he breathed in the smell of lemons and Liza.

"Jocelin, Jocelin, not here."

"Honey, you got to quit trying to put the bees back in the hive once you've stirred them up."

She gasped when he nibbled at her ear. "You're doing it again, turning gunfighter. Now you stop that, Jocelin Marshall. I'll not—"

He shut her up by taking her mouth. He sucked hard, found her hips, and pressed her close. When he lifted his head, she tried to speak again, but he covered her lips with a finger.

"Quit, honey. No use giving orders when nobody's listening."

"Then I'll have to make you listen."

He stared into those challenging tricolor eyes, noting the mischief in them. He felt her hips wriggle against his own.

"Why, you little—"

"Ah—hem."

He sprang backward off her. Liza popped up into a sitting position, and they both faced Loveday.

"I did knock, my lord, but we were otherwise engaged and failed to respond."

Jocelin yanked on his necktie and brushed his hair back from his eyes. "Hang it, Loveday."

"I beg pardon, my lord, but there is a person who insists upon entering the house."

"A person?" He glanced at Liza, but she shook her head in confusion.

Loveday's posture, already stiff, became as upright as one of Reverie's fluted columns. "A person of low station who threatens violence, my lord."

At that moment a loud voice boomed at them from the foyer.

"Gor! Where're you at, you bleeding toff?" Toby Inch burst into the room, brandishing a club. "Missy, there you are."

Windmilling his arms, he brushed past Loveday and headed for Jocelin.

"You leave her be, you puffed up, rutting swell."

Liza cried out as Toby launched himself at Jocelin. Jocelin sighed, then ducked and stuck out his foot. Toby stumbled over it and crashed to the ground. His head bashed against his own weapon, and he howled. Jocelin put his arm around Liza's shoulders, and they surveyed the moaning intruder.

"Toby," Liza said. "I'm sorry I didn't send word. The viscount and I have reconciled."

Toby sat up rubbing his head. "You coulda bleeding told me."

"You curb your language in my wife's presence, sir," Jocelin said.

"My language? Mine? Have you heard hers?"

Jocelin groaned and looked at Liza. "Is this the way it's going to be?"

She pressed her lips together, and he could see she was fighting not to smile.

"I'm afraid Toby is rather forthright." She drew closer within the circle of his arm and lay a hand on his chest. "Can you bear it?"

He grinned at her. "If you provide me with consolation for the burden."

"Ah-hem." Loveday oozed over to stand above the grumbling Toby. "My lord, shall I conduct this person to the kitchen, where he can be attended to?"

"Who're you calling a person, you stuffed oyster?"

"An excellent suggestion," Jocelin said.

With the lift of a brow, Loveday managed to intimidate Toby into rising and shuffling out of the room. Loveday bowed to Jocelin.

"If I may point out, my lord."

Jocelin was already backing Liza over to the sofa again. He gave her a little shove, and she dropped onto the cushions. He put his knee on the cushion beside her thigh.

"It has not been our custom," Loveday continued, "to conduct private encounters in the library."

Jocelin barely heard the valet, so intent was he on counting the flecks in Liza's eyes. She put her hand on his thigh, and he couldn't have spoken to Loveday if he'd wanted to. She flushed, rubbed his thigh, and then darted a look past him at the valet.

"We're starting a new custom, Loveday. Now go away."

They both grinned when the door clicked shut. Jocelin nuzzled Liza's cheek.

"Wait," she said, pulling away from him.

He noted the set of her chin and sighed. "I know what you're going to say." He sank down beside her on the sofa, stretched out his legs, and fixed a grim stare at the toe of his boot. After a moment he turned to her and whispered. "Sinclair and the others, I didn't murder them, you know. I didn't have to, but, Liza, I don't want to end up like Ash."

Launching herself into his arms, Liza began kissing his face and chattering at the same time. "I was so afraid you wouldn't see it. So afraid you'd be unable to give it up, this crusade of yours." She laid her cheek against his.

"Nick said I couldn't continue, that it was tearing me in pieces."

"He was right," she said as she pulled away from

him and looked into his eyes. "You can't continue this crusade, this playing God."

"But I can't just let it happen."

She smiled at him. "Nor can I. And there's no reason why we can't, between the two of us, ruin anyone who needs ruining. Legally, that is. We can still rescue the ones who need it."

"But it's not easy to remain balanced. I see those predators, and I want to kill."

"No, it won't be easy." Liza squeezed his hand. "Perhaps we should establish a home, and a foundation. I don't know what's best."

"Neither do I."

"But at least," she said as she turned to face him, "at least we can work on the solution together."

He smiled and kissed her quickly. Then his smile faded. "You realize I'm going to have to deal with your father."

"You mean the gunfighter will?"

"Yep."

She squeezed his hand. "May I watch?"

He laughed, and suddenly his spirits lifted.

"You give me respite, sweet, sweet Liza. You give me tranquillity."

She leaned toward him and put her hand on his thigh. He sucked in his breath.

Liza grinned at him. "Well, honey," she drawled, "seems there's at least one part of you that's not so tranquil."

With a laugh he lunged at her, bearing her down to the sofa. "Not right now, honey, but it will be. In a little while."

Liza pulled him down on top of her. As their bodies met, she gasped and whispered to him. "Maybe not such a *little* while."

ABOUT THE AUTHOR

SUZANNE ROBINSON has a doctoral degree in anthropology with a specialty in ancient Middle Eastern archaeology. After spending years doing fieldwork in both the U.S. and the Middle East, Suzanne has now turned her attention to the creation of the fascinating fictional characters in her unforgettable historical romances.

Suzanne lives in San Antonio with her husband and her two English springer spaniels. She divides her time between writing and teaching.

SUZANNE ROBINSON
loves to hear from readers. You can write to
her at the following address:

P.O. Box 700321
San Antonio, TX 78270-0321

And coming next from
the spectacularly talented

Suzanne Robinson. . .

LORD OF
ENCHANTMENT

Here is a glimpse of this
enthralling new historical romance.

Pen Fairfax leaned out over the battlements of Highcliffe Castle and felt her skin prickle as if she wore a hair shirt next to her flesh. She had no cause to feel so skittish, and yet she'd left her bread and ale to climb to the top of the Saint's Tower and scour the horizon.

Agitation tingled in her bones as she looked out at the sea. League after league of azure met her gaze, topped by a sky without clouds and riffled by a teasing breeze that burned her cheeks crimson. The glare of the sun, the sea's moisture, and the icy breeze combined to turn the air almost silver. Far below the steep cliffs upon which the tower sat, the surf foamed and crashed into the jagged black giant's teeth that were all the island could claim as a beach.

Again the flesh on the back of her arms prickled. Shading her eyes with one hand, Pen studied the sea. She didn't turn when Nany Boggs labored up the last stair and puffed her way across the tower roof carrying a cup of ale. Nany's generous chest heaved under the strain of hauling her bulk up the winding staircase. Teetering to a halt, she steadied her precious cargo and took a long sip. Then she wiped her face with her apron and tucked a strand of silver hair beneath her cap.

Before Nany could scold, Pen lifted a hand and pointed out to sea. "There's going to be a storm."

Nany Boggs looked up at the unblemished sky, at the calm sea, at Pen.

"Prithee, how do you know it?"

"We'll have to get the grain inside, and the hay and the animals. No threshing this morn."

Pen avoided her old nurse's stare. She breathed in the fragrance of crisp sea air. The breeze caught a strand of her hair and played with it as she surveyed the blue plain of water that stretched from the island to the horizon. She shivered abruptly and rubbed her upper arms.

"Aha!"

Pen tossed her head and scowled at Nany, but the nurse only planted a fist on her hip and glared back at her.

"I knew it," Nany said. "I saw you go still in the hall and bolt like a frightened hedgehog. You're going all fantastical again, aren't you? Listening to spirits and fell creatures of magic."

Pen rolled her eyes and giggled. "Not spirits and creatures—"

"Hearken you to me, Penelope Grace Fairfax. If you rush about like a demented harpy, your secret will be out and we're all o'erthrown."

Pen took a deep breath of cold air, spread her arms wide, and lifted her face to the sun. "God's patience, Nany, I but warned of a storm."

"Under a cloudless sky, mistress."

"You're always complaining that I'm addlepated and fit only for Bedlam, yet when I give cautious warnings and thought to the protection of those under my care, you complain of that as well."

Never one to let logic impede her way, Nany drained her cup and then shook a thick finger at Pen. "You're going all fantastical again."

Pen smiled at Nany and touched the end of her nurse's red nose with the tip of her finger. Nany swiped at her hand, but Pen danced away from her grasp. She left the embrasure but paused to glance out at the tranquil water, then went to Nany and patted her shoulder as she headed for the stairs.

"There will be a storm," she said brightly, "a storm nonpareil, with waves as high as towers and sideways rain and sleet. A storm of trouble and wonder, Nany. A storm of trouble and wonder."

Out of sight of Penance Isle, a carrack chased a swift pinnace westward from the coast of England. On the carrack, Morgan St. John raced across the deck toward the stern, his arm clamping his sword to his side. He'd pursued the spy-priest Jean-Paul from England to Scotland and back again and wasn't about to give up because of a few clouds. He veered around a coiled rope and swooped down upon the ship's master. Before he could speak, the master nodded to the boatswain, who began to shout.

"Stand by your lines!"

Morgan turned and gazed past the prow and the rapidly vanishing pinnace on the horizon. He rounded on the master. "You're not coming about."

Sunlight vanished as he spoke, and the sea and wind picked up. The master pointed to the sky behind them.

"That be a black squall, my lord."

Morgan gazed up at a line of ebony clouds that seemed to fly across the sky, swallowing all light. The leading edge was as straight as a sword blade. Several men scurried past them and climbed up to loosen the topsails.

"You know nothing of the sea, my lord. A storm like that can slap my ship to the bottom of the sea. I know you want to catch that pinnace, but the squall will reach her before we can." When Morgan remained silent, the master pressed his lips together and continued. "After all, I got a wife to think of, and my men—"

"Mean you that you're turning this ship around because of a *woman*?" Morgan's eyes rounded and widened. "God's blood, man, that pinnace carries a French spy. If I don't catch the bastard, he's going to cause the deaths of more than just a few English sailors. A pestilence take you, man, that priest serves the Cardinal of Lorraine and the Queen of Scots, and you prate to me of a stupid woman? I'm trying to prevent a war!"

As Morgan finished, the wind hit them, and the boatswain began to yell again.

"Lower and reef the main course. Lower the mizzen course."

A driving rain mixed with sleet pelted them as the master's gaze darted from the topsails to the mizzen course and spritsail.

"Boatswain," the master yelled. "It's too late. Trim the spritsail."

A heavy swell pitched the ship, and Morgan gripped the gunwale. His feet began to slide out from under him, and he tasted rain and salt water. Now the swells blocked out the sky. The ship ascended the next wave, and he caught a glimpse of the horizon before the deck rolled and pitched beneath him. Cursing, he got his feet back beneath him. Across the deck, sailors had uncoiled ropes and strung them down the length of the ship.

The master had worked his way amidship to join the boatswain. Morgan followed, but a great swell broke over the stern, dashing him to the deck. He landed facedown and felt his body begin to slide. He grabbed a cask as the ship pitched almost vertical to the seafloor. When he'd gotten to his feet again, he gripped the gunwale and slowly maneuvered forward. He reached the master in time to hear him bellowing at a young sailor, little more than a boy, who was hugging the mast. The master pointed at the mainsail, which lay across the deck with its spars extending out past the gunwale.

"Get out there, you pissant cur!"

Morgan glanced at the men reefing in the sails. Soaked, sails were heavy and dragged, requiring great strength to haul. The master was still yelling. Morgan watched another swell nearly carry a man overboard, and made a decision.

Removing his sword and letting it fall to the deck, he lurched past the man reefing sail on the port side and climbed out on the spar. A swell rose up as he edged out over the sea. Morgan hugged the spar as an ocean of water broke over him. When it was gone, he straightened, spat water, and began to drag in sail.

To his right he heard someone yelling. It was the master, but he dared not take his gaze from the sail. A blast of horizontal sleet hit him in the face, and he gasped. The ship rolled, and the world turned sideways. Morgan clutched the spar again. He heard the master screaming at him. He couldn't see for the spray and the wind that blew his hair in his face.

Then he felt it—the crack and sudden drop of the end of the spar. Voices shouted at him, and he lunged in the direction of the gunwale. As he leaped, the spar broke. The sail tore as he grabbed for it. A gray wall of water loomed high above him, topping the mast. Morgan grabbed for the jagged end of the spar and then plunged into the sea.

He hit the water like a pat of butter hitting a brick. The sea swallowed him. As he sank, he twisted his body and looked about, his lungs on fire. His clothing dragged at him as he fought his way to the surface. He popped, corklike, into the air and gulped in a deep breath. Another swell slapped him underwater once again.

This time it was all he could do to claw his way to the

surface. A wave batted him again, and he went down into darkness once more. It was as if he were swimming in cold pitch. His muscles were stiff, and his chest burned.

Rapidly losing his senses, he broke to the surface. He tried to remain afloat, but his strength was fading. Another wall of gray rose in front of him, and he knew he couldn't survive it. The carrack had vanished.

In desperation, Morgan turned and tried to swim away from the giant swell. He threw out an arm, and it hit something hard—the end of the spar. Clutching the wood, he wrapped himself around it and braced himself as the swell hit. This time he went down, but the wood helped him pop back to the surface quickly.

How long he rode those swells, he couldn't judge, but his arms froze in their clutched position around the spar, and the rest of him went numb. Suddenly the blast of the wind dropped a bit, and the pelting rain let up. His vision blurred, he could just make out great mountains of waves under a ragged black sky.

He fixed his whole attention on remaining afloat and kept it there until he heard a sudden crash. Swinging his wobbling head around, he beheld sea foam and white tops. A wave rocked him. As he was carried on its crest, he saw the reason for the foam and the crash—rocks. Tall, jagged, and black, they littered the coast of an island.

Morgan tried to turn and swim away, but the swells were carrying him toward the rocks. He kicked uselessly, and a high swell picked him up as easily as the wind blows a feather. His body sailed high. Then he plummeted into the base of a pair of rocks that looked like giant's teeth.

His body slammed against pitted black stone. Air rushed out of his lungs. He lost his grip on the spar as he was sucked back out to sea by the return wave. Half-conscious, he flailed his arms and legs, only to be lifted once again and thrown. He saw black teeth and white foam, then cried out as his body was rammed between the two rocks. As he hit, his head smacked into stone. He felt the exploding pain just before the blackness overwhelmed him.

The morning after the storm, Pen stood in the outer bailey listening to Dibbler and Sniggs. Behind her she could hear and catch the smells from the piggery, which backed against the south wall between two towers. Dibbler began shouting at Sniggs as the castle's herd of pigs trotted outside. Pen waved at the swineherd, a girl by the name of Wheedle, then winced as Dibbler cuffed Sniggs on his ear.

"Stop it at once," Pen said.

Dibbler gave her a glance of pretended remorse and dug his toe into the mud. "Your pardon, mistress, but fell asleep at his post, did Sniggs. What if Sir Ponder had decided to attack last night?"

Sniggs reddened and burst into speech. "It were a fairy, mistress. A wee fairy with gold wings and silver hair cast fairy dust in me eyes and put me to sleep. I didn't even hear no thunderclaps nor nothing."

"Fairy dust."

"Aye, mistress."

Pen's gaze traveled over Sniggs, from his grease-caked hair, patchwork vest, and hose to his worn and cracked boots. She caught a whiff of ale and cheesy breath, and stepped back.

"It weren't no fairy," Dibbler said.

"No?" asked Pen.

"Nah, mistress. Everyone knows that fairies don't come out in no storm. They hides under toadstools and leaves and such."

Sniggs sputtered. "Well, this one hid in my tower last night."

"It did not!"

Pen waved her hands and tried not to smile. "Please, both of you. I like not this quarreling. No harm was done."

"But, mistress—"

"Dibbler, I thank you for your diligence, and now I must catch up with Wheedle. One of her sows took ill last night."

Pen left the two men to finish their quarrel without her and walked across the wet ground, avoiding puddles and lakes of mud. She passed the beehives and the dovecote, rounded the corner of the deserted kitchen building, and entered the gatehouse. She passed beneath the rusting portcullis, through iron-studded double doors, and over the drawbridge. The moat was littered with leaves and moss blown by the storm.

Free from the confines of Highcliffe, Pen emerged onto the stone outcrop upon which the castle had been built and hurried down the slanting path that led to the fields. A patchwork of soggy mud lay before her, and Pen thanked God once again that the harvest had been gathered and most of the grain threshed before the rain came. Her warning had come in time to shelter both animals and wheat.

Nany Boggs wasn't pleased, though. She was still disgruntled, but Pen couldn't be bothered. Her life was almost perfect, except for that foul blemish, Sir Ponder Cutwell. Nany resented their lack of servants, the shut-up and boarded towers, the plain food, the isolation of Penance Isle. Pen loved it for these very reasons.

Reaching the base of Highcliffe Mount, Pen saw that Wheedle had already reached the edge of the forest that lay between Highcliffe and the realm of Ponder Cutwell. She took in a deep breath of rain-washed air. She could ask about the sick pig when the girl returned.

In the glare of the newborn sun, yesterday's apprehension and prickling expectation seemed but a whimsy.

Her spirits lifted as she beheld the masses of gold and copper of the turning leaves of the forest. The sea breeze whipped at her cloak and skirts and danced in her hair. Another ordinary day in which she must needs see to the salting of meat, the making of preserves, the storing of grain and wood, all in preparation for winter. But first a walk in the open air.

Pen skirted fields and gardens and took the path that bordered the cliffs. She would walk to the caves and back before resuming the day's chores. As she went, Pen glanced down at the surf breaking on the rocks. Gulls and terns cawed and screeched as they sailed over the waves. She paused while three dolphins skimmed by, then took the path around a rock outcrop. As she walked she gathered stones. When she had a handful, she stopped and began tossing them over the cliff. She was determined to throw one out beyond the farthest rocks in the sea.

Three stones hit the fan of boulders that marked an old cliff slide. Pen grimaced and walked farther down the path where the sea had carved more land from the island. She clamped a hand around a stone, drew back her arm, and it stayed there. Something white had flapped in the air. She narrowed her eyes against the sun's glare and peered down at two high rocks that jutted out of the roiling surf. It wasn't foam, this white. Was it a sail?

Pen turned abruptly and went back to the rock outcrop. Climbing it, she looked down on the jagged black teeth swimming in surf. A shirt! And someone was in it. A torn shirt covered the torso of a man. Now she could see him. His body was wedged between the rocks, lodged just above the water. His arm hung loosely, his fingers dangling in the waves at the base of the rock.

Hopping down from the rock, Pen ran back toward Highcliffe Castle. She was breathless by the time she reached the drawbridge. She waited there to regain her breath, put two fingers in her mouth, and let out a piercing whistle. Dibbler's head appeared out of an arrow slit in the gatehouse.

Pen bent her head back and shouted. "I've found a man on the rocks below the south cliffs! Bring a litter."

Without waiting for an answer, Pen raced back to the cliffs. There was a terraced stair to the beach, but she had to scramble over rocks until she came to those upon which the man was cast. Leaping from boulder to boulder, she stood on a flat stone, bent her knees, and jumped onto the black rocks. She lodged her feet in a crevice and touched his hand. It was cold, and at first she thought he was dead. Her gaze drifted to wet hair blacker than the rocks he lay upon. She lifted his head, and he coughed.

"Saints!" Pen's hands slipped across his skin as the surf sprayed them. "Sir? Sir, can you hear me?"

He muttered something but failed to wake. With his long legs and the bulk of his muscles, he would be far too heavy for her to lift. Pen glanced over her shoulder and saw Dibbler and the youth Erbut carrying a litter along the cliffside.

The surf had drenched her. She moved so that she could support the man's head in her arms and shelter against the rocks at the same time while she waited. Shivering, she felt the man lurch and flail his arms.

"No, no." She stroked his head and shoulders. "Don't move and hurt yourself further."

Of course he didn't hear her, but her caresses must have reached him somehow, for he stilled into her cradling arms. Pen shifted so that she supported his head against her breast. Glancing at the men carrying the litter and then back to her charge, she found herself staring.

She had never seen a man with perfect features. Mayhap not perfect, for the lips were those of an ascetic, a bit thin, and yet somehow in complete proportion to his nose and brow. A blue shadow beneath his skin told her his beard would be as black as his hair. But then he was a young man.

Casting a covert glance at Dibbler and Erbut to assure herself that their attention was on the terraced stair, Pen returned to her study of the man. This might be her only opportunity to see a man's body. His shredded clothing left much of this one's exposed. Much of it was bruised and scraped. Pen was touching the hill of flesh that formed the muscle of his upper arm and wondering at the silken feel of his skin when it bunched and turned hard. The arm came up, nearly striking her. The man moaned again, but Pen captured his arm. Murmuring reassurance, she tried to hold his hand. It was too large, so she held his wrist instead.

His head had turned in his thrashing, and she noticed the blue tint of the flesh beneath his eyes. Without warning, his eyelids raised, and she beheld eyes as black as his hair. His body writhed, and she writhed with it.

"Marry, I do believe the Lord has sent me a night-black leopard in the guise of a man. Be still, sirrah."

Behind her, Dibbler and Erbut climbed over the rocks with the litter between them.

"Leave it there," she called to them. "Help me lift him to it."

Their combined strength got the man off his rock perch at last. Dibbler and Erbut lowered him onto the litter, and Pen covered him with a blanket. She waved at Sniggs and his son, Turnip, who were hurring down the terraced stair to join them. At her feet, the man moaned and thrashed about as Dibbler tied him to the litter. Erbut was trying to lash his legs. He bent over the man's boot, then straightened and held something up to Pen.

"Look at this, mistress. It were in his boot."

Lying in the youth's hand was a dagger. Not a yeoman's dagger, nor even that of a gentleman. This was the weapon of a nobleman. A polished blade of steel with an evil edge to it. A hilt wrapped with gold and black enamel in a design of writhing snakes. A pommel inlaid with jet.

Pen stared at the dagger, and as she stared, the snakes began to twist and squirm. She stuffed her hands behind her back as Erbut tried to hand the blade to her.

"No!"

Erbut jumped at her sharp cry.

"I mean, put it in your belt and we'll store it in the Saint's Tower after we've seen to this poor man."

Erbut gave her a confused look but did as he was told. Dibbler was stuffing the blanket tightly around the man's body.

"That be a lord's weapon, mistress."

"Oh?" Pen clasped her shaking hands together. She'd almost touched the dagger.

"I seen plenty of them kind of blades in London town. That there is a fine blade. And this boy here, he's no sailor. Look at them hands. Palms got no calluses. Rough where he grips a sword. Got no sword, though." He produced a belt and pouch.

"Dibbler!" Pen said. "No filching and picking, remember."

"But we got to find out who he is."

Pen snatched the items from him and pointed at the stretcher. Sniggs and Turnip had arrived, and the four lifted the litter. Pen followed them as Dibbler resumed his treatise upon their castaway.

"He's a lord. Look at that shirt. Finest cambric it is."

"And how would you know cambric from a camp stool?" Sniggs asked.

"Probably stole plenty of them, by our Lady," said Erbut.

Pen looked at the man on the litter. His head was turned to the side, exposing a gaunt jaw and a long, smooth neck. Somehow the sight of that exposed flesh turned her insides to custard. She studied the fan of black lashes against his cheeks, stumbled and nearly fell. Catching her balance, she glared at the backs of her men, but none of them had seen her foolishness. And that's what it was, foolishness, near madness to allow the sight of a man's neck to nearly break hers.

Pen stopped for a moment and watched the litter and its burden. The storm had brought him to her. Erbut stumbled, causing the man to moan, and Pen fought the urge to rush to him. She clamped her teeth together as she watched his body writhe beneath the bonds that held him to the litter. Though he was covered with a blanket, she could follow the movements of his legs, torso, and arms.

Suddenly he arched his back, and his hips thrust upward, nearly sending Dibbler and Sniggs to their knees. That movement, its violence, its suggestion, attacked her senses. She felt as if the storm of last night had suddenly entered her body, and that he had put it there. As abruptly as he'd begun, the man lapsed into stillness.

Pen blinked, then shook her head. "Saints. God's patience. Holy Mother . . ."

The storm had given him to her; she knew it. She knew it the way she knew so many things, things she usually didn't want to know. Only this time, these presentiments—they were different. She wasn't afraid of them. And they remained with her rather than fading like mist. They turned her world to gold and diamonds.

She shook her head again, then smiled the bright smile of a suddenly rich pauper. He was hers, though he didn't know it, this offering from the sea. Gathering up her skirts, Pen danced from rock to rock following the lord the storm had brought her.

Captivating historical romance from the pen of

Suzanne
Robinson

"An author with star quality... Spectacularly talented."
—*Romantic Times*

LADY VALIANT

Thea Hunt was determined to help her friend Mary, Queen of Scots avoid a treacherous marriage. But in the thick of an English forest, Thea suddenly finds herself set upon by thieves...and chased down by a golden-haired highwayman who'd still her struggles and stir her heart--with one penetrating glance from his fiery blue eyes.
—29575-6 $5.50/6.50 in Canada

LADY DEFIANT

Disarmingly handsome and one of Queen Elizabeth's most dangerous spies, Blade Fitzstephen is given the task of romancing the secrets out of a clever young beauty named Oriel Richmond. Together they plot to thwart a conspiracy to topple the queen from her throne.   ____29574-8 $4.99/5.99 In Canada

LADY HELLFIRE

After she braved the perils of the wild American frontier, there wasn't a man alive that Kate couldn't handle—or so the reckless spitfire thought—until she found herself on British soil and in the presence of the devilishly handsome Marquess of Richfield.
____29678-7 $4.99/5.99 In Canada

LADY GALLANT

A daring spy in Queen Mary's court, Nora Becket risked her life to rescue the innocent. Yet it was Nora who needed rescuing when cutthroats attacked her—and when Christian de Rivers, a lusty, sword-wielding rogue, swept her out of harm's way...and into his arms.
____29430-X $4.50/5.50 In Canada

Look for these titles at your bookstore or use this page to order.